RUMOUR

A. C. LAWRENCE

To Judi,
Best wishes
Angela C. Lawrence.
December 2009

Sandlings Press

R<small>UMOUR</small>

ISBN 978-0-9562446-0-4

Published by: Sandlings Press, The Shipway, Mallard Way, Hollesley,
Woodbridge, Suffolk. IP12 3QJ
Email: lawrenceac@aol.com

Printed by: The Lavenham Press Ltd, 47 Water Street, Lavenham,
Suffolk, CO10 9RN

To Brian, for his encouragement.

* * * *

'I could not love thee, dear so much
Loved I not honour more.'
Richard Lovelace
To Lucasta, on Going to the Wars. 1649

'In war, truth is the first casualty.'
Aeschylus

* * * *

Prologue

𝕰𝖆𝖘𝖙 𝕬𝖓𝖌𝖑𝖎𝖆𝖓 𝕯𝖆𝖎𝖑𝖞 𝕿𝖎𝖒𝖊𝖘
Monday June 29 1914.

**Royal couple assassinated. Austrian heir and his wife shot.
Bomb and revolver outrages. Murder in a Sarajevo street.**

The Archduke Francis Ferdinand, the heir to the Austro-Hungarian throne, and his wife, the Duchess of Hohenberg, were assassinated in the street at Sarajevo, the capital of Bosnia yesterday.

As commander in chief of the army, the Archduke was on a visit to Bosnia for the forthcoming military manoeuvres in that country and his headquarters were pitched at Llidze near Sarajevo. Yesterday he was motoring with the Duchess to the town hall to receive an address of welcome from the mayor and corporation when a bomb was thrown at the royal car. The motor car immediately following received the full force of the explosion and an aide de camp was badly injured.

After the ceremony at the town hall the royal couple drove off to visit the wounded colonel and at the corner of Francis Josef and Rudolf streets were both fatally shot by a Serbian student. Both the bomb thrower and the assassin were captured by the police.

At ten o'clock yesterday morning the Archduke and Duchess left the military camp in their automobile for the town hall. The car halted for some minutes while a number of young girls, who were drawn up in festive attire, greeted the royal pair who accepted some flowers from them and spoke a few kindly words. The car moved on, but it had not proceeded more than a few yards when a man who has since been identified as a printer named Cabrinovic sprang out from the crowd and hurled a bomb, full at the royal couple. The infernal machine fell at the back of the car, just where the Archduke was sitting, and rebounding onto the road, exploded. The royal car by this time had moved several yards and the full force of the explosion fell on the following automobile, which contained four members of the suite. The Archduke, after ascertaining the extent of the injuries to the aide de camp and seeing he was medically attended to, gave the order to proceed and the royal car soon afterwards arrived at the town hall.

At the entrance to the building were the members of the town council with the Bürgermeister at the head. The Bürgermeister was about to read an address to the royal visitors when the Archduke raised his hands and spoke as following,

5

in a voice in which resentment was blended with emotion.

'Mr Mayor, we came to Sarajevo to make a friendly visit and are greeted by a bomb. This is outrageous.' Then after a pause the Archduke said, 'You may now speak.'

The city fathers stood thunder struck and could not conceal their chagrin. The Bürgermeister, however, recovered himself and delivered the speech he had prepared. The Archduke made a suitable reply and with his wife then spent half an hour inspecting the town hall. The Archduke then stated he was going on to the garrison hospital to see how Lt Colonel Eric von Merizzi was progressing. The royal couple, escorted by the town councillors, descended the steps leading to the entrance to the building, re-entered their automobile and drove off.

The car had reached the corner of Francis Josef and Rudolf Streets when two revolver shots, in close succession, rang out. The first struck the Archduke in the right cheek, inflicting a mortal wound while the second penetrated the body of the Duchess, severing a main artery. The unfortunate lady sank unconscious into the arms of her spouse who, a few seconds afterwards, also fainted. With all speed the car was driven by the chauffeur to Konak, the governor's residence, but almost before a doctor could reach their side the royal couple had expired.

The assassin, who was a Serbian student named Gavrilo Princip, was seized and disarmed. The crowd made a desperate attempt to drag the murderer from the protecting police, but they succeeded in rescuing him and conveyed him to the police station.

Part 1

Uneasy Idyll

Chapter One

Sunday June 28 1914

The day Archduke Ferdinand and his wife were assassinated in Sarajevo, being a Sunday, Alma Delina Theophilia Smith and her husband William went to church.

The student's bullets found their mark at about the time Alma and William were dismissing their Sunday School classes. And by the time they rose from their pew at the end of Evensong the Archduke and his beloved Sophie had been dead for many hours. Their corpses by now cold and rigid, their reputations, and the significance of their sudden end, subject to hasty dissection by journalists for the following day's newspapers.

While the lives of one devoted couple, celebrating their wedding anniversary on a state visit to Bosnia, had been extinguished in the flash of a gunman's eye, the modest existence of another passed wholly unremarkably in a Suffolk village.

The summer of 1914 was dominated by the heatwave. For some it was a glorious season, the best they could ever remember. Endless days of unclouded, metallic blue skies suffused them with well-being, giving them an air of confidence, of unshakeable complacency.

They discarded their clothes with their cares and headed for the beach or river, the cool waters soothing their parched skin. In town the parks came alive with striped deckchairs and awnings as workers snatched a brief respite from the stifling heat of office, shop or factory, seeking the deep shadows cast by plane and sycamore trees. They spread their rugs on grass the colour of coconut matting. Women in sprigged muslin and large-brimmed hats sat decorously beneath parasols accompanied by men in flannels, shirt sleeves and panama hats. Wicker hampers lay open invitingly.

For others, though, the long drought was exhausting of body and spirit, beast and soil. A time of mute anxiety.

Months without rain had seared and scarred the wide Suffolk landscape. What had once been productive pasture was now reduced to a dessicated, buff-coloured desert.

Dust covered everything. It lay in drifts across the streets, kicked into swirling clouds by the occasional passing motor car and tired, dirt-encrusted horses drawing carts or waggons or tumbrils. It dyed the pink-washed Suffolk cottages and coated the thatches a dreary grey. Dust clouded the windows like half-forgotten blinds and tinged swathes of poppies and cornflowers in hedgerows and gardens so that there was barely a hint of colour to be seen.

Inevitably the people of the countryside took on its exhausted hue. Clouds of fine dust billowing from the corn and hay fields mingled with sandy Suffolk soil and rose in draughts to cling to their clothes the instant they stepped out of doors. It etched their faces palely. Their throats rasped and their lungs choked. The stinging grit inflamed and reddened their eyes. Yet still they prayed the fine weather would last into August so that every field could be harvested.

The air was humid when the evensong congregation emerged from the cool interior of Wangford parish church into sunlight streaked grey. The church-goers blinked their eyes against the glare, having become accustomed to the softness of light filtered through stained glass. In their Sunday best suits and freshly laundered dresses they'd welcomed the clean caress of untainted air. They'd felt the cold stone slabs beneath their feet. The gentle organ voluntary at the end of the service had lulled them into a communal stupor of well-being. God had bestowed the gift of fine weather to ensure a good harvest, they'd been told.

The congregation spilled through the church door in order of rank. Gentry first, agricultural labourers last. Alma accepted this as quite proper. With William at her side, she watched from her pew as the Vicar, the Rev. Trevor Edwards, shook each worshipper's hand and blessed them.

The residents of Henham Hall were first to leave. The Earl of Stradbroke, his bearing that of a military man, led the way. As he moved between the pews he bestowed nods of recognition. Village worthies, estate workers, even the lowliest parlour maid – all found themselves encompassed by his benevolent smile.

All eyes, though, were on the Earl's younger Countess following a few paces behind him. With her delicate porcelain skin, sage-green eyes and chestnut curls she was a classic English beauty. Yet Alma, gazing at the nape of the Helena Stradbroke's neck as she picked her way decorously down the aisle, detected a rebellious streak. The strands of hair escaping beneath the demure brim of her Ladyship's hat had about them a wantonness, a carelessness.

But the Countess's was oblivious to the stares. Her attention was focused solely on her wayward children. She shepherded the eldest six down the aisle and out into the churchyard as masterfully as she could. Only the young Viscount Dunwich, a handsome youth of eleven, was careful to maintain a dignified poise as he followed her closely. A nursery nurse brought up the rear of the little procession, carrying the latest addition to the Stradbroke dynasty wrapped in a lace-edged shawl.

Alma and William stood with the rest of the congregation at the church gate as the Earl and his family clambered into their open carriage. It was a weekly ritual.

The entire village gathered after church to raise their hats, doff caps or wave off their aristocratic neighbours with fluttering handkerchiefs, before strolling from the churchyard themselves.

They watched as the Stradbroke children squeezed into the carriage. A coachman and four greys waited patiently, the horses immobile and steaming in the heat. Arms and legs flying as the children leapt about, laughing and chiding each other with relief at being freed from the strictures of the front pew.

What a handful, thought Alma, shaking her head. She turned to glance up into William's sun-beaten face. His eyes furrowed to a frown. She knew his opinions of ill-disciplined children. It made no difference whether they were high or low-born.

The village of Wangford was small and unassuming, a remote community buried deep in the folds of Suffolk's undulating landscape. George Edward John Mowbray Rous, third Earl of Stradbroke, owned most of the village, just as his father and grandfather before him. His father had endowed the school and lavished money on the imposing flint and brick church. It was full of memorials to his family; a couple of fine stained glass windows for his father and mother and a lectern to his uncle, the Admiral Henry John Rous, sometime Member of Parliament.

The church itself stood on a slight incline in the centre of the village. A long pathway led down through the churchyard to an iron gate and into the main street. Around it clustered dozens of small shops, workshops and cottages. The road meandered and curled in both directions. On the gentle slope to the south it passed through Henham, the principal village on the Earl's estate, eventually arriving in Ipswich. Northwards it bore traffic to Lowestoft and Yarmouth.

With so many travellers on the turnpike Wangford was able to support several coaching inns and public houses. Opposite the church stood the 'Lion Inn' and on either side of it the 'Swan' and the 'Angel Inn'. Several beer-houses scattered amongst the smaller cottages and shops also made a healthy living from passing traffic.

Although the schoolhouse where Alma and William lived lay to the south, they turned northwards out of the gate. It was their custom, on a Sunday evening, to walk the length of the village.

'Our usual Sunday constitutional,' William called it. 'A good couple of miles walk will keep us agile and healthy.' After spending the entire day in church or teaching Sunday school he itched to stretch his legs.

Alma agreed, though sometimes reluctantly. So whatever the weather or time of year they were to be seen each Sunday strolling past the shuttered shops, admiring gardens, greeting pupils playing hopscotch or marbles in the street, or stopping to exchange pleasantries with the adults sitting idly chatting on doorsteps.

On this particular evening they had just drawn level with the 'Lion' when the door was flung open. They stopped, surprised by the violent crack of wood against ancient hinges, and turned to glance inside.

The interior of the low, rough-beamed bar presented a very different picture from the cool spirituality of the church they had just left. The air was thick with the haze of tobacco smoke, beer-fuelled laughter and raucous singing. They saw it was full of young men. Some were standing in small groups, others lolled on the wooden bar or crowded around small tables.

Nearly all were in khaki uniform.

The room was too confined to contain them all. As the door swung back one of the groups spilled out onto the roadway. They emerged clutching tankards and cigarettes.

One, too young to hold his beer, leant against the wall of the pub and vomited, spewing yellow liquid into the gutter. The others, just as young, guffawed unkindly at his innocence and thumped each other on the back. They were *men*, their laughter implied. Yet, like erratic bean-poles blown in a summer gale, they teetered uncertainly, supporting one another with arms around shoulders and necks, unable to stand alone. There were half a dozen of them, their ruddy, sunburnt faces reddened further by the effect of quantities of strong ale.

The young men knotted untidily together were only half-aware of the schoolmaster's presence a few steps away and continued to laugh and sway. Then a couple spotted him through the blur of alcohol. Their demeanour changed. They straightened themselves, pressing back their shoulders. Grins were wiped from their faces. It was instinctive. A natural reaction on seeing William Smith.

Alma felt William's fingers tightening on hers. 'They're all our boys,' he murmured softly. 'All of them. Our boys.' He sounded reproachful. He regarded drink as a destructive demon, especially among the young. Still, she detected a note of endearment.

Every man standing before them, ranging in age, she guessed, from eighteen to twenty-eight, had been a pupil at their school. Each had started as a terrified five-year-old and had been in their care until he'd left at fourteen to find work.

'Evening sir. Evening Mrs Smith.' One touched the brim of his khaki cap.

'Good evening Baxter,' William said. Then with some irony added, 'It certainly appears to be a good evening.'

'Yessir,' slurred Baxter. 'Weekend training camp just broke up. Fourth battalion Suffolk's. At Leiston, sir.'

'Jolly good it was too, sir,' chimed a young lad, not many years out of school and still mindful of the respect he should show his old headmaster.

'Glad to see you doing your bit for the colours, too, Parsley.' William smiled, for he remembered the boy more for the number of entries he and his brothers had achieved in the punishment book than for any academic prowess.

'We were two hundred men in camp. They've just brought us back,' Parsley rushed on, anxious to explain why he and his fellows were now celebrating. 'Terri.... Terri....' he tried to make sense of the word, but his mind and tongue failed him. '....Torrials. General training, bayonet practice, basic drill, marching up and down . That sort of thing. You know, in case there's a war, sir,' he added as an afterthought.

Alma pursed her lips anxiously. *God help us if any of these boys have to fight a war. Some of them are barely out of the schoolroom.*

She tried to picture Baxter and Parsley marching in unison with two hundred others across Leiston Heath, Lee Enfield rifles sloped across their shoulders. She wondered if they practised with live ammunition and how dangerous such a venture might prove in such inexpert hands. All she could see were these young men, their faces burnt by the sun as they marched across the heath, concentrating on skills that would enable them to kill other young men. It distressed her to think of it.

Baxter pulled himself upright in deliberate fashion and attempted to re-join the conversation. 'We learnt all sorts of other useful things, like putting up tents and cooking on camp stoves,' he explained. 'Old sargeant from the South Africa campaign showed us how.'

'Well, lads, you're doing the village proud. Back to work tomorrow though, eh?' They nodded in unison, taking his remark as a dismissal.

Alma watched them lurch uncertainly, not sure which way to turn. Behind them lay the warmth of the cramped bar, the softening of the senses with each fresh pint of ale and the camaraderie of other young men in uniform.

William shook his head and sighed. Tonight, he imagined, they would hang their dust-covered Territorial Army uniforms in a cupboard and forget about them until the next drill night or next year's training camp. Tomorrow they'd be back at their work-benches, behind the counters of village shops or working with the horses on one of the Earl's farms. Their lives intimately woven into the fabric of the village. A weekend at a training camp in Leiston, not twenty miles away, a major expedition, a break from dull routine and drudgery. The idea of travelling overseas never, realistically, entering their heads. The prospect of fighting some foreign war, like the Boer War, too remote to entertain.

He wound a protective arm around Alma's slim shoulders. He sensed her anxiety. 'Don't worry. They'll come to no harm. Now, how about our walk?'

She slipped her arm through his and, as they made their way up the street, the strains of men's raised voices and raucous singing faded, note by note, until they became a distant echo.

Around them older children bowled metal hoops. Their parents, with little ones sitting at their feet, gathered in groups to chat to neighbours or passers-by, braving the clouds of dust thrown into their faces as pedantic cartwheels rumbled over cobbles.

In the trees fringeing the churchyard blackbirds and linnets vied for the top-most perches from which to warble their evening serenades, their song trickling across the street, a fragile, liquid sound. And above them, rising into the air from surrounding fields, a tumult of exultant skylarks.

They had walked some distance before Alma wriggled her arm free from William's. She swung round with uncharacteristic urgency and gazed back towards the 'Lion'. Stood there, still. Her serious grey eyes fixed on the ordinariness and familiarity of the scene.

So orderly. The faces, the smells, the sounds. So predictable. Yet something about it is out of place. Doesn't fit. She couldn't explain, even to herself. But what she felt was a deep unease, a bewilderment welling up from deep within her imaginings.

The knot of young men outside the 'Lion' had faded away, like their singing. Swallowed by the yellow-grey fog of sunlight shafting through wreaths of dust.

All she could see were insubstantial shadows in a sepia landscape.

Chapter Two

Monday June 29 1914

The day after Archduke Franz Ferdinand was shot in Sarajevo a postcard arrived from Germany. It was addressed to William Smith, Henham and Wangford School, Suffolk, England.

The sepia tinted picture showed the Bavarian Alps, snow-capped even in summer, towering over lush green meadows. In the distance, huddled beneath the shadow of the mountains, was a turreted castle and wooden chalets, their balconies a riot of tumbling flowers. White star-like blooms decorated the foreground.

The scene could hardly have been in greater contrast to the yellowing decay of the countryside during the heatwave.

The young postman laid the card on top of a pile of official letters from County Hall. Despite the early hour he was already feeling the effects of the heat. Beads of sweat trickled in rivulets down his cheeks, dropping onto the envelopes as he handed them to Alma at the door.

'Bit different to here, Mrs Smith.' He nodded at the picture.

Alma smiled gently into the eager young face as he attempted to make polite conversation. 'Manners maketh man', she'd drummed into the older scholars as they'd prepared to face the world. She liked to see her years of tuition bearing fruit. 'Yes indeed, Thomas. Wouldn't it be lovely to feel that cool here? This heat is so enervating,' and she fanned herself gently with the letters as if to accentuate the point. With that he nodded again. He accepted her gesture of polite dismissal, bade her 'Good day' and trudged down the garden path. Alma lingered at the door, watching him.

All those years she'd taught him. Eased him through the traumas of coming to school from a home that sneered at such unnecessary fripperies as education. A home where a boy was expected to earn a few shillings picking flints from the fields to sell to road builders or scaring birds from newly-sown crops, not sit at a desk all day tussling with addition and subtraction, reading and writing. But she had persisted and now he had a job. A job, moreover, that entailed reading proficiently. No longer a scholar but a working man.

She'd been patient, coaxing him to learn. Patted his hand when discouragement and disapproval at home made learning hard. As he retrieved the bicycle he'd propped against the gatepost she closed the door.

The picture of lofty snow-covered mountains and verdant pastures amazed Alma. Such an intensity of whiteness. Such a living greenness. It took her breath away. The thrill made her fingers tingle.

Mountains had never been part of Alma's experience. In all her fifty years she'd known nothing but the undulating flatlands of East Anglia and the winding lanes of her childhood home in the rural Forest of Dean. It was there, as a pupil teacher, that 21-year-old Alma Morse, the daughter of a prosperous mine owner, had met and married her husband.

She gazed at the picture, feeling the chill of the snow-covered peaks as she held the card delicately by its edges. Imagined the smell of meadow grass and sweet-scented flowers.

She turned the card over. The message was from Eva. She and her sister Marianne were walking in the Alps with their father Josef and their elder brothers, Rudolf and Walter. Father had been given command of a new ship. She and Marianne had become teachers themselves. Most surprising of all, she was inviting William and Alma to Germany. The news overwhelmed her.

Alma flicked through the rest of the post before taking it into the breakfast room. Most were official reports from the Education Committee, which William would deal with. 'Nothing of great interest today....' she began as she laid the letters beside his plate, 'except this. A postcard from our little frauleins. On holiday in the mountains!' The delight in her voice made him glance up from the remnants of toast and marmalade.

'Well, well! How wonderful that they should remember us, after all this time. Well, well,' he repeated, tickled at his own surprise. 'What do they say? Read it to me.'

She read the message, written in quaint, translated English. 'We are walking with our father and brothers in the Alps at Berchtesgaden. It is very beautiful. Since we stayed with you we talk of you often. We have good memories of Suffolk. We are teachers now and Papa is captain of a submarine. Next summer you come and stay with us in Aachen? Yes? Fond wishes, your friends Marianne and Eva.'

'Let me see,' William said. She thrust the postcard into his eager hand and he flicked it back and forth, looking first at the scene, then the message, then back again. Stabbing at the mountains with his forefinger, he laughed. 'How wonderful! How extraordinary!' He was in fine spirits this morning. 'The little frauleins have remembered us after all these years. Well, I never! Now remind me, my dear, how long is it since they stayed with us here? Five years is it? Maybe more? I've lost count.'

'Mmm. It must have been the summer of…er…' Alma stopped, then counted back on her fingers as she made rapid mental associations. 'I think it must have been 1910.'

'My goodness. The excitement those girls caused. Do you remember, Alma? Such pretty girls too, with their fair hair and embroidered costumes. And didn't our boys just adore them?' William laughed again, remembering the teenagers who had descended on the village. They could have been alien beings from another planet, for all the stir they'd caused. Any outsider, even from neighbouring Norfolk, would have been viewed with suspicion as a 'furriner'. But the arrival of two German students wishing to learn English had been so unlikely as to be almost scandalous. 'They must be quite grown up by now, though.'

'Alex was only 17 then and still studying in Aachen. It was just before that dreadful winter when he fell sick and you had to travel to Germany and bring him home,' Alma prompted.

'Well, well now,' William shook his dark, close-cropped head several times in disbelief. The passage of time had caught him by surprise. He could think of nothing else to say. The mention of his son's name stirred dark misgivings within him. Alex's prolonged absences abroad troubled him greatly, although he never admitted as much to Alma.

Alex had left home to study in France and Germany, having shown great promise as a language scholar at school. Then two years ago, in a move that William and Alma thought bordered on lunacy, Alex announced, quite out of the blue, that he was moving from Germany to teach languages in Guatemala. The very name of the Central American country, ruled by a dictator, sounded exotic and dangerous to his parents.

William wondered if Alex would ever settle back in England again after seeing how very different life was abroad. A restless young man it was doubtful whether the close-knit, claustrophobic community of his birthplace would ever contain him or satisfy his yearning for freedom and novelty.

Ted Alexander Montague Smith was mature beyond his 21 years. He had no need of home or stability nor even any desire for news of home. In return he volunteered no information about himself. He wrote few letters to his parents. Consequently they couldn't begin to imagine how he lived in Guatemala City, or how he was coping with the language and the culture. They wondered what kind of exotic food he was eating. What did it taste like? His parents found it unfathomable. William knew Alma was fearful that Alex's already delicate health would deteriorate in such an inhospitable climate, that the fever he'd suffered in Aachen would return and once again leave him close to death. Sometimes William wondered if he would ever see his son again.

'Do you see what it says at the bottom?' Alma prompted, peered over his shoulder, lightly resting her cheek against his. A chilly silence had descended at the mention of Alex's name. She wanted desperately to dispel it. 'The little frauleins have invited us to go and stay with them in Aachen next summer.'

'Would you like that?' He reached up and touched the greying wisps of chestnut hair that curled around her pale cheeks. His deep brown eyes glowed affectionately. He knew what her answer would be.

'You know I would. And the Reimann's were so good to Alex when he was ill. I'd like to be able to go and thank them myself.'

'I shall write back today, thanking them for their invitation,' William said, turning in his chair and taking her hands firmly in his. 'And we *shall* go to Germany next summer. But there's one, small thing,' he paused, teasing. He watched the anxious creasing around her eyes.

'What's that?'

William jabbed his finger at the postcard again. 'I'm afraid you won't be seeing mountains like these if we go to Aachen. It's a beautiful city with streets full of fountains and fine old buildings. And it has some splendid hot sulphurous springs that are very good for the rheumatics, but snow-capped mountains? No.'

'I shall love it, whatever the geography,' she smiled back at him. With that she picked up the postcard and put it in the pocket of her dress. She had thought of a use for it in her schoolroom.

The schoolhouse stood next to the flint-walled village school and each morning William and Alma walked there across the adjoining yard. It was a popular school, with many children travelling long distances from villages several miles away, often on foot. One hundred and sixty children between the ages of five and 14 were on roll. But even in summer full attendance was a rarity.

Sickness, which rampaged through the close-knit community during the cold winter months, depleted the numbers. At other times pupils were kept home by parents desperate for an extra pair of hands to earn a few extra shillings. Often they were needed to care for younger siblings. An assistant and two pupil teachers, 16 and 17 years old, helped with the younger children.

Like the house itself, the school was of austere flint and brick. It was built in 1859 as a Public Elementary School on land benevolently provided by the second Earl of Stradbroke. The scholars were divided between three classrooms according to age; infants, Lower Standards and Higher Standards. The classrooms were daunting places with their lofty, arched ceilings and long, narrow windows. Windows, Alma suspected, set high to thwart daydreamers gazing at the freedom that lay beyond the dull green distemper walls.

At the end of each classroom stood a raised platform and on it a desk and high teacher's chair. The dark wooden floors were pitted and splintered with age and harsh use, yet Ida, the housekeeper and cleaner, worked hard to keep them clean and polished. The only form of heating was from enclosed iron stoves.

Sometimes in winter it was so cold that the smaller children, many in ragged, threadbare clothes, could barely hold their slate pencils. Then they'd be commanded to jump up and down in well-drilled unison or throw a ball back and forth to each other to keep warm.

Adjoining the Upper Standard's classroom was the headmaster's small office and beyond that a lobby which was used as a cloakroom. Around the back of the building and across the yard were the children's toilets. Small, squalid little outhouses with a smell that stubbornly resisted Ida's liberal applications of Lysol disinfectant.

A porch sheltered the front of the building and the roof was crowned with a bell-tower, although William preferred to summon the children into lessons using a large brass hand-bell he had bought himself. Along the front of the school was a low flint wall that offered some protection from the comings and goings of the traffic on the turnpike between Ipswich and Lowestoft.

The small playground at the back of the building was unfenced, the ground falling away gently to a hedged area of gardens where pupils cultivated vegetables. Further down the slope was what William proudly termed 'the playing field', but which in reality was a roughly-mown meadow. Beyond that was the little River Wang.

A bathing pool, which had been constructed from a meander in the river by William and men of the village fourteen years previously, lay less than a hundred yards away.

The older pupils in Upper Standards listened enviously as beyond the grimed windows they could hear the younger children splashing in the pool and plunging with shrieks of delight from the diving board. Their turn would come, they knew, but they were impatient to be there instead of sweating at their desks in a fetid, airless classroom. They ached to feel the cooling water on their skin.

Alma pinned the postcard prominently on the wall beside her desk. 'See how high the mountains are,' she pointed out, trying to distract them. 'So high that the snow never melts, even at the height of summer. See how different their houses are.' The postcard had then been passed around the class, sticky hand to hand, so that each child could peer at it.

'Observe the small white flowers in the foreground,' Alma instructed. 'They look like stars. Have you ever seen such flowers before?'

None of the children could recall finding flowers like this in the meadows or the marshland, nor deep in the woodland of the Henham Estate.

So, having studied this foreign landscape, the children were finally set the task of writing their compositions. How would they compare this mountainous scenery to that of their own country? Since all they knew was the flat pastureland of Suffolk the contrast could not have been greater. How would the cool of that mountain air compare to the heat-wave they were now experiencing? What would the lush grass of that meadow smell like? How would it feel beneath their feet? Alma knew she was demanding an impossible stretch of the imagination. After all, she'd never seen mountains herself and could only imagine their magnificence.

There was silence as fifty pupils obediently set to work, each hand tracing immaculately even, looped letters across the pages of their exercise books. Only the tapping of pens in inkwells, the scratching of nibs and the dull hum of insects among the rafters broke the quietness. Although the threadbare, black blinds were pulled down, the sunlight still penetrated, casting pale ribbons of dust across the rows of bent heads. The air, thick with the smell of unwashed young bodies, was stultifying. Drowsy heads began nodding towards the desks as pupils struggled to stay awake.

They worked on without a murmur. Alma stepped quietly across to the long window where, if she stood on tiptoe, she could just see over the stone ledge. Outside in the schoolyard the dust was playing a solitary game. Eddies of corn-husks and straw had formed a lazy whirlpool which were being whipped gently by a sea breeze wafting over the fields from Southwold. She thought its rhythmic circling mirrored the elegant curls of her pupils' lettering.

Occasionally she'd catch a glimpse of her husband and the younger children, splashing about in the pool at the bend of the river. She liked to stand at a distance, unobserved, watching him. Even now she marvelled at their unlikely pairing. She'd been a plain, somewhat reserved young woman, blessed only with delicate features and a gentle disposition. He, dramatically handsome and ebullient, his enthusiasms often bordering on obsessions. Yet their union had been fulfilling beyond all their imagining.

She fixed her gaze on William's athletic body as he cut with animal swiftness from one group to another, encouraging and cajoling, demonstrating the strokes of the crawl or breast-stroke with his arms from a vantage point on the bank. He was finely developed; an abdomen that was flat and etched, legs that were powerful and in symmetry. His upper body, bared for swimming, was strongly muscled and well defined and his skin had a distinctly olive tone. It marked him out. As a Devonian of Celtic stock, he looked quite unlike the lanky, fine-boned men native to Suffolk. His silky black hair and dark eyebrows and moustache only served to accentuate this difference.

Sports of all kind and physical fitness, William had declared, were supremely important for developing young minds and bodies. He was most emphatic about it. Alma often wondered if his determination to foster sporting prowess, whether at swimming, cycling or athletics, was to the detriment of other, more academic studies. But the school always achieved glowing reports from His Majesty's Inspectors when they arrived on their periodic inspections.

Creating a swimming pool had been his obsession from their earliest days at the school.

'All our children must learn natation, it's one of the noblest of our pastimes,' he'd said, racking his brains as to how it could be achieved. 'And life-saving, too, for they live so close to the sea that many will be destined to earn their livelihood from it, not to mention the large numbers who'll swim off the beach for relaxation. Anyone possessed of ordinary human pluck must be taught the best methods of rescue and resuscitation.' And so the germ of his idea for a pool had been born.

William had organised a special parish meeting in the schoolroom to discuss his notion of damming the River Wang and to his delight the Earl of Stradbroke had attended. At the end of the meeting he'd applauded William as loudly as the rest of the villagers.

'Mr Smith, this is a fine idea. You're to be congratulated. When you have your pool constructed I've no doubt you'll be producing some worthy competitors for the swimming galas in Ipswich and Lowestoft. Who knows – we could one day have a champion in Henham,' he'd said enthusiastically. It was an ambition that won appreciative applause.

The villagers who had crowded the larger of the schoolrooms that evening sensed that times were changing. A new, young headmaster with go-ahead, revolutionary ideas about what children should be learning and with a strong sense of discipline, had taken over the school. The old Earl had died seventeen days short of his ninety-third birthday and into his shoes had stepped his 24-year-old son, George, who had brought fresh vigour to the estate, its farms and the village as a whole. Both men had thrown themselves wholeheartedly into the life of the village, so that there was a feeling in Wangford and Henham that life in the new century was definitely changing. And for the better.

'How fortunate we are!' William had exclaimed when all the villagers had left. Grabbing both Alma's hands in excitement, he'd swung her off her feet, kissing her.

'We have such a wonderful benefactor in the Earl. We have this school and now we're to get our pool. I must be, without doubt, the happiest man in Suffolk!'

She remembered how William had flung himself, emotionally exhausted, limbs flying erratically, into the hard wooden chair behind the desk she now occupied.

Long after the Earl had married and brought his bride to Henham and they'd produced a clutch of children, his Countess had unexpectedly arrived one afternoon at the school.

Glimpsing her carriage halting outside the gate from his office window, William had scrambled to his feet with not a little trepidation. He'd watched as out of the open carriage tumbled the three older girls. Then the Countess, a slender, statuesque figure dressed in a pink linen suit and matching straw hat set at a fashionably rakish angle, stepped down. As she picked her way up the brick path the seven-year-old Viscount Dunwich clung reluctantly to her skirts.

Hastily William had commanded his pupils close their books and stand silently to attention behind their benches to await the guests.

'Good afternoon, headmaster,' Helena, Countess of Stradbroke smiled and inclined her head slightly, firstly at William and his wife, then around the room, as she and her children made their entrance into the larger of the three classrooms.

'Good afternoon, your Ladyship,' William and Alma replied in unison. Then turning to the children, William nodded in silent signal. On cue fifty or more children chorused, 'Good afternoon, your Ladyship.'

'Children, you may sit.' William said in carefully measured tones, though feeling far from calm. They scrambled quietly back onto the benches ranged in straight rows behind the long heavy desks. They sat bolt upright, not daring to whisper a word.

An older boy, a monitor, crept forward and moved Alma's round-backed wooden chair from behind the desk to the front of the small dais. He held out his hand with exaggerated courtesy, motioning the Countess to be seated. Her bemused children clustered around her in a circle.

'Mr Smith, I have been hearing great things from his Lordship about the success you're having with teaching your scholars' natation. He's particularly proud, since he's chairman of your School Managers, that the life-saving team was awarded a trophy at the gala in Ipswich last week. Well done, all of you.'

'Thank you ma'am,' William hardly knew what to say. Such an unexpected visit and now such compliments.

Helena twinkled disarmingly, realising her sudden appearance had caused some consternation among both scholars and teachers. 'Now. To the reason for my visit. I would like our son John here, and all our older girls to learn to swim. His Lordship and I sadly came to realise, through a most tragic family accident, that being able to swim is a very necessary skill for both boys and girls.'

She turned and spoke directly to the children ranged in rapt silence before her. 'Six years ago, children, on a beautiful summer's day just like this one, in August nineteen-hundred-and-four, the Earl's dear sister, Hilda, drowned while trying to rescue an eleven-year-old boy from a river.' There was a sharp sigh from the assembled children.

'Yes, I know how shocking that must be to you. Lady Hilda McNeill was an extremely brave woman. She'd seen Glen Pritchard fall into the waters of the River Taw at Fremington, where she was spending a holiday, and leapt in to try and save him. Unfortunately neither she nor the boy were able to swim. Both of them were swept away by a very strong current and drowned. It was courageous and selfless of her, but you can imagine the dreadful sadness this tragedy caused the families, both ours and the Pritchards. Especially as Lady Hilda's own son, Ronald and Glen's sister, Mary, saw the whole frightful event from the bank.' She smiled gently at their solemn faces. 'That's why I'm so delighted you're all learning natation, and doing so well at it. And so his Lordship and I want Mr Smith to teach our own children, too.'

'I would consider it a great honour, your Ladyship,' William said deferentially.

'So, headmaster. If it's not an inconvenience to yourself, perhaps they could start next week? Their governesses will bring them down from the Hall at a time convenient to your swimming timetable.'

'I should be only too happy, your Ladyship,' he'd replied. 'I'm sure you're aware that the Honourable Lady Agnes Eden already entrusts us with her nephew, Anthony. During his frequent visits to her on holiday from Eton he's been training in life-saving and is now a most creditable member of our life-saving club.'

Helena nodded. She had learned as much from her close friend Agnes and was confident in the rightness of entrusting the Earl's son and heir to William's tuition.

'If there's anything we can do to help in your venture, please don't hesitate to ask. I'm sure his Lordship will be only too delighted to ensure it's carried out,' she'd added.

'Now, I'm sure your scholars will wish to return to their studies. I'll detain you all no longer. Good afternoon Mr Smith,' and with that she had gathered up the extravagant skirts of her dress with one hand and young John with the other and swept from the building, down the brick pathway and out to her waiting carriage.

Her three daughters remained rooted to their tight circle, spellbound by the ranks of silent pupils and their dress; the boys in cut-down corduroys and shirts with holes in the elbows, the girls in faded pinafores and high button boots. So mesmerised were they by this show of obedience and the poverty of the pupils' dress that they failed to notice the rows of eyes and mouths narrowing in suspicion and hostility.

This view of a childhood regimented by class was indeed a novelty for the Rous girls. They were more accustomed to governesses who failed abysmally to maintain any semblance of order or silence in their schoolroom at Henham Hall. They seemed reluctant to leave, entranced by the large number of children assembled for their benefit and amusement.

'Pleasance, Catherine, Betty! Come along, don't dawdle!' Lady Stradbroke's imperious tones rang out across the schoolyard. Her bevy of pretty daughters swiftly obeyed.

Now, in the searing heat of the summer of 1914, Alma witnessed another generation of children learning to swim in the green pond. She was proud of her husband. He had trained champions. So many children, so many triumphs brought home to Henham from the swimming galas of Lowestoft and Ipswich and beyond.

She watched the young Viscount Dunwich, now a strong, athletic youth, execute a neat dive from the diving board. He slipped with barely a splash into the deepest part of the pool and disappeared beneath the surface. There was no sign of him. The new governess who had brought him down from the Hall looked on in consternation. She leapt from her chair beneath a shady willow and shrieked, 'Mr Smith, Mr Smith! Where's John?'

Hearing the note of panic in her voice the ever-vigilant lifesaver, Dick, the black Labrador, leapt into the water and paddled enthusiastically out to find him. But John eluded him. Suddenly the boy emerged from beneath the water, close to the farthest bank. Laughing, he grabbed the dog's tail, the customary method of rescue if there were no members of the lifesaving club present, and allowed Dick to haul him back to his hysterical governess.

'There Miss Potts. I told you I could swim,' he yelled as he scrambled up the bank, aware of the panic he'd caused. Governesses, in John's book, were fair game.

'Well I don't know. I really don't.' Miss Potts sounded flustered. She flapped a small white handkerchief in front of her nose to ward off the fainting fit she was sure she was about to suffer. A fit induced by fear that the Viscount had drowned. 'Wrap yourself in a towel now, Mr John. I don't want you catching your death of cold.' She pursed her lips. This boy was proving quite a handful, and she knew when she was deliberately being made a fool of.

Alma laughed quietly under her breath and moved reluctantly from the window. She glanced up at the clock. Half past three. 'Tommy, go and ring the bell, please.'

A tall, serious-faced boy in the back row of desks closed his workbook, then taking the large brass bell from the cupboard at the back of the classroom went out into the empty yard. He shook the bell enthusiastically, his whole underfed frame tolling with it.

'Time to pack away, children. You may finish your compositions tomorrow.' Alma knew these were the sweetest words of the day to young ears. Quickly they put away their pens and books. They stood to attention behind the rows of desks, hands clasped neatly together, heads bowed ready for prayer.

Alma started intoning quietly. 'Lighten our darkness….' They took up the refrain, parrot fashion. Chanting the habitual words with solemnity, yet without thought to their meaning. It was the way of all children. 'Defend us from all the perils and dangers of this night. Amen.' An obedient chorus of 'Amen' echoed back at her and they raised their heads. 'Good afternoon girls and boys.' They replied as one: 'Good afternoon Miss.'

Alma watched them from the door as they walked in single file across the schoolyard, past the little stone hay barn that separated the school from the house. Once across the yard they became joyful creatures, careering and leaping through the grass. Some to join those in the bathing pool, others to head across fields to farms and cottages. Most made their way up the main street to homes clustered around the centre of the village, younger brothers and sisters from the infant and Lower Standards classes tagging along behind.

Older children bicycled to and from school, and she watched in amusement as the Boggis brothers, Clement and Charlie, indulged in their daily argument as to who should have first turn on the shared bicycle that got them home to the butcher's shop in Southwold market place. One would ride the adult bicycle, far too big for them, standing on the pedals. The other would trudge down the lane on foot. At a given point the rider would dump the cycle in the hedge and start to walk while the walker picked the bike out of the hedge and eventually caught him up. Such was the routine for children who had to cover many miles to and from school each day.

For many, the end of the school day only marked the start of their other, working day. Even quite young children were expected to go gleaning, picking up beans and other crops, left behind by harvesters, or helping their mothers stone-picking in the fields. On long summer evenings they would be working until the light faded. Working like little donkeys, until they dropped through exhaustion. Only then would they eat a sparse supper before collapsing onto straw-filled mattresses on the floor.

'I'm walking to the store,' Alma called to William as she passed the pool, once her class had disappeared from view. 'Watch that boy doesn't drown.' she added, pointing to the Viscount now sprawled panting on the bank with Dick lying contentedly beside him.

'John's not a bad swimmer for his age. We'll turn him into a champion yet,' William laughed easily, racing up the river-bank to deliver a light kiss to his wife's cheek before she could pass him by.

It was a short walk from the school to the centre of the village. In wintertime, or if the weather was inclement, she would take the pony and trap. But leaving the cloying atmosphere of the classroom Alma needed to feel the faint whisper of sea breeze on her skin, feel it wafting the skirts of her muslin dress. As she picked her way daintily through the drifts of dirt in the cobbled street people sitting in doorways bade her 'Good afternoon, Mrs Smith.' Some stopped to engage her in conversation, but all they could talk about was the weather.

The heat wave.

There was no other topic in this remote, agricultural corner of Suffolk that was of any importance. This was no longer a glorious summer, to be basked in and enjoyed. It had gone on far too long for that. To those who lived so close to the soil and whose livelihoods depended on its fertility, nothing caused greater anxiety than the lack of rain. As each cloudless day dawned to scorch their crops and exhaust their animals they could do nothing except shake their heads dismally and mutter dire predictions. The spring that fed the River Wang was close to exhaustion so their wells were running dry. There grew an unspoken fear that soon there would be no water left.

They scanned the local newspaper for the latest stories about the weather.

'How terrible. What a dreadful way to die,' Alma heard someone say. A small group had gathered outside the village store and was listening as a proficient reader read aloud. The intense heat had been responsible for the death of a 60-year-old man, a miller named Robert Kerry, who'd worked at Steggall's Mill in Stowupland. Just as he was about to enter the mill, where he was accustomed to take his meals, he collapsed and died in the yard. The doctor was sent for, but could only pronounce life extinct. 'Shocking,' they all agreed.

Meanwhile, at Ipswich meteorological station, the thermometer had risen to 89.5 Fahrenheit. The highest temperature reached in many years, the newspaper reported with confidence.

No other topic merited such deep deliberation and discussion. Not the intractable question of Home Rule for Ireland. Not the efforts of the suffragettes to win the right for women to have the vote. Certainly not a violent assassination in a far-off capital the previous day. Why, in the suffocating heat of that summer, should the shooting of an Archduke in Bosnia impinge on *their* lives?

Alma flicked through the pages of the Daily Times as she left the store. The headline on a downpage story caught her eye.

Royal couple assassinated
Austrian heir and his wife shot

She read the item, but without absorbing it. Then something made her stop and read it again, this time with greater attention. When she'd finished she folded the paper and placed it on top of the basket of groceries, staring with unseeing eyes down the narrrow street.

She pictured the couple, dying in each others arms, their bloodied bodies clinging together. Curious crowds staring, dumbfounded at what they were witnessing. Jostling and shoving for a closer view. The very public death of a royal personage, heir to the Austro-Hungarian throne and his Duchess, in a sordid side street.

How terrible to die in such a fashion, with the eyes of so many people upon you, thought Alma. *But to go with the one you love, surely that's a fate we would all devoutly wish for?*

As she walked home across the harvested cornfield she couldn't get the image of the dying couple out of her mind.

Chapter Three

Thursday July 16 1914

The Countess of Stradbroke stared critically at her image in the dressing table mirror. After hours of preparation she was satisfied. The evening gown she'd chosen for the ball was perfect; an exquisite creation designed especially for her by Maison Beer to show off her lithe, whisper-thin figure and emphasise her firmly-rounded breasts. The cloth was a dark cyclamen Liberty, covered with a black tulle tunic and embroidered in gold and amethyst shades with stones of the same colour. A big bow of black satin, edged in gold and fringed with amethyst stones, dramatically highlighted the hem of the dress as it cascaded into a train.

In her hair she'd carefully positioned a tiara of diamonds and pearls with three stunning central amethysts that picked out the fine tracery in her gown. It sat confidently among the rebellious riot of dark, glossy curls, which her maid had pinned high on the crown of her head. The final touch had yet to be made, she observed, applying just the slightest hint of rouge to her cheeks. And that would be in the hands of her husband.

At forty-one Helena Stradbroke was now regarded as one of the 'matrons' of the royal court, yet she was still one of the most stunningly beautiful women currently gracing English society. Her face had lost none of its sensuality. High cheekbones accentuated her peachy complexion while dark eyebrows and a long, aquiline nose bestowed on her an almost Mediterranean mystique.

Sir James Shannon, one of the most sought-after society artists of his day, had painted her some years earlier and it was generally acknowledged he only chose to paint the most beautiful women and that he'd painted more lovely women than any other artist of his day.

He had managed to capture, with uncanny accuracy, the very qualities that had entranced the Earl when he had courted and married this stunning 24-year-old in 1898. Beneath the demure, porcelain-like delicacy he had discerned a determined and resolute spirit. Helena, perhaps because of her upbringing in a military family with roots in Scottish society that stretched back to King Robert the Bruce, was very much her own woman.

George had marked her out as potentially a formidable mistress of Henham Hall. And so it was to prove. Helena's prodigious energy enabled her to run his huge household efficiently, yet with concern and compassion for all those who worked for her. She was also a woman of enormous generosity, a trait which revealed itself when it came to throwing lavish balls, house parties and shooting parties at Henham at which they had entertained fellow members of the aristocracy. Even the King had graced Henham with his presence.

Most of all, though, the Earl's heart had been won by the promise held in those luminous emerald eyes. There lurked beneath the fluttering dark lashes a daring coquetry that never failed to stir his passions to an almost uncontrollable intensity. He knew he had to have her.

Their marriage had been more than simply a love match. Both acknowledged that fact, although love had been the overwhelmingly driving passion in their union. It had brought together two families with not just royal roots but with a long tradition of military service.

Helena Violet Alice Fraser was the only child of a soldier baronet, Lt General James Keith Fraser, Colonel of 1st regiment of Lifeguards. Her great-uncle, Brigadier General Robert Crauford – popularly known as 'Black Bob' – was one of Wellington's ablest commanders during the Peninsula War. He was killed while leading his troops into battle at the siege of Cuidad Rodrigo in 1812.

Her grandfather, Sir James Fraser, 3rd Baronet, also served under the Duke of Wellington. He was Aide de Camp to the unfortunate Earl of Uxbridge, Wellington's second in command. Lord Uxbridge achieved notoriety for having lost the Duke his cavalry in 1815.

Later Helena's uncle, Major Charles Crauford Fraser of the 11th Hussars, won the Victoria Cross at Lucknow during the Indian Mutiny of 1858. He'd volunteered, at great personal risk and under the sharp fire of musketry, to swim to the rescue of a captain and some men who were in imminent danger of being drowned while in pursuit of the rebels. He succeeded, despite being disabled by a wound he'd received while leading a charge against the enemy some months earlier.

George's father, John Edward Cornwallis Rous, the second Earl of Stradbroke, had been a professional soldier who saw extensive action in the Peninsula campaign, being present at the battles of Salamanca and Vittoria, the sieges of Burgos and San Sebastian and the investment of Bayonne. His older brother, Henry, became an Admiral as well as a Westminster MP.

Coming from such families, where public service was an accepted adjunct to the wealth and power of inheritance, Helena loved in George the same qualities she had so admired in her own father. He was, she felt, the epitome of the most admirable kind of Englishman; restrained yet determined, honourable and upright, good-humoured and public-spirited and certainly capable of leadership under fire. He was also an accomplished sportsman and horseman and his trim physique, even in later years, was testament to that athleticism.

But what she adored most about him was the warmth and laughter he spread like a comfortable blanket around him, wherever he went. His children adored him and were frequently to be seen tumbling in a noisy mass on top of him as he romped with them on the nursery-room floor. There was never a time he turned down the opportunity to play, even if it was past bedtime and nanny was looking on with silent disapproval. George himself often shamefacedly admitted he spoiled his children terribly, especially his four fine boys. But he was unrepentant and in Helena he found a willing, giggling conspirator in outwitting nanny or the governesses.

Together tonight at Buckingham Palace Helena would be in her element. She adored parties and especially lavish evening soirées thrown by the King when she would be mixing with members of the Royal family and other members of the English aristocracy, not to mention those who had been invited from the world of opera, the stage or entertainment. An accomplished mezzo-soprano herself, she was looking forward to the chance to talk informally with singers like Melba. Her husband, an ADC to King George V, as he had been to King Edward VII, would be much happier talking farming, shooting, politics or military matters with fellow members of the House of Lords or the smattering of foreign ambassadors who were usually present.

She was wondering who else would be on the King's guest list when the door to her dressing room opened.

'Come in George. How do I look?' Helena swung round from the mirror, lifting the train of her dress as she rose so she could spin a graceful circle before him.

'Nellie my dear, you look absolutely divine.' George Stradbroke gazed at the glittering apparition before him, tossing her jewelled curls in a mocking, careless gesture.

'Wonderful. Without doubt you'll be the most beautiful women in the room tonight,' he added, with feeling.

'Thank you darling. You're such an old flatterer. But there's something missing.'

'Oh?' He frowned, the corners of his blue eyes crinkling with concern.

'Why, my diamonds, silly!' she chided him.

'Of course,' he smiled with relief. He had momentarily forgotten the intimate routine they had initiated on the first day of their marriage. 'I shall do the honours, as usual.'

George took a key from the bureau in the corner of the dressing room and unlocked a large case. Inside lay a glorious diamond necklace and matching earrings. A priceless family heirloom that had adorned many previous Countesses of Stradbroke at court functions. He lifted the necklace gingerly and with well-rehearsed precision placed it around his wife's neck and fixed the complex clasp together. It lay glistening against the pale ivory of her skin. Now, he thought, she looks even more breathtaking.

He bent over and brushed his lips gently along the nape of her neck. 'I am madly in love with you. You know that don't you Nellie?' he whispered.

'Darling George.' Her hand reached up to pat his greying moustache. 'Behave.' She twinkled her eyes at him. His face, she thought, was now showing signs of his fifty-two years, yet still he was the handsomest of men, with an intensity in those blue eyes that never failed to melt her.

She was well aware that their passionate relationship was the source of much unkind gossip among acquaintances. So unlike *their* formal, empty unions. They chided her for producing so many children, seven of them so far and the latest only a few months old. Yet how were outsiders to know how much they adored not only each other, but all of their offspring?

Earrings set in place, cloak fetched, Helena was ready. It was a short journey from their elegant London home in Kensington's Lexham Gardens to the Palace. Parties there never began before eleven o'clock and carriages came at dawn. It would be an exhausting night of dancing, eating, drinking champagne and gossip.

For many years, in Helena's younger days, London entertaining had been in the doldrums. Queen Victoria had abdicated her position as head of society and without a sovereign to give a lead it had virtually gone to pieces. Split into sections, each cotterie going its own way, the disparate parts had little or no connection with the others. The effect of this disintegration had been to put an end to general entertaining and so Helena, and other young debutantes of her era, missed the glitter of court life and subsequently felt badly done by.

But when Victoria's son, Edward, came to the throne that was quickly remedied. Shortly after his accession in 1901 he announced that he and his Queen would honour their greater subjects with their presence at balls and receptions. The effect had been instantaneous. The stately homes of England threw open their doors as the leaders of society vied with each other as to who could provide the most lavish hospitality. His son, George and his Queen, in their turn, were equally as lavish.

So now Helena found herself with invitations during the Season not only to the four evening Courts, but a series of brilliant parties at the Palace and this was to be the most glittering of all, the event that wound up the Court festivities of the season.

Some two thousand guests, including members of the Corps Diplomatique, government and opposition MPs, Dukes and Duchesses, Marquesses and

Marchionesses, Earl and Countesses, Viscounts and Viscountesses, Lords and Ladies, Baronets, Knights and officers of the Navy and Army, were all born by their carriages up the Mall to the Palace for this spectacular event.

A wealth of beautiful flowers had transformed the galleries and chambers into a garden of enchantment. The air was scented with the fragrance of exotic blooms mixed with equally tantalising perfumes.

The great ballroom, with its dazzling white walls adorned only by two panels of priceless Gobelin tapestry, was lit by crystal chandeliers hanging from the lofty ceiling, casting their irridescent light on shimmering silks and satins and extravagent uniforms.

In Victoria's days myriads of wax candles had shed a soft golden radiance. Far more becoming to the complexion, Helena felt, than the searching light of electric lamps. But they had also diffused an amount of heat, which on a warm July night like this had made the atmosphere intolerable.

At one end of the ballroom was the musician's gallery where his Majesty's band was stationed and facing this at the other end was a dais, surmounted by a crimson and gilt canopy. This was reserved for the royal personages, often accompanied by some crowned head or other illustrious visitor from abroad.

By eleven o'clock most of the guests had assembled in the ballroom and in the vast corridors leading into it. Helena, with head held high, entered the ballroom on the arm of her adoring husband. *How beautiful everyone is*, she thought, as the glittering chandeliers blazed down on crowds of England's fairest women and most aristocratic men. Diamonds flashed in soft hair and gleamed on white shoulders. Amidst the men in evening dress was a peppering of colourful dress uniforms. Most remarkable of all were the gorgeous dresses of the Indian guests who, as a rule, took no part in the dancing. The Maharajah of Kuch Behar was a notable exception and, as Helena had experienced, was a waltzer with few equals.

The brilliant throng did not have long to wait. Punctually, at eleven o'clock, the strains of the National Anthem heralded the approach of the Royal procession. The Lord Chamberlain, ramrod straight back and alert in his blue, gold-laced coat, knee-breeches and white silk stockings and bearing his long wand of office, backed slowly into the ballroom before the King and Queen. He conducted them to the dais where they, their guests of honour and other members of the Royal Family took their places.

Helena quivered with excitement. This moment never failed to entrance her. George took her hand, knowing the expectancy that was welling up inside her.

He whispered, 'This is the moment you've been waiting for, isn't it?'

She nodded and her bejewelled head twinkled with a million lights.

The dancing was about to begin. The State quadrille, danced to Strauss's 'Methusalem', was immediately formed and beside the Royal family members, ambassadors, high officials and their wives, a privileged few would be invited to take part. Those usually singled out for this distinction always included such leaders of society as the Duchesses of Sutherland, Portland and Westminster as well as Lady Londonderry and Lady de Grey. Others in that small phalanx which constituted the King's immediate entourage were also included. As ADC to the King, the Earl and his lady were a part of that select circle.

Helena's moment had come. She stepped forward with a natural grace to take her place in the quadrille with her husband. She heard someone whisper among the watchers, 'A daughter of the gods, divinely tall.' She smiled to herself. She was aware she stood out from the throng, the diamond tiara adding inches to her stature.

The State quadrille completed, the dancing became more general. There were waltzes by Lehar, Gilbert, Fortoni and Strauss, another quadrille and a lively polka – eleven dances altogether. Helena loved every one of them.

Those among the Royal party who enjoyed a waltz were in the habit of sending an equerry to inform their intended partners of the honour in store for them. On past occasions, Helena remembered, the old King, Edward, had invited her to dance in just such a fashion. She had dined out on the experience for months. Now, with King George on the throne and so many delightful young ladies to choose from, she doubted whether such an invitation would come her way again. It wouldn't be long, though, before their eldest daughter Pleasance, would be presented to the King and Queen as a debutante. At fifteen she was almost of age and was being groomed for this nerve-wracking occasion.

George was anxious to take his place with the gentlemen and after fulfilling his quota of dances gratefully deposited Helena on a sofa where she was surrounded by several other be-jewelled ladies, including the Duchess of Westminster and the Duchess of Marlborough. Dancing was a necessary social skill, he acknowledged, but he found it tedious.

The conversation among the military men and landed gentry he discovered lolling against the exquisite furniture in the corridor, had turned from the worn and seemingly insoluble dilemma of Home Rule for Ireland to the shooting of Archduke Franz Ferdinand.

'Rum old do, this business in Sarajevo,' muttered the elderly Duke of Marlborough. 'Yet another royal house in Europe laid low by an assassin.'

'It's the third time Herbert Asquith has had to move a humble address to the King expressing the sorrow of the Government at such a death,' the Duke of Portland volunteered. 'Why, only last year the King of the Hellenes, the brother of our own Queen Mother, was assassinated in his hour of triumph in the streets of Salonika. And do you recall, six years ago, King Carlos of Portugal met a similar fate while riding out in his own capital?' Those gathered around him nodded knowingly. There had been a shocking toll of violent royal deaths in recent years.

The United States ambassador, looking exceedingly plain alongside the finery of the aristocracy, wearing a simple black coat, knee-breeches and black-silk stockings, injected a note of cynicism. 'Some I've spoken to are of the opinion it's good riddance to the Archduke. He was stirring up a hornet's nest visiting Sarajevo in the first place,' he said. 'Fancy choosing to go there on Serbia's National Day. No wonder the Serbs felt insulted and plotted his death.'

'You know, of course, he married a Magyar,' Portland threw out haughtily. 'That may have endeared him to the Hungarians, but everyone else was quite appalled, particularly the Emperor. Why he couldn't have chosen a Hapsburg or a member of one of Europe's other ruling dynasties, I can't imagine. She was a commoner, a lady-in-waiting. Not a wise match, I think.'

Heads nodded again, dismissing Archduke Franz Ferdinand because he had married beneath him.

'Surely we should be wary of the consequences of such an assassination?' suggested the Earl. 'After all, the Austrians and Serbs could well come to blows over this?'

Marlborough laughed confidently. 'Good God, no, George. Haven't you read the papers today? The student who shot him has confessed to being an anarchist. An odd cove, acting on impulse I would say. It'll all die down in time.'

A tall, distinguished man in the full dress uniform of an Admiral stopped as he ambled along the corridor.

'I beg to differ, my Lord. Too many nations are simply spoiling for a fight. Germany, for instance. This situation between Austria and Serbia could be the very tinderbox that sets them all off. Then who knows who might join the fray?'

The Admiral's prognosis was met with stunned silence. The distinguished lords, having gathered at the Palace in relaxed mood, found it hard to turn their minds to the complexities of international treaties that bound nation to nation or to envisage how these might colour the present situation.

'The King reviews the Home Fleet at Spithead at the end of this week,' the Admiral went on. 'It'll be, incomparably, the most formidable assembly of fighting ships ever seen in British waters reviewed by a monarch. A larger fleet, by far, than Nelson ever had at his disposal in the Mediterranean a hundred years ago.'

He reeled off an impressive list: 59 battleships, - 24 of them dreadnoughts and 35 pre-dreadnoughts; twelve squadrons of cruisers and light cruisers; 78 destroyers; nine flotillas of 59 submarines and 23 of the latest type sea-planes, plus a large number of auxiliary vessels. 'But we shouldn't be complacent,' he warned. 'We may need to use these ships sooner than we think. I'm sure Winston will be watching the situation closely.'

It was indeed an ominous thought. George suspected the Admiral was being unnecessarily pessimistic, but refrained from saying so. What good would a navy be if conflict erupted in middle Europe, between land-locked Austria and Serbia? And why would England be troubled by such a conflict, anyhow?

In the carriage on the way back to Lexham Gardens, as the first pink light of dawn spread across the sky, the Countess, still lively as a cricket, recounted with much laughter the latest court gossip she'd acquired from the other ladies. George listened, but only with half his attention. His mind was troubled by the remarks he'd heard in the corridor, those brief snatches of conversation he'd been party to before he'd moved on to join other groups where life, more predictably, revolved around hunting, shooting and farming.

East Anglian Daily Times
Monday July 27 1914

London Letter.

Out of the Near East has suddenly loomed up another war cloud. On Thursday it seemed no bigger than a man's hand. Today it has enveloped Europe, indeed there are rumours that hostilities have broken out in places and that along the Serbian frontier fighting has commenced. Certain is it that diplomatic relations between Austrian and Serbia have broken off and that the Serbian capital has been shifted from Belgrade, which is close to the frontier, to Kragujevakce.

The peace of Europe has not been in such grave peril for a generation. The grouping of powers that has been the outcome of European diplomacy since Bismarck called into existence the Triple Alliance, may have warded off war for 30 years, but at the same time it has involved the peace of the continent being imperilled over a very small matter.

The grave question now is; can the quarrel between Austria and Serbia be confined to those two powers? Strenuous efforts are being made to ensure that, but the mischief is that in *that* event Serbia is certain to be humiliated and her humiliation may reflect on the power and influence of Russia, a powerful protector.

In this way a revolver shot in a squalid street in Sarajevo may be the signal to let lose the dogs of war in almost every state in Europe. It is certainly to be hoped that in the next few hours assurances will be given that neither the Triple Alliance nor the Dual Alliance, to say nothing of the Triple Entente, will take up this quarrel and make it their own. The whole of Serbia is not worth to us a single grenadier or to France, a curasier.

Chapter Four

Monday August 3 1914

The storm eventually broke, bringing the drought and suffocating heat to an end. The countrymen knew it was coming, long before the clouds vent their anger with deafening intensity.

'Watch them li'le ole birds,' the older villagers told the children, pointing skywards at the dizzying swirls of swifts and house martins, drawn by swarms of insects being driven eastwards and upwards by a looming weather front bearing rain from the south-west. Their shrill whistles filled the air as they indulged in a feeding frenzy.

'We'll be having rain a-fore we're a-bed,' the old men predicted and they weren't mistaken.

The children dutifully wrote these observations in their school gardening diaries, alongside notes made of the crops they had planted in the school allotments and the methods of horticulture they had used. William encouraged them to be observant of natural phenomena and so, beside their entries for planting lettuce, beans or peas were comments such as 'the first frog spawn was seen in the pond' or 'robins have built their nest in our privy.'

Entries made later that summer, however, bore the signs of ink smudged with tears of frustration. 'All our lettuces and beets have perished for lack of water' or 'We have no water to put on our seedlings so they quickly withered and died.' The sight of the school garden, which that spring had been a hive of activity as rows of green shoots required hoeing and thinning, now distressed them. Nothing remained but hard, dry earth. Except for a few hardy weeds, which incredibly seemed to grow whatever the conditions, the entire garden had been reduced to a yellowing desert. It was indistinguishable from the surrounding meadows and pastures, simply part of a landscape bleached of colour.

Conscious of how upsetting the children found their losses, William tried to comfort them. 'Next year we shall plant again. Plant new crops, perhaps different, more hardy crops. There's always another spring, another summer,' he told them. 'This summer, which we all thought to be such a blessing, has turned out to be a terrible curse. If you're distressed at seeing your vegetables shrivel and die, how much more terrible do you think it must be for the farmers who need a good crop to sell at market? And for your parents, who rely on the vegetables they grow to feed you?'

His pupils had grudgingly nodded. They understood. They'd seen the anxiety on grey adult faces. There had been little food that summer. Pay, as well as water, had come to an abrupt end when farm workers were laid off. For some the threat of the poorhouse beckoned. There had certainly not been sufficient water for washing either bodies or clothes. A swim in what remained of the depleted bathing pool beside the River Wang had now become a daily routine for them all, an essential cleansing to relieve the stench of sweaty bodies that pervaded the classrooms.

Thankfully the harvest, such as it was, had been gathered in early. With no rain the grain heads had failed to fill. The hay needed no drying in the field. It had meant some hard decisions for William. He had been forced to allow many of the children to take valuable time off school to help with the harvest. Time they could ill-afford to lose if they were in their final year. For the others he was philosophical. 'There will be time for them to make up their studies in the next academic year,' he said to Alma as they surveyed the poor absence record for the summer term.

The countrymen were right. The heat wave broke in cataclysmic style. Thunderstorms arrived at the farthest fringes of the East Coast long after the rest of the country had felt the benefit of cooler air and refreshing rain. With the thunder came torrential rain that fell incessantly all night and throughout the following day. After the brilliant sunshine of the previous months the gloom of overcast skies was welcomed with upturned faces and smiles. Rushing streams filled the streets, forming waterfalls across the uneven cobbles and washing away the drifts of grey dust. The dried-out, cracked bed of the River Wang trickled as a stream once more and with the re-birth of springs the villagers' wells re-filled.

But the smiles soon faded when the musical sound of rain beating on cobbles turned to floods as the dry earth rejected the onslaught. People rushed to help their neighbours, wading through the swirling mud that engulfed the cottages along the high street. The dirt floors inside became baths of filth where straw-filled mattresses and fragile furniture took on lives of their own, floating away through open doorways and away down the hill.

Suffolkers born and bred, it was not in their taciturn nature to rail against the elements. They shook their heads meaningfully and clenched their lips, but refrained from outward shows of emotion. The rain had come.

But no sooner had the storms abated and the torrents died to a whisper than the villagers ears were tuned to another, more distant rumbling. The talk now was not of the weather, but of war. To the people of rural England this was a distant thing, dismissed with a shrug of the shoulders. A petty quarrel between states of little consequence when compared to the mighty British Empire.

Yet their daily papers were full of foreboding. Austria had declared war on Serbia. Armies were mobilising and shots had already been reported. Although the rumours of actual hostilities between Austria and Serbia hadn't been confirmed it was clear that other powers were watching for any opportunity to leap into the fray and flex their military muscles. There was no need to mention the word 'Germany'. British efforts to broker a peace conference had failed.

Even when Russia massed eighty thousand troops along the German frontier 'as a precautionary measure' a spirit of calm optimism persisted in this remote Suffolk hamlet, as elsewhere in England. The area of conflict would be restricted, people were assured by their newspapers. There was little possibility Britain would become involved.

None of this bothered William. He was far too busy organising events to mark the end of the school year to be overly concerned by what he read in newspapers. He spent days in his study, engrossed in sorting out enough villagers' waggons, carts and cars to take a hundred and fifty children to Southwold beach for the School Treat on August Bank Holiday Monday. Then there was the annual sports day and cycling races to organise. They were always held on the Henham Estate and schools from around the district would be competing.

'Her Ladyship has promised to present the prizes this year,' he announced at the end of morning assembly. 'It's a great honour.' He waved a piece of blue notepaper in the air. 'His Lordship has written to me telling me how sorry he is he can't be at our sports this year, but he's away in Wales, training with the colours. Nevertheless, he says,' William paused to read the actual passage for maximum effect, '"I expect the children of Henham School are throwing themselves wholeheartedly into their practice and will do well on the day".'

The children grinned expectantly at each other. They looked forward to the end of the summer term. It meant a release from their desks and books as instead they practised for the sports. A time to relax and stretch their limbs, to laugh and play with a purpose. Each child was entered for something and expected to shine. Dozens of cyclists of all ages were sent careering through the narrow lanes under the watchful eye of one of the older boys, pitting their bikes and strength against each other.

The villagers knew to leap out of the way as they hurtled past in an untidy mass of metal and limbs. Cycling, like swimming, was one of William's passions and his pupils invariably brought home trophies from the major county events.

There were other, less energetic pleasures, to look forward to in summer. Nature walks through the meadows and woodlands became a frequent feature of the timetable. Even as they were encouraged to name wild flowers and trees or listen to a bird's song, William insisted they recite their times-tables as they walked. So as they made their way in a crocodile along the main street, fifty or more voices chanted in unison, 'five nines are forty-five, six nines are fifty-four......' until they reached their destination.

The glorious weather over the weekend preceeding Bank Holiday Monday encouraged large numbers of people to flock to the seaside by train and car. Hotels, boarding houses and apartment houses in resorts all along the Suffolk coast were bursting with visitors. There was a bustle of excitement and anticipation that no amount of gloom-mongering in the newspapers could dispel.

On Bank Holiday Monday Alma and William were up at dawn to prepare for the School Treat. Alma quickly dressed in her best muslin dress and covered it with a fresh white apron. A new straw hat, bought especially for the occasion, hung on the side of the mirror on her dressing table. While William was out in the yard harnessing the pony and tying ribbons on its bridle, Alma prepared food for the picnic, which she then packed carefully into wicker baskets. William placed them on the floor of the small cart, along with cricket bats and balls, a rug to sit on and a lantern to see them home by. Dick watched all the activity patiently.

'Come Dick old boy,' William called him. The dog leapt into the cart, perhaps knowing what the day held. A day of swimming in the sea, playing with countless willing children and an orgy of forbidden titbits.

'It's a grand day, Will,' Alma glanced upwards at the clear blue sky from beneath the brim of her new bonnet as she shut the schoolhouse door behind her. 'A wonderful day for the children. How lucky we are!'

Will took her hand and helped her gracefully up into the cart. He beamed at her, his black hair and moustache gleaming in the early morning sunlight. She looked so serene, sitting in their little cart in her new bonnet. His heart was full of joy. The day, which promised so much, had started well. Once Alma was settled in her seat he clambered up beside her. He jangled the reins and set the pony trotting at a brisk clip up the lane.

By nine o'clock a throng of scholars, parents and clergymen, along with a motley collection of pony carts, larger horse-drawn waggons and tumbrils and even a couple of motorcars, had gathered outside the church, ready to make their customary procession along the winding lane that led to Southwold.

Everyone was in their Sunday best. The horses and ponies were decorated with bright ribbons and gleaming horse-brasses, the men were in light suits and panamas while the women wore their best floral summer dresses and straw hats. Even the poorest children had turned up in clean clothes; white aprons over cotton frocks for the girls, some proudly wearing new sashes and fresh bows in their hair; pressed shirts for the boys.

The children scrambled to sit in the best places on the waggons and tumbrils. Twenty could sit on the straw that covered the worn floors while others sat on the broad sides built to carry sheaves of corn. A privileged few were able to dangle their legs over the tailboard, watching the village gradually disappear into the distance as the horses bore them steadily towards the sea.

It was a joyful day. A day of swimming in the chill grey waters of the North Sea and paddling along the shoreline with trousers rolled and skirts held primly at the knee, of games on the sand and races along the greensward on the cliff top. There were sweets for prizes and feasting from picnic baskets laden with fresh produce from the farms. It was a day of rare and real happiness, of unaccustomed indolence for adults as well as children. A day when families, long familiar with each other, chatted and gossiped in a desultory fashion, enervated by the heat of the sun.

At the end of the day the rector and his wife produced enormous bags of sweets and scattered them across the rugs that had been spread over the sand for picnicing. It was the signal for a boisterous gaggle of children to plunge with a melee of arms and legs to reap an unexpected harvest.

As the light began to fade William and Alma slipped quietly away to stroll arm-in-arm along the water's edge, while Dick continued to splash excitedly through the waves in search of playmates. As the sun set behind them every breaking ripple at their feet reflected a kaleidoscope of pink and purple.

There was peace between them. A natural, unspoken tranquillity. *Even Will, with his constant seeking after perfection and his black moments of despair, must recognise this,* thought Alma. She squeezed his fingers. She wanted to tell him how much she loved him. How passionately she needed him and wanted him. How his very physical presence gave her life. But she couldn't. She hoped he knew. She felt sure he did.

It was dusk when the little procession set off, leaving behind the seafront with its gaily-coloured bathing machines and Punch and Judy stands, the broken sand-castles and remnants of gargantuan picnics. Horses and ponies wearily bore their loads home at a gentle plod. The way lit only by flickering lanterns swinging from the backs of carts, beams dancing like demented fireflies, casting ghostly shadows against hedges and overhanging branches.

At first the children, still bubbling with excitement, sang and counted their prizes or showed off treasure trove they'd disentangled from seaweed left by the retreating tide. But tiredness eventually overcame them and the homeward journey ended in contented silence.

East Anglian Daily Times

Tuesday August 4 1914

London Letter, Monday night, 3rd August 1914

Once or twice in the course of every century a great nation finds itself face to face with a fundamental crisis. Either by or through its constituted leaders or else in some more representative capacity it has to say 'aye' or 'no' on some fateful issue from which there is no subsequent drawing back. This time for Great Britain came today.

Members of the House of Commons assembled on a Bank Holiday, but in something far from a holiday mood. They crowded the chamber to its upmost capacity. They even sat in chairs on the floor of the house. The galleries were as crowded as the House itself. In the Peers gallery the Marquis of Lansdown had only room to peer at the drama going on on the floor.

This government has been noted for the way in which it has kept its secrets. Everybody knew this afternoon that the Cabinet had at last decided upon action. What that action was, nobody knew, apparently unanimity in the Cabinet itself was only obtained with some difficulty and it is said tonight of the price of more than one withdrawal.

On the lips of everyone was the question: 'Are we going to war?' Then a strange rumour, which increased the intensity of feeling, spread like fire in the bracken of a hot summer night. The House of Commons was to decide. The grim necessity of casting a vote for war steadied most men. A sigh of relief went up indeed when it was found the government were not going to shift the onus onto parliament. Members were perfectly ready to vote for war, but they preferred to vote for the support of a government that had declared on war. As always in time of war and strife some truculence and bravado, but there was little of it apparent today.

Part 2

From Sad Shires

'And bugles calling for them from sad shires'

Anthem for Doomed Youth
Wilfred Owen

Chapter Five

Tuesday August 4 1914

'Hart! Haaart!'

Ten slender, almost girlish fingers – nails shaped like almonds – hesitated above the keys of an ancient Imperial. Frozen between inspiration and dull yellowing copy paper.

'Hart?' This time the word bounded and re-bounded the length of the corridor between the editor's office and the reporters' room, ravenously seeking its prey.

Ernest Hart rested his hands momentarily on the scarred desk and smiled a weak smile of resignation at the eight faces watching him. Eight mouths barely concealing grins of relief that the call wasn't for them.

Ernest Hart, Chief Reporter. If there was a problem he got The Call. Ernest quickly grabbed a notebook and pencil and ran down the corridor as fast as his crippled leg would allow.

The editor filled the open doorway as he stood with hands gripping bulging hips. He didn't wait for Ernest to reach him before demanding, 'Hart. Have you seen this?' He waved a scrap of paper above his head, snatched simultaneously with his outburst from the wire service.

Ernest hadn't. The editor always got to the wires first. 'No Chief,' he said with mild innocence. 'Is there a problem?'

'A problem? Of course there's a problem, yer dimwit!' He fluttered the ragged paper under Ernest's nose, flapping it against the glass of his spectacles. 'Read it! Read it for yourself. It says we're going to declare war on Germany some time later today. Madness. Absolute madness! And to make matters worse we'll be fighting on the same side as the damn Frenchies. Can you believe it? Madness,' he muttered, banging his heavy walking stick violently on the wood block floor. It echoed down the corridor and everyone who heard it shuddered a second time.

He held the paper closer to his own dim eyes. '"England to mobilise - *today*",' he announced. 'Today, d'yer hear? Troops at the ready".' Then flung his head back with an energy belying his seventy years, causing a pair of unruly grey whiskers to erupt like overstuffed cushions.

A huff of contempt issued from the pursed mouth. His disgust was directed not at the Germans nor at Ernest, but at the old enemy. The French. He wheeled heavily in the doorway and stomped back to his desk.

'Come into my office. And close the door behind you.'

'Yes Chief.' Ernest addressed his employer in the respectful fashion adopted by generations of reporters before him.

It would have been unthinkable to call the editor 'Sir Frederick' or even just plain 'sir'. 'Chief' was the title Sir Frederick Wilson preferred. He'd unashamedly bestowed it on himself. He'd founded the East Anglian Daily Times in 1874. It was his newspaper, his creation, and for the past forty years he had been its editor. He'd been responsible for turning a four-page, half-penny rag with an uncertain birth into one of the most respected newspapers in the region. Seven years previously King Edward had knighted him for services to journalism. He was, most definitely, in position, stature and voice 'The Chief'.

Ernest Hart was less fearful of Sir Frederick than the other reporters. A studious young man of 26, he had ambitions to leave what he viewed as the provincial pettiness of the Daily Times for something more erudite, something more worthy. He fancied himself as a Times or Daily Graphic reporter covering important stories of national interest. He was bored with the daily round of council meetings, courts and agricultural markets. Perhaps Sir Frederick had heard gossip in the reporters' room or on the subs' bench that he was itching to try his luck on Fleet Street?

But if his editor was about to find fault with something he'd written, or boot him out as unceremoniously as he was wont to do with young reporters, Hart was prepared for it. He'd simply shrug his shoulders and move on. It was only Lizzie's pleading that kept him in Ipswich.

Wilson peered sharply at the slight, spare young man standing with almost military erectness before him. He observed the wire-rimmed spectacles balanced on a thin nose; the neatly trimmed, fair moustache that vanished into a pale complexion; the almost childish blond curls framing the mild-mannered face and quizzical sidelong glance.

'Hart. This war business. It'll all be over by Christmas, of course, you can bet yer life. A few short, sharp engagements and the Germans'll know who's top dog. That's the general view, anyhow.' The editor paused, his breath rasping. 'Anyway, that's why I called you in. You're a good reporter and yer still young. You could do better.'

'Yes Chief,' Ernest said respectfully. *So, this is it,* he thought. *He's booting me out. But what's the war got to do with it?*

'I've got something special in mind for you, Hart. There's going to be one hell of a lot of changes to this paper with a war on. Lots more war news. Wire service stuff from the battlefield, more reports coming down from London office. That sort of thing. But what I want *you* to concentrate on is the *local* angle. What will the young men of Suffolk be doing? Will they join the fighting forces? What'll be the effect of the war on people living in this region? Their jobs, their livelihoods. D'yer get m'drift?'

'Yes Chief.'

'So what I'm offering you is the job of Special War Correspondent. How about it?' He flung himself violently back in the battered leather swivel chair so that it creaked and bounced ominously. 'Well?' he demanded. His pugnacious gaze drilled into Ernest's face.

'Well….' Ernest found himself stammering, 'I don't quite know what to say. Yes, of course. Excellent.' The editor's offer seemed like an answer to his secret ambitions. 'I'll do it.'

'Make a good job of it Hart and there'll be a few extra shillings in your pay packet. Can't say fairer than that, can I?' The editor's large florid face relaxed and broke into a beaming smile, which once more precipitated the seismic shuddering of side whiskers.

Ernest replied quickly, 'No, Chief. Er...very fair.' He tilted his head sideways, trying to get a grip on this rare moment of generosity. Sir Frederick, grinning conspiratorially at him.

Just like uncle Sydney when he was a child. Sydney the music hall conjuror, who used to produce threepenny pieces from out of thin air for him and his brother. Grinning and throwing out his gaudily waistcoated chest with delight at confounding the youngsters with his magic.

But Ernest found the Chief difficult to read. The man's overwhelming physical presence veiled any inkling of deep emotions. Except, perhaps, anger or frustration. He would never know that beneath the gruff exterior the Chief harboured a soft spot for him.

Sir Frederick acknowledged that it wasn't simply because Ernest was a talented writer. Despite their obvious differences he identified with the young man, had something of his vulnerability.

Both of them had suffered accidents involving horses. He himself had fallen and broken his hip while hunting and was now forced to walk with the aid of a stick. Hart's leg had been mangled by a horse-drawn bus. 'Bloody creatures. Can't trust 'em,' he was frequently heard to mutter, although as a young man he'd been an exceptionally keen huntsman. He'd even ridden in the Parliamentary Steeplechase during his brief sojourn in the House of Commons as Liberal MP for Mid-Norfolk.

Wilson had witnessed Hart's accident from the window of his office. The young reporter had been crossing the road on his way to work. Probably not looking where he was going. Daydreaming. Mind on something else, as usual. Shame about the leg. He was otherwise a good-looking chap with a pretty little wife.

'May as well start today, Hart. You're relieved of other reporting duties. Get that chap Gilbert to stand in as chief reporter and take over the diary. I want the Daily Times's war reporting to be second to none. Yer hear that?'

'Yes Chief. I'll get on with it right away. I think some of the Territorials and reservists are returning today from their summer camps. I'll check and see what's happening at the barracks.'

'Good man.' The editor waved his arm. Ernest turned quickly for the door. 'Leave it open. I like to hear what's going on.'

'Of course. And thank you.'

The other reporters were lounging idly about the newsroom when Ernest returned. It was a cramped room and barely large enough for nine of them to work in, yet none of them seemed to notice how much of their precious space was taken up by paper.

The room was a jungle of paper. Old yellowing newspaper cuttings were stuck to every inch of dingy khaki-coloured wall space. There were heaps of moth-eaten newspapers mounding up in the corners. Mice had nibbled their way into the heart of these mountains, leaving a confetti trail that a cleaner occasionally swept away.

Each pitted, ink-stained desk, on which countless reporters had carved their names, was awash in scraps of paper and ill-typed folios. Spikes overflowed with more superfluous paper. In-trays, out-trays, boxes full of clean folios and discarded notebooks, all juggled for space. More paper spewed out of half-closed drawers and cabinets. Only the nine ancient black typewriters were at this moment devoid of paper, awaiting inspiration.

It was the dingiest of rooms, even though it had windows on two sides. On one side a single, high window overlooked busy Carr Street and its traffic. Set in an elegant Renaissance-style façade it was now covered in dust and grime. It afforded no view to speak of, except of shops on the opposite side of the street, and let in only the merest hint of light. On the other side of the room a window faced onto a narrow gallery, which ran around three sides of the typesetting and compositing floor below.

The clatter of the typesetting machines and the hammering of metal on metal as the pages were set on the stone, penetrated the thin glass, playing an accompaniment to creative thought the reporters quickly grew accustomed to. In the basement beneath the rows of typesetting machines were the printing presses. When the presses were running the rumble and roar shook the entire building to its foundations and made conversation well-nigh impossible.

'Well? What did the old Croc want with you *this* time?' a pudgy face appeared above a lowered newspaper to peer at Ernest with an ill-concealed sneer. The click-clack, click-clack of the editor's stick tapping on the uneven woodblock floor was as fearful a warning of his presence as the Crocodile's ticking clock in *Peter Pan*. It was a story still fresh in their young minds. They giggled mischievously at their own daring. The Chief, they imagined, had no inkling of his nickname.

Ernest looked around the room. He was *their* chief. Working long hours cloistered together in this sweating, dingy, rodent-infested hole, he'd grown to care for the other chaps as comrades. Almost like brothers. He knew they wished him no harm at the hands of the editor. He'd earned their respect, not simply because he was a good, honourable reporter, but because he cared about each one of them.

'Sir Frederick's given me a special job to do,' he said, peering over his spectacles with a solemnity that belied the excitement he felt at this assignment.

No bawling out? No sacking? Not this time. There were surprised glances between them at the announcement.

'First of all, Alf is to take on my job as Chief Reporter. Temporary like,' he added hastily, lest Alf Gilbert thought the job was his for good. 'I say temporarily because I'm to be a Special Correspondent while the war is on.'

'Well, that won't last long, will it?' piped up seventeen-year-old John, the youngest of the reporters whose desk was consequently in the farthest, darkest corner.

Ernest ignored the jibe. 'Alf will be responsible for the diary and the duty rota as well as covering council meetings. Tom,' he turned to the pudgy-faced fellow who'd greeted him, ' you'll take over courts from Alf. The rest of you will have to help cover where necessary. Is that clear?'

'Yes Ernie,' said Alf, thrusting out his burly chest with an air of authority. 'But what will *you* be doing?'

Ernest had no idea. He shrugged his shoulders with contrived nonchalance as though the answer was self-evident. He pushed a bundle of papers from the corner of his desk and perched a lean hip uncomfortably on the edge, his crippled leg dangling inelegantly. His gaze passed over eight faces fixed raptly on him.

'I can't tell you at the moment. All I know is, I'm to start right away, covering the mobilisation of troops. You know,' his voice dropped to a whisper as though thinking aloud, 'This could be the most important event we've ever covered here.'

As he hurried through the centre of town Ernest sensed a strangely subdued air of excitement. Tuesday being market day, Ipswich was always bustling, but this Tuesday there was more urgency in the jostling of the crowds, more knots of people gossiping on the narrow pavements, more exchanged hushed, whisperings in shop doorways. It was as though the whole town was party to a secret, but was keeping it from him.

Stalls were laid out on the Corn Exchange, laden with produce brought in from the countryside by farmers and their wives. They crowded into their

49

customary haunts, the ale and beer houses in the narrow back streets and the air was full of broad, ripe Suffolk voices. Their rough tweeds rubbed uncomfortably with the bright holiday finery of returning Bank Holiday crowds, back in Ipswich after their day at the seaside.

But to Ernest's mind the town had taken on an entirely alien character. Everywhere he walked there were men in khaki. It was as if, in the course of the couple of hours since he'd been called into Frederick Wilson's office, every young man had decked himself out ready for war.

He headed for one of the drill halls near the canal. It was a long walk and he was limping badly. There would be much walking today as he went in search of the stories the editor demanded, and his leg was hurting. Hands in pockets, he fingered the dog-eared notebook and pencils. He would, he vowed to himself, describe as accurately as he could the scenes of feverish activity that he saw. Report the conversations, the comments of men on the eve of battle.

All around him outside the drill hall in Portman Road young men thronged, looking purposeful and confident, their faces bronzed from days spent marching and drilling. Inside there was feverish activity as stores and camp equipment were got ready. This hall was headquarters to the largest territorial unit, the half battalion of the 4th Suffolks, which had returned from their annual training camp in Yarmouth the night before.

Ernest watched as the men, still in the uniform they'd worn at camp, formed into alert ranks on the parade ground. Kits were inspected and a list of deficiencies and unsuitable articles was made so that an order could be placed for substantial boots, shirts, socks and other clothing for distribution as soon as possible.

He approached a young Major, the notebook now in his hand. He introduced himself and briefly described his mission. The Major, a lean faced, moody-looking man, nodded. He understood, yet was impatient to get on with his tasks.

'What's going on here?' Ernest asked, pointing to where a sergeant was holding the attention of a large group of men on the parade ground by shouting out their names.

'Most of these men are bandsmen. The headquarters companies had a large number of them and they're being redistributed to other sections. Some will be changed into stretcher-bearers, others will become fighting men,' the Major explained. 'We've also seen a large number of former Territorials under the age of 35 re-join the colours, too. Most gratifying. There's plenty of spare kits in store and they'll be quickly equipped. Excellent, don't you think, to have received such a good leven of trained and mature men so soon? And the war not declared yet.'

Ernest nodded his appreciation of the importance of experience, but the reorganisation of bandsmen into roles they were ill-equipped for appeared to be a lengthy process. It took hours, though he couldn't for the life of him see why.

After the last musician had been allocated the job of stretcher-bearer, the men were dismissed and told to re-assemble later in the evening. No-one was returning home this night.

A large crowd of onlookers had gathered while these small, domestic military manoeuvres took place. Men and women from the back streets around Portman Road, with their modest red-brick terraces set back-to-back, were fascinated. It was an entertainment as engrossing as the circus which had recently rolled into town, but this time they were being entertained at no expense to themselves.

The Major took out his pocket watch. 'If I were you, I'd head for the station. The third East Anglian Howitzer Brigade is due back from its summer camp in Wales this evening,' he said, watching Ernest's face crinkling with curiosity as he watched the distribution of kit and the redistribution of men.

'What time? Any idea?'

'They're due in at four, but with so many horses and men to load, the trains will probably be late,' said the Major. 'When you get there the person to ask for is Major Hugh Mellor. He's in charge. Oh, and you might get the chance to talk to their commanding officer, Colonel Stradbroke.'

'What, the Earl of Stradbroke?'

'Mmm, the same.' The Major was growing increasingly anxious to be relieved of the task of press informant. 'Must dash. See you around, no doubt. Plenty going on,' and he gave a half salute, half wave as he headed through the door of the drill hall.

It was a short walk to the station. When Ernest arrived he found himself engulfed in a milling throng of relatives, friends and the merely curious, all awaiting the arrival of the three trains bringing home the Territorials of the 3rd East Anglian Howitzer Brigade of the Royal Field Artillery. Travellers trying to reach other platforms to catch trains to London or Norwich wormed their way through the press of bodies with difficulty.

The crowd became increasingly restive as the due time came and went, with no sign of the trains. An hour passed and there were anxious enquiries made of the station manager. 'Has there been an accident?' 'Has a train broken down?' But the station manager merely shrugged his stooping shoulders inside an ill-fitting uniform jacket and answered as politely as he could that he knew no more than they did.

It was twenty-five to six before the first train arrived. As it pulled into the far end of the tunnel Ernest could hear singing echoing hollowly outwards. Men's voices raised high, long before their heads leaned from carriage windows to catch a glimpse of the waiting crowd.

They're looking remarkably fit, considering the long cross-country journey they've endured, thought Ernest studying their sunburnt faces.

This train bore the larger portion of the men and more than a hundred horses. As the men leapt out of the carriages in a flurry of khaki and kit bags and fell into the arms of their loved ones, the officers responsible for the horses unclasped the sides of the wagons.

Large, sturdy horses of good farming stock stood three or four to a wagon, side by side. The journey from summer camp in North Wales had taken all day and the heat had exhausted them. Some kicked out petulantly as they were released and led from their temporary imprisonment. Others, more docile, too cowed by the vicious hissing of the steam engines, the cacophony of shouted orders and the press of the crowds to do anything but meekly follow their masters. They were led away in pairs, across the station concourse and the short distance to the grassy field opposite the drill hall, which was usually given over to fairs. There they were to be fed and watered and given fresh hay.

Ernest was transfixed by the joyful chaos around him. These men had been away just ten days, but in those ten days the whole tenor of public expectations had changed. Now these khaki-clad men, many of them with the mature looks of seasoned campaigners, were on the verge of fighting for their country. They would be going to war, possibly to die in battle, yet he could see only confidence and cheerfulness in their demeanour. *What did I expect?* he wondered. *Fear and misgiving?*

The other two accompanying trains arrived shortly afterwards, bearing more territorials and all the brigade's equipment. There were several dozen horse-drawn Howitzer guns on carriages as well as covered supply waggons, bundles of tents, a field kitchen, medical supplies and tack, food, water and bedding for the horses. The platform began to resemble a battlefield as it overflowed with men and equipment.

Slowly and methodically it was moved, piece by piece, out of the station and into the street.

Ernest now found himself surrounded by men far taller than himself. He was forced to jump onto a station luggage trolley to catch a glimpse of the man he'd come to see.

There he was, standing on the topmost step of the train, quietly surveying the activity along the length of the platform. Lord Stradbroke's customary summer attire of oatmeal linen jacket, buff-coloured trousers and panama hat had been replaced with an outfit altogether more sombre. He was wearing a well-cut dark khaki uniform jacket and beneath it a lighter-coloured shirt and regimental tie. Across his chest was strapped a buckled, leather gun holster which secured around his waist. The four stripes around the wrists of the jacket proclaimed his rank and the hat badge his regiment; the Royal Artillery.

Ten days of intensive drilling and training in the rough North Wales countryside had taken their toll. Despite the characteristic jaunty curling of his grey-flecked moustache, the Earl's face was lined and his eyes drooped with weariness. The brigade – numbering around 120 and recruited from the East Anglian flatlands – were unaccustomed to the mountainous terrain. It had taxed both men and horses.

Yet here, at the end of their long journey, he was amazed and gratified by the way the men's spirits lifted. He observed the efficiency with which his unit patiently marshalled horses, guns and supplies into a well-disciplined column, ready to march in correct formation back to its base. He knew they'd be under close scrutiny from the waiting crowds and they wouldn't disappoint. They'd put on a grand show.

'Your Lordship! Lord Stradbroke!' Ernest called from his perch on the trolley, trying to attract the Earl's attention when he saw him step from the train. But the reporter's passage along the platform was blocked by men and machinery. Eventually, by elbowing his slender form between the pressing bodies, he reached Lord Stradbroke's side.

Ernest was breathless from the effort. His pale face was flushed. Beads of sweat chased across his unfurrowed brow and his glasses were slipping down his nose. 'Your Lordship! Good afternoon. I'm so glad to see you,' he gasped. He stopped dead in his tracks. Perhaps the Earl would think it presumptuous of him to have spoken first. He pursed his lips, annoyed with himself.

'Ah, Mr Hart,' Lord Stradbroke sounded surprised, if not a little amused. 'What brings you here today? Part of our little welcoming party, eh?'

'Pardon my intrusion, your Lordship, but I wanted to speak with you about the brigade and what your plans are in the event of war being declared today.'

Lord Stradbroke smiled wearily. 'We fully expect the King's proclamation today. I think I can safely say that by this time tomorrow we shall, most definitely, be at war with Germany.' Then he frowned and in a voice of mock severity, said, 'By the way, Mr Hart, I suppose you should not, by rights, be calling me "Your Lordship", nor even "Mr Chairman", as is customary when we meet at County Council meetings. Now I'm wearing the uniform of a Colonel I fear you'll have to get used to calling me Colonel! Most confusing, I know,' he laughed loudly.

Ernest was glad of the Earl's good humour, relieved he hadn't overstepped the mark. The Earl was, without doubt, the most influential man in Suffolk; chair of its county council, the Freemasons' Provincial Grand Master, not to mention a dozen or more other honorary presidencies and chairmanships.

'Look here, Mr Hart. I'm a trifle busy at the moment with all this going on,' George Stradbroke waved his hand airily towards the melée further down the platform. 'I suggest you talk to my Major, Major Hugh Mellor. He's the man in command. Come and see us tomorrow when we'll be a bit more shipshape, down at the drill hall.'

'I'll do that. Thank you sir. Er, Colonel,' Ernest corrected himself.

'You know Mr Hart, this war......' The Earl paused, staring thoughtfully at his well-polished boots. 'It's all over a quarrel between two states in the Balkans, far from Suffolk. Yet we mustn't forget that within our county borders we have the naval base at Harwich. This coast lies very close to the continent of Europe. It's not to be wondered at that it feels the obviousness of the present crisis more than most parts of England.' He hesitated again before looking Ernest fully in the face. 'I believe its citizens have recognised that they'll soon be eye-witnesses to stirring events and possibly participants, in a colossal struggle.'

He gripped Ernest's hand in a handshake of surprising intensity and headed into the crowds. The soldiers, still densely pressed together, rapidly cleared a path for their Colonel. In a matter of seconds he'd disappeared from Ernest's view. The young reporter sighed wearily. It was now well into the evening and the light was fading. He needed to get back to the office in Carr Street to write his story. He feared it would be the first of many long days spent chasing news of the war.

Just after eleven o'clock on Tuesday night the news finally broke: Britain was at war. The London crowds, many in evening dress spilling onto the pavements from theatres and restaurants, heard it first. A whisper spread among the large number milling around the West End that an announcement was imminent. They were reluctant to go home in case they missed it.

While Londoners learnt of the Government's decision to go to war late on Tuesday, the information only reached the rest of the country the next morning, with the arrival of the morning newspapers.

East Anglian Daily Times
Wednesday August 5 1914

Britain declares war on Germany. Reply to ultimatum. Summary rejection by Germany. Ambassador handed his passport. Hostilities already begun.

Great Britain has declared war on Germany. Mr Asquith announced in the House of Commons yesterday that the British government has sent an ultimatum to Germany which would expire at midnight requiring Germany to respect Belgian neutrality.

The German answer to the ultimatum has been received and is unsatisfactory. A council, which the King had arranged to be held at midnight, was held in consequence at an earlier hour and certain proclamations which follow a state of war were disposed of.

Chapter Six

Wednesday August 5 1914

It was clear to Ernest, when he awoke next morning in the cramped bedroom of the terraced house in Upper Barclay Street, that this was to be the pattern of his life from now onwards. Or at least for the duration of the war. Lizzie had railed at him relentlessly the previous night because he'd failed to turn up in time for supper. He'd been shocked at what a fishwife she could be. She was still feeling peevish this morning. Like a wild cat with a bird, reluctant to put it down.

'Considering you work not a stone's throw from this house,' she hissed at him over breakfast, continuing the row from the night before, 'you might have popped in here on the way back from the station. I'd prepared a special mutton stew and it was completely ruined. Good food, totally gone to waste.' Lizzie's elfin face puckered as yet again she threatened to burst into the tears that had greeted him at the door last evening.

Elbows propped on the scrubbed wooden kitchen table, Ernest drooped his head into his hands. 'Lizzie, how many more times do I have to say I'm sorry? I truly am. It was such a long day, so much to see. You can't imagine what a day yesterday was. Amazing. Historic, really, when you think about it. Thousands of Suffolk men joining their regiments, queuing for hours in the blazing sun to join the colours. Such a sight as I've never witnessed in my life before. And then I had to go back and write it up.....' His voice petered out. He raised his gaze warily. Lizzie had taken a commanding position in front of the range, where she was ladling porridge.

'Well,' she retorted petulantly, 'I don't give a fig for this stupid war and I don't think much of this Special Correspondent's job if it means you're going to have to work harder than ever. I hope old Sir Frederick is raising your salary. That's all *I* have to say on the matter.' She slammed the metal ladle down hard on the stove as if to prove a point, then waved it under his nose like a conductor's baton, blue eyes blazing and long, fair hair ferociously tossed from her face.

Ernest pushed his chair back and stood up wearily. He took Lizzie's arm and gently prised the ladle from her. 'Lizzie, my dearest girl, we mustn't argue about such things. I know I was wrong not to get word to you, but there wasn't a moment to spare. It's the way I have to work now. You must understand.

There's a war on. And that's more important than you and I arguing about a spoilt mutton stew. Isn't it?' His pale, wide eyes beseeched her forgiveness.

They stared at each other in silence. Faces close together, feeling each other's warm breath, yet separated by a barrier of resentment. He hated arguments. It wounded him, cut him with an almost physical pain to the heart. Their young marriage was in constant turmoil and usually over such stupid things. They'd wind up shouting at each other. Then there would be bitter, angry tears. He couldn't understand why. *Why couldn't he get through to her? What was he doing wrong?* He tortured himself with such questions into the long night as she slept beside him. Too often she'd turned away from him. Ernest ached to be close to her, to feel her touch and know that she loved him just as he had loved her since their schooldays. He had no doubt that his need for her engulfed and overwhelmed all other emotions, all other ambitions.

He stroked her hand softly and watched as her pert bow lips unclenched and spread into a reluctant smile that warped her mouth upwards. It was the cue he'd waited for all night. Gently he pulled her towards him. Then tightly, clasping her slender back, covering her in kisses. First her cheeks, then her forehead, then deluging her lips. She buckled under the onslaught, unable to withstand his overflowing emotions. Their mouths locked hard together, their hands moved across each other's bodies urgently, as though in a desperate search.

They fumbled to undo buttons, undressing each other with a furious intensity. Clothes were tossed across the room with a delicious abandonment of caring. Now, as they writhed naked on the bare stone of the kitchen floor, they gave vent to the intensity of their desire for each other.

There was peace between them afterwards. The cold stone of the floor cooled the sweat of their bodies, as they lay there, legs still passionately entwined and arms circled. It was Lizzie who moved first, reluctantly lifting her slender white body from Ernest's embrace.

'Porridge will be spoilt,' she laughed softly, and Ernest knew that in poking fun at her own ill-temper of the night before, he'd been forgiven.

Ernest headed that morning straight for the drill hall in Portman Road that was the headquarters of the 4th Suffolks and the East Anglian Howitzer Brigade. It was a busy place. The companies based there had assembled early, at seven o'clock, and from then onwards there hadn't been an idle moment for those in charge. They'd already distributed a considerable supply of boots and socks, identification badges and first aid sets and 150 rounds of ball cartridges to each man.

Others were busy filling out papers for separation allowances for the married men. Ernest watched the men queuing. He was curious as to the large numbers who were helped with reading and writing. Those with wives signed away three-quarters of their pay to augment the small sum allowed to wives and children. The vast majority of the single men did the same, leaving half or three-quarters of their pay to their mothers and other family members who depended upon them.

Ernest found Major Hugh Mellor, a sandy-haired man in his thirties with an intelligent face, checking on the progress of this necessary administration.

'Colonel Stradbroke told me to find you,' he said, pulling out his notebook. 'I saw him when he arrived at the station yesterday. I'm Ernest Hart, Special War Correspondent for the Daily Times.'

They shook hands and exchanged amiable grins.

The Major pointed to dozens of men bending over long tables as they filled out forms. 'There must necessarily be a few cases of hardship, I fear,' he said. 'Young men earning good wages and maintaining a widowed mother will from now onwards only be in receipt of an ordinary soldiers' pay of one shilling a day. And though they devote nine pence of it to her, it must be a struggle with rent to pay.'

Ernest nodded. He thought of his own meagre wages from the Daily Times. It covered the rent on their house, their food and clothing, but treats were few and far between. Perhaps Sir Frederick's promise of a few extra shillings for his war reporting would bear fruit.

'This mobilisation will hit the inhabitants of the poorer quarters of town far harder than any others,' the Major went on. There was sorrow and regret in his tone. 'In the district between Fore Street and St Helens, and again around the Mount, many homes have lost one and in some cases more, male members who, as reservists in the regulars or as Territorials, have responded to the call to the colours.'

Ernest knew the area well. Knew that the women and children left behind would experience real hardship, possibly hunger or even greater deprivations. Was there nothing that could be done to help? Their menfolk were prepared to serve their country, so what was the country doing for the families left behind? He'd seen the knots of women with their children clustering around, discussing the grim reality of war. They had about them an air of calm seriousness. Hysterics were conspicuous by their absence.

Major Mellor led him into an adjoining hall. Men were lined up, stripped to the waist, waiting to see the doctor. 'Dr Jefferson's our medical officer, attached to the battalion. He's giving them the once over.'

The medical examination looked fairly perfunctory. Ernest was curious. 'Will everyone pass?'

'No, about two per cent will be rejected, perhaps 'cos they're too short and don't meet the height requirements, or have an injury or ailment that'd make military action difficult. About another two per cent will be put back for a month.'

Just then a hearty cheer went up. Ernest peered through the doorway into the main hall. The troops were greeting the battalion commander, Lt. Col Frank Garrett. *Evidently a popular commander*, he noted.

Milling around among the young Territorials was a large number of older, former members, anxious to rejoin. Their disappointment was palpable when they were told there was no more equipment and that the companies were practically up to full strength. Major Mellor told him the battalion would be moving on that afternoon to the station allotted them, so Ernest headed off to another of the town's many drill halls in Woodbridge Road, that of the Ipswich section of the Cyclists, which formed the 6th Battalion of the Suffolk regiment.

He'd never seen so many bicycles gathered in one place before. Some 200 cyclists had fallen in at the drill hall that morning, all on uniform black bicycles. They looked a cheerful crowd, he thought, almost enviously. And fit, too, with their wiry, well-honed bodies and sturdy, muscular legs. Many of them were fanatical cyclists who had taken part in races. Some had won cups for their speed and prowess on a bike. Now here they were, enthusiastically offering up their pastime to the service of their country. There was a good deal of laughter among the cyclists and their commander, Lt. Colonel Pretty, seemed to have difficulty bringing the gaggle of men and machines to order.

It was late in the day before they moved off for their destination in Saxmundham. The long string of riders, now organised into ranks two abreast, making a fine display for the large contingent of friends and onlookers who had spent the greater part of the day outside the hall, waiting to wave them off.

Ernest wandered from drill hall to drill hall. An ever-changing crowd outside the headquarters of the 4th Suffolks and the Howitzer Brigade in Portman Road, were watching with interest the evolutions of the sentries on duty and the arrival and departure of khaki-clad officers and men.

The Howitzer Brigade, much to their entertainment, not only had sentries posted over their headquarters, but their guns and waggons were parked on the ground opposite. There the crowd watched as all hands busied themselves cleaning the artillery and the horses' harness that had become encrusted with dirt during their stay in North Wales.

Wonder-struck children edged close to touch the shiny metal of the howitzers' barrels and stroked their hands around the wooden spokes of the wheels. Each of these awsome five-inch guns required a team of six horses to pull them. The children would have tried lifting the high explosive shells they fired, which were laid in a pile close by, if a sentry hadn't shooed them good-naturedly away.

Seeing Ernest among the crowd, Major Mellor called out to him, 'Best get down to Ipswich railway station. There's a large party of reservists leaving at noon. You don't want to miss it. Something to report for your newspaper.'

'Thank you, sir, I'll get there straight away.'

It was a short walk, but Ernest was tired and had eaten nothing since breakfast. He grabbed a pie from the pie stall outside the station and joined an even greater throng on the platform than had been there the day previously.

Most of the reservists and Territorials had already boarded the trains. A large number of women had gathered. They crowded around the carriages, balancing precariously on the very edge of the platform, anxious for a final glimpse of their menfolk. The younger men and women were the most demonstrative, clinging to each other in a final, lingering embrace.

One man clasped his baby to his breast while it smiled and gurgled, unaware of the heightened emotions of this moment. But the wife being left behind stood by, discreetly dabbing her eyes with a handkerchief and looking longingly at her husband. Their parting was barely minutes away. Neither had any idea how long it would be before they saw each other again, although everyone was reassuring themselves with whispers of 'It'll all be over by Christmas.'

Ernest heard the guard's whistle. Saw him signal. There was a frantic final clutching of hands through the open windows and tears in the eyes of waving women as the train slowly moved out of the platform, heading southwards. One woman, overcome with emotion, fell in a faint.

There was no cheering or shouting from the men hanging from the fast-receding carriage windows. No patriotic songs. They looked sombre and serious. Separation was more painful than any of them could have imagined.

The women dragged themselves away from the station in disconsolate knots as the last puff of smoke mingled with the clouds above the bend in the track. An unnatural silence hung about them as each privately bore her own thoughts and feelings, burying them deep beneath layers of hardness and bitterness cultivated by years of scraping a living. Without a breadwinner the future looked grim. And what if the breadwinner should never return?

News of the war filtered through slowly to the rural areas. The daily and evening papers were eagerly awaited and speedily scanned at the little railway stations as bundles of papers were unloaded. Wednesday's East Anglian Daily Times arrived in the villages and outlying towns throughout the morning, bearing the biggest, blackest banner headline it had ever set.

'Britain declares war on Germany'

The news had been expected, but it shocked all the same. Groups of labourers listened to the more important portions being read out to them by mates more fluent in reading. Visitors alighting from the train were bombarded with anxious questions. 'What's the latest?' 'What's happening?' 'Has the fighting started?'

At Henham Hall the effects of the declaration were immediate. Government agents had descended on Lowestoft, where market day was in full swing, and commandeered half-a-dozen of Lord Stradbroke's horses and waggons. He wasn't the only landowner to suffer this unexpected blow; many others found their animals snatched without having any right to protest to the military. Quite suddenly the farming community had a new problem to face; how would it cope with not only its men draining away but horses and transport, too?

William and Alma were appalled at the news that war had been declared. This being the school holidays, they had taken a leisurely stroll together across the meadow from Henham to the village store in Wangford High Street to buy their morning paper. There was a small knot of people outside and Alma knew from their solemn faces that the announcement had been made.

'It can't be true,' she said, turning to William for reassurance. 'We're to fight the Germans?'

'Yes, my love, I'm afraid we are.' William opened the paper and slowly read aloud: '"Mr Asquith announced in the House of Commons yesterday that the British government has sent an ultimatum to Germany which would expire at midnight requiring Germany to respect Belgian neutrality. The German answer to the ultimatum has been received and is unsatisfactory".'

'How can that be right? How can we possibly be on the opposite side to people like the Reimanns in a war? They're decent, honourable folk. You've met them yourself. You must see how stupid this is?'

'I know. It's hard to believe.'

'I can't bring myself to hate the Germans simply because our government has declared war on them,' Alma said with a shrug of her shoulders and turned away in disgust.

It occurred to William at that moment that the Reimann's sons, Walter and Rudolf, were of an age to fight. So, too, was their own son, Alex. *Thank God he's so far away. Safely out of harm's way in Guatemala,* he thought. *What a terrible twist of fate it would be for the friends to find themselves in opposing armies.*

'But why should men from Suffolk have to fight?' Alma persisted. 'We're far removed from any war in Europe. Just because German troops are marching into Belgium it doesn't mean *our* menfolk should be involved.' A note of obstinacy crept into her voice.

'There's no rhyme or reason to any of it,' William agreed. His dark eyes reflected her bitterness. 'And I fear, from what I've read in the newspapers over the past week or so that this is a war we can't possibly win. I'm sure even Mr Churchill feels the same way.'

People standing around him shook their heads in disagreement. This was not what they wanted to hear. This was the voice of defeatism and despair.

The village undertaker and wheelwright, George Mallett, still in his long leather apron, had dashed from his shop the moment the newspapers had arrived and was leaning in the shop doorway. 'Surely with such a sizeable navy at his disposal, the First Lord of the Admiralty can have no such doubts?' he argued confidently. 'Look at the large number of ships we have here on our very doorstep, in Harwich harbour. Three flotillas of destroyers, not to mention submarines, cruisers and seaplanes. I've been down and seen 'em for meself. A magnificent sight.'

'But we don't have enough trained troops or guns to put up a fight against the Germans on *land* and that's where it counts,' said William patiently, as though delivering a homily to his class. 'Our professional army is minuscule in comparison to the standing armies in Europe. We only have about four hundred and fifty thousand men under arms and hundreds of those are reservists.

'The Germans have been preparing for years for this, building up their army as well as their navy with great single-mindedness and efficiency. The Kaiser's been spoiling for a fight, looking for the slightest pretext to prove his supremacy and grab our Empire. Now they've pounced on the assassination of the Archduke as an excuse to make war. And we won't be able to stop them.'

As William warmed to his theme Alma watched with growing alarm the glares of hostility being shot in their direction. The crowd around him was becoming increasingly sceptical. Some scoffed quietly behind his back, but William seemed not to notice. Alma feared open disagreement would erupt on the street and William would find few defenders for his outspokenness.

'Mark my words, the British government will rue the day it allowed itself to become aligned with the French. A perfidious nation!' His voice rose as he became more indignant. 'We've been dragged into a war that's none of our making because of this Entente Cordiale – this meaningless piece of paper!' He waved his newspaper excitedly in the air as though clutching the very document itself.

'My boy's already joined his regiment,' a middle-aged woman said quietly, turning from her paper to look up into William's reddened face. 'He's with the Cyclists, the sixth battalion. Do you remember him, Mr Smith? He was school champion five years ago?'

'Of course I do, Mrs Harvey.' His tone softened. He sensed his outburst had upset her. 'Alfred was the best we've ever had. A fine boy. A credit to you and the school. I have no doubt he'll acquit himself well in whatever role the army has in mind for him. And all the others.'

His placatory tones did little to quell the unease he'd stirred among the villagers. William Smith was a patriotic man. They had always thought him to be so. He'd taught their children about the military exploits of the nation's past heroes; men like Nelson and Wellington, Clive of India and Gordon of Khartoum, even Lord Kitchener. Pride of place was given in the Upper Standards classroom to a book he'd compiled on these and other great Englishmen and women.

But his implicit praise of German thoroughness and preparedness, while criticising their own government's lack of forethought, was at odds with their own unquestioning patriotism.

Alma quietly slipped her arm through her husband's and tugged it gently. It was a hint that her honest, outspoken husband should walk away. Now. Keep his opinions more discreetly buttoned. These, she knew, were criticisms that had frequently been aired by politicians and trades unionists in the London newspapers over the past few weeks as the war clouds gathered, but among country folk these anti-war views had no credence. They were enthusiasts for the war. The Germans would be beaten; they were not invincible. The might of the British Empire would prevail.

𝕰𝖆𝖘𝖙 𝕬𝖓𝖌𝖑𝖎𝖆𝖓 𝕯𝖆𝖎𝖑𝖞 𝕿𝖎𝖒𝖊𝖘
Thursday August 6 1914

New spies bill. 21 arrests in 24 hours.

A Bill was introduced into the House of Commons yesterday to enable his Majesty, in times of war or imminent national danger or great emergency, by Order in Council, to impose restrictions on aliens. It was claimed the object of the measure was to remove or restrain undesirable aliens, especially with a view to removal or detention of spies. Espionage has been much increased in recent years, and during the last 24 hours 21 spies have been arrested in various parts of the country, chiefly in important naval centres. The act will cause as little inconvenience as possible to 'alien friends'.

Chapter Seven

Thursday August 6 1914

The narrow streets in the centre of Ipswich were stifling, despite the early hour. Ernest twitched his nose at the sweet smell of fruit and vegetables rotting in the gutters where they'd been left since market day. The sweepers hadn't yet got as far as Upper Barclay Street and the rats, crows and seagulls were picking over the feast around his feet.

As he made the leisurely five-minute walk to the newspaper office in Carr Street he gazed longingly at the cloudless sky overhead, slivers just visible between the cramped rooftops. It would have been pleasant to take Lizzie on the train to Felixstowe for the day, just as they had done on Bank Holiday Monday. To paddle in the sea together and enjoy a stroll along the promenade. She'd looked so pretty twirling her new parasol.

But this promised to be another day plodding around the town between drill hall, barracks and recruiting office.

He sighed and hauled his aching leg up the flight of stone steps leading to the imposing main entrance. Often when he arrived for work he'd stop in the street for a few seconds, simply to gaze up at the unusual, bell-shaped turret that topped the newspaper's offices and admire the magnificent doric columns guarding its doorway. He was proud to work in such a fine building. Built in Queen Victoria's Jubilee year, it had become a landmark in the town centre. Its composing rooms and printing rooms were among the largest and most modern in the country. Pity the conditions in which he and the rest of the reporters worked were so dismal, he reminded himself wryly.

When Ernest arrived he was curious to see the editor sitting not in his own office, but overflowing the hard wooden chair behind *his* desk in the reporters' room. The Chief was always first to arrive in the morning from his home in Felixstowe, generally well before seven o'clock, and the last to leave in the evening.

His dedication to the newspaper he'd founded was legendary. It was his reporters' belief that he had no other care in life, despite having a wife. What other pastimes or pleasures did he have, except his newspaper? Yet his staff, who saw only the eccentricities of an elderly man, weren't to know that in his younger days he'd been a fanatical sportsman; one of the early golfers, a keen cricketer and tennis player and also a crack rifle shot.

The newspaper belonged to him. It *was* his family. After forty years in the editor's chair Sir Frederick Wilson was obsessed with news. Woe betide any unfortunate reporter who missed a story. The editor's wrath loomed large in their lives and they taunted each other with its consequences. Legend had it, in the reporters' room, that some years earlier the Chief had been to Germany to interview the Kaiser.

'Hart!' The corpulent frame rose slowly, like a monster emerging from the depths of the ocean, but the voice that welled up with it rang with panic-stricken overtones. 'Thank God you've arrived! I nearly came up to yer home to fetch yer!'

Ernest almost fainted. The thought of Sir Frederick coming to his humble residence appalled him. It was unheard of. An editor visiting a reporter, even his chief reporter, was unthinkable. 'It's only seven o'clock, Chief, I'm actually early,' he tried to point out reasonably. 'We don't normally start until half-past-seven.'

'I know that, yer dimwit! But I've just taken a telephone call, not five minutes ago. A doctor someone-or-another. Said there's something big happening out at Shotley barracks. He's just off there and he advises you to get out there at once if you want a good story.'

'Yes Chief. You mean right now?'

'Of course I mean right now, yer nitwit!' The editor's voice rang with exasperation. 'Doctor whoever-he-is will be driving past the door in his motor car in two minutes. If you're not waiting on the front step you'll have to make your own way out by cab. Now get moving!'

Ernest grabbed his notebook from the top drawer and a couple of freshly sharpened pencils and ran. He'd just reached the front door when Dr Francis Ward's car pulled up, his chauffeur at the wheel.

'Ernest, my man, jump in.' A smiling face with a neatly pointed beard peered from the back passenger seat and held open the door. Grateful for a ride in such style, Ernest climbed in. 'You're in luck,' pronounced the elderly Scot who had delivered him into the world 26 years earlier. 'A couple of minutes later we'd have been on our way. I gather there's been a disaster of some sort. Can't tell you what, though. I thought I'd best get down there and see if I could be of any assistance.'

A *disaster*.

The very word produced a frisson of expectation in the young reporter. He felt a tingling sensation spread down his spine and quiver along his limbs. It was a sensation he invariably experienced when faced with a story of some magnitude. A story that would be his. His scoop. The anticipation, the slow-burning fuse of gathering the facts. Then he'd ignite the touch paper of the shocking truth. It was like the approach of an orgasm, only somehow more satisfying.

As they motored towards Shotley along the bank of the River Orwell, past the parklands of a great estate, through quiet villages and fields of waving wheat and newly-reaped crops, Ernest found it difficult to believe peaceful England was at war. Yet only yesterday, one day after war had been declared, a flotilla of destroyers and other ships had steamed out of Harwich and into the North Sea. It had been a gallant sight. They'd made a wide sweep of the sea off the East Coast to ensure there were no German battleships lurking. *Only yesterday*, Ernest thought. *And only four days ago we were enjoying Bank Holiday by the seaside.*

The jagged shard of Shotley peninsula stood at the point where two rivers, the Orwell and the Stour, joined forces and flowed into the sea, opening a gaping mouth to the Harwich approaches and providing a safe haven for large naval vessels. As they approached Ernest could see the naval barracks and boys training centre, *HMS Ganges,* standing on the highest point. It was a superb vantage point, overlooking Harwich naval base on the opposite bank.

As their car turned between the high metal gates guarding Shotley barracks a sentry waved them in. The doctor was evidently expected. Everywhere uniformed men were running about while dozens of younger men, the trainees, were carrying stretchers. A member of the medical staff was shouting orders, directing operations.

Dr Ward pointed him out. 'That's the chap to talk to. We worked together some years ago at the East Suffolk Hospital. Mention my name. I'm sure you'll find him co-operative.'

The car ground to a halt on one corner of the gravelled parade ground. Ernest leapt down before it had barely stopped and ran over to the naval doctor. Explaining he'd come with Dr Ward he asked, 'What's going on?'

'Afraid I can't tell you. You'd best come down and see for yourself,' the doctor answered curtly, and hurried out through the gates.

'I'm heading down to the waterfront,' Ernest told Dr Ward, who was lifting his black medical bag from the back of the car. 'Are you coming?'

The older man shook his head, peering thoughtfully over the top of his spectacles. 'I'll find out where I'm needed most. Could be, with all those stretchers being taken out, that I'll be more use up here, if there are injured people being brought in.'

When Ernest reached the waterfront a large crowd of onlookers had already gathered. He pushed his way to the front of the quayside, notebook in hand. 'Ernest Hart, Daily Times,' he introduced himself to the man he'd elbowed next to. 'What's happening?'

'There's been a disaster,' the man said bitterly. 'Bloody German mines. Blew up one of our ships earlier this morning. Sank it.' All around him there were sharp gasps of incredulity. Even though the news had earlier filtered through to the waiting crowd, its re-telling still shocked them. They thought it unbelievable. Just two days after war had been declared and one of Britain's ships had been sunk.

'What about casualties?' Ernest waited, pencil poised.

'Not sure. There must be hundreds. They've already taken one group up to the barracks. More are on their way. Just you wait and see.'

Ernest looked back over his shoulder and saw signalling going on within the barrack enclosure. Within minutes an orderly ran down with an officer's sword. One of the waiting officers fastened it to his belt before marching with several others onto the Admiralty Pier.

They were followed by a contingent of naval trainees, *HMS Ganges* lads who quick-marched smartly along the waterside then wheeled onto the pier and formed up on the pier head. Others were drafted into the waterside shed where they brought out stretchers. They stood silently on the pier, stretchers at the ready.

The crowd didn't have long to wait.

'There's a destroyer coming in!' went up the shout from several who had positioned themselves on higher ground. Ernest stood on tiptoe, but could see nothing. Then, looking towards Harwich, he saw two aeroplanes and two submarines coming towards them. *They must be the advance guard for the rest of the Harwich flotilla,* he thought.

Moments later, looming against the bright easterly sunlight, he saw the dark hulls of a dozen or so destroyers, moving in a sinuous crocodile through the sparkling water towards the Harwich approaches. He shaded his eyes to watch their progress. Slowly, leadenly, they followed each other down the deep channel into Harwich as though in some well-prepared drill.

The first steamed well up the River Stour to take the farthest deep-water mooring whilst others moored as close as they could to the two piers off Shotley. It was the signal for feverish activity. Steam pinnaces and other craft approached from all directions as well as Red Cross boats and cutters manned by *Ganges* lads.

Stretchers were passed up to the destroyer moored nearest to the public pier. A chute was let down. Minutes passed. Then the first stretcher emerged. On it was the sprawled body of a wounded sailor, arms trailing over the edge. He was passed over the side of the ship with the greatest care, to be followed by another and another.

When the small craft was fully laden with injured men it moved away from the looming shadow of the destroyer's starboard flank to the pier head. There the wounded were as carefully passed up and carried to hospital by the lads from the barracks.

It was a tense moment when the first stretcher passed within a yard of where Ernest stood. The man had been very badly hurt in the legs. His face was livid and his eyes were closed. *Evidently a very bad case and so he's been sent first,* Ernest thought, scribbling a couple of lines in his notebook. The seaman looked close to death.

The young stretcher-bearers stumbled on the rough pathway with their unfamiliar burden. The stretcher tilted sideways and with it the sailor's body. Something fell with a barely audible *clink* onto the stones, but only Ernest heard it. The bearers struggled onwards and up the hill to the barracks.

The reporter knelt down. It was a bent copper coin that had fallen from the seaman's breast pocket. A penny. He felt the edges between his fingers. Such was the force of the mine's explosion that it had not only bent the coin but torn the edges. He put it carefully into his trouser pocket. *A grim souvenir of the first engagement between the British and Germans*, he thought. *The first casualty to come ashore.* But there was something heart-rending about this modest keepsake. He wrote a line in his notebook, 'It will forever remain among my greatest treasures'. He meant it.

Other stretchers followed. The occupants had obviously been the victims of an explosion and he could hardly bear to look at them. The faces of many were blackened and disfigured beyond all recognition. Case after case was born past him to the hospital, some with faces ominously covered. Involuntarily Ernest, and many of the other men watching, took off their caps and hats and bared their heads in respect.

The silence was broken by the firm step of marching men. A contingent of the 5th Essex regiment marched onto the pier and halted. More men were unloaded from the destroyer and herded together into a tight knot. A short time elapsed before the soldiers marched back, this time with fixed bayonets. In their midst was a group of German prisoners.

The onlookers craned their necks with intense interest. The prisoners were grimed, tattered and battered but for the most part bore themselves carelessly enough, looking at their unexpected surroundings with evident curiosity. Some were lame or slightly wounded.

In the front rank was a handsome fair boy, a young giant, who looked Ernest full in the eye with grim determination as he passed close by. Next came a couple of German officers without a guard, but accompanied by the British officer who'd required his sword at his side in order to do the honours. He was chatting to them cheerfully in what Ernest could only suppose was fluent German. One was tall and fair-bearded with flaxen hair. *A typical Tuton,* Ernest noted. The other was short, swarthy and thick-set, scowling miserably.

A gunboat came tearing in shortly after the destroyers. She had evidently been having a rough time for every scrap of paint had been stripped from her sides. She, too, landed a contingent of prisoners and wounded. The onlookers were shocked at their condition. Some were just able to raise their heads and glance around. Others had only a scrap of features showing while a few had their faces completely swathed. Nearly all were suffering from bad burns and shock after the explosion.

Again the contingent of soldiers returned to the pier head and escorted yet more prisoners ashore. And still the wounded came. Four men, British bluejackets, though there was nothing left of their uniforms to show their rating, bare headed and bare footed, came into view, limping painfully and helping one another along. They tried to bear themselves jauntily, but it was an effort. They were tight-lipped as they staggered over the stony road to the hospital gate.

More British wounded followed on litters and then a couple of young naval officers, their clothing torn and their faces smoke-blackened and one with both hands swathed in bandages, trying to walk bravely past the crowd. But there were no smiles from either side.

Ernest tried to calculate how many casualties and prisoners he'd seen that morning. Perhaps 60 German wounded and prisoners and about a score of British officers and men, he thought. He'd gathered 20 were victims of the mine-laying engagement and the others of another engagement involving a disaster to one of the British destroyers.

Such care, such tenderness, he thought as he watched the German prisoners being taken ashore by British naval officers. A woman in the crowd had similar thoughts.

'D'yer think *our* soldiers or seamen'd get such fine treatment from the enemy if *they* was taken prisoner?' she asked angrily, not addressing anyone in particular. There was a grumble of 'No.' Heads were shaken. They doubted it.

Ernest turned to walk back up the hill to the barracks, leaving the quayside and the crowd behind him. He needed to speak to someone in authority; someone who might know what had happened to cause such a disaster. He needed to find Dr Ward.

'Which way's the hospital block?' he asked the sentry at the gate who had waved him through earlier. The sentry pointed across the parade ground. Ernest skirted around the edge, afraid that without a uniform he'd look conspicuous walking across the middle. He wasn't even sure he should be there.

Once inside the main corridor he darted from ward to ward. Every bed was occupied by a casualty. Some of the men groaned quietly to themselves, others sobbed and cried out for their mothers. All were desperate for morphine.

Anything. Just kill the pain. Dr Ward was bent over one of them when Ernest found him. The old doctor's hands were bloodied. So, too were his white shirt front and cuffs. He looked up quickly.

'You shouldn'a be here, laddie. This is na' the place for you,' he whispered hoarsely in his soft Edinburgh brogue.

'I know. But I need to talk to some of the officers and men who've been brought in. I need to find out what happened.'

Dr Ward pointed to a corner bed. 'Talk to him. He's an officer from the *Amphion*.' He continued bandaging the gaping wound in his patient's stomach.

The officer was sitting on the bed, head in hands. He was a slim young man, no more than mid-twenties. *Probably younger than me*, Ernest guessed. Only his mouth, darkly pained eyes and nostrils were visible amidst the swathe of bandages around his face. A tuft of matted blond hair protruded from the back of the bloodstained turban.

Ernest sat on the bed next to him.

The smell of burnt flesh and charred clothing that hung from the young officer and the man in the neighbouring bed threatened to overwhelm him. He momentarily clamped a hand over his nose and mouth, desperately holding back the vomit rising in his mouth. He swallowed hard and cleared his throat loudly. He introduced himself and said gently, 'Tell me what happened to you.'

'Those damn mines,' the seaman whispered into his bandages as though no-one was there. Then he raised his head and stared at Ernest for a few moments before gathering his spirits. 'Never mind. We'll give it to them in a week or so,' he tried to sound bullish. 'Just as we were celebrating, too. Our destroyer flotilla had been tracking a German mine-layer, the *Koenigen Luise*, across the North Sea for hours. We caught up with her just off the Dutch coast. One of our destroyers fired a couple of shots and sank her. First blood of the war, so to speak. We stopped to pick up the survivors.

'The *Koenigen Luise* had managed to lay a line of mines from Aldeburgh Ridge to a point opposite Bawdsey, right in the track of any vessel leaving or coming to Harwich. We hit one of them about 45 miles south east of Lowestoft. Smack! Right on the bow,' he punched his right fist hard into his left palm to illustrate the force of the explosion.

Hearing the ferocity in his voice an older man lying on the bed next to him, a petty officer, sat up. He'd been blinded. Both eyes as well as his arms were swathed in bandages. He swung his legs carefully over the side of the bed. They, too, had evidently been badly burnt.

He spoke with difficulty, his voice hoarse from the acrid smoke he'd inhaled. 'It was hell. There were men lying everywhere. One minute they were standing there with me, the next – boom! They were gone. Bits of their bodies. Heads.

Legs. Blown across the deck.' He stopped. His bandaged arms were shaking. Whether it was with grief or anger Ernest couldn't tell.

'Then she started to go down. Slowly at first, then as she took on water, faster and faster. The noise was terrible. A creaking, splitting sound. Men were jumping into the water off the stern, even some of the injured. Some of us tried to get down below to find our mates. The fire was spreading fast. I managed to drag a couple of chaps up the companionway, but we couldn't reach all the men in the fo'c'sle before she sank.'

'Is that how you got like this?' Ernest asked, but the petty officer couldn't see the reporter pointing at his bandaged arms with his pencil. 'Going into the flames?'

'We had to try. It's done now,' was all he would say.

Ernest turned to the young man sitting beside him on the bed. 'How many men did you lose?'

The swollen lips moved painfully beneath the bandages. 'Paymaster Gedge and over a hundred men were killed outright. Captain Fox, sixteen officers and I'm told 135 men were saved by the other ships of the third flotilla. Harry here, and I were lucky to get out alive.'

'Thank God they were close by,' Harry said. 'The gunboat came right alongside, braving the fire and taking a scorching herself. She lifted many of the injured to safety and plucked a good few from the sea, too. I was one of the lucky ones. We were only a few hundred yards clear of the *Amphion* when she sank.'

Both men lowered their heads. The loss of their new ship, so early in the conflict, was like a death itself. The cruiser, whose crew had been so proud to lead the third destroyer flotilla, had been launched only the previous year. Now it rested on the ocean floor to rust like any other ancient hulk.

'And what of the German prisoners? I saw some being brought ashore.'

'Twenty prisoners picked up from the *Koenigen Luise* and confined in the fo'c'sle of the ship perished. Killed by their own bloody mine. You could say it was divine retribution.' The corners of the petty officer's mouth twitched in a vain attempt at a cynical grin.

Ernest gazed down the long ward, with its score or more beds, towards the double doors which in turn led into the next ward. Each injured man would have his own tale to tell of this war. This bloody war. It had hardly begun yet the navy had already lost more than a hundred men. Most likely from Suffolk seafaring families, too. *Would that the young recruits flocking to join up so cheerfully at the drill halls in Ipswich could see these poor souls,* he thought.

The young blond officer's dark eyes glimmered with tears. 'What'll my wife and kiddie say when they see me? This face. They won't recognise me.' He poked at the bandages petulantly.

'Last time I saw them was when we went off to Spithead for the King's review. What a grand day that was. They were there, waving flags and cheering like the rest of them. Crowds of people, all along the seafront at Portsmouth and Southsea. I've never seen such crowds, nor so many ships – you'd never believe it. Hundreds and hundreds of them, too many to count. And sea-planes, too. Ships stretched in long lines all the way from Spitbank Fort as far as Cowes. Lines and lines of grey ships, as far as the eye could see.

'As each ship steamed past the Royal yacht their band played the National Anthem. Oh, that was a grand sound! After we'd sung 'God Save the King' our ship's company gave three hearty cheers for His Majesty. I saw him standing on the bridge of the *Victoria and Albert*, with the young Prince of Wales at his side, acknowledging our salutes. How proud I was, to see the King for myself. Can you believe it? It took more than six hours for that line of warships to pass before the King? What a wonderful day! I felt we were unbeatable, invincible.

'We all thought we'd get manoevre leave after that, because we were due to have manoevres, but no, we were sent back here, to battle stations, so I never saw my family again before this happened.' The officer buried his head in his hands, the recollection of more glorious times only serving to heighten his disbelief at becoming such an early casualty of a war which had only just begun.

A young officer came striding purposefully down the centre of the ward. Ernest recognised him as the fellow who'd requested his sword in order to accompany the German officers ashore. He was heading straight for the end bed where he was still sitting with the two injured *Amphion* officers. Ernest feared he'd be told to leave. That a newspaper reporter wasn't welcome here.

'You're from the Daily Times, aren't you? I'm glad you're still here,' the officer said chirpily, holding out his hand. 'Lieutenant Briggs, at your service.' He perched his tightly uniformed buttocks uncomfortably on the end of the iron bedstead opposite.

'I've got some *good* news. You might want to print it in your newspaper.' He smiled inanely, running long fingers through the sleek dark hair which framed a delicate, bird-like face. Ernest thought him far too foppish to be taken seriously as an officer.

'People will certainly be grateful for some good news after reading my report about what's happened to the *Amphion* and her crew.' Ernest's dour look quickly wiped the smile off the officer's lips.

'Well,' Lt. Briggs snorted, 'one of the German officers I accompanied ashore, and who is now being held prisoner, holds the rank of Naval Commander. Most fortunately he had about his person, when we captured him, the complete plan of the mine-laying scheme, showing that one hundred of these death traps had already been laid before the *Koenigen Luise* was caught and sent to the bottom.' He sounded triumphant.

The injured men sitting beside Ernest shook their heads cynically. What good would the plans do them now?

'Thanks. I'll use that information in my report,' Ernest replied. 'I'm most grateful for you seeking me out to tell me this.' He thought it best to be civil. He didn't know when he might need to use this young officer's willingness to spill the beans again. 'If you get anything further happening, any more incidents, you'll let me know, won't you?'

It was early evening when they left, yet the heat bouncing off the parade ground was still intense. Even so, Ernest and Dr Ward were glad to be out there breathing the dust-filled air rather than in the wards with their fetid stench of men; the burnt, bleeding flesh and the sweat and vomit of their pain and fear. They climbed into the car without a word. The chauffeur roused himself from a doze to begin the journey back to Ipswich.

They sat in the back, silently staring out of the windows as Shotley barracks disappeared from view. Back past the rolling acres of wheat and snatched glimpses of the tan sails of barges reflecting in the opalescent mud of the River Orwell at low tide.

They'd left behind a human detritus washed ashore after a terrible storm. Men without limbs, skin ripped from their faces and blinded forever. Young men the same age as Ernest.

Ernest rubbed unconsciously along his crippled thigh as though their pain had been transferred to his own limb. Felt again the power of the black hooves as they pounded flesh into bone. Heard his screams muffled by the rumble of overpowering wooden wheels. How much worse must be the pain of fire and shearing metal? He resolved to put self-pity behind him from now on.

'Leg giving you a bit of trouble, laddie?' Dr Ward was glad of an excuse to open the conversation.

'It's been bad of late,' Ernest admitted. 'Too much walking isn't good for it.'

'You should come and see me soon. I'll take a wee look at it.'

'I'll do that.'

Both men returned to their reveries. They contained images they'd rather forget, rather never have seen.

Ernest thrust his hands into his trouser pockets. There was the penny. He clasped his fingers around it. Spontaneously he pulled it out and held it in his open palm. A large, heavy Victorian penny, although the Queen's head had been worn almost to a shadow. *What a story it could tell*, he thought. Then he remembered that at Central School the English master had set them, as the subject for a composition, "The Adventures of a Penny". What had he written? Something fantastical, no doubt. But nothing to compare with what must have befallen this particular coin.

'What's that?' Dr Ward leaned forward, peering over his spectacles to see what he was holding.

Ernest told him how it had dropped from the mortally wounded seaman's pocket and that he'd picked it up as a souvenir.

'Look how badly the explosion pierced the edges and dented it.'

Dr Ward plucked it delicately from his palm. 'Poor wee fellow,' he muttered quietly and handed it back.

When they reached Ipswich the chauffeur stopped outside the newspaper office on the corner of Little Coleman Street and Carr Street. Ernest thanked the doctor for his kindness and they shook hands.

'Don't forget. Come and see me,' Dr Ward ordered, waving briefly through the window.

Sir Frederick was still in his office. He listened as the car door slammed then heard the heavy oak front door of the office swing open and close quietly behind his chief reporter.

'That you, Hart?'

'Yes Chief.' He put his head around the door to see the editor bent over wire service tapes.

'What have you got for me, then?'

It was difficult to put into words. He stuttered and stumbled but eventually managed to convey the gist of what had happened.

'Were you the only newspaperman down there?' Wilson peered at him suspiciously.

'Yes. I think so.'

'Good man. You know what this means?'

Ernest hesitated, suspicious of what Wilson could be driving at. 'No?'

'If you were the only newspaper there, then the Daily Times has the biggest exclusive of any newspaper in the country. Anywhere. The first battle in England's war against Germany. The first casualties - brought ashore in Suffolk. The East Coast comes face to face with the grim realities of war. In the front line of sea battles yet to come!' The editor's voice rose, becoming more dramatic with each phrase. He spoke in dramatic headlines.

Headlines Ernest assumed he'd already written for the next morning's edition. 'So, get on with it. And show me first before it goes to the subs.'

'Of course.' He left the door open, knowing the editor took pleasure in hearing the rattle of old typewriters from down the corridor.

From the moment he spun the first folio into the machine he wrote as though possessed. He hardly referred to the copious notes he'd made. The scenes, the conversations he'd had, were in his heart. The folios lay in a white drift on his desk when he'd finished. It seemed as though there were hundreds. Enough to fill several columns of small, dense type.

When his gaze finally lifted from the keys he saw it was dark outside.

Frederick Wilson heard the typewriter stop. Pricked his ears for the faint rustling of papers being stacked in order. He lifted himself from his swinging chair and stomped with his stick along the echoing woodblock corridor. He loomed in the doorway of the reporters' room.

'Finished?'

'Yes Chief.'

'Good man.' The editor grasped the proffered copy in his thick hands. He skimmed through the top three or four folios, reading fast. For a moment he seemed at a loss for words. His red-veined eyes were shining with a kind of madness Ernest had never seen before. He wondered what he was thinking.

'Best get off home, young man. Don't want that pretty little wife of yours fretting because you're late for supper, eh?' The heavy body swung out of the room and tip-tapped urgently back to his office. Ernest watched him go then shrugged his shoulders. He supposed the editor wasn't displeased with what he'd written.

It was only after he'd heard the reporter close the front door behind him that Frederick Wilson added, with huge satisfaction, a line at the bottom of the copy. He wrote "by Ernest Hart, Special Correspondent". It was the first time in his newspaper's history he had ever allowed a journalist a by-line. The first time a writer had been anything other than anonymous. It was the Chief's mark of respect for his chief reporter and a remarkable eye-witness account of the aftermath of the first engagement of the war.

East Anglian Daily Times

Saturday August 8 1914

Loss of the Amphion. Mr Churchill and use of mines. Opening of Press Bureau.

In the House of Commons yesterday the first Lord of the Admiralty, who was loudly cheered on rising, made a statement with regard to the loss of the *Amphion* and announced the establishment of a Press Bureau for the supply of official news for the press. In reply to a question by Mr Bonar Law, Mr Churchill said the House would have read with sorrow of the loss of *HMS Amphion* the day before yesterday. A flotilla of destroyers patrolling in the approaches to the Channel found a German mine-laying ship, the *Koenigen Luise*, and pursued and sank her.

About 56 members of the crew, which numbered 120 or 130 in all, were humanely saved by the flotilla. The *Amphion* continued to scout the flotilla and on her return journey was blown up by a mine. The greater part of the officers and men were rescued by the boats, but nearly 130 persons were killed outright by the explosion and in addition to that 20 prisoners being confined in the forepart of the ship.

There were no other losses of any kind and there had been no other fighting so far, as far as we are aware.

The indiscriminate use of mines not in connection with military harbours or strategic positions and the indiscriminate scattering of contact mines about the seas, may cause to destroy not only enemy vessels or warships but peaceful merchantmen passing under neutral flags, possibly carrying supplies to neutral countries. This use of mines in warfare deserves to be attentively considered, not only by us who are engaged in the war, and be prone to hasty judgements on such matters, but it deserves to be attentively considered also by the nations of the civilised world.

The Admiralty is not at all alarmed or disconcerted by such an incident. We have expected a certain number and we will continue to expect a certain number of such incidents and our arrangements provide for reducing such occurrences to the minimum possible.

Chapter Eight

Friday August 7 1914

With the outbreak of war Lord Stradbroke, as Chairman of the County Council, hastily arranged a public meeting to set up an East Suffolk Defence Committee. Despite the event's short notice, crowds converged in huge numbers on the new County Hall.

The audience congregated well before the appointed time of ten o'clock, cramming through the doors and jostling each other good naturedly in the street outside. It was a crowd composed almost exclusively of men. Not young men, full of pent-up enthusiasm and bravado for battle, but mature men of some rank in the community: doctors and lawyers, headmasters, magistrates and members of the county council and other public bodies, their dark attire presenting a sombre and monotonous sea of grey and black. Only the merest fragment of colour here and there indicated a woman's presence.

Once inside the hall they were forced to sit crammed closely together, shoulders wedged between those of their neighbours, in the breathless air. Even so, there wasn't room for them all. Latecomers stood in the passageways adjoining the main hall or squeezed into the high gallery at the back. The windows were flung open, not purely for ventilation, but to allow those standing outside to hear the proceedings. It seemed that anyone who considered himself of importance was there. Anxious to be seen by his fellows to be contributing to the war effort.

To William Smith's surprise the Earl had sent one of his footmen down to the schoolhouse the day before with a hastily scrawled note, asking him to attend and urging him to encourage other schoolmasters to join him. 'Your skills at organisation are vital at such a time as this,' the Earl had assured him. 'And your fellow headmasters should also be aware they have an important role to play in persuading local people to set up committees to help ensure troops stationed in our midst, and the poorer classes in society, are properly cared for.'

William had secured a place at the front of the hall, having caught the early train from Blythburgh with his old friend and colleague George Busby, the headmaster at neighbouring Yoxford village school.

Alma had driven him to the station in the dog cart, but had refused to accompany him to the meeting. 'I'm having nothing to do with this war,' she said petulantly, 'I can't bear it. Our men fighting and dying. It's so needless. Such a terrible waste.'

As the two schoolmasters sat waiting for the meeting to begin they turned to watch the crowds pouring in, filling the rows of seats behind them. The atmosphere of suppressed excitement infected everyone and the hubbub of voices grew louder and more animated as the minutes ticked by.

The hall was almost full by the time a fair-haired young man, limping perceptibly, came to a halt in front of William. He twitched his hand, slightly apologetically, towards an empty chair at the end of their row. A printed notice hung from its topmost rail: 'Reserved for the East Anglian Daily Times'.

He removed his hat, nodded his disorganised curls politely and introduced himself. 'Good morning, gentlemen. I'm Ernest Hart, the special war correspondent for the Daily Times. Would you mind if I joined you?'

'Not at all, not at all,' said William jovially, motioning to the seat next to him. He and Busby introduced themselves in turn and all shook hands amiably.

'What do you think of all this?' Ernest said, waving his hand towards the crowd. 'D'yer think we'll achieve anything by it?' He took a notebook and pencil from the pocket of his worn black jacket.

As they exchanged views on the merits of setting up a defence committee Hart made notes. William wondered if their patriotism didn't sound a trifle absurd. Hart might imagine they were both in favour of this war. That, like everyone else, they believed in the infallible might of the British Empire. *Yet that couldn't be further from the truth*, he thought grimly.

The reporter's brow creased quizzically and he tilted his head to one side as he looked up from his notebook. He paused, tapping the chewed end of the pencil on his front teeth. 'And what effect do you think the war will have on schools like your own?'

Only three days previously Busby had attended a meeting of the National Union of Teachers and so was able to recount the apprehension expressed by fellow schoolmasters that the war, if prolonged, would have a detrimental effect on children's education. 'There's already pressure being brought to bear on schools in some parts of Suffolk to allow older scholars of between 12 and 14, especially boys, to leave school early to work on the land now that so many agricultural workers have joined the colours,' he told him.

'And do you think that'll happen?' Hart asked.

'I certainly hope not,' Busby said indignantly. 'They have precious little time at school as it is.'

William leant forward, his dark head close to the young reporter's as he bent to make a note. He laid his hand on the young man's arm, as though to reinforce what he had to say. 'And you must see, too, that if fathers and brothers leave their jobs in order to enlist, who will be the breadwinners? I fear many poor families will starve as a result of this war. Or, as my colleague so rightly pointed out, our young scholars will be taken away to labour instead.' His voice trembled with anger.

Hart nodded. He'd noted the grim set of both teachers' mouths. Perhaps they were being unduly pessimistic. He scribbled something in his notebook and closed it discreetly so they were unable to glance down at what he had written.

Suddenly a shout from the back of the hall broke through their thoughts and the din around them.

'Three cheers for Lord Stradbroke! Hip hip....'

They turned in their seats to see a khaki-clad figure entering the hall through a side door. As the Earl came into view the crowds cheered loudly and stamped their feet on the bare wooden floor, like unruly children, irrepressible and almost joyful.

William found it hard to believe that this was a gathering brought together to discuss the war. It was more like a concert party. The cheering quickly gave way to thunderous applause.

The Earl's rugged face flushed. He felt somewhat bemused. It was the first time he'd appeared in public in the drab khaki of a Royal Artillery Colonel rather than in his customary red robes as chairman of the council. He was quite overwhelmed by this response to his appearance. Such spontaneous, patriotic fervour. It was quite unexpected. The crowd continued to clap and cheer as he made his way to the front of the hall where he took his seat in the centre of the dais.

Lord Stradbroke was followed by the Chief Constable. Captain Jasper Mayne was an tall, imposing figure. In his fifties, a tightly clipped grey moustache emphasised the severity of his steel grey eyes. As he took his seat it was with a rigid stiffness in marked contrast to the easy manner of the Earl. The audience applauded him respectfully.

William, just feet away, gazed up at him and for a lingering moment their eyes met. Yet if they did so it was only fleetingly. The policeman's impersonal stare glided away, across the sea of upturned faces that was spread in a surging, agitated mass before him. He then tilted his chin to glance coolly upwards at the eager heads craning over the gallery. The steel eyes missed nothing. They bore through the open doorway to take in the crush of people jostling in the corridor. All the while his face was impassive, betraying nothing.

This man, thought William, *is sitting in judgement, assessing the worth and honesty of every man before him.* Who had Captain Mayne singled out as wanting in those qualities? William shifted in his seat. What was it about him? His aggressively military bearing? The cynical turn of his mouth? A sense that suspicion lurked in every fibre of the well-fleshed body? William found it hard to understand why he felt such unease in the police chief's presence. It was an entirely foreign emotion.

Lord Stradbroke stood. Leaning one hand on the carved, eagle-winged lectern he held up the other to silence the applause. 'Thank you, thank you!' His deep voice rumbled to the rafters. 'Thank you for your kindly welcome. I'm delighted to see such a large number of you here today. As you're aware, I've summoned this meeting at this time of great national emergency to help our King and country.'

A loud cheer broke out in the hall and echoed down the corridor among the crowd straining to hear him through the open doorway.

He held up his hand again to quell their enthusiasm. 'I hope we're able to calmly discuss the present situation and allay any feeling of panic that might arise. I know everyone is anxious to do what he can to assist our country at the present time. But we want to make the best of that assistance. We can only do this by careful organisation. We don't want to waste our energy.

'We'll have to make use of everything. There's a danger of the enemy managing to do harm and there's also a danger of shortage of food supplies. We must do everything we can to economise where food is concerned. Who knows how much will be required or how long the war will carry on for?'

There were murmurs of assent. The Earl was a popular, down-to-earth fellow. A farmer before all else, a lover of the land before a soldier. He understood the problems of food production and animal husbandry. He, like the rest of the nation's landowners, would have to face the winter with fewer farm hands as the forces claimed their reservists and Territorials.

'This war is an infamous war,' he declared. 'Infamous. But we're not here to stir up bitterness or ill feeling. We're here to meet the great danger we face. There are many ways we can assist the government. In times of stress and emergency there'll be breakdowns in organisation. Large numbers of troops might be pouring into the district. Who knows where the fight will take place? If we organise in advance we'll be able to help.

'For example, men on the march could be suffering from thirst and hunger. Having local committees means we can meet the troops and serve them water or supplies as they go along. Farmers would be able to lend them horses for transport up hills or where the roads are broken up. Boy Scouts could help in a number of ways, such as taking messages to the troops. They'd have to look after the wounded and help men who might fall out of the ranks from sickness or slight accidents.'

A kindly, practical man. His audience felt comfortable that such a man had taken charge at this critical time and with such sensible solutions. His East Suffolk Defence committee would be a nucleus for smaller local committees, which would help people in their own communities.

'We also have a great responsibility to look after the poorer classes,' he went on. 'Not merely working men who receive wages, but others whose income is very small. It's our duty, as a committee, to organise their food supplies so their suffering is minimised as much as possible.' There were rumbles of 'here here'.

'Finally, I'd like to move a resolution,' he said. 'That this meeting pledges itself to be loyal to the government and the assistance of all classes in the defence of the country and the protection and maintenance of the general community.'

The cries of 'Here! Here!' and 'Bravo!' echoed in the streets outside. He bowed slightly to the audience and took his seat next to the Chief Constable.

Captain Mayne then rose and the hall fell quiet. He straightened himself to his full height and contemplated what he needed to say. His audience, however venerable, had no inkling of what currently posed the greatest threat to the nation's safety.

Spies. Spies and aliens who could pass military secrets to the Germans, thus delivering England into the hands of its enemies.

He cleared his throat, pulled at the hem of his uniform jacket to straighten it then read in a monotone from a single typewritten sheet of paper. 'This notice is from the Privy Council and is with regard to aliens. Aliens of whatever nationality. They must report themselves at once to the nearest police officer who will direct them to their registration office in my district.' He looked up from his papers and added, 'I've been appointed the official registration officer for East Suffolk.'

'What are aliens?' someone shouted from the gallery. The question threw him for a moment. He assumed everyone would know.

'The Germans are most definitely "alien enemies",' replied Jasper Mayne tersely. 'But all others are "alien friends". At present. That is all I have to report on the matter of aliens. Thank you.' He sat down with as much precision as he'd risen.

The Earl nodded graciously in the direction of the Chief Constable. Then, drawing a crumpled piece of blue writing paper from his uniform pocket, he surreptitiously glanced down. There was something he'd forgotten. Something of vital importance. Helena would never forgive him if he failed to mention it.

He leapt hurriedly to his feet again. 'And finally,' he raised his voice to quell the rising hubbub of chatter, 'and finally….we mustn't forget the ladies.'

He ignored the cries of 'hear, hear!' and 'hurrah for the ladies!' and pressed on.

'We must impress on our womenfolk that they are just as important to the war effort as we are. They can form sewing and work parties and organise charitable events to raise money, not only for the troops but for those left bereft and destitute. I therefore implore you to go back to your villages and workplaces and enlist their assistance.'

Having done Helena's bidding the Earl finally sat down.

The business of setting up a Defence Committee over, a voice from the front of the hall called for a vote of thanks to Lord Stradbroke. It was an excuse for another burst of cheering and then, just as spontaneously, the singing began.

A few voices at first, then the hundreds assembled in the hall, the corridors and around the gallery, as one, took up the anthem; 'God Save Our Gracious King, Long Live Our Noble King......'

It was an emotional moment. An outpouring of patriotism never before as heartfelt or fervent as this day, in this place.

William found himself singing as lustily as any man there. As tears welled in his eyes he felt his heart would burst.

Having been fortunate enough to secure front seats William and Busby were among the last to leave. As they waited patiently for the crowd to disperse through the double doors at the rear of the hall William caught sight of the corpulent figure of Sir Frederick Wilson, pushing urgently forward, against the flow of bodies, voice and whiskers exploding simultaneously. He was waving his stick wildly above the heads of those jostling against him, trying to attract the attention of the Earl and Captain Mayne who were still seated on the stage, deep in conversation. Sir Frederick wasn't to be ignored.

'Excellent turn-out! Wonderful! Wonderful!' he boomed as he barged his ungainly form between the two schoolmasters. The Earl and Mayne both nodded, leaning forward in their seats to acknowledge the venerable newspaper proprietor's presence, although his remarks seemed to be addressed to all and sundry. 'I congratulate you, your Lordship! Fine idea. We're certainly in the front line of this war, without a shadow of doubt.'

Then turning to Captain Mayne he lowered his voice to a melodramatic stage whisper. 'And what about these *aliens*, eh? *Spies* in our midst, wouldn't you say? No doubt about it. No doubt at all.'

Mayne knew better than to be contemptuous of the eccentric figure before him. This grey-haired old man tottering on his stick, who looked as though he'd been squeezed into a second-hand suit several sizes too small for him and whose moustache was sadly in need of a barber's discipline, was, he knew, an influence to be reckoned with. He ran a flourishing newspaper that was widely read. He could help promulgate his message.

'Sir Frederick, so glad you could join us.' The Chief Constable rose to his feet and extended his hand. The weak smile that tweaked the corner of his mouth never softened the icy glaze of his eyes. 'You're right, of course. There *are* spies and we need to root them out before they can do too much damage. I fear that we've already seen the tragic results of their work with the terrible disaster that befell one of our ships. Here, off this very coast. I have no doubt there were spies who signalled the enemy that the flotilla's departure from port was imminent.'

He paused and glanced at the knot of people standing close to the stage, waiting for the crush around the doors to subside. Once again his eyes locked into the mesmerising darkness of William's. Again he noted the sleek, almost unnatural blackness of the hair and moustache, the sallowness of the bronzed face.

The face of a foreigner.

'Perhaps you and I should discuss how best to overcome this imminent danger? In my office? Shall we say tomorrow? Same time?' Mayne uncoiled the gold chain across his chest and flipped open his pocket watch.

'Capital idea! Capital! Patriotic newspaper, the Daily Times. Always has been. Always will be. I'll see you at eleven tomorrow. Good day your Lordship. Captain Mayne,' Sir Frederick said, tipping his misshapen black hat at the Earl.

Having achieved his mission he stomped back through the waiting crowd which, sensing a person of some importance in their midst, grudgingly parted to allow him past.

Once in the street William and Busby struggled to get through the press of people spilling across the pavements outside the hall. It was a good quarter of an hour's walk to the station and their train was due. They were in danger of missing it and neither relished a long wait for the next one. They set off at a run, Busby panting in William's wake. The sight of two middle-aged men in dark suits and stiff collars, darting recklessly amongst the traffic like a couple of naughty schoolboys escaping a prank, set heads turning.

It was with huge relief that they discovered their train was late. 'Lowestoft train's been held up for a troop train going up the coast,' was the stationmaster's explanation.

When it finally pulled into Ipswich station the doors cascaded open and hundreds of young men erupted onto the platform in a volcanic lava flow of khaki. The vaulted roofs of the station echoed to their shouts and laughter and the clatter of their boots.

As William and Busby took seats by the window vacated by soldiers they watched the grey-brown tide ebbing slowly away, flowing disjointedly along the platform. Then, as the train pulled out of the station, the cacophony of voices and footsteps receded as the tranquillity of the Suffolk landscape closed in around them.

It was familiar. It comforted them. The seething mass of high-spirited young men clamouring for war was not an England they recognised or felt comfortable with. Their roots were here, in this unremarkable, quiet landscape. Bound to the soil and the people who lived close by it. Their lives and livelihoods as schoolmasters lay among the reapers in the harvest fields; the men and women who straightened their backs to stare at the train as it sped past and the young children gleaning along the margins where the corn had already been carted away on the horse-drawn waggons.

The pupils who'd sat in hushed rows of desks were now this army of wives and girls passing bundles of fourses among the men to eat where they worked. No time for rest for any of them.

There was an added urgency about this harvest. Enfield rifles would soon be slung across the reapers' shoulders in the same casual way that they now carried their pitchforks or scythes.

As the steam engine toiled through the gently undulating grainlands the glorious smell of wild mint wafted from the stubble through the open carriage window.

'There's much to be done when we get back home if we're to satisfy the wants of Lord Stradbroke's Defence Committee,' William said, eventually breaking their reflective silence. Then glancing anxiously at his pocket watch he added, 'but my most pressing engagement today is with my young swimmers.'

'Surely you allow yourself a day off supervising your pupils during the holidays?' Busby looked surprised. 'Especially when you have important business to attend to, such as today's meeting?'

'My dear friend, if you saw the enthusiasm these children show for swimming, and the respite it brings after long days' toiling at the harvest, you'd understand why I must be there.' Will smiled into the rounded, amiable face of his colleague.

Busby shook his head ruefully. He felt Will took his devotion to his pupils too far, but politely refrained from saying as much.

When the Earl returned in his chauffeur-driven Siddeley landaulette to Henham Hall, flushed with the morning's triumph in Ipswich, he was surprised to find his wife standing in the centre of the ballroom with his estate manager, William Mitchell.

Helena was pointing out various items of furniture set around the room, waving a rolled newspaper as a pointer, while Mitchell wrote a note of what she was saying in a small, leather-bound book. She spun round when she heard George's footsteps behind her.

'George! You're just in time! How did your meeting go? Did it go well?'

'Very well. Very well indeed. In fact.....' and he blushed again at the recollection, 'the audience gave me three cheers. I was terribly moved by it all, I must say.'

Helena grabbed his arm and reached up to kiss his cheek. 'Oh darling, that's marvellous.' She was about to ask for more details when George interrupted her.

'Mr Mitchell, what brings you into the ballroom on a fine morning like this? What's her Ladyship scheming now, eh?'

Helena released her grip on his arm and frowned. 'Oh George, it's not a scheme. It's far more important than that. I'm sure when you hear what I'm planning you'll agree with me. Don't you think so, Mr Mitchell?'

Mitchell nodded, but with no great enthusiasm. A tall, rangy man in his early forties, dressed in tweeds and with the weather-beaten complexion of a countryman, he had run the Henham Estate and its several dozen farms for many years. He was also a consummate diplomat when it came to differences of opinion between the Earl and Countess.

'It is a most worthy cause, your Ladyship, but I do have some concerns over the... what shall we say... *practical* implementation.' Marshall shuffled his feet backwards very slightly as though distancing himself from Helena's scheming.

'Right ho, Nellie, out with it. What's this all about?' George smiled indulgently at his wife and wrapped an arm round her shoulders, nudging her playfully.

Helena took a deep breath and he felt the straightening of her shoulders beneath his hand. 'It's no laughing matter, George. It something I feel very, *very* strongly that we should be doing. I.....I really do believe that.....', she faltered, staring hard at William Mitchell, '.... that we should do our bit for King and Country by....,' she hesitated again, anticipating an explosion from her husband at what she was about to suggest. 'By turning Henham into a hospital. A hospital for wounded soldiers and sailors.'

George was momentarily at a loss for words. He saw, out of the corner of his eye, Wlliam Mitchell raise a quizzical eyebrow as if to say 'I hinted that this might come as a shock to you.'

'That's an absurd idea, Nellie. Totally absurd,' George said shaking his head emphatically. 'How on earth are you going to run a hospital here? In this house? It's not fit to be a hospital. It's.....well,' he grappled for words, 'it's.... too ..... too... *grand*.' As soon as he'd uttered it he realised the word *grand* was totally inadequate for how he truly viewed Henham Hall.

But Helena would brook no opposition. Head down, not daring to look at her husband, she rustled through the copy of the Daily Times she'd been carrying, until she found Ernest Hart's description of the casualties rescued from the *Amphion*.

'Have you seen this?' She demanded, thrusting it under his nose. 'George, the war is *here*. Now. Here in Suffolk. Right on our doorstep. There are already wounded men in our hospitals. Men are dying for the want of medical help.

And the war is only days old. We *have* to do something to help. Don't you see?' Her jade eyes sparkled with tears as they met his.

'But my dear, what do you think you could possibly do here? How could you even *begin* to turn this place into a hospital?'

'I've already discussed it with Mr Mitchell,' she nodded towards Mitchell, confidently expecting his complicity in the scheme. 'The furniture will be moved from all the state apartments and stored in the first floor rooms. This,' she waved her hand around the ballroom, 'would make an excellent ward for a large number of patients. We could also use the drawing room and I think the large hall would make an ideal place for receiving cases as they arrive. And, of course, we'd have to have an operating theatre......' Her voice tailed off. She hadn't quite decided which room should be allocated for the purpose, but George's snuggery was a definite possibility.

George wasn't about to cave in. 'And what about staff? Where on earth will you find doctors and nurses to run such a hospital? It'll take months to find people who're qualified for such a task. And by then the war'll be over!' he said, trying to insert a grain of reason into the argument.

'I very much doubt it. It's my belief that here on the East Coast we'll be inundated with casualties. There'll be more naval engagements in the North Sea such as we've witnessed this week and hospitals in towns like Ipswich won't be able to cope. And what of the men who'll be injured in the land battles that Kitchener is assembling his army to fight? Where on earth will they be treated, if not in specially organised hospitals such as Henham Hall?'

'That could well be the case, but as Mr Mitchell very sensibly pointed out, the practical implementation may not be so easy.'

'Darling, there's really no need to worry about any of that. I've already made arrangements. We start tomorrow,' Helena announced with an air of finality.

'What? Start *what* tomorrow?' The Earl could hardly believe his ears. What on earth was his wife doing to his ancestral home? The beautiful country house that had been built in the 1790s for John Rous, the first Earl of Stradbroke, to the designs of James Wyatt? Stripping it of its beautiful furniture, its works of art, to turn it into something as utilitarian as a hospital?

'Tomorrow the men and women of the local Red Cross Society are coming to remove all the carpets and furniture upstairs. Then they'll set up the beds that have been generously lent by some of our local boarding schools for the purpose. We could have a hospital for nigh on a hundred patients up and running very shortly,' she said, an air of quiet triumph in her voice.

George could hardly believe that Helena had organised such a major upheaval to his home in such a short space of time. Had she achieve all this during his absence in Ipswich that very morning? The euphoria with which he'd returned

86

to Henham had completely dissipated. He knew things had gone too far for him to argue. Almost apologetically he threw out a final, hasty objection. 'And who's to run this hospital? You know I won't be able to. I shall be with my regiment. I could be anywhere. Who knows? We could be sent to France at any time.'

Helena bit her lip pensively. 'I know, George. Don't you think I worry about that every single moment of every day? I'm just praying the war will be over quickly so you're not taken away from us. But I've engaged a Dr Mullock to take charge of the hospital. He has promised me a team of six doctors and five trained nurses. And that's not counting more than thirty certificated Red Cross nurses who could be called on, if needed.'

There was no more to be said. Henham Hall would be a hospital within the week.

George took Helena's hands in his. He smiled wanly at her. He felt drained. The past two weeks of manoeuvres with the men of the Howitzer Brigade in the harsh mountainous environment of North Wales had exhausted him. The tension he'd felt as rumours of war escalated day by day had stretched his nerves. On top of all his other civic responsibilities he'd taken it upon himself to organise the county's war effort, raising money for the poor and dispossessed.

None of this would have been insurmountable if he'd been able to come home. But this would no longer be his home. No longer his refuge. This ballroom, where he'd danced with Helena on their wedding day, would be stripped of its beautiful furniture.

He tried to imagine the walls lined not with silk-covered chairs and the portraits of his ancestors but with beds. Utilitarian metal-framed beds at that, covered in cheap white cotton sheets. Instead of floating ball gowns and the sparkle of tiaras there would be the rustle of starched uniforms as nurses in stiff caps moved purposefully from patient to patient.

And what of those patients? Wounded men? Arriving at Henham not in cars or carriages drawn by four fine horses like his own, but ambulances? George bowed his head and his eyes rested on the rich earthen threads of the soft carpet beneath his feet.

Dark red threads, like drops of blood spilled on the floor. Men's blood.

At that moment he realised Helena was right. The Stradbroke's owed it to the country that had given them so much.

He sighed deeply and linked his fingers gently through hers. 'You're absolutely right, Nellie. As always. It's the right thing to do. We're at war now and we must do whatever's in our power to help. We'll do it together.'

Her green eyes shone back at him. This was all he'd ever wanted. This was his refuge. Not a fine ancestral building, but this fiery-spirited woman, this green-eyed Celtic warrior with the determination of King Robert the Bruce. His Countess.

'Come with me, my lady.' George's eyes twinkled mischievously as he whipped round in a sudden burst of energy, still clutching her hands. 'You too, Mr Mitchell,' he called over his shoulder as he disappeared down the corridor.

When he reached the closed door of his snuggery he stopped. With a deliberately dramatic flourish he flung the heavy door wide open. They stood gazing into the room, Helena and Mitchell mystified, not knowing what to expect. This was the Earl's room, his private sanctuary, his retreat from domestic chaos.

The afternoon sun greeted them, slanting through the tall, dust-covered bay windows and blushing the faded, red velvet drapes. There was his desk and chair in front of the window and his battered leather armchair beside the bookcase. There was the worn Persian rug where the dogs would lie contentedly while he smoked and read or worked at his correspondence. Occasionally a child would be allowed to lie there too, having promised to remain very still and quiet. There were the walls lined with books on his passions; the breeding of Suffolk Punches, sheep and Red Poll cattle and on land management. There, too, were his father and grandfather's collections of military books.

George took a deep breath and wheeled round, a look of triumph in his blue eyes. 'I think *this* would make an excellent operating theatre, don't you agree?'

Ernest Hart checked his watch as he shuffled slowly with the crowd out of County Hall and into the street. Eleven o'clock. Still time to get out of Ipswich and down the Shotley peninsula before lunch. He felt an irresistible compulsion to return to the barracks. The horrific images of the two seamen, burnt and shrouded in bandages, urged him onwards. All night their pained eyes had drilled into him yet he'd been unable to meet their gaze. They had haunted him throughout the long hours of darkness.

Lizzie knew there was something wrong. She'd told him over breakfast that he'd done nothing but toss and turn all night. At one point he'd launched himself bolt upright, yelling and waving his arms about. Then he'd flung the counterpane from the bed, leaving her shivering in her nightgown.

She'd been quite indignant. He'd apologised. Tried to explain that yesterday had been quite an extraordinary day. But then so, too, had the day before. And the day before that.

Now, as he watched the crowds from the meeting disperse excitedly he knew he had to see the men once more. Today, in the cold light of a new day, he needed to be convinced that what he'd seen and heard was real. That the gouged, bloodied bodies lying in neat rows of beds hadn't simply been a figment of his nightmares.

Perhaps, he reasoned, viewing them anew wouldn't be so bad. He'd chat to them. Have a laugh and a joke. Share a cigarette. Try to elicit more information from them on the disaster that had befallen their ship.

Sir Frederick had given him the use one of the newspaper's motorcars. It was a privilege not bestowed lightly. Ernest had been behind the wheel a couple of times before, yet still he moved the gears gingerly and steered cautiously until he was well clear of the busy town centre streets.

There was a more orderly atmosphere in the naval hospital than on the day previously. The floor was no longer splattered with blood, nor were there open, blood-soaked wounds on display. The rows of ashen faces lying back on crisp white pillows, many shrouded in clean white bandages, were laid out as though for critical inspection as he made his way tentatively down the ward. A young medical orderly had grudgingly granted permission for him to visit after updating him on the casualties.

'Overnight there've been eight deaths,' the orderly told him, flicking through lists of names which covered several pages of foolscap. 'Four of our own countrymen and four Germans.' Ernest peered across and noted the letter D pencilled into the margins beside some of the names.

'And how have the prisoners who were wounded been treated?' enquired Ernest, quietly fingering the notebook and pencil in his pocket.

The orderly frowned as though this was an impudent question to ask. He paused. 'With the consideration Britishers usually display towards those whom they've defeated in a fair fight,' he said stiffly. It sounded like the official line. 'What I mean is, the German officers have been admitted to the Ward Room and have been allowed all the liberties compatible with discipline. Nor have they been debarred from any of the little pleasures usually given to privileged prisoners, such as smoking, reading and freedom of intercourse.'

'That sounds very fair,' Ernest commented, scribbling briefly in his notebook.

'Mmm,' the orderly sniffed non-committally. 'Except that such humanity and courtesy isn't appreciated, I'm afraid. The officers have refused to give us their word of honour that they won't try to escape. And their men are just as contumacious. Well, they're the losers for that. As a precaution they're all being dispatched to a prison in Sussex without delay.'

The orderly stuffed the list back in his pocket. 'You can talk to the chaps in the next ward. They're making good progress.' He pointed at the adjoining doors. 'But some of them are very shocked and confused about what actually happened. Hard to get any sense out of some of 'em.'

Ernest thanked him and made his way between the long rows of iron beds, each covered with a white counterpane. Nurses and medical orderlies were moving among the beds, administering drugs to deaden the excruciating pain. The pain of limbs torn away, of faces left ragged by fire and of torsos stripped bare and pitted when metal was scattered like so much confetti. The only sounds were the occasion sharp cry or low moan, the crackle of starched linen aprons and the murmuring of concerned voices conferring at the foot of a bed.

He pushed through the double doors connecting the wards. Sunlight was flooding through the long south-facing windows at the farthest end, casting a soft glow across the white nightshirts worn by four men sitting huddled together. They were drawing relief from cigarettes and mutual pain. Ernest recognised two of them as the seamen he'd spoken to the previous day. They looked up as he approached and one waved him to a vacant chair.

'Morning,' Ernest smiled his welcome around the group and sat down. 'How are you feeling?'

'Better, better,' the fair-haired young officer who'd regaled him with the account of how he'd met his injuries the day before tried to sound chipper. His bloodied bandages had been changed and his head was now bound in a neatly woven white turban. The purple swelling of his lips had subsided, but the dark pools of his eyes still betrayed the pain he was suffering.

'They say we'll soon be out of here,' said a tall, gangling young man with dark hair and an arm in a sling. He blew a ring of smoke so that it drifted through the slanting rays. 'Soon as they find other hospitals to take us. God knows where,' he tailed off, a bitter note to his voice.

'Is that the newspaper reporter we spoke to yesterday?' Harry, the petty officer he'd seen the day before raised his head. Both his eyes were still covered. His arms pinioned now by plaster.

'Yes, it's Ernest Hart.' Ernest rose from his chair and leaning over took one of the blinded man's hands gently in his own.

'Well, we've got some more information you might want to print in your newspaper. We've been debating which ship administered the coup de grace to the German minelayer what did for us. We reckon it was us chaps on the *Amphion* what fired the first shot, the one which blew away the *Koenigen Luise's* bridge and killed her captain. But more than four shots were fired altogether.'

'Yes, at least four shots,' agreed another, a stout young officer with the well-fed, ruddy complexion of a Suffolk countryman. '*Linnet, Lark and Lance* also did some fine shooting. We all think, though, it was *Lance* which delivered the Parthian shot.'

'The bombardment was fast and furious. I'll never forget the noise of it as long as I live,' wheezed the rangy young man. 'We all cheered when we saw the white flag hoisted on the *Koenigen Luise* and immediately lowered our boats to pick up survivors.'

'Bastards! Fucking bastards! You won't believe what those German bastards did next.' Harry spat violently on the polished wood floor. 'They started firing on our ship's boats! The boats we'd lowered to pick *them* up. Bastards! Fuck'n bastards! Fuck them! Fuck them! Fuck them.....' His voice wailed upwards into a painful, falsetto crescendo, the vehicle of his seething hatred careering out of control and off the scale. The ward fell into awed silence.

'Steady on, old chap, steady on.' The red-faced young officer sitting next to him clutched the petty officer's arm in both hands to calm him. A dull murmur passed around the group. Harry's unrestrained outpouring of invective embarrassed them.

'The rest of the flotilla gave them what for, though and eventually they capitulated. But they don't play the game. They don't play fair.' The young officer who'd been raised in the shires pursed his lips. War, he'd quickly discovered, wasn't like a game of cricket on the village green.

Ernest scratched a quick note in his dog-eared notebook and looked around the group. He was about to put it back in his pocket when the turbaned officer piped up. 'And that's not all. As our officers and men boarded the minelayer the rank and file of the crew were bellicose and offensive. That's no way to behave in defeat! Why, one German officer even refused to yield his sword when it was demanded by one of our officers!' He lunged his foot hard against the leg of the chair opposite. His indignation was palpable.

'So....?' Ernest had no idea what the penalty for such an unsporting act might be.

'Our officer, the one who made the order, drew his revolver and shot him through the shoulder. Serves him bloody well right,' came the gruff reply.

Between them the men described how they'd played their part in shepherding all the survivors down the gangway and onto the *Amphion* and the rest of the ships of the flotilla. The wounded were taken aboard and had their injuries attended to by fleet surgeons as promptly as possible. Shortly afterwards the *Koenigen Luise* sank.

But then the story took on a new twist, one which puzzled Ernest deeply. He made a careful note of what his informants told him, yet aspects of it didn't ring quite straight or true. Left him with more questions than it answered.

They told him that the flotilla, headed by *Amphion,* then made for Harwich and entered the harbour that evening. There they landed the wounded and some of the prisoners and took on fuel oil. On Thursday morning they once again headed for the open sea. They were only a short distance out when the *Amphion*, which was in the vanguard of the procession, struck one of the mines the German ship had been caught laying.

Among those blown to eternity were 20 of the German prisoners confined in the forepart of the cruiser. Hoist by their own petard.

But why, Ernest wondered, if some of the prisoners had been landed on Wednesday night, were there still German prisoners confined in the fo'c'sle? Why weren't they *all* taken ashore that night? Had the flotilla been in such a rush to return to sea? Were the German seamen being kept on board as hostages? Had they been the least compliant of the men the British officers encountered when they boarded the *Koenigen Luise*? Or perhaps these young officers were in such a confused state they'd lost track of times and events? That in fact their ship had struck the mine on its return from sinking the minelayer? He remained silent, unable to voice his confusion for fear of causing offence. He made a mental note, however, to check the reports of what Mr Churchill had told Parliament about the affair.

The seamen went on to describe how the oil tanks, now full, exploded with deadly effect. How they, and dozens of their shipmates, had rushed about the deck, their clothes a mass of flames ignited by the burning oil which sprayed over them. The unbearable screams of pain still rang in their ears as they spoke, the acrid smell of burning flesh forever in their nostrils.

Once more the *Amphion's* boats were lowered. This time to save the lives of her own crew.

'Perfect discipline prevailed,' was how the ruddy-faced officer described it. Factual. Unemotional. 'Our chaps displayed remarkable heroism. Other vessels in the flotilla also lowered their boats and every survivor was got off safely before the *Amphion* gently sank by the head, twenty minutes later,' he added.

The lanky young man dragged violently on his cigarette and drew his thin shoulders into his chest as he recalled his ship's final moments. 'She went down in what must have been shallow waters. I was one of the last to get off and I swear I felt her touch the bottom,' he said.

'What makes my gorge rise is how unsporting the Germans are when it comes to fighting a war.' Harry leant into the centre of the circle. 'We've been discussing it between ourselves and we reckon the Germans'd been laying their mines for a considerably longer period than the time which has elapsed since England declared war against Germany last Tuesday. The plans our officers captured show about a hundred had already been laid. We don't think she could possibly have accomplished this between Tuesday night and Wednesday morning. And we found another two thousand of these floating mines on board, waiting to be put down. God help our navy if she'd given us the slip.'

There were more mutterings of 'bastards', 'atrocious', 'barbaric', 'not playing the game'.

Ernest was struck by the deep resentment these young sailors harboured towards their foe, not so much for the appalling injuries they'd suffered at his hands but for the unsportsmanlike way he was waging this war. It had induced in them all an eagerness to get back to sea again and have another turn at the enemy.

Ernest had left the car in a shaded corner of the parade ground and after leaving the wards he walked slowly downhill to the quayside. He squatted down on a large iron bollard and lit a cigarette. He felt uneasy, confused by what he'd heard. It all sounded so unbelievable. So unbelievably dreadful. Could this really be happening to Englishmen? He gazed across the wide mouth of the River Stour to Harwich on the opposite bank. The turning tide was idling slowly with hardly a ripple. A line of destroyers lay grey and silent at anchor along the deep central channel.

He watched with some curiosity as a tender wove in and out amongst them. When it pulled up alongside the jetty the oarsman threw a line with expert deftness over a bollard and despite his considerable bulk leapt agilely up the stone steps. It was the ferryman who normally operated the motor ferry service between Shotley and Harwich.

'Waiting to go 'cross?' he called to Ernest.

Ernest considered for a moment. 'Yes, why not. I don't see no ferry, though.'

The leathery-faced ferryman looked thunderous. He slouched his body closer and loomed over the figure straddling the bollard. 'Ain't no ferry, bor. Service suspended. Orders of the military. Daft buggers are a-feared I'll be taking spies out to look at their blessed warships. Bloody stupid, I calls it.'

'So.......'

'I'll row yer across. Same price.'

'Fine'. Ernest pushed himself painfully from his temporary seat and limped down the steps behind the ferryman's rolling buttocks. He gingerly lowered himself into the wooden dinghy and consigned his fate to the strong hands of the rower. Once more the ferryman steered a course beneath the looming grey flanks of the destroyers, adroitly weaving in and out between them. It was the first time Ernest had been so close to such large ships. *It would be so easy to be crushed beneath these bows,* he thought. *Sitting here in the stern of this decrepit rowing boat. We wouldn't stand a chance if it suddenly upped anchor and started its engines.*

'What on earth are *those* doing here?' he shouted at the ferryman who was groaning loudly with each heave of the oars. Ernest pointed to a long line of barges, with all their tan sails hoisted to catch what little breeze there was, crossing their path from the Felixstowe side of the harbour.

They looked like floating pantechnicons. He could see wardrobes and chests of drawers, rolls of carpets and beds, pianos and sofas and jumbles of miscellaneous kitchen utensils, cramming the barges from bow to stern in precarious piles. A small dog keeping watch on the bow of the *Beatrice Maud* yapped angrily at them as they passed close to its starboard side.

'Thems taking the furniture and goods of people living in Felixstowe up river to Manningtree,' he puffed between strokes.

'What on earth for?' Ernest frowned at the absurdity of the sight of these floating households stretching several hundred yards as they made their way serenely upriver.

'Didn't you hear 'bout that? Felixstowe folk bin turned out'a house an' home 'cos of the war. Them's sending their things by river 'cos of the difficulty and cost of taking the stuff by rail or road,' he roared back.

'Who's turfing them out?'

'Why, the military a'course!' The ferryman answered huffily. It was a sore point. The all-powerful military, as far as he was concerned, had taken his livelihood away without a word of explanation. Now they were grabbing people's homes.

'D'yer know why?' Ernest asked.

'Who knows? Maybe they wants the houses for billets. Maybe they're a-feared there's spies living along the coast what'll signal to the enemy whenever the fleet leaves harbour. Who knows.'

Another mystery, Ernest decided, that demanded definite answers.

The ferryman had promised to be at the bottom of the quayside steps in an hour's time to take him back to Shotley. An hour to find out what was going on in Harwich.

Ernest headed for the Great Eastern Hotel. Its ornate, pale brick and stone facade gleamed like a welcoming beacon in the sunlight, a solid four-storey boast to Victorian railway prosperity. Today he felt too subdued to indulge his normal custom of raising his cap with a respectful, 'Good morning' to the idiosyncratic busts of past kings and queens ranged along its walls. Since 1864 they'd stared out across the river, impervious to the weather or the ravages of history; Henry VIII, Queen Elizabeth, James I and II, George II and Queen Anne.

The Great Eastern was a pleasant watering hole, a favourite haunt where he often stopped for a glass of ale and lunch on days he was sent to cover events in Harwich. He glanced up. The large clock at the building's apex - appropriated, he imagined, from one of the London termini - told him it was one o'clock.

Pushing open the double glazed doors he came to an abrupt halt. This wasn't what he'd been expecting. The familiar faces and smells were gone. He shook his tousled head in disbelief as he peered wide-eyed over the top of his spectacles.

Instead of being met by the heady whiff of roast beef and the familiar beaming face of the landlord and his lady, he was faced instead with a bustling army of Red Cross nurses. The smell of strong disinfectant tickled his nose.

The hotel had overnight been transformed into a make-shift military hospital.

The place was humming with frenetic activity. The hallways were so crammed with beds and mattresses he had difficulty squeezing through. When he reached the spacious dining room, with its ornately plastered high ceilings, he found it had been converted into a hospital ward. Eighty of the wounded German prisoners from the *Koenigen Luise* were already lying there. Beds were also being hastily erected in the smoking lounge while the Yacht Club rooms were being equipped as an operating theatre and nurses quarters.

So much is changing, yet it's only three days since war began, he marvelled, dumbstruck at the sight.

Ernest was silent on the return trip across the river. His favourite hostelry had been turned into a hospital. He could hardly believe the transformation. It depressed him and he tried to erase from his memory the image of wounded men lying in rows of iron beds along the walls of the dining room where he'd so often eaten.

As he motored past the outskirts of Shotley he caught sight of a coffin standing on its end outside the wheelwright and undertaker's shop. It hadn't been there when he'd driven through that morning. It intrigued him so he drew up outside.

He found the undertaker and his assistant inside the dilapidated barn that served as a workshop, surrounded by lengths of pale wood. They were engrossed in making coffins. *Plain, unadorned coffins. A rush job by the look of things,* he thought.

'I assume they're for the casualties up there?' Ernest ventured, nodding in the direction of the barracks high on the hill.

The undertaker viewed him suspiciously. 'Who wants to know?' He stood with arms folded defensively across the chest of his long leather apron.

'Sorry. Should have introduced myself. Ernest Hart, special war correspondent for the Daily Times. I've been told eight of the men brought in yesterday died overnight.'

The undertaker relaxed. 'Tha's right, bor. Four of these 'ere elm coffins'll be finished for the morrow. Four for the day after. The funeral of the four German sailors'll be held in the graveyard of Shotley parish church tomorrow. The four English seamen will be interred in the same place Sunday morning.' He delivered the precise details as methodically as he hammered the joints.

'Thanks. Sorry to interrupt you,' Ernest said, touching his forehead politely before heading back out into the sunshine. Sitting in the car he pulled the notebook from his pocket and wrote briefly 'eight plain elm coffins'. He needed no more descriptive reminder.

Speeding back to Ipswich as quickly as he dared along narrow, twisting lanes, he was surprised to find tears trickling down his cheeks. *The horror of war,* he thought. *The horrible suffering.* He was overcome by the unfairness of it all. The randomness of the way fate picked its victims. The seamen blasted from the decks of their own ship. Suddenly and inexplicably. They had done no wrong. They had performed no evil. Still, God had plucked them from the living world. Or worse, maybe, left them incapacitated and in pain for the rest of their mortal days.

Yet what choice was there? He decided he'd have to temper his report of death and loss with an encouraging, patriotic message. The nation, the British people, had got to see this thing through. See it through with all the determination and courage which had made her respected on sea and land.

Beneath the headlines 'How the *Amphion* Sank' and 'Heroism of British seamen' he also wrote 'German abuse of the White Flag'. Boldly he added the words 'By our Special Correspondent' and at the end typed his name. He felt sure Sir Frederick would approve.

East Anglian Daily Times
Saturday August 8 1914

Heavy German Defeat. Armistice asked for at Liege. 25,000 casualties.

A message was received from Brussels last evening stating officially that the Commander of the German force attacking Liege has asked for a 24-hour armistice. The town of Liege, it is added, has not been occupied by the Germans who acknowledge casualties to the number of 25,000. This message shows how serious is the check administered to the invaders at Liege by the gallant defence of Belgian troops.

Chapter Nine

Wednesday August 12 1914

'Where the blazes are they?' Sir Frederick Wilson's corpulence filled the open doorway to the reporters' room. It was eight o'clock in the morning, half an hour after the working day had begun, and the Chief was in a foul mood. His dark presence swirled unpredictably about the occupants like a circling flock of crows.

Three reporters were absent without his permission. Three typewriters silent. Three desks unoccupied. 'What's the meaning of this?' He waved his stick belligerently at the empty chairs as though demanding answers from inanimate objects.

Ernest flashed an uneasy glance at Alf Gilbert sitting at the next desk. Around them, bent over their work and hoping for invisibility from the Chief's piercing gaze were the remaining four reporters. Who would tell him? Who would dare?

'Er....hmm....Chief......' Ernest cleared his throat. He knew it had to be him. Reluctantly he rose to his feet and adopting as dignified an air as he knew how, slowly pulled his spectacles from his nose and placed them neatly on top of his typewriter. His colleagues viewed the gesture with some awe. It meant serious business.

Ernest looked his editor full in the face, unflinching. 'Chief, I think I can explain. It's my belief that Mr Martin, Mr Allan and Mr Hobbs have gone to...to....'

'Gone? Gone?' the editor roared. 'Gone where? where? Go on, tell me! Or am I to be the last person in the building to know what the young scoundrels are up to?'

'They've gone....erm... down to the recruiting office. To enlist, Chief. To join up. In Lord Kitchener's New Army.'

'What?' To enlist?' Without my permission?' It was like three blasts of cannon fire, shot from deep within him.

The young men at their desks instinctively ducked their heads lower into their shoulder blades. Some began typing furiously. Others made great play of winding folios of copy paper into their machines or flicking through the pages of their notebooks to pour intently over scribbled notes.

Sir Frederick spluttered again in disbelief. 'Without my say so? How dare they? Never heard anything like it. Impudent young buggers.'

'I think, Chief, they felt they should offer their services. King and country and all that, yer know.' Ernest shrugged with well-practiced casualness.

'Hmm,' the old man snorted. His thunderous eyebrows twitched round the cramped reporters' room. No-one moved a muscle. They all held their breath.

'Yes, Chief. And they're not alone, either,' Ernest added cheerfully. 'Thousands of Suffolk's young men are joining up. The call to arms is being met with tremendous enthusiasm here.' Ernest wanted to reassure the editor that his newspaper wasn't alone in being deprived of its manpower. 'I toured the recruiting offices on Monday and they're all absolutely besieged by men eager to join the services. There are long queues of young men, all waiting their turn. You would hardly believe it possible.'

'And it could be that Joe, Ed or Clem could be turned down,' Alf chipped in helpfully. 'Any one of them could fail the physical tests or might prove not to be tall enough.'

'So, answer me this,' Sir Frederick bellowed, waving his black cane at all and sundry. 'What on earth possessed these fine young fellows to think Lord Kitchener would want the likes of them? That they'd make good soldiers? Have any of them ever handled a rifle or loaded an artillery piece? Or driven a team of horses? Eh? Eh? They're soft buggers, the lot of 'em! The biggest thing they've ever worked on in their entire lives is one of those damned old typewriters!'

A raucous, choking roar emerged from the Chief's throat and reverberated along the narrow, high-ceilinged corridor, down to the compositing floor below. It was laughter. Laughter at his own joke. At the incongruity of the image he'd conjured up. The editor's mirth was a rare sound indeed.

The reporters sniggered quietly to themselves. Secretly they, too, had wondered whether their colleagues had taken leave of their senses. The occupants of the empty desks had been swept along on the wave of indignation following the agonising fate that had befallen British sailors the previous week. They'd been infected by the excitement that was creeping like a fog into every nook and crevice, every street corner and every ale house. They'd succumbed to the belief that the Hun were, without exception, evil bastards and had to be overpowered – at any cost.

Even with their own, inexpert, soft-handed lives.

Three young men out of nine. 'Well, well,' Wilson sighed at last, his bulk visibly deflating. 'I suppose it was inevitable. But I don't know how we'll manage without them.'

'Shall I tell them to come and see you when they get in?' Alf, emboldened by the responsibility of his new role as chief reporter, enquired.

'Yer damn right yer will. And I'll be docking a day's pay for their absence. You tell 'em *that* when they deign to arrive for work.' With that he stomped down the corridor to his office, rattling his stick impatiently along the metal railings around the balcony. The compositors glanced up as the clanging juddered around their heads like an out-of-tune peal of bells. The boss was not in the best of tempers. Their ears were ringing with the warning notes.

The ringing of the phone broke the tension in the newsroom. Alf answered it.

'Fine. Yes, yes. I'll tell him. Yes, right away. Yes, yes, I won't forget. Good morning doctor.' His answers were brief, he'd taken a note. He put the receiver back on its hook.

'Ernie, it was for you. Scottish chap, Doctor Ward. Says you're to go up to his house right away. The address is... er.... um....' he glanced at his notebook, 'Gatewick, number 20 Park Road. Says it's urgent. He's got something of interest for you.'

'Thanks.'

'Any idea what that could be?' asked John from the farthest corner. 'Yer see, he's my doctor. Decent old boy. Treats yer right and doesn't charge too much. Me ma says he brought all of us Middleditchs into the world.'

'More fool him, then!' quipped Tom, always the joker of the pack.

'No idea at all,' Ernest smiled at John and shrugged his shoulders. He grabbed his glasses from the top of the typewriter, his jacket from the coat stand, checked his notebook and pencil were in the pocket and headed out of the building. He was glad of the excuse not to be around when Joe, Ed and Clement returned to bear the brunt of the Chief's wrath.

Perhaps, though they won't come back. Perhaps they'll be tricked out in smart khaki uniforms or more likely temporary Kitchener's Blues and shipped straight out of town to a military training camp. And what if....? What if? No, no. He shook his head vigorously. He didn't even want to allow himself the luxury of macabre thoughts of 'what if we never see them again?'

The walk from the newspaper's building in Carr Street up to Park Road provided a welcome reprieve from the dusty streets. It took him through Christchurch Park and although the usually well-tended green lawns had been reduced to dust and clay, he felt calmed by this natural oasis in the centre of town. He headed past the ancient Christchurch Mansion, skirting the ornamental pond where nurse-maids and young mothers took their young charges to feed the ducks with stale bread, then dawdled through a long avenue of mature chestnut trees until he reached the gateway at the top of the park leading into Park Road.

Doctor Ward's house was an imposing Victorian red brick mansion which doubled as a consulting room. The brass plate beside the door informed callers that Dr Francis Ward, M.D. C.M. Edin, was a physician and surgeon and honorary medical officer for East Suffolk and Ipswich Hospital. Ernest rang the bell and waited. A maid answered and when he gave his name said 'Ah yes, he's expecting you. I'll show you straight in.'

Dr Ward was standing behind a large leather-topped desk, hands plunged into his trouser pockets, staring out at his garden from the open French windows. He turned and smiled as Ernest closed the door behind him, welcoming him with a 'hello young man. Glad you could get here to see me,' but Ernest thought he looked distracted and anxious.

'Do sit down,' he waved Ernest to the chair beside the desk. 'Now. First things first. Let's take a look at that leg.'

This hadn't been quite what Ernest was expecting, but he acquiesced and dropped his trousers. The doctor examined his right femur and hip closely, manipulating the joint back and forth, feeling its action. It still bore the vicious scars of the hooves. Unsightly purple lances criss-crossing his flesh. The damage had not repaired as well as he'd hoped.

'It's showing signs of arthritis, I'm afraid,' Dr Ward said, straightening up. 'I imagine that's what's causing you some distress. I'll give you something you can take to relieve the pain.' He moved to a glass-fronted cupboard beside the door and began rummaging along the shelves. Ernest watched him, at the same time pulling up his trousers and re-attaching the braces.

The doctor returned to the high-backed chair and leaned across to hand him a small bottle. 'Take this when the pain gets bad. And come back and see me again when you need more.'

'Thank you, Doctor. You're most kind.' Ernest tucked the small bottle into his jacket pocket. 'But Alf said you had something for me. A piece of news, maybe?' he hinted diffidently.

'Yes, of course, of course,' Francis Ward said irritably. ' Even now I find it incredible. Unbelievable. The most ludicrous rumour. All lies, of course. You must have heard it yourself. Everyone's talking about it, apparently.'

'What rumour? What are you referring to?'

'Why, the rumour about my chauffeur, George, of course. The ridiculous assertion that he's been discovered to be a German spy. That he's been in disguise these past few years, living under the cloak of my employment and all the while collecting information of use to the enemy. It's apparently flying around the town like a swarm of bees.'

'Well, yes, I did hear something. A chap in the White Horse told me a couple of days ago there was a spy living in Ipswich. He didn't mention any names, but I suspected it was all nonsense.'

'Of course it's all nonsense!' The doctor's voice rose in frustration. 'But how do you stop these silly rumours? How do you answer such ridiculous lies? Why, it's even come to my notice that people are saying he's accumulated a small fortune by means of his espionage and established a banking account. And as a consequence he's not only been arrested, but found guilty and summarily shot. Shot! I ask you! Have you ever heard anything more ridiculous?' The doctor slumped back in his chair. 'Ernest, you're a newspaperman. What can I do to impress upon people that this scurrilous yarn is totally untrue?'

Ernest tapped his pencil against his teeth. 'I suppose', he began thoughtfully, doodling in his notebook, 'I could write something. How about something along the lines of "Dame Rumour is a lying Jade and she's been busy in Ipswich as elsewhere" because I've certainly read of other such cases in the papers over the last few days?'

'Yes, yes. And you must print the truth. You must state quite clearly that George has been in my service for three-and-a-half years, is still with me and is likely to remain so. And that instead of being a German or in the secret service of Germany he is, in fact, an ex-Artillery man having served this country for 21 years and who fought all through the Boer War.' Dr Ward's hands fluttered in agitation as he strove to control his emotions.

'Then how on earth did the rumour start that he was a German or a German spy , if he was nothing of the sort? It makes no sense.'

Dr Ward leaned forward. 'Exactly! Exactly my point. It's a total nonsense. So perhaps your article will give the *coup de grace* to this ridiculous rumour.' He rubbed at his neatly-trimmed beard nervously, elbows jabbing the leather desktop. 'As ye can imagine, it's not only caused *me* a great deal of annoyance but my chauffeur too.' His lilting Scots vowels were tinted with anguish.

Ernest watched the familiar face crumple and his heart went out to him. 'I'll do what I can,' he promised and rose to leave.

'You're a grand laddie. Thank you.'

Germans. German spies. Alien enemies. Dame Rumour. A thousand tongues. Ernest tossed the words around in his mind as he walked back through the park. *What on earth is going on? Where are these pernicious rumours coming from? Is the Chief Constable right to be so fixated on spies and aliens or is he fuelling paranoia so that innocent men like Dr Ward's chauffeur suddenly find themselves suspect?*

There was another message waiting for him when he returned to the office.

'Lady Stradbroke rang. She asked for *you*. Personally.' Alf sounded deeply impressed.

'Oh yes? What did her Ladyship want?' Ernest said with an air of deliberate insoucience.

'She wants you to visit her hospital. She said she'd seen in the paper that you'd already been to the new hospital at the Great Eastern Hotel in Harwich, but that the military hospital she's set up at Henham Hall is on a *far* greater scale. She said to tell you,' here Alf consulted his notebook, 'that the hospital was ready last Friday and is already receiving cases sent there from the VAD hospital in Saxmundham. And that 100 of the 150 beds have been ready for over a week.'

'Mmm. When does she want me to call?'

'This afternoon, she says.'

'Fine.' Ernest hung his jacket on the coat stand and glanced around the reporters' room. The three empty desks glared at him. 'So, is anyone going to tell me what happened?'

'They've not returned, Ernie,' John said dismally.

'Hart!' His name came rumbling down the corridor. The editor had heard him return.

Ernest sighed and at the door plucked the notebook and pencil from his coat pocket.

'Yes Chief.' He hovered in the doorway of the editor's office.

'Come in, come in. Got your notebook?' The Chief was now somewhat calmer than he had been earlier. More himself, Ernest thought. Perhaps he'd realised he was powerless against the blandishments of a recruiting officer who was offering young men the chance to escape the dull grind of farm, factory or shop work, the endless poverty and the narrow horizons of rural life. The chance to exchange all that for the glamour of a foreign adventure, a noble cause and the comradeship of men.

'Those foolish young fellows,' Sir Frederick waved his stick in the direction of the reporters' room. 'Joining up. Bloody stupid. Untrained chaps like that. All they're fit for is the bloody infantry. A pair of boots on their feet and a rifle in their hands. Canon fodder, that's what they'll be. No chance.....no chance.....'
He turned abruptly to the window. Hiding his face.

Ernest didn't ask what he thought there'd be no chance of. *Perhaps the old devil actually cares about these chaps,* he mused.

The Chief gazed unseeing at the traffic churning back and forth along the street below. Young men's bloodied bodies writhing on the cobbles. Crying out in pain. He'd seen it himself. How many years ago was it? How many years since he'd picked up a weapon and fired it in anger against an enemy? The memory was as clear as though the battle had occurred the day before.

It was in 1867. He was a young man then, just twenty-three. He'd just moved from the Liverpool Post to edit the Chester and Birkenhead Observer. As a crack shot in the sporting field he'd joined the town's Rifle Volunteer Force.

The Fenians were at the height of their activities, fighting for independence from British Rule in Ireland. So when their leader, Thomas Kelly, led a group of supporters to attack Chester Castle in an attempt to get their hands on weapons and ammunition, he'd been called in to help defend it.

He and the other Volunteers had held the Castle, beaten off the Irish Nationalists in a brief but glorious battle. Kelly had been arrested. It had been an historic day. Without doubt the most exciting in his entire seventy years.

How paradoxical then, that years later, after being elected Liberal MP for Mid-Norfolk in 1895, he was to rub shoulders with Michael Davitt, the leader of the Fenian Party and a fellow MP, in the House of Commons.

'Anyway,' he said, pulling himself back from his memories and turning to Ernest, 'it set me thinking. I want you to write something about this demand by Lord Kitchener for a hundred thousand more soldiers. Although it's an important step I believe it's being taken very late in the day. Perhaps *too* late in the day. Creating a new force after the war has actually commenced is a difficult task. Obviously there are plenty of chaps like ours able and willing to serve. But why can't this government see that what we *really* need is an army trained in peacetime in order to be ready for war? I think, as an independent newspaper, we should express such a criticism.'

The Chief was on one of his hobby horses and Ernest knew better than to interrupt him in mid-rant. He scribbled furious notes as the editor swung his rotund form into his desk chair while he thought aloud.

'Men being enlisted into the new force will be of no earthly use in the artillery or engineers unless they've had previous experience,' he declared emphatically. 'Yes, it'll be possible to lick the likes of our three chaps into shape as infantry soldiers in a comparatively short period, but it takes time to train artillery men.

'I've contended for many years that we can't have too many soldiers. Not necessarily regulars, but men like the Special Reserve and Territorials who learn their business in peacetime. But the great mass of the population of this country has never realised the situation. It's hopeless trying to rouse the nation during peacetime to a sense of its responsibilities. How much better it would have been had these fellows come forward in time of peace instead of coming forward now, as untrained men.'

'Mmm. So is this what you want me to write?' Ernest sounded unsure. 'Is this, er *wise*, Chief?' He was astounded at his own temerity. Reporters did not lightly question the Chief's judgement on news.

Sir Frederick paused only momentarily. 'Of course it's what I want you to write, yer nitwit. The truth, Hart, the truth. Unpalatable as it may be, we must point it out.' The editor spat the words out, his whiskers twitching irritably as he did so. 'Better get on with it. ' He turned to leaf through a pile of wires, then glanced up, remembering something. 'Oh and by the way. What was your visit to my old friend Francis Ward all about?'

Ernest was startled. He hadn't known of the editor's close connection with the doctor, but he should have guessed. Sir Frederick knew everyone of any note in town.

'Well, I find it hard to believe, but there's a rumour circulating that Dr Ward's chauffeur has been unmasked as a German spy.' Ernest couldn't keep a tone of amused scepticism from his voice. 'Not only that, it's being said he's been arrested and actually shot! Well, you can imagine how shocked Dr Ward was to hear of this. The whole thing's a total fabrication, of course. From beginning to end. In reality the man's a former soldier in the Artillery who fought in the Boer War. I was about to write something when you called me in. I feel it's our duty to expose such calumny for what it is.'

Sir Frederick leaned back so that his chair creaked ominously. He held Ernest's gaze steadily for a moment. 'And do you believe what the good doctor tells you? Or do you hold to the view that we're nurturing spies in our bosom? Spies who are lurking in the most unexpected places? Which, after my conversation with the Chief Constable the other day, is most definitely the view of the military in these parts.'

'I believe Dr Ward's chauffeur to be innocent of such accusations. I can't understand how they've taken root in the first place. And, I have to say, I think Captain Mayne is somewhat affected by paranoia where spies and aliens are concerned. But the war's only days old. It remains to be seen if such spies exist. I'm sure the Daily Times will be told of them if they do,' Ernest said, struggling to find a diplomatic path through the confused minefield of rumour and truth.

'Quite right, quite right. Good man.' Satisfied with the answer, the Chief waved Ernest away with a flapping gesture of his huge hand. 'Mustn't keep the Countess waiting. Better take the car. It's a fair old journey to Henham Hall.'

Afternoon tea in the low-beamed snug at The Angel in Wangford served to remind Ernest how very different was the pace of life in the remote villages along the East Coast. To the young journalist brought up amidst the noise and clamour and dirt of the narrow streets of Ipswich the hamlet exuded a peaceful, old-world charm. It was one of the few places he'd visited in the past week which showed no signs of any incipient warfare. There were no young men in khaki on the streets, no recruiting offices, no fluttering posters urging men to enlist.

As he turned the car up the long carriage drive to Henham Hall, game birds skied in all directions and pheasants rose on the wing, their raucous warning cries filling the air. Glimpsing for the first time the lofty Wyatt mansion set in rolling parkland, he began to appreciate the extent of the sacrifice its owners had made in transforming it into a hospital. *How could they bear to give up such a fine house?* he thought.

He felt it best to ring at the tradesmen's entrance. He pulled the bell several times before the door was at last opened and he was admitted.

'Her Ladyship isn't in,' explained the footman who greeted him, 'but she gave instructions that you were to be shown over the building by the Matron, Sister Methold.'

Sister Methold, he soon discovered, was a formidable woman. Tall and erect, her uniform immaculate, she quickly made it known she had impeccable references. She had been a nursing sister for many years, most recently at Guy's Hospital. She made it clear, too, that she had little time to waste showing reporters around. Ernest had difficulty keeping up with her as she darted from room to room.

'As you can see, the most important state apartments and living rooms have been converted to hospital wards,' she informed him brusquely.

Ernest's eyes were drawn upwards to the ornate ceilings and lofty windows. There was a lightness, a cheerfulness about the place which he found refreshing in a hospital. Yet the lines of beds, with their fresh white linen sheets, were empty.

'And this is the operating theatre which has been fully equipped from the Southwold Hospital,' she said, throwing open the door to one of the drawing rooms.

Marching onwards down the corridor she reached the door of the Earl's snuggery. 'While Lord Stradbroke is away with his regiment he's given up his own snuggery and it's been completely turned out to make space for a smaller ward for patients.' She allowed only seconds for Ernest to peep inside before pulling the door behind her. Time enough to see that some of the beds were occupied.

'And what's been done with the handsome furniture from all these apartments?' he asked with some timidity.

'Come, I'll show you.' Sister Methold made an abrupt turn and led him up several flights of sweeping staircase to the upper floor. There, in one long gallery, tightly packed like a furniture repository, were the entire contents of the state rooms. A miscellaneous store room of priceless antiques and paintings now hidden away behind closed shutters and drawn curtains.

'So where does Lady Stradbroke live, now that all her furniture is stored up here?' he asked.

'Her Ladyship, with great self-sacrifice, is contenting herself with very limited accommodation,' Sister Methold replied primly. 'You must understand that converting her home into a hospital has involved great personal inconvenience and not a little destruction and wear and tear of valuable furniture and household treasures.'

Their tour of the house over, Ernest enquired about the patients.

Sister Methold sniffed. 'We've received several cases sent by Major Gibb from the Saxmundham VAD hospital. Those were the most serious cases. We should have had many more here, but for a most unfortunate mishap. Most upsetting. About fifty beds, which had been lent by one of our local girls' schools, were taken back when the proprietor decided to re-open. As a consequence they all had to be dismantled and dispatched away and others with bedding sent to replace them. Subsequently we have only one new case today, a Territorial suffering from pneumonia.'

And what of the staff? Ernest wondered. Sister Methold rattled off the details; six doctors and five trained nurses and thirty-three certificated Red Cross Society nurses of whose competence she'd formed a high opinion. With that she curtly dismissed him with a 'Will that be all, Mr Hart?' and he was escorted by the same footman to the tradesmen's door. He wished he'd had the opportunity to speak to Lady Stradbroke herself. He had a feeling she might have been more forthcoming than the tight-lipped Matron.

As he drove from Henham Hall, through the landscaped park, he wondered if perhaps the sacrifice of the Earl and his lady didn't represent true patriotism. Here was a man who had given his house, his money and best of all himself in the service of his country. *Noblesse oblige* amply fulfilled, Ernest decided.

East Anglian Daily Times

Friday August 14 1914

Defence of the Realm Act. Wide Powers for Military. Spread of Alarming Reports Forbidden.

A second supplement to the London Gazette issued last night contained an order in council under the Defence of the Realm Act giving the naval and military authorities wide powers for securing the public safety.

The competent military or naval authorities are given full powers to take possession of any land, buildings, water supplies and private property and if necessary can require the inhabitants to leave any area specified by order in the neighbourhood of a defended harbour. No persons must trespass on any railway or loiter near any railway bridge or culvert and the authorities have the right of entry to any building or ships suspected of being used in any way prejudicial to the public safety. The photographing or sketching of any naval or military work, dock or harbour is prohibited and the spreading in the neighbourhood of a defended harbour of reports likely to create disaffection or alarm among his Majesty's forces or civilian population, is forbidden.

Spies and persons contravening the regulations are liable to trial by court martial.

Chapter Ten

Thursday August 20 1914

William awoke before daybreak. He slid silently from the bed, taking care not to wake Alma, then stooped to pick up the clothes he had left draped across her old nursing chair. Barefoot, he crept downstairs, the old oak boards creaking as they always did. He headed for the squat little scullery at the back of the kitchen. A full harvest moon was shining through the small window above the stone sink, giving him just enough light to dress by. Dick had been asleep in his basket in one corner, but on hearing his master's footfall on the stairs had staggered sleepily to his feet. Time for a walk, instinct told him.

'Come on, old chap,' William patted the Labrador's head, but his movements were distracted and mechanical. His mind at this hour was not inclined to the cheerful pursuit of dog walking, but to a more melancholy act. He lifted the storm lantern from its peg by the scullery door and stood it on the wooden draining board. He struck a match. Its sudden flare as he touched it onto the wick so startled him he almost cried out. The tension within him was unbearable. Carefully he wound the wick down until it provided just a glimmer of light.

Closing the door quietly behind him he made his way across the school yard with Dick loping along at his side. Out of the walled yard and through the meadow sloping gently down to the bathing pool, deserted at this hour, except for a few mallard dibbling among the weeds. Dick's senses immediately awoke and he plunged into the water after them. They took off, with much indignant flapping of wings to land on the opposite bank, well out of harm's way.

William stopped on the grassy slope beside the water's edge and put the lantern down so that its light shone feebly on the water. In what had become a dismal annual ritual he took off his shoes and trousers and rolled up his shirt-sleeves. Then, treading his way tentatively down the muddy bank, he waded into the pool until he could stand thigh-high in the murky green water.

Taking a pocket-knife from his breast pocket he leaned out to reach for a patch of lilies and methodically cut through the tough stems. The pink lilies were still tightly budded. He chose just nine of them to cut.

His task over, he hauled himself out through the reeds with his free hand, holding the lilies aloft so as not to break the delicate petals or bend the fleshy stalks. Oblivious to the water and chickweed dripping from his legs he quickly shrugged on his trousers and plunged his wet feet back into the pair of sturdy boots he'd placed neatly on the grass.

From the pocket of the trousers he pulled a folded sheet of thick, official school notepaper. Across the top was printed 'Henham and Wangford School'. Beneath it William had written the same brief message he'd written each year for the past eight years: *In loving memory of Benny Crowe who died this day in 1906, aged nine.* His throat caught. Tears welled in his eyes as he gazed at the simple words then slowly trickled down the deep lines of his face, falling on the lilies as he wrapped them in the white paper.

Why, Benny? Why? William rubbed at his crumpled face with his free hand, clutching the flowers to his chest with the other. *Why didn't you listen to me?*

Before him, as always on this day in August and too often in his nightmares, he saw again the terrible moment of Benny's death. How he wished he could bring the boy back, undo what had happened. William never ceased to blame himself. *If only I'd reached him in time.* The refrain ran through his mind like a haunting tune. Over and over again his inner voice chastised the man he tried to be.

Each day that he stood beside the pool, teaching a new generation of children to swim, he was tortured by the recollection. His pupils never knew of the agony he endured. All they saw standing before them was the strict disciplinarian, the strong athlete urging them on to achieve better things.

As was his custom on the last day of the summer term, William had gathered the entire school together to wish his scholars a happy and productive holiday. He'd admonished them to be helpful to their parents and reminded them the bathing pool would be open for swimming each day, but certain rules had to be observed. Children who couldn't swim were forbidden from bathing at all and the bathing hours for others would be from twelve noon until half past twelve for girls and half past twelve until one o'clock for boys. These were the hours when he would be at home and able to supervise them.

Benny had been at the pool that day with his friends, larking about in the water in an excess of high spirits, splashing the girls as they lounged in careless knots on the bank and giggling coquettishly at the boys. William had watched. Benny was an excellent swimmer for his age. A possible champion in the making. Six weeks earlier he'd swum fifty yards and William had presented him with a bathing costume to mark the achievement.

But he's a boy that needs discipline, thought William. *He's gone off the rails since his father died. Little wonder. His poor mother can't cope with eight children on her own.*

'Benny! Alfred! You boys! Try to swim to the other side!' he'd bellowed.

'Yes sir!' There was no disobeying an order from Mr Smith. The pool was fifty yards wide, bank to bank. Benny and the other boys struck out. 'Race you,

Benny,' one shouted above the splashes as they kicked and flailed in valiant attempts at the crawl.

William had turned away to comfort one of the girls, in tears because a couple of the boys had yanked her leg and tried to pull her down among the reeds. When he looked up the boys were scrambling up the bank, yelling argumentatively at each other, 'I won.' 'No, I won!'

'I won, sir!' called Benny, waving his arms triumphantly in the air.

'Come over here. I need to speak to you all.' William's voice rang with a hint of steel.

The boys quickly ran around the pool and stood to attention before him. The headmaster spoke quietly, reprimanding them for their ungentlemanly behaviour towards the girls. As he spoke his attention was drawn to Benny's face. The boy's lips had turned a bluish colour.

'The rest of you may finish your swim. Benny, get dressed. I think you'd best go home.'

'But sir.....' Benny began to protest feebly.

William would brook no argument. 'I don't think you should swim again today, Benny. You don't look at all well.'

The boy's head drooped and his shoulders slumped. William didn't see the resentful scowl, nor the frustrated kick at the grass as Benny headed to the bathing hut to change.

When all the children had left, quietness descended on the riverside. Only the sounds of waterfowl dibbling in the stagnant dykes and summer bird song from the overhanging reeds and willows, punctuated the silence. William felt contented. Now he would spend the afternoon with his family, picnicking on the beach at Southwold.

As he brought the pony and trap round to the front entrance he heard his younger daughter, Gladys Valletta, calling out, 'I can hear him! Father's here with the trap. Come on, hurry!' His heart ached at the sound of her voice. At fifteen Gladys had blossomed into a sweet-faced and sweet-natured young woman. Yet his beloved daughter had been paralysed and totally blind since infancy.

'Father, father,' she called, hearing his footsteps in the doorway.

'I'm right here, my dear,' he said, and even though she couldn't see his face she heard him smiling at her. He lifted the fragile body from the chaise longue by the window, feeling her bones beneath the scant flesh, and carried her out to the trap.

Alex, a bundle of swimming costumes and towels beneath his arm, had bounded ahead to hold the door open. Alma and Evelyn, their elder daughter, followed behind with the hamper and rugs.

When they reached the promenade the pony was released from the trap and put to graze on the grass. William carried Gladys down the flights of steps onto the beach where Alma had spread a rug in readiness for her and there she lay for the rest of the day while they swam in the warmed ocean or played tennis on the sand. Occasionally her brother and sister brought her shells to hold and feel, buckets of seawater to bathe her hands and feet or trailed slippery wracks of seaweed up the beach for her to smell and feel.

They were as tender and attentive as they could be, yet could hardly understand her limitations. Gladys was a constant gnawing sadness in all their lives. William and Alma often wondered how she would be cared for when they became too old and infirm themselves. Who would bathe and feed her? Who would love her as they did?

Dusk was falling as they made their way home, the gentle clip of the pony's hooves and the rattle of the metalled wheels lulling the children to sleep as they slumped together along the bench at the back of the trap. Alma sat beside William on the high front seat, watching his strong hands lightly flick the reins over the pony's rump. She turned to catch a last glimpse of mellow sunlight fading over the treetops as they headed inland. A linnet sang from an overhanging branch as they passed, its liquid melody filling the air. 'If only we could capture days like this forever,' she'd whispered to him.

The school was eerily still and quiet and the only light from the schoolhouse was from Ida, the housekeeper's room, as four boys crept through the gate, across the school yard and down to the bathing pool. The last rays of light were fading fast yet there would be enough brightness in the sky for another hour. Long enough for a swim, they'd reasoned. Thomas Crowe, at 14, had left school and was the only one of the four permitted to bathe at the pool without supervision. With him were his eleven-year-old brother Herbert and nine-year-old Benny and a classmate, Alfred Doddington.

Thomas and Herbert undressed quickly and dived naked into the water from the diving board, Alfred following them more tentatively, slipping into the black water from the muddy bank. Benny was still struggling with his boots as the three swum towards the opposite shore.

Five minutes passed before anyone noticed that Benny hadn't joined them.

'Where's Benny?' called Herbert as he clawed his way up through the grass and looked about him. All he could see in the gathering gloom were the outlines of willows along the bank and the looming darkness of the school in the distance.

'Must be swimming this way,' replied Thomas carelessly, his head bobbing above a patch of rippling water lilies.

'He's a good little swimmer, in't he, for his age?' said Alfred enviously, aware of his own lack of skill in the water.

They sat together, feeling the damp grass against their naked bodies, and listened. The quietness of the evening was all-consuming. There were no sounds from the water. Nothing splashed. No enthusiastic boy with wildly kicking legs and out-flung arms emerged from the dark waters.

'Where's he got to?' Herbert frowned, a sense of unease sending a chill down his spine. He called out, 'Benny! Where are you? You hiding?'

'Bet he's hidden up somewhere. I'll go and search the bathing hut, you look behind them trees,' Thomas directed, running off towards the wooden hut where the children changed. But when he looked inside its emptiness set his heart racing. 'No, he's not here,' he called to the others. 'He's not here neither,' yelled Alfred when he reached the nearest clump of willows.

The three boys stood and looked at each other in silence. 'My God! He must be in the water,' Thomas clutched at his brother's arm, a terrible fear gripping him. 'I'm going in.'

'No, no! I'm a better swimmer than you. I'll look for him,' and with that Herbert ran down the bank and plunged headlong into the pool. Three times he dived down to the murky depths of the pool, each time coming up for air, gasping and draped with weed. Each time he shook his head. There was no sign of Benny.

'Get dressed! Go and get help!' he spluttered as he struggled to crawl from the water. 'Go and get Mr Smith. He'll find him. Quickly!'

Their wild hammering on the schoolhouse door and panic-stricken shouts roused the housekeeper.

'Headmaster's not here. He's taken his family to the seaside for the afternoon. Best run to the village for help,' Ida said simply.

Still wet and half-dressed they ran across the yard and down the brick pathway. As they reached the gate a pony and trap drew up.

'What the devil.....?' William stood up in the front seat of the trap at the sight of half-naked boys haring down his pathway, the pony's reigns still in his hands. He got no further.

Thomas Crowe yanked the reins from his hands and in a blind panic grabbed his arm and tried to pull William from his seat. 'Sir, Sir! Come quickly! It's Benny. You must help. He's in the water. We can't find him!'

William leapt from the trap, throwing the reins to Alma to hold. He'd flown across the yard and down through the meadow within seconds, yet it seemed an eternity. Blindly he tore off his boots and plunged fully clothed into the pool.

Over and over again he dived down to the muddy bottom, coming up to gasp at the fresh air before spiralling downwards again. How many times had he dived? Ten? A hundred? There was no counting.

And then he'd seen the tell tale sign he'd been looking for. A line of small bubbles, rising to the surface. As he lowered himself through the entangling weeds, moving more gently this time, he saw in the dank greenness of the pond's lower depths the shadow of a body.

Benny was lying face upwards in the silt beneath the lily-pads. He prayed he wasn't too late, that there was still life left in the tiny body.

William seized him by the head and with his left foot on the ground he put his right knee into the small of Benny's back. One vigorous push sent them both to the surface. Turning Benny onto his back he gripped his face with both hands so that it was out of the water. He supported him along the length of his body and kicked out in a back-stroke. His desperate mind willing his exhausted body, *faster, faster*.

Eager hands helped to pull Benny from his grasp and haul him up the slippery slope. They laid him on the grass, then froze back into a circle of fear around him. The boy's face was dark and congested, the veins gorged with blood. Venous blood, starved of oxygen. William knew the signs. He urged himself, *stay calm, stay calm*. But even years of life-saving drills hadn't prepared him for the horror of this moment.

'Herbert, run and fetch Dr Acton,' he rasped, hardly able to draw breath. Herbert was rooted to the spot at the sight of his brother's body lying on the ground.

'Go!' William shouted. Herbert turned and ran. Up through the meadow and out along the main street he ran, half-naked and wracked with fear. 'Thomas.' He turned to the older boy. 'You must help me.'

Still gasping for air himself, William set to work. A moment's delay could prove fatal. There wasn't a second to spare. He had to get Benny breathing again.

'Help me turn him over,' he directed, kneeling down to cradle Benny's head while Thomas held his brother around the waist. They laid him face downwards, his head resting on one arm. William gave three sharp blows with his open hand between the bony shoulder blades while Thomas ripped the tail from his rough shirt to wipe Benny's blue lips and clear his mouth and nostrils of the slime that covered him like a silken cocoon.

'Tear another strip,' William commanded as he turned Benny carefully onto his back again, 'so we can pull his tongue forward and hold it secure.'

Thomas did as he was bidden. He rolled the rest of his shirt into a ball and placed it beneath Benny's shoulders. William bent close to the boy's face, putting his ear first to his mouth and then his chest, listening for a sound of breathing or the tremor of a heartbeat. He heard nothing.

Then holding the thin arms below the elbows, William drew them upwards and outwards. He raised them gently above the boy's head to expand his chest, then back down again to his sides.

Pumping up and down, carefully and deliberately, he paused for a second at the climax of each movement. He tried to time the motions. Each pattern repeated fifteen times a minute. He imagined the child's lungs exchanging air, bad for good, just as in natural respiration. Everything he'd ever taught about life saving was now for real.

How long it lasted he couldn't tell. Thomas tried to warm the lifeless body by rubbing it with a rough towel while William persisted with artificial respiration, but it was no use. All he heard was his own breath and the sharp, silent horror of the watching boys. There was no sound from Benny. No sudden whisper of a breath inhaled spontaneously.

Where's Charles Acton?

The children stood at a slight distance in stunned silence, horror and fear etched on their young faces. *Such a shocking thing to witness. Benny of all people. And coming so soon after the tragic death of his father.* Realising the finality of it, Thomas and Alfred began sobbing uncontrollably. 'Poor Benny.' Their barely audible whispers were like evening mist along the river bank.

William slumped with exhaustion. Water and weed still dripped from his clothes, his hair was matted and his face grey with grief. He picked up the small body and rocking back on his haunches, cradled it in his arms. He bent his head close to Benny's face and wept. The tears flowed uncontrollably. It was a terrible burden, this mixture of grief and guilt that overwhelmed him.

At that moment he knew his God had deserted him. If He could take Benny, the lively boy who'd created so much mischief and laughter in his short life, then how could He be a compassionate, loving God?

A hand gently squeezed his shoulder. He glanced up. It was his friend Charles Acton. 'William, my dear chap. Let me take a look.' William reluctantly pushed himself to his feet and Dr Acton took his place beside the limp body. He felt for a pulse, listened for the slightest breath. There was no question the boy was dead. But Dr Acton's examination, however brief, had revealed something unexpected.

He looked up to see William's grief-stricken face and the wide-eyed terror of the boys huddled next to him. 'There's nothing any of you could've done to save him,' he said, trying to sound reassuring. 'He died only a minute or two after entering the water. My conjecture is that he was seized with syncope, a sudden loss of consciousness, and thus met his death by drowning. His father died of syncope, too, you know.'

William nodded numbly.

As the last glimmer of light faded from the sky he suggested they should carry Benny's body up to the school before the undertaker was sent for. He would lay him out in his study. 'Thomas, I'm afraid you must fetch your mother. Perhaps it would be wisest not to tell her the worst. The shock would be too dreadful for her. Let me break the news to her gently," he'd said.

Standing now in his sodden black boots, usually so well-polished, William bowed his head as he recalled the moment eight years earlier when Phoebe Crowe had arrived at the school. She'd come in great haste, fearing the worst. 'Is Benny in trouble again?' Her thin, careworn face was lined with enquiry.

When she saw Benny's lifeless corpse lying on the floor of the headmaster's room, covered with one of Alma's freshly-ironed linen sheets, she shook her head in disbelief. He heard again, as he did so often in his dreams, her screams filling the air of that small space. Such a tormented outpouring.

Only seven months earlier she had buried her husband, Will, at the age of forty-seven. She had cried then, too. But those had been tears of fear. Fear of a future without a breadwinner rather than of a passion lost.

It was not as though death had been an unexpected visitor to the Crowe household. She'd born ten children, but had lost two in infancy. Twins William and Phoebe had been sickly from the start and had given up the struggle to survive after only three days. They'd died five years ago, almost to the day. This time, though, her favourite son had been snatched from her. It was too much to bear.

The inquest three days later had presented a heart-breaking sight. Benny had been a popular boy and his death had cast gloom over the whole village. It was no surprise to William to see so many people crowding into Wangford's Drill Hall to hear how the lad had met his untimely end. As the coroner Arthur Vulliamy gently questioned Thomas about the last moments of Benny's life, his mother, still in her widow's weeds, sat listening intently, her thin fingers twisting at her shawl.

Then William was called. He, too, was questioned. About the depth of the pool, his whereabouts that afternoon and about his actions.

'Before the holidays you gave instructions as to the use of the bathing place?' Arthur Vulliamy asked.

'Yes, the day before the holidays I gave an address to the children as to their conduct during the holidays and the help they should be to their parents and the regulations to be observed with regard to swimming.' He'd gone on to explain his daily timetable and why non-swimmers were barred from the pool. 'These regulations have been in force from the time bathing started, in 1900, six years ago,' he'd added.

'The deceased was an excellent swimmer?' The elderly coroner had peered over his spectacles at William. William recalled the hush in the hall as everyone awaited his answer.

'Yes, he'd been swimming that day in my presence. About six weeks ago I presented him with a bathing costume for swimming fifty yards.'

'What did you notice about the deceased?'

'After swimming across I noticed a blueness in his lips after he'd been in the water for about two minutes. He wanted to go into the water again, but I wouldn't let him and told him to dress.'

Then Charles Acton had presented his opinion as to the cause of Benny's death. 'I judged from the pleasant expression on the boy's face and the absence of signs of struggling, that he'd fainted when he entered the water, sank and was drowned. Some time ago he suffered from St Vitus' Dance, which often leaves a weakened heart. An attack of syncope was extremely probably, especially as he'd partaken of a hearty meal before swimming.' He'd delivered his evidence in the formal language of the medical profession.

The Coroner's jury had returned a verdict of accidental death.

But then Arthur Vulliamy had added, somewhat harshly, in the minds of those gathered there, 'This was an accidental death due to neglect on the part of the deceased to follow the instructions given by his master. It was a lamentable occurrence, but no-one was to blame but the boy himself.'

In an unexpected gesture of kindness Charles Acton and the twelve members of the jury had afterwards given their fees to Benny's mother.

William raised his eyes to gaze once more across the pool. The first pale light of dawn caught the ripples, a pale blue sky wisped with fine clouds, their edges fringed with pink. *It's a beautiful place we've created here*, he thought, *but a terrible place, too. A place of despair.* A despair he could share with no-one, not even Alma.

He was alone, except for half a dozen Suffolk Punches, barrel-bellied and the colour of beaten bronze, grazing beneath the cool branches of the tall elms and an aspen on the far river bank. The horses raised their heads only briefly in curiosity at his presence.

A melancholy whisper echoed around him as a breeze sprang up, swishing through the straggling beds of brown reeds and grasses that grew around the margins of the pool and the dykes. The tranquillity and secretiveness of these lonely marshes mirrored the very being of this village, folded away from outside eyes in a shallow valley that dipped down towards the sea.

This was a wild, bleak corner of England, where people as well as trees bent compliantly before the bone-chilling winter winds that blew straight from the North Sea. It spoke to him of its mystery. Its bleakness was his bleakness. Its murky depths were the darkest fathoms of his innermost soul. It folded him in its arms, but offered little comfort.

There was a last ritual to perform. Leaving the pool behind he crossed the meadow and made his way up the back lane to the church, avoiding the main street where people were already stirring.

He pushed open a small, rusty iron gate at the back of the churchyard. Close to the back wall, overhung with lime trees and a single weeping ash, was the plot where children were buried. He swung the lantern high to find the spot he was looking for, even though it was almost daylight. Beneath the trailing bough of the ash was the unmarked grave in which Phoebe Crowe had buried firstly the two tiny corpses of her newborns and then Benny.

William closed his eyes momentarily. He tried to pray. Pray for Benny's soul in heaven. But he was no longer certain there was a heaven for innocents. It simply added to the weight of guilt he felt each Sunday in church when he recited the Creed and knelt to pray, or taught the gospel with such fervour in Sunday School.

He calculated how old Benny would have been, had he lived. Seventeen. Almost old enough to volunteer, like half a million others, for Kitchener's Army. Almost old enough to fight and kill other young men. Only four days previously the British Expeditionary Force had landed on French soil and in the first two weeks of this war hundreds of innocent young men had already met with a violent, meaningless death. And this was just the start of it. How many more were to die and be mourned before Christmas?

He placed the lilies at the foot of the wall. Even without a gravestone he knew where Benny lay. He knew, too, that there would be no other flowers on the grave to mark the anniversary.

Mrs Crowe had gone, too. Her husband's death while labouring on one of Lord Stradbroke's farms meant she'd lost not only his wages but also their tied cottage. She'd been evicted from Wangford Lodge and forced to take a small cottage in Church Street owned by her mother-in-law's family. There she took in sewing to make a few shillings to supplement what she received from Parish Relief. It was never enough to adequately feed and clothe them all. Then Benny had been taken from her.

In a desperate bid to cast off the ill-fortune that had dogged her, she turned her back on England and emigrated to Canada, taking her seven surviving children with her. That was the last anyone in the village had heard of her.

William ensured Benny's grave was kept neatly mowed. Once a week, in summertime, a small contingent of pupils would be sent up to the church to tend it with hoes and scythes. One autumn they had planted daffodils there. It was the least he could do.

He shuffled his boots through the long grass, damp with early morning dew, to another well-mown grave that stood a few yards closer to the vestry door. This one, though, was marked with a low scroll headstone bearing a clear inscription. He ran his hand along the curved smoothness of the pale stone, then traced the letters with his forefinger. 'In ever loving memory of Gladys

Valletta the beloved daughter of William and Alma Smith who died July 25 1909 aged 18 years. Resting.' His ritual was complete.

Alma turned fitfully in her sleep, sensing the emptiness on William's side of the iron-framed bed. He'd gone. It jolted her awake. She sat up with a start, seeing the light tingeing the eastern sky away over the thick bank of willows at the bottom of the garden. Then it came to her. The date. She laid her greying chestnut head back on the pillow, closed her eyes and awaited his return.

She feigned sleep as William crept back between the stiff cotton sheets beside her. His legs and feet felt cold and clammy. She moved her body closer, pressing the warm flesh of her breasts and stomach around his back to comfort him. Her arms moved around his shoulders and with gentle fingers she caressed his chest and abdomen. Her cheeks moved against the glossy dark hair. She felt the dampness of the early morning mist in it. She knew where he had been. She drew him tighter to her. With these unspoken gestures of love the melancholy welled up inside him yet again and his body heaved with sobbing.

East Anglian Daily Times

Friday August 21 1914

Call to Arms.

We are now waging war with the greatest military nation in Europe, a nation in arms of 70 million people with an army of over two million ready, of which she can send one million into a single fighting line and defend the Russian frontier with the other. With time she is further organising her resources and calling up every available reserve to the extent of another three millions.

Lord Kitchener believes he may want – and wanting he may have – another 500,000 men. He has asked for 100,000 by way of a commencement and more than half of these are enrolled. But there is no time to be lost. A day wasted in the present campaign may mean perhaps a battle lost. Those men who are hesitating whether they would give their services to their country must hesitate no longer. They must seek the recruiting officers who are to be found in almost every important centre of population and join the colours.

The young man must throw away his tennis racquet, put aside his cricket bat, take off his blazer, put on khaki and shoulder a rifle. The lawn and playing field must be deserted for the parade ground and the camp; the mansion and villa for the barracks, the student and philosopher must give up study and dreams, the artist his art and all must face the stern facts of the moment. The wastrel who has felt he has missed his chances and no hope is left to him of social and moral recovery must seize the golden opportunity, which will restore to him his pride and self-respect. For what man will dare to recall that he was a 'rotter' when he has fought and bled, and maybe died, for his country?

This is no time for slothful ease and paltering. Before long many a man will feel himself marked and despised because he didn't offer himself to his country in the time of her emergency. Not one but should ask himself the question: 'What can I do for my country?' If his heart and conscience tell him he can and should leave his desk, his counting house, his bench, his plough or whatever his work and fight for her, he must go where duty and patriotism call him, and go at once.

Captains of industry and large employers of labour should be the first and foremost in encouraging their men to enlist. There are others, and of these very many in the fair and fertile Eastern counties, with their stately mansions and great estates, the homes of rich and leisured people employing staffs of servants, many of them men of fighting age and capacity. Country gentlemen should be willing to dispense with some of their footmen, gamekeepers and valets if not gardeners, for the last may be needed to keep the ground profitably tilled. Let them employ women as far as possible, especially the wives of soldiers, sailors, Territorials, recruits and all those whose duty has called them to rally round the flag.

Men must fight and women must work and work must be found for the latter or they and their families will starve. But what the country wants now and at once is men. Clubhouses must cut down their staffs to the lowest possible. Employers of all sorts must, if needs be, work short-handed and increase the hours of labour and the rates of pay commensurately for those who remain.

There is one way in which employers can immensely encourage recruiting and that is by giving an assurance to their men that, in the event of their enlisting, their places will be open for them on their return. Doubtless fears for the future rather than for the present may be deterring some from coming forward at the moment and a public statement from employers to the above effect would give an additional stimulus to the response to Lord Kitchener's call.

There may also be a national assurance that while breadwinners are away fighting for King and Country those dependant upon them will not be left to want. The Prime Minister and Lord Kitchener have both said that the country will need 500,000 additional men for the army, and where are these to come from unless there is a ready response from all classes, from the highest to the lowest?

We see the King's sons - one serving in the army, the other in the navy. The Queen's brothers are eagerly offering their services. Over 100 members of the House of Commons have joined their regiments and about 50 more have offered themselves for service. A large proportion of members of the House of Lords have done the same and the new recruits include all sorts and conditions of men from Peers to peasants. Distinctions of class and caste count as nothing. All Britishers have a common cause; their country, their common rank, their manhood.

Is there any need to express the hope that the men of East Anglia – to whom we now particularly appeal – will respond to the call with eagerness and alacrity? That they will take up arms in this most righteous struggle with a fixed and stern determination to fight for their country's honour and for the hearths and homes which they cherish in order to crush once, and forever, a menace even more serious than that which overshadowed the country just 100 years ago?

Let them remember the words of a famous writer. 'Every sword drawn against the Kaiser is a sword drawn for perpetual peace'. We are fighting not only that our dear country may be free from the blighting tyranny which overshadows Europe and that we may have peace in our own time, but we are fighting for an era of perpetual freedom and peace.

'For us the glorious dead have striven.

They battled that we might be free.

We to that living cause are given.

We arm for men that are to be.'

121

Chapter Eleven

Wednesday August 26 1914

Ernest opened the Daily Times at the centre pages. The large broadsheet flopped loosely across his typewriter. Dense knots of grey type, topped with layers of headlines and sub-headlines and accompanied by a detailed map, conveyed the latest news from the Front.

He pressed his face to within an inch of the sprawling pages, peering through inadequate spectacles. Just as he'd done as a child, nose pressed against the dingy window of the cake shop on the corner, except that then he hadn't had spectacles. They had been far too poor for that.

The news was bad. Worse than anyone had expected this early on in the war. The headlines were as sombre as they were sober.

2,000 British losses. Hard Marching and Hard Fighting. Invasion of France. Offensive resumed by German troops. Aeriel attack on Antwerp.

The British Expeditionary Force, which only eight days earlier had landed in France without a single casualty, was now engaged in the first battle of the war. A fierce confrontation with the enemy, raging along a front of nearly a hundred miles in southern Belgium. Ranged against them, along a line from Mons to the Luxembourg border, was almost the entire German army.

Herbert Asquith found himself having to announce in the House of Commons that the Commander-in-Chief, Sir John French, had estimated the British casualties at over two thousand. These had been largely sustained in the 'withdrawal' of British troops from Mons. Withdrawal. The word itself was like a dagger blow to the heart. It was painful and shocking. Surely withdrawal meant retreat? And retreat, so early in the game, wasn't what readers avid for news of victory were expecting.

'Two thousand casualties. Unbelievable,' Ernest muttered to himself. Alf and John were leaning close, their elbows weighing heavily down on his slim shoulders, reading the grave bulletins from the battlefield. Their silence was deadening.

When he'd read enough John looked up, his child-like blue eyes clouded. 'This won't play well in Ipswich. Not coming just before tonight's big recruiting meeting. If blokes see this they'll have second thoughts about enlisting.'

'Nah. You're wrong.' Alf was in confident mood. 'When Sir Ian Malcolm stands up to speak on the steps of the Town Hall they'll be like putty in his hands. You mark my words. He's a most persuasive speaker and once he lets rip into the Hun ...well... just you watch. They'll be flocking into the arms of the recruiting officers in their *thousands*! Just you wait and see.'

There was much scoffing at his exaggeration. 'Well, maybe not thousands. Hundreds...yes, I reckon hundreds at least,' he shrugged.

'They're calling the battle at Mons a "turning movement".' Ernest looked up from the newspaper and peeled the wire-rimmed spectacles from his nose. He folded them and clenched them tightly in his fist. 'Two thousand casualties. That's no light number by way of executing a turning movement. Just imagine. What must it be like in many soldiers' homes today? Women fearful that their men have been in the thick of this fight? Waiting for news. Wondering "is my husband, son or brother one of those two thousand?" And not knowing. Waiting for the list to come out. That's the worst part of it. The not knowing.'

His leg twitched painfully. He grimaced and clenched his eyes shut. Two thousand dead. And how many more had suffered horrific injuries? How many more were left lying on some Godforsaken Belgian battlefield, screaming in agony? Limbs blasted from torsos by artillery fire. Faces burnt. Blinded. Like the casualties he'd seen brought ashore from the *Amphion*.

He clutched at his aching thighbone with his free hand. The deadening weight of the horses' hooves, the blackness as one of the creature's bellies collapsed over him. His ears were full of their whinnying and the screech of wheels skidding on cobbles.

What compelled me to do such a thing? Why on earth did I step out into the road like that? What was it? What did I see on the other side of the street? He constantly racked his brain to remember. *Was it something in a shop window? A person? Someone on the opposite pavement? If so, who?*

Every time the accident flashed across his mind's eye he tried to remember. Tried to conjure up the picture. *Carr Street. An early frosty morning. A short walk to work. Walking between the electric tram lines. Then what?*

But the pain of those heavy metalled hooves pounding into his flesh had driven it totally from his memory. Yet still he hoped that somewhere, festering deep down within his subconscious, was an image that would one day rise to the surface. Unlock the nightmare.

He relaxed the grip on his spectacles and hooked them behind his ears. Only then did he dare look up and challenge the stares of the others.

A freckle-faced reporter with an unruly mop of red hair was leaning back in his chair, feet crossed nonchalantly on the edge of his desk, chair wobbling precariously on its back legs. He sat up abruptly, boots thumping to the floor. 'I agree with Alf. I think this might just do the trick. Hatred of the Hun will be boiling over after this. It'll spur them on. They'll want to avenge the deaths of our brave lads. And if the young men of this town are slow to offer themselves you can bet their young women will shame them into it.'

'Aye, Stan, and what about all those idle fellows who hang around on street corners and in the pubs?' A rangy, athletic young man leaned from his chair to point at the street below. 'A poor apology for manhood, that lot, wouldn't you say? And what of the well-to-do idlers? All those mothers' boys who plead "my mater would be just too, *too* upset if I were to go off to be a soldier." George leapt from his seat, lisping the words and apeing the young men he'd jealously watched promenading in the park in fine clothes, with pretty girls on their arms.

'Now then, now then,' Ernest chided as the others fell about laughing. He could see their larking around was about to get out of hand. Their laughter would reach the ears of the Chief and then there would be hell to pay.

'Yes, but Ernie,' John protested. 'If every mother's son made the same excuse, how many men would now be serving their country? It won't wash, yer know! It's better to make no excuse at all than to advance your mother's opposition as a reason for not joining the colours. Don't you agree?' The seventeen-year-old looked around the room for approval.

Alf slapped him on the back. 'Well said, young John.' He thrust his hands aggressively on his hips. 'Now. Who's for coming along tonight to the Corn Hill with Ernest and meself to see the fun? Stan? George?'

Stan, nodded, flicking back a strand of auburn hair that had fallen over his eyes. He would go, but reluctantly. He had no intention of joining the colours. In his late twenties he was the main breadwinner of the house. He was responsible for a widowed mother and younger sister, so pursed his lips tightly rather than say anything.

George called out 'Aye, Alfie, count me in,' and John added his name to the roll call. 'I'll come with you. We'll all go.'

Ernest looked from one to the other. He feared any one of them could succumb to the rhetoric of a consummate politician like Ian Malcolm. Three had already gone. He couldn't bear it if more of his lads left.

He looked down at the pile of papers on his desk to be dealt with for the following day's edition. Top of the pile was a typed letter from Lord Kitchener. He wondered if every newspaper in the country had received something similar, exhorting the editor to give it prominence.

'You'd better listen to this, then. All of you.' He rapped the letter against the typewriter to gain their attention. 'It may well influence the number of local men deciding to join up. It's from the great Lord Kitchener himself. He says....' Ernest paused to adjust the glasses on his nose. '"East Anglia, with which I'm personally associated, will I'm sure respond enthusiastically to my call to arms. The best way to obtain recruits willingly to serve their country is to call a meeting in every parish; in the open air, in the school room or any suitable room and get local speakers to address it, for they know the place best.

'Take down the names of men willing to join, who must be between the ages of *nineteen* and thirty". There you are, John, you're too young so don't be getting any ideas tonight!' The other reporters smirked nervously. They were well aware that Ernest's weak attempt at humour hid a serious anxiety.

Ernest continued. "Enlistment is for the duration of the war or three years. The pay for infantry is one shilling a day with threepence a day messing allowance".'

'That don't sound much. A shilling a day,' George interrupted. 'Not a lot for getting your head shot off.'

There were murmurs of assent all round.

'But older men get more. Listen to this,' Ernest went on. "Old non-commissioned officers will be taken over the age of 30 and under 42 and their pay is higher". D'yer think any of them next door will be tempted to sign up?' He nodded towards the sub-editors room next door.

Contemptuous sniffs were all he got in reply. The idea that any of the staid, middle-aged men in the subs room would join up brought all discussion to an end.

One by one they drifted back to their desks. Some to shuffle papers and notebooks and pound on heavy typewriters, others to head out to meetings or courts, or to chase up stories of how the war was affecting the price of staples such as flour and milk. Life in the county town seemed to be going on as normal, yet every aspect of it had become inevitably tinged by the war.

Ernest turned from his typewriter to stare out of the window. Not that he could see much. The traffic below threw up a continuous cloud of dust which filmed the glass, turning it opaque. He could vaguely see the outline of shopfronts on the opposite side of the street. People were merely dim figures in nondescript clothing. He leaned over in his chair and with both hands edged the window up a fraction, carefully, so as not to break the frayed sash cord. It creaked uncertainly as he did so.

The air that insinuated itself under the crack was as fetid as that in the stuffy room, but now he had a clearer view of the activity outside. There were far more people in uniform than he'd seen even on the previous day. He watched as the dust particles rose into the air, driven past the narrow opening by people hurrying about their business. Even the dust was khaki-coloured.

The ringing telephone broke across his thoughts. He bent his left ear to the receiver and said automatically, 'Good morning, East Anglian Daily Times. Ernest Hart speaking.'

It was Cyril Alcott, the landlord of a pub in Dovercourt, a village on the Essex side of the River Stour, not far from Harwich. Alcott was a useful contact. Ernest had courted his good nature for years, drunk in his bar and bought him beers.

Consequently he always rang when he heard something newsworthy. This morning he sounded more excited than usual.

'Got a tip-off for you Ernie, old chap. Only just heard it meself and thought I'd better ring you. Can yer believe this?' He paused for effect. Ernest waited patiently without answering. 'They've caught some German spies!' Cyril sounded triumphant. He knew he'd got hold of a good story.

'Where? Not around these parts, surely?'

'Yes, a'course in these parts! Where'd yer think?'

Ernest quickly pulled a notebook from his desk drawer and grabbed a pencil. 'Fine. Tell me what you've heard.'

'You won't believe this, but they've picked up *three* o'the buggers. Couple of Germans close by Shotley - your side'a the river - and another one in Dovercourt. They're all over the bloody place! Can you believe *that?*'

Ernest murmured into the receiver that he couldn't. Cyril could hardly contain himself.

'Arrested two of 'em at me mate Charlie Poole's pub on the road to Ipswich from Shotley. 'Course, what with the fleet being in the river off Shotley like, it looked mighty suspicious, didn't it? Ole Charlie knew immediately their speech was foreign and he suspected they were spies as soon as he clapped eyes on 'em. Course, he called the police, didn't he? So there they was, drinking in 'The Boot' as cool as yer like. Sitting there with their beers, whispering to each other in them's furrin words when the police arrives and arrests 'em.'

'So.... where are they now? Do you know what's happened to them?'

'Well, ole Charlie says they wus slung straight into Ipswich jail. Like as not they'll stay there till the war's over.'

'I see.' Ernest hesitated. Cyril hadn't finished and he could hear him harrumphing in disgust at the other end of the phone.

'Now what's even stranger is what's happened to this chappie from Dovercourt. I knows him quite well, actually.' Cyril stopped abruptly and corrected himself. He didn't want Ernest to think he was boasting or that he consorted regularly with spies. 'Well, rather I should say....we're *acquaintances*. We says good-morning to each other if we pass each other in the street. He keeps a hotel just around the corner. He's got an English name, Joseph I think it is, but he speaks with a German accent. He's a German who's been naturalised. The chap may be quite innocent, a'course. But we're fighting a war, aren't we? So.... makes sense to believe he's guilty until he's proved innocent, eh? Don't yer think?'

'Mmm,' Ernest mumbled non-committally. 'So what's he supposed to have done?'

Cyril's laughter rumbled down the phone. 'Would you believe it? It seems he's suspected of dispatching carrier pigeons to the enemy with news of the fleet movements in and out of Harwich! Hah!' He sounded sceptical, but was reluctant to quash a good story. 'Leopards can't change their spots, though can they? D'yer think getting naturalised is going to make the average German into one of his Britannic Majesty's loyal subjects? Huh! And here they are, mixing free and unsuspected with us Britishers!'

'So,' Ernest prompted, 'what's happened to this Joseph fellow?'

'Arrested, a'course. Like the other two German spies.' Cyril's reply was curt and to the point. 'There's more to this than meets the eye. See what yer can find out, Ernie. You knows ole Captain Mayne the Chief Constable, don't yer? Why not ask him?'

'Yes, I'll do that. Good idea. Thanks.'

'Not at all. Always like to keep you in the picture, Ernie. Yer know that.'

'I appreciate it, Cyril. Thanks for letting me know.' Ernest said farewell, hearing Cyril breathing heavily and emotionally down the line. He'd worked himself into a real stew over these spy stories.

Ernest sat staring at the typewriter. It was true, then. There *were* spies in their midst. Men with English names, but German accents. Naturalised Germans, pledging their loyalty to the King yet still, in their hearts, loyal to the Kaiser. The Chief had told him as much after he'd returned from his meeting with the Chief Constable. Captain Mayne had been most emphatic; he'd said he knew for a fact that a large number of Teutonic chaps had recently – very conveniently – transferred their allegiance from Kaiser Bill to King George.

When war was declared there had been a rush on the part of hundreds of Germans to become naturalised. They'd used it as a ruse to escape the compulsion to register and report themselves to the police. Yet how many of these fellows secretly remained faithful sons of the Fatherland? Captain Mayne had wondered. He fancied there would be no more naturalisations until the war was over. If then.

Ernest furled a fresh folio into his machine. He typed the story Cyril had given him. Perhaps people needed to be warned. He added a final line; "For the present it behoves us all to exercise the greatest vigilance with respect to the stranger within our gates. If we have any suspicions of his *bona fides* we should not hesitate to communicate them to the right quarters".

When he'd finished writing he leaned back in his chair. He held the typed folios in his hands, fanned out like a pack of playing cards. He studied them, pouring over his words. But with each reading and re-reading he felt less certain.

Spies drinking in a local pub, another sending carrier pigeons to the enemy. It sounded just too fanciful. Yet these men were flesh and blood, certainly no figments of Cyril's imagination. They'd been apprehended and thrown into jail. So there could be little doubt as to their guilt; the accusations had to be true. It occurred to him it might be a wise move to send a reporter to the county jail to try and talk to these men.

Yet what of that other so-called 'spy'? His own doctor's chauffeur, who had been labelled a traitor by malicious gossip? Someone had set that false hare in train. Someone, perhaps, with an axe to grind, maybe a patient holding a grudge against Dr Ward? All revealed as fantasy. A pure invention. He felt uneasy, recalling the doctor's anguished plea for the lie to be put to rest by airing it openly in the newspaper. How many more of these spies, now languishing in police cells, were there unjustly?

He rolled his copy inside a cylindrical metal tube, screwed on the lid and sent it humming along the overhead track which crossed the ceiling of the reporters' room and then descended into the subs' room, dropping the tube into a wicker basket. *Let them decide*, he told himself.

'I'm sick to death of it. War, war, war. That's all you talk about nowadays.' Lizzie spat at him in frustration as he walked through the door. 'I'll be mightily glad when it's all over, I tell you *that* for nothing.' She was taking her peevishness out on a mound of creamy pastry spread across the marble kitchen slab. The wooden rolling pin thumped hard against the marble, deadening the last breath of air within the pastry as she leaned into it with the full weight of her body.

Ernest had appeared for supper on time, which was unexpected, but only because he would be disappearing within the hour to cover the recruitment meeting on the Corn Hill.

How dismal, how depressing everything's becoming, he thought, gazing at the drizzle slowly greying the sky beyond the back scullery window. He hardly ever saw Lizzie smile these days. Her pale skin was stretched taut across the high cheekbones making deep hollows for her eyes and her narrow lips were permanently down-turned in a scowl. She was invariably vexed with him and he couldn't blame her.

She was right. All he talked about was the war.

It had, in the space of three weeks, taken over his life, his every waking hour. He was obsessed with it. He could find no space in his mind for any other topic. Certainly not people outside the closeted environment of the newspaper; not his wife nor the parents he hardly saw, despite the fact they lived on a direct tram route only a couple of miles the other side of town.

All his emotions; his anger, pity, love and bewilderment were directed towards the war and the casualties of war. These alien feelings conflicted so totally with the unconsummated yearning he felt for his wife that they were tearing him apart.

'I shan't be long. I'm sure the meeting will be over within an hour or two.' His excuse sounded lame and he knew it.

'So. Who'll be there? Who else is going?' She looked up, pushing stray strands of hair from her face with floury hands.

'Me, Alf.....some of the other lads. Er ....George, Stan....oh, and young John. Why?'

'I saw a notice up outside the Town Hall as I was passing today. I saw Sir Ian Malcolm was visiting Ipswich on a mission to recruit men into the army. It looked important.'

'It is.'

She stopped pounding and looked him straight in the face. 'And will there be *women* there?'

'How should I know. I doubt it. Why?'

Lizzie shrugged. The gesture was more aggressive than casual. 'No reason.' She turned back to the inert pastry waiting to be turned into a meat pie for supper.

Ernest was shocked. Lizzie didn't suspect, surely, that he was casting his eyes towards other women? 'I....I....imagine......'

Lizzie didn't let him finish. 'It's just that I think women *should* be there. *Should* know what their menfolk are letting themselves in for. Signing up to become soldiers. Women should have just as much say in all this as men. It's men who've taken us into the fighting, just because some silly ass shoots a tinpot archduke, but it'll be women who suffer the consequences, you can be sure.'

Ernest was tired, but managed a smile. 'If you care so much why don't you come along? Come with me. Go on! It'll be a big night for the town. Probably the most exciting we've ever seen. I'll keep a tight hold of you so you don't get pushed around in the crush, I promise.'

She straightened her pinafore with her hands and bit her lip, considering. Then seeing his smile she softened. 'Yes. I'd like that. I'll come. I'd like to....to see what's going on. See what it is about this war that's *eating* you so.

'Splendid, splendid! ' Ernest grabbed one of her floured hands. He felt an unexpected surge of cheerfulness. Felt a sense of shared interest. At last they would be doing something together. Maybe the meeting would convince her of the importance of this war. 'But first .....we'll *eat* supper!' He laughed sheepishly at his feeble attempt at a pun. 'So get that pie in the oven, my girl! I'm starving!'

Ernest and Lizzie found the other reporters waiting impatiently for them on the steps of the newspaper office. Lizzie's fussing over which dress she should wear, the grey or the green, had delayed them. Finally she'd settled on a sombre black skirt and white blouse which she covered with a light shawl. She'd pinned up her hair beneath the new straw bonnet she'd worn for Bank Holiday which gave her an air of elegance and sophistication. Being seen with a pretty wife on his arm brought out a rare confidence in Ernest and he forced himself to walk jauntily, disguising his limp by swinging a slim black cane.

As the little group walked the short distance down Carr Street and into Tavern Street they were surrounded by rowdy groups of young men, all heading in the same direction. Others were arriving by rattling tram-load from the outskirts of town, the open upper decks crammed with waving, shouting youths, some brandishing union flags. Hundreds more streamed up from the station. The narrow streets in the centre of town were filled with the heavy tramp of sturdy boots on cobbles.

There were shouts and taunts of 'Bet you don't do it!' as rival gangs found themselves with a common purpose. A few scuffled in alleyways, rolling together in gutters, but with no serious animosity. The rain failed to dampen their high spirits and laughter lightened the reason for this masculine surge; the recruitment of volunteers to Kitchener's Army.

Had it not been for a threatening storm the meeting would have been held in the open air, on the Corn Hill, a wide square flanked on one side by the Victorian red brick Town Hall and elaborately porticoed Post Office and on the others by grandiose, stuccoed buildings that declared their importance as banks and hotels.

Ian Malcolm, who'd once been a Conservative MP for Suffolk North-west and was now the member for Croydon, had been due to deliver a rousing address from the Town Hall steps, but the military authorities decided they couldn't risk the event being washed out at such a time of grave emergency so it had been hastily set up inside the Public Hall. Even so, the crowd was so large that it overwhelmed the hall, filling the Corn Hill with a sea of patient umbrellas.

As they took their seats in the hall Lizzie whispered in awe, 'I've never seen anything like it. So many people.'

Ernest was preoccupied writing in his notebook. 'Mmm. I thought it would be well attended.'

Alf was buoyant. 'Splendid isn't it? Beats all the excitement of election nights, eh?'

Ernest nodded. He'd seen the town in times of national sadness as well as gladness, rejoicing in the deeds of valour of men fighting during the South African war or mourning their loss. But he'd never witnessed patriotism on such a scale as this.

He stood up, his slender frame stooping slightly, and glanced quickly around. He spotted only three other women, further back in the crowd.

They were sitting together. He thought they might perhaps be nurses, thinking of volunteering their services abroad. His Lizzie made it four. Mostly there were sombrely dressed young men who he guessed to be between the ages of 19 and 30. The eligible age. *How many of these hundreds will volunteer?* he wondered, scribbling a few lines. His eyes caught John's, sitting the other side of Lizzie and drinking in the atmosphere of feverish excitement. Alf, George and Stan, meanwhile, had adopted a deliberately casual attitude, joking among themselves.

The hubbub fell to a whisper as the Mayor, accompanied by Colonel Travers, the recruiting officer, and Sir Ian Malcolm, marched up the platform steps to take their seats. As the Mayor got to his feet, a hush fell on the hall. It was immediately imitated by the crowd outside as the message was whispered from mouth to mouth, down the corridor and out to those huddled beneath umbrellas, that the meeting was about to begin.

The Mayor welcomed the audience, declaring his pride in Ipswich men and their record of service to King and country in past conflicts. But now, he warned, an even greater threat had to be met. He paused and the silence remained unbroken. Then he plunged his hand into the pocket of his scarlet robe and produced from it a hand-written piece of blue notepaper. Fluttering it before him he cleared his throat importantly.

'I've received a letter from the Earl of Stradbroke which I wish to read to you. The Earl has written as follows: "I'm sorry I shan't be able to support you when you hold your meeting, but I urge you to impress upon the people of Ipswich and East Suffolk the need there is for recruits for the army. I'm sure that the people of Suffolk will come forward to support our country in its hour of need and that they will come forward the more readily because it's been brought home to us very clearly that we might be called upon in a day to fight for our homes".' The Mayor looked up from the letter to gauge the response. Hundreds of pairs of eyes, burning intensely, stared back. The deaths of British seamen so close to Suffolk's shore had brought the war home to every man there, he had no doubt.

'And the Earl goes on to say: "Many Suffolk men are now out with their regiments. But the country requires many more to enable us to carry out the war in the only way we can, before it's being finished. I feel sure that their response to Lord Kitchener's appeal will be a very hearty one". It's signed "Yours sincerely, Stradbroke".' The Mayor sat down to loud cheers. Outside on the rain-soaked Corn Hill, the cheers returned like an echo.

When the cheers subsided Colonel Travers, portly figure held tightly within his faded uniform, got to his feet to appeal to the cohesive spirit among the town's young men. 'If two hundred of you volunteer tonight, those accepted will form a distinct Ipswich Company, training together as 'pals'. A Pals Brigade,' he assured them. 'So that all will know each other and work and fight together as old friends and comrades.'

Many in the audience shot cheerful glances at each other. Joining up with their mates, training with them, fighting alongside them – it appealed to their simple, innate kindliness and loyalty. The devotion they felt for their local Association football team, now to be honed into a fierce pride for regiment or battalion. There were yet more loud cheers which sent the Colonel beaming back to his seat.

It was left to the flamboyant politican and diplomat, Ian Malcolm, to make the most stirring appeal. 'I bring you tonight a message, red-hot from the great Field Marshal and High Steward of Ipswich – Lord Kitchener himself!' he cried, balancing his feet precariously on the edge of the platform and flinging his arms wide in a dramatic gesture. The hall burst into spontaneous cheering and applause.

'I call on 500 men of Ipswich to respond to Lord Kitchener's call.' His sonorous voice boomed across their upturned faces. 'One doesn't envy the feelings of those young men who still hold back. Many, yes many of them, may soon find themselves more or less objects of *contempt!* ' He flung the word out and let it hang in the air. ' The young women of the country can do something by shaming the shirkers.' He waved his hand towards Lizzie, the nearest woman in the hall. 'And I call on all mothers to let their sons join the service of the King.'

There were more loud cheers and stamping of feet which echoed beyond the walls of the hall to the crowd outside.

'No girl should be seen abroad with a young man who isn't wearing the King's uniform.' His voice lowered to a more ominous warning note. ' This may be rather an extreme course, for many a would-be recruit has been - and will be - rejected through no fault of his own, but for physical and constitutional reasons. I would suggest that a badge might be issued to every man who has tendered his service to the country, whether he's been accepted or not. It'll show willing and relieve the wearer of the suspicion that he's a craven or a *shirker.* Yes, a *shirker,* ladies and gentlemen. And there are others, who for good or sufficient reason, can't join the colours. But it must be remembered that conscription admits of no such exception!'

The floor vibrated with the uproar of feet as they stamped their approval.

Ernest noted Ian Malcom's pronouncements carefully in his battered notebook. He shivered involuntarily. This event, which he'd viewed as an occasion where others would participate and he'd be in his customary role of observer, had now taken an unexpected turn.

He was taken aback at the depth of the shame and guilt he felt. It burrowed deep within him. It was a physical pain. His face reddened, burning with embarrassment. He would be one of those shirkers, one of those who didn't join the colours. Yet what use would he be as a soldier? Barely able to walk with his crippled leg, let alone charge across a muddy field with a Lee Enfield?

He eyed Lizzie sideways, hardly daring to look at her. Her ashen face was fixed and unsmiling, gazing up into the bloated, middle-aged face of the famed MP. She would be one of those young women seen on the arm of a young man not in uniform. How shaming for her. Was she already sensing that shame for him?

He bent his head low and wrote frantically to hide his confusion.

The evening was coming to an end. Ian Malcolm held up his hand to command silence. 'In a moment those who intend offering themselves as volunteers will come forward and pass into the large vestibule at the back of the platform. But first, now that Mr Price has taken his seat at the organ, we'll all sing our most patriotic song.' With that he threw out his chest and intoned in a deep bass voice the first notes of 'God Save Our Gracious King....' As the entire assembly scrambled to stand at attention, hands clenched tightly to sides, the sound of young men's voices filled the hall; vibrant and full of life and expectation.

As the last reverberating note of the organ died away all that could be heard was the steady step of young men's boots making their way down the middle aisle towards the platform.

Slowly they faded from view, dim shapes disappearing into a haze of cigarette smoke as they turned into the small vestibule behind the stage. Groups of workmates, brothers and cousins, members of cycling or cricket clubs clung together, glad to be fighting alongside trusted friends and family. Others came singly, hesitantly or with cocky bravado. Out of public view they would take the oath and write their signatures. The deed would soon be done.

In a split second John made his move.

Slipping away from Lizzie's side, pushing sideways along the row, shoving urgently past the bodies barring his way.

'Er, watch it!' someone warned. But John, unthinking of the consequences, was born along on a wave of hysteria and emotion, wrapped in the glorious sentiments of the National Anthem. He wanted to be part of the closeness of an Ipswich Pals Brigade. Old friends and work comrades, training and fighting together. His heart swelled with an overwhelming happiness. It sang to him, urging him to join the shuffling queue snaking along the central aisle.

But Lizzie was too quick for him. Shaken from her grim trance she lunged out as he lurched down the row. 'No John! No!' Her scream tore into the respectful silence. She managed to clutch the tail of his jacket. Clinging on as though her own life depended on it she hauled him back with surprising strength.

It was several seconds before Ernest realised what was happening. He launched himself after John and caught his arm. Between them they yanked him back and thrust him down into his seat.

'Let me go! Le'me *go*!' He struggled in vain.

'What the hell do you think you're doing?' Ernest was shouting uncontrollably, unaware of the disapproving stares from people around him. 'What are you thinking of? You're only seventeen. You're not old enough, you stupid ass.'

'You can't stop me, Ernie,' John looked up. His lower lip curled in resentment. 'You're not my father. You've no right. No right to stop me doing what I want.'

'Your father, God rest his soul, wouldn't want you to sacrifice yourself as he did, fighting the Boers. Don't you think your mother's suffered enough?'

Tears clouded John's wide eyes. 'But Ernie, I'm not a shirker. I don't want people to point at me in the street and say "He's a coward. He didn't join the colours".'

Ernest drew a deep breath and sat down beside him. 'Listen,' he hissed quietly, 'there can be no argument. You're not old enough. Nineteen to thirty. That's what the letter from Lord Kitchener said. Remember? I read it to you this morning.'

'I'm nineteen in a couple a'years. It's not long. I could have lied about my age.'

'Don't be so bloody stupid. If the war's still going on in two years' time – which I very much doubt - well, maybe you can join then. If you still want to. Besides, everyone says the war will be over by Christmas. But don't enlist now. Not now. You haven't seen the bodies coming ashore like I have. You haven't seen the terrible injuries inflicted on the wounded. War's not all glory. It's a terrible thing. Cruel and unfair.'

John snivelled into his sleeve. 'Who's to say I'd get injured or killed? I'd make pretty damn sure I killed a German before he killed me.'

The other reporters gathered in a circle around them. Alf shrugged his shoulders in disbelief. 'Don't be daft. See sense, John. You may be brave, I'm sure you are, but Ernie's right. You've no business trying to enlist tonight. You're only doing it because everyone else is. What would your ma say? She'd go out of her mind if she thought you'd gone off to fight. You're her only son.' He kicked John's leg gently to accentuate his point.

John slumped forward in his seat, head between his hands. 'I really, really want to go. I want to join with all the other Ipswich lads. Fight alongside other Ipswich men. It would have been a fine thing to do. A glorious thing. To serve King and country.....' His voice tailed off, muffled in his throat.

'Come on. We'll take you home.' Ernest put his hand beneath John's elbow and gently eased him up. Lizzie slipped her fingers through his other arm, holding it firmly as though fearful he'd try to escape again.

Ernest bent to pick his cane off the floor and led the little group from the hall and out into the square. Almost without thinking his limp became more pronounced. Clutching John's arm with one hand he leaned a little more heavily on his stick with the other. As though aware it was to be his only defence against the callous jeers that were to be cast his way in the days and months ahead.

East Anglian Daily Times
Monday August 31 1914

Heroic British Army. Official account of four day's battle. 5-6,000 losses. Reinforcements already at the front. German bomb on Paris.

The epic story of the little British army's glorious stand against tremendous odds is told below in the matter of fact language of the War Office. There was a four day's battle extending from Sunday August 26th until Wednesday evening in which the Kaiser's legions evidently made determined though unsuccessful efforts to crush our men out of existence by sheer weight of numbers. Again and again they came to the attack, often across open country and in dense formation only to be hurled back. On Wednesday, when the Germans brought up five army corps to storm the British lines, the battle was of a desperate character. But the superb resistance of our troops eventually enabled them to withdraw to their new defences. Our losses during the whole period are estimated at 5-6,000 while the German casualties were out of all proportion.

Chapter Twelve

Saturday September 5 1914

William Smith took a step backwards. He eyed the two new maps he'd pinned on the wall of Higher Standard's classroom, making sure they were straight. One on either side of the large map of the world. A map which proclaimed, in its predominant pinkness, that Britain proudly ruled a disproportionate part of the globe.

These new maps, though, held a grimmer purpose; to help his scholars follow the progress of the war. Make sense of the nightmare that had descended on the country since they'd last sat at their desks. The map closest to the long, arched window showed the eastern European nations now at war; Serbia, Bosnia, Russia and the Austro-Hungarian empire.

The other was a map of northern Europe – France, Germany, Belgium and Holland separated from England by a merciful strip of blue.

He stepped closer to northern Europe. Tracing his finger across the hard, shiny surface he searched along the border between France and Belgium for the name of the town that was now on everyone's lips. Le Cateau. Spoken of in hushed tones, for it was here that one of the county's own regiment, the 2nd Suffolks, had met with terrible destruction after nine hours of incessant bombardment from the German army. Bit by bit, day by day, the details of the battle had filtered past the censors and into the newspapers; from reporters in the field and men invalided home.

As the murky dawn mist of August 26 faintly streaked the sky, the men of the Suffolks, already dog tired from three days' marching in retreat from Mons, had been crouched in their miserable shallow scrapes, gripping their rifles in readiness for the inevitable German assault. They had no choice; their commanding officer, Lieutenant Colonel Charles Brett, had been ordered that under no circumstances were they to retreat. 'The position will be held to the last man and the last round.'

That was the order.

Eleven hundred men, lying on the hard baked, sun-scorched earth, amidst the corn stubble.

Waiting.

William's eyes drifted to the mellow harvested fields undulating into the far distance beyond the classroom window. He imagined how the soldiers' arms and faces would be cut to ribbons by the harsh razor-like edges of the scythed corn as they crouched low. He remembered his own childhood, playing hide-and-seek among the hayricks with his brothers. His skinny, sunburnt arms bleeding as he ran to his mother for sympathy.

Eleven hundred men, willing themselves invisible in their exposed position a-top the hill above the sleeping town of Le Cateau. Skylarks rising in tune to the earth's rotation around the sun on what was to be their last day on earth. Unconcerned little brown birds with a song of such incessant sweetness as would break your heart.

But daybreak did not bring the expected infantry attack. Instead a barrage of artillery and machine-gun fire systematically and relentlessly pounded them into the dirt. A ceaseless deluge of shrapnel and high explosives raining down upon their heads, hour after unbelievable hour.

The noise had been horrendous. One hundred German guns firing directly at them, shells bursting overhead. Answering their fire, the English artillery, lined up two hundred yards or so behind the Suffolks' trenches. A few men, numbed and deafened beyond endurance and reason, climbed blindly out of the inadequate trenches. It was a suicidal act. They were quickly scythed down by machine-gun fire.

Only then did a vast surge of grey-uniformed enemy soldiers deem it safe enough to bear down upon the Suffolks, as well as the companies of 2nd Manchesters and 2nd Argyll and Sutherland Highlanders who'd come to their assistance. The Germans encircled them from the front, both flanks and the rear.

Tightening the noose.

Determined to go down fighting, the surrounded British troops desperately met the enemy with rifle fire and bayonets.

Now there were still more dead amd wounded. Men shot at close range. Men clubbed to death with rifle butts. Men bayoneted. The trenches filled with their agonised cries. The stench of torn flesh and blood. Then silence.

After nine hours of incessant bombardment they lay like broken wheat stalks amidst their own stubble.

Hundreds were taken prisoner and carted away to suffer uncertain tribulations in a prisoner-of-war camp inside Germany. All dreams of glory dashed.

Despite the courageous tenacity of the gunners and steady marksmanship of the Suffolks, the regiment had been virtually wiped out. Colonel Brett was dead. Killed within the first half-hour. Lieutenant Phillips had been wounded, whilst the names of no fewer than 21 Suffolk officers appeared on the list of missing.

William's newspaper carried an eye witness report from a private who'd been invalided home from the front. He reported that out of the eleven hundred men of the 2nd Suffolks who went into action at Le Cateau only 219 answered the roll call next morning.

'I saw Colonel Brett killed,' Private William South told a reporter. 'He was walking about as cool as a cucumber when he was struck. I was the only one to get out of my trench and in retreating across a mangold field I had the K of the word 'Suffolk' on my shoulder shot away.'

Another survivor, a sapper officer, was moved by the piteous sight of artillery horses, wounded by German gunfire. 'One of the saddest things I've seen was the wounded horses trying to keep themselves on their legs by leaning against the stooks of corn which had been lashed to the gun wheels as camouflage.'

That, particularly, wrenched at William. Made his gut heave. It moved him more than the thought of disfigured human casualties.

His earliest memories had been of the strong, burly form of his father in the blacksmith's forge in Drewsteignton, shoeing horses. He remembered the crackling of the fire and its acrid plumes of woodsmoke, the pungency of charred hoof after the hot shoe was offered up to the animal's foot.

The smells had filled his lungs and made him cough and spit. His father had merely laughed, and, slapping him on the back, had sent him out into the fresh Dartmoor air. The fires of hell. Fire and brimstone. That's what they preached in church every Sunday. He knew about the all-consuming power of fire and the hell it represented. That must be what the battle had been like.

The overwhelming cacophony of heavy artillery, the rattle of rifles and the cries of men. He knew that, too. He heard again the relentless clanging of hammer on anvil and the hissing sound when new shoes were plunged into a barrel of cold water before being bonded to the animal's hooves.

He'd cried in infant terror at the fear the horses were being hurt, running to cringe behind his father's leather apron-clad bulk with imaginings of inflicted pain. But his father had reassured him the beasts felt nothing.

And when he was older, being allowed to hold the horses' heads while each hoof was raised in turn to be shod. The huge cart horses towering powerfully above him, patient and statuesque. He'd stroked their coarse-haired noses to calm them, smiling encouragingly into their liquid brown eyes. Even though he couldn't have been more than a lad of seven, it was a task he'd taken seriously.

Horses were in his blood.

Yet it was his brother John who'd taken over the smithy when his father grew too frail to carry on. He'd left home for Culham College in Oxfordshire to fulfil his dream, his true vocation as a schoolmaster.

As darkness fell across Le Cateau the enemy's pursuit eased off, then died away. The Suffolks who'd survived withdrew southwards. Exhausted and with only a cigarette or pipe for comfort as drizzling rain soaked their mud and blood-spattered uniforms, they were simply glad to be alive. At the end of the bloodiest nine hours imaginable British losses numbered 7,812 men, including 2,600 taken prisoner. Thirty-eight guns had been captured. The horses lost - too numerous to mention.

William wondered how many families in the neighbourhood would be grieving, once telegrams from the military authorities arrived. He knew it would be for him to explain to the children what had happened when school re-opened the following Monday. It was a task he dreaded. Fathers and older brothers, uncles and cousins. Men who'd been either regular soldiers, reservists or Territorials. The 2nd Suffolks drew its strength from Suffolk and Cambridgeshire and there was no knowing how many local men had been caught up in the mayhem of Le Cateau.

He remembered the young men spewing across the pavement from the pub one sunlit Sunday evening in late June. Young men in khaki, returning in high spirits from the 4th Suffolks Territorial training camp. Parsley and Baxter and their comrades. *Where are they now?* He rubbed his brow hard with his fingers, feeling the furrows deepen. He closed his eyes, a desperate refrain painfully pounding at the inside of his skull. *Keep them safe, please God, keep them safe.*

But how to explain? How to make sense of this nightmare to the children? He perched his buttocks on the edge of the front row of desks, staring at the maps.

There was so much to say. The cause of the war, the unpreparedness of the British military, the pathetically small number of regular troops and reservists shipped to France with the Expeditionary Force, and the call by Lord Kitchener for half-a-million volunteers for his New Army. He'd avidly consumed every account of the political manoeuvrings.

Now the appalling statistics of death loomed before him in black headlines. Two battles fought, thousands dead, no hint of victory and still only a month into the war. He doubted the optimism of those who'd predicted it would all be over by Christmas. Another year, more like.

He thought it ironic that the battle at Le Cateau should have been fought only hours before the big recruitment meeting at Ipswich Town Hall. While Suffolkers spilled their blood and lay dying, young men with no military training whatsoever were volunteering to take their place.

The ripples from Ian Malcolm's rallying cry had spread outwards to every town, village and hamlet through the medium of the press and by word of mouth. Volunteers fresh from the harvest field were daily pouring into the county town. Country folk whose only skills were as butchers and blacksmiths or farm labourers. Broad-shouldered, deep-chested men of the soil. There was even a stationmaster amongst them.

Three hundred in a single day. More than 1,200 in just four days.

Village lads had arrived at Ipswich station by special train early in the morning to be greeted by cheering crowds. Marching into town, joyful almost to the point of frenzy. Led into the welcoming arms of the recruiting sargeant by a troop of the town's boy scouts and a scout bugle band. Crowds of laughing children marching alongside, waving Union Jacks and egging them on. Entertained with refreshments, papers and magazines and a sing song in the Corn Exchange. Such excitement, such a novelty for men more accustomed to grinding farmyard drudgery and the narrow horizons of rural life.

Every day fresh batches of men arrived, were tested and dispatched without delay to Woolwich, Aldershot, Chatham or Bury St Edmunds. Some were brought in motor cars by landowners willingly shuttling back and forth. Their cargo safely deposited they returned to their villages for more.

A band of well-dressed young men came into the recruiting station to make the beginnings of a shop-assistants and clerks corps. When they failed to match up to the required chest measurements they went away disappointed. Others tried to secure places in the Royal Flying Corps, but a short discussion elicited only a negative reply. There was nothing they could do but grin and bear it. Their future lay in the infantry.

The eagerness of the county's young men to join up was proving an embarrassment to the military. Suffolk Territorial Association's recruiting committee received a telegram from Lord Kitchener saying the numbers had outstripped the accommodation available at depots and training centres, not to mention the resources of the depot training staff. Yet undeterred, they continued to pour in. Driven, William suspected, by opportunism. They saw it as their one chance to escape from the land, its lack of opportunity and its poverty rather than an overwhelming spirit of patriotism and a wish to defend little Belgium or to fight for their country.

William found the jingoistic newspaper reports of this rush to the colours discomfiting. There was, he felt, a deeper dishonesty about the inducements to young men to take up arms and fight.

He thought of his friends in Aachen. The Reimanns were a gentle, amiable family, devoted to intellectual pursuits such as music and literature. They'd cared for Alex as though he were one of their own sons. Rudolf and Walter had treated him like a brother. Their sisters had proved delightful company when they'd come to stay at the school house.

But now they were on the opposite side in a war. Herr Reimann had command of a submarine and would have been charged with destroying British ships, he had no doubt. The hated Hun. Beyond contempt, if the vitriol pouring from the pens of newspaper editors was to be believed.

He wondered if he alone in Suffolk, maybe the entire country, felt unable to hate. The only man not galvanised into a frenetic desire to kill.

It was another irony that as a member of the village Defence Committee it had fallen to him to organise a recruitment meeting for the coming Tuesday evening. He was already uneasy that there wouldn't be a single young man volunteering who'd not been a scholar at his school.

Boys whose eyes had gazed up at him over the past thirty years from these battered and carved rows of desks as he stood at the blackboard or sat at his desk on the raised wooden platform.

He saw again the carefully combed heads bent over their books, the painstaking attempts at perfect handwriting, the ugly blots as the hard metal nibs refused to yield. The worried frowns of boys attempting to fathom the complexities of arithmetic and failing miserably. Boys mischievous, lazy or downright disobedient; their reputations living for ever in the neat columns of the Punishment Book.

Worse though, were the echoes of past summers. Summers when the sound of cheerful chatter and laughter filled the valley as boys hoed and planted the school vegetable garden. Of raucous yelling as boys were sent spinning along tortuous lanes on bicycles in training for the annual sports at Henham Park.

Most melancholy of all were the images of boys, now young men, swimming and diving in the bathing pool. Boys who'd swum for the school team in the indoor baths at Ipswich and Lowestoft and returned home county champions.

Lost in recollection he was unaware that Alma was standing in the doorway behind him. She'd been watching him for several minutes. Appraising with concerned grey eyes the strong, athletic body braced against the dark wood of the desks as he stared unblinkingly at the map. Even from behind she sensed his intensity. The tautness of the square shoulders, the rigidity of the spine, a slight tilt of a questioning head to the right.

Her soft green cotton dress rustled against the edge of a desk as she approached and he turned quickly to greet her. The black shadow of the Labrador trotted along behind her.

'The gig's outside and I've prepared a picnic,' she said. 'Have you done everything you need to do in here?'

William nodded. There was a forced cheerfulness about his smile. He shook himself back into the present, attempting to dismiss his demons like a dog shaking burrs from its back. 'Yes, all done. Let's go. It'll most likely be our last picnic of the summer. Where shall we go?'

'I thought our favourite spot, Southwold? We could tie Polly to the railings and take a stroll along the Green. If the tide's out a picnic on the beach would be pleasant. Some of our friends will probably be there with their families, too.

And maybe, if there's time, we could go shopping. I could buy a new winter dress.'

'Excellent idea. Perhaps at Southwold we'll be able to forget about this damnable war for a few hours.'

As they shut the door of the classroom behind them Alma tucked her arm through his. 'I do hope so, Will. I'm worried that you're taking it all too much to heart. I know you're anxious about our lads going off to fight. But it's their duty, you know. You mustn't blame yourself if terrible things happen to them. You've done your best for them. Given them a good education, a good start in life.'

He smiled down her at. 'I know. It's just that I can't believe that the Germans are our enemies. That we're killing them and they're killing us. Does it make any sense to you, knowing as you do what fine people the Reimann's are?' The shadows cast across his face as they walked down the dingy corridor only served to accentuate the deep worry lines around his mouth. She shook her head, saying nothing.

The heavy door to the school closed quietly behind them. In the middle of the playground Alma came to an abrupt halt, clapping her hand to her mouth, annoyed at a moment's forgetfulness.

'I've just remembered something. The lantern. I left it on the draining board in the scullery. I'd better go back for it. It'll probably be dark by the time we return home and we'll need to hang it on the back of the gig.' She turned as she walked towards the school house. 'I'll bring our books as well. There won't be many peaceful hours for reading once term's started.'

Outside the school gate the pony stood expectantly in a small trap. Polly was tied to a metal ring in the wall, although it wasn't in her nature to attempt an escape. She'd been well-schooled, just like everything else in William's life.

Dick the Labrador bounded up first, taking his seat in the trap. William handed Alma up into the front seat beside him and while she settled her skirts and straightened her straw hat he took the reins. Along four miles of dusty lanes shaded by overhanging branches, past multi-coloured meadows fringed with cornflowers, purple thistles and dandelions, the gig swayed to the leisurely beat of the pony's hooves and rumble of metalled wheels.

The journey was a time for idle conversation; about the coming term and what they were planning for their pupils, about their friends and neighbours and the latest goings-on at Henham Hall. It cheered William immensely.

Alma was nestled tightly beside him. He felt the warmth of her body against his and the touch of her small hand laid lightly on his thigh. A huge wave of closeness and affection enveloped him. He was calm and happy, however fleetingly.

But if they were expecting an escape from reminders of war they were to be disappointed. As they drove into Southwold's main street they spotted a large crowd gathered in the market place.

William stood up, the gig swaying from side to side as he did so, to get a better view. Polly stopped instinctively. 'Some sort of parade. Let's drive up and see.' He clicked his tongue at the pony to walk on and arrived at the fringe of a circle of onlookers.

In the centre of the market square fifty or sixty young men were standing in neat lines. They were in civilian clothes; smart suits, rough tweeds and corduroys. Standing erect, side by side. It was obvious they were destined for the military. They were Southwold's volunteers answering Kitchener's call, parading for the benefit of the townspeople. And there, rather self-consciously on a makeshift wooden platform before them was the mayor, resplendent in scarlet robes, his ornate regalia glinting in the late summer sunshine. The mayor's words boomed out over the heads of the crowd. Words of patriotism and encouragement for the men who'd volunteered.

His speech over and roundly applauded, the small band of recruits marched off in as tight a formation as they could muster, heading for the station, where a special train awaited them. The crowd jostled behind them, eager for a front-line view. They packed the whole of the station enclosure, children pushed forward to stand dangerously close to the platform's edge, and as the train moved off a hearty cheer went up.

'Well, what a sight!' Alma was amazed at the large number of recruits and the size of the crowd. It occurred to William that she'd not been out of the village since the start of the war so had seen nothing of the spontaneous fervour with which local people were throwing themselves into the war effort. A fervour he'd witnessed in Ipswich during the Earl's meeting to set up a county Defence Committee.

'Amazing, isn't it?' he agreed. 'But I think we should carry on. I've seen enough. Let's find a quiet spot on the Green for Polly and take our walk.' He felt irritated that such a scene should mar their day. The high spirits of the ride into town had dissipated and the old melancholy had come flooding back.

He was put in better spirits by walking and when they found several of their old friends encamped on the beach with their children and capacious hampers of food, he was once again his jovial, public self.

Dr. Charles Acton was there with his adorable pink-complexioned wife and twins, the vicar was seated on the steps of a bathing machine with his heavily pregnant wife while Agnes Eden watched proudly as her nephew, Anthony, confidently swam far out from the shore, enjoying his last weekend with her before returning for his final year at Eton.

While Will and Alma walked hand in hand along the margin of the foam, Dick chased the sticks they threw for him, diving into the sea to retrieve them, diverting only to help the children burrow holes in the sand.

As the evening drew in the families drifted away one by one, retrieving their ponies and traps for the ride back to Wangford and Henham. A mellow light played on the ripples that gently rustled the pebbles. Alma was reluctant to leave. This might be the last time they'd gaze across such a benign sea. Soon it would be made angry by strong northerlies or north easterlies, wind against tide rattling the waves up the beach and pounding the cliffs so that the whole town trembled.

'Let's take the gig up the coastal track and sit on the clifftop for a while with our books,' she suggested. Will agreed and soon Polly was walking carefully up the rutted pathway to the topmost point of the red sandstone cliff. Modest in scale, for this was an unpretentious landscape, it could barely be called a cliff, yet it afforded them a satisfyingly expansive view across the ocean.

William flung himself down on the hummocky grass. Lying on his back and gazing at pink-whisped clouds he said dreamily, 'I love this place. It's so tranquil. So beautiful. D'you know, I think I feel far more akin to Suffolk than my own birthplace in Devon? This is home. We're fortunate to live in such a fine community, don't you think?' He flung a hand towards the beach they'd just left where the last picnickers were packing away their hampers.

'People. That's what matters most. People are worth far more than anything else I can think of. Far more than wealth or high office. I can't imagine living anywhere else now, can you?'

Alma carefully sat beside him, smoothing her dress as she did so. She placed a hand on his knee and patted it. 'You're getting old, Will,' she joked. 'Being so philosophical. But then you'll soon be a grandfather, so perhaps it's not surprising you're getting so set in your ways.'

He sat up and shook his head ruefully, indulging her little joke at his expense. She knew he was looking forward to Evelyn and Johnnie producing their first child.

He picked up the book that lay beside him. 'I thought I might read this to the Upper Standard this year,' he said, waving the cover under her nose. He read the title aloud. '"The Life and Explorations of Dr Livingstone" written by the great man himself. Now there's a man of independent spirit and enormous courage and faith. I think he sets a fine, heroic example to our scholars.'

She nodded in agreement. 'I'll light the lantern so we can both read for a bit. I'm afraid my book is far less erudite. It's "Oliver Twist". A wonderful story. I think it's Dickens' best. Do you think the children in Lower Standard would understand and appreciate it?'

'I do, my dear. Most certainly.'

As the sun set behind them, casting its last purple swathes across the sea, the lamp gleamed brightly between them. Soon it was the only pinprick of brightness shining high above the dim lights of the town. Two hours passed in complete absorption before the thud of Polly pawing at the ground with a front hoof distracted them.

Alma looked up. 'Time to go, I think. Polly's letting us know she's hungry and impatient to be home.'

The new maps proved to be a natural catalyst in broaching the topic of the war. From the moment they entered the classroom, with its smell of freshly polished wooden floor and desks, the Higher Standard pupils were transfixed. The sun shafting through the easterly window glinted on their varnished surfaces creating bright reflections that while drawing attention to them, made it impossible to see exactly what they were. None of the children dared step from behind their desks to take a closer look. Curiosity was generally rewarded with a reprimand.

'What's them things he's put on the wall?' a white-pinafored 12-year-old whispered to her neighbour.

'Looks like maps o' some sort,' was the reply.

'Not *more* geography,' moaned another under his breath.

William caught their muttering from his high desk on the dais where he was taking register, but deliberately ignored it. He was relieved that to each name he'd called out a positive 'present, Sir' was returned. At least the school year would start with full attendance, but as the term, and the war, progressed he feared the oldest among his Higher Standard scholars would be withdrawn to fill the jobs left vacant by recruits to the fighting. Their education would be irrevocably ended. There would be no second chance.

He'd set them some simple arithmetic as a first exercise. After a summer spent working, either on farms, helping their mothers in the home or tending the half-acre patches of scarlet runners, cabbages and potatoes, their minds had become dulled to academic pursuits. He wanted to ease them gradually back into the discipline of sitting still at a desk, exercising their brains and manipulating pen and paper.

'Pens down,' he said as he closed the register. The command was instantly obeyed. William rose from the chair behind his desk and walked deliberately along the narrow platform to where he'd hung the two new maps. He turned a sombre face towards his class. Fifty children, aged between 11 and 13 waited expectantly.

'Today we begin a new school year. For many of you it'll be your last. When you reach the age of 14 you'll leave, either to go to work or to study at other educational establishments. You must make the most of it. I expect you to work diligently and apply yourselves and set a good example in both your studies and your Christian behaviour to those younger than yourselves.

'Since we all last assembled in this room much has happened in the world outside our village. Our nation is at war, as I'm sure you know. Our men are at this minute laying down their lives for the very preservation of all we hold most dear. It is a noble and worthy cause and they do not die in vain or unmourned. Those of us who are left behind must honour their names. We must never forget their sacrifice.'

The children listened in rapt silence. They'd never heard him speak this way before. Some cast their eyes downwards at the arithmetic books on their desks, hardly daring to hold his gaze. When he paused all that could be heard was the distant murmur of Alma's voice in the adjoining room and the penetrating song of a blackbird intruding through the open window.

They heard how the Archduke Ferdinand had been shot in Sarajevo; how the complexities of treaties throughout Europe had dragged Britain reluctantly into war following the assassination; how the race to build ships over the previous decade had made war a virtual certainty, yet how their country had embarked on this venture with a pathetically inadequate army.

A hand crept up, tentatively.

'Yes, George?'

'Sir, if we don't have enough soldiers, how can we beat the Germans?'

'A very sensible question George. I fear the answer to that is; with difficulty. It won't be a quick victory and it won't be easy. I've read that we have only about seven hundred thousand trained soldiers and that includes reservists and Territorials. Some of the men from our village number among them. I'm sure you know them yourselves. Maybe your own father or older brothers, or uncles are now serving with the colours when two months ago they were still here among us. Working at their labours on the Earl's estate, on farms, in the wheelright's and the carpenter's shops and in the various inns and on the railway stations. These men have trained hard so that they might rush to our country's defence in her hour of need. But they aren't *professional* soldiers and they're being put at great risk because they're fighting a far bigger and better prepared German force.

'Not only that,' William continued, warming to his theme. 'The German troops are better equipped than ours. Instead of relying on horse-drawn vehicles to carry their arms and ammunition and necessary stores they have motorised transport. It's clear from telegrams from the Front now being received by our newspapers that the Germans are using motor traction to move a goodly number of their men from one place to another. A properly equipped motor corps whose sole duty is the transport of troops. I fear that when the history of this war comes to be written it'll probably be found that the motor lorry and the wagon have played a great part in it.'

He picked up a copy of the Daily Times, open at the war reports spread across its middle pages. 'Those of you who care to, may read the reports for yourselves. I think it essential that you should be aware of what's going on. You're of an age to understand the gravity of the situation and the criticisms being levelled at our government for its lack of preparedness. Even in these past few days Lord Kitchener's been forced to issue an appeal for hundreds of thousands of young men, who've never carried arms before, to join his New Army. That in my opinion, is a most serious step with consequences too awful to contemplate.'

'But Sir, God *is* on our side, isn't He? The Hun are cruel and wicked, so God'll make sure they're defeated. My father says so.' A girl at the front raised her arm ramrod straight to gain his attention.

God. Did He take sides? If so, who could rightly claim Him? It was an agonising question.

William stalled. 'Maudie, I'm sure God will watch over all our soldiers, but I'm not sure He takes sides in a war. The Germans are a God-fearing people, too, just like us. They're no worse, nor no better than us. Certainly no more wicked nor cruel.' His brown eyes mellowed.

'Do you remember the two frauleins who came to stay at the school when you were in Lower Standard? The pretty young ladies with long blonde pigtails? Well, they're Germans and they're our friends. Their father and mother and their two brothers are also good, honest and gentle people and we like them, too. We must never assume that because we happen to find ourselves on opposite sides in a war that these people, who have been kind to us in the past, suddenly become evil, monstrous beings.'

Another hand shot up in the back row. A tall skinny youth whose father worked with the Suffolk Punches on the Earl's estate. 'When I'm old enough I'm going to be a soldier,' he announced. 'So that I can join his Lordship's artillery regiment, and ride the horses that pull the howitzers.'

'Me too, me too.' The mutter echoed around the room.

'Is that what your father's doing, Albert?'

'Yes, Sir. And my oldest brother, Percy,' Albert said, pulling himself up to his full height with pride.

'The Earl is a fine and brave man and leads an excellent group of men. Men like Albert's father and brother,' William replied. 'We must remember them all in our prayers.'

He turned and pointed to the maps arranged along the wall behind him. 'You're all familiar with the map of the world, showing the extent of the British Empire, but now we've acquired two new maps which I want you to pay particular attention to. Here,' and he pointed to the map of central Europe, 'Here is a map which shows the countries at the centre of the dispute that led to this war; Serbia, the Austro-Hungarian Empire, Bosnia and Russia. There's intensive fighting now going on across all these borders.

'And here.' He took several steps along the platform. 'Here's the map of northern Europe showing France, Belgium, Holland and Germany.' His finger hovered over the border between Belgium and France. He peered closer then stabbed the map on a small dot that was Le Cateau. He turned to face them, finger still glued to the spot. This was the moment he'd been dreading. When he'd hear the bitter truth from the children he loved.

'This is the small French town of Le Cateau. The place where one of the county's regiments, the 2nd Suffolks, fought a terrible battle with the enemy just a few days ago. We lost some of our finest men, some of our best soldiers.'

William's finger began to tremble and he took it from its spot on the map and clasped his hands tightly behind his back. His voice dropped to a tentative, almost nervous, questioning. 'Do any of you know of anyone who was injured or perhaps taken prisoner at Le Cateau? Or even.... even.... anyone who....who fell and made the ultimate sacrifice?'

His gaze took in the entire room. Slowly three hands rose, one by one. The answers came in whispers. Tears were wiped away on sleeves. A cousin missing. A brother injured. An uncle – his fate not known.

There was silence.

'All stand.' William commanded gently. 'We will say a prayer for our loved ones who have made such sacrifices in preserving our country's honour.'

Fifty desk seats squeaked in unison as they swung upright on heavy iron hinges. Fifty young heads bowed over clasped hands. A new maturity had settled upon them.

In the hours before Wangford's recruitment meeting William was beside himself with nervous anticipation. He paced the small sitting room of the school house, rehearsing under his breath the short speech he'd written for himself. As the time grew nearer he became increasingly agitated.

'For goodness sake, Will. Sit down. Relax. It's going to be fine,' Alma smiled up from the book she was reading.

'What if the meeting is a complete failure? What if no-one volunteers? That would reflect badly on the entire village and on me in particular because it's been my task to organise it.' He absently rubbed his forehead, pressing strong brown fingers into the deepening furrows.

'Of course men will volunteer,' she soothed. 'Haven't you read the papers these past few days? There've been meetings held in practically every town and village in the county and everywhere there are young men coming forward.'

He stopped beside the low leather armchair where she sat amidst plump, embroidered cushions. Alma placed her book face downwards across the arm.

She'd given up trying to concentrate on "Oliver Twist" while her husband paced the floor. He bent his face close to hers and clasped both her hands tightly.

'You know how I feel about this war. The entire country is going into it ill-prepared. Our enemy's forces are far better trained and equipped than ours. How can we hope to beat them? And yet....' he faltered. 'And yet I've been given a job to do; organise the village's recruitment, persuade young men to join the colours. Young men you and I have taught. So I must do it to the best of my ability. It's hard, though....do you *know* how hard it is?.....' His voice petered into a whisper.

'I know, my love. I know. They're our boys. They're *all* our boys. They'll never stop being our boys wherever they are. Whatever happens to them.'

'That's the problem, isn't it? "Whatever happens to them". Who knows what that'll be? And yet it's my duty as a loyal Englishman to do all I can to serve my King and country, just like everyone else.'

William's fears were unfounded. The recruitment evening he'd organised proved a resounding success, a great social occasion for the entire village. William had organised a full evening's entertainment, with local people singing and playing musical instruments. Some recited patriotic poems. He'd also recruited friends from Southwold to perform string quartets and popular music hall routines.

After the songs, the jokes and the laughter there was a rousing call to arms from the constituency's former MP, Harry Foster. As the applause for his speech died away, the door to the hall opened to reveal a late arrival; the Countess of Stradbroke.

Her entrance was electrifying. Her appearance totally unexpected. Gone was the well-tailored fashionable suit and in its place the severe, navy blue serge jacket and matching skirt of a Red Cross nurse's uniform.

Beneath the buttoned jacket she revealed a discreet triangle of plain white blouse, clinched at the neck with a black crepe de chine tie. Instead of the latest in London millinery, an unbecoming navy blue straw hat, bearing the ribbon and badge of the Red Cross, was firmly anchored to her upswept curls by a plain black hatpin.

As she made her way to the front of the hall spontaneous applause broke out.

William took her gloved hand to help her onto the small stage. 'Perhaps your Ladyship would care to say a few words?' he said, *soto voce*.

'Of course, Mr Smith. I'd be delighted to.'

Helena turned to face the large crowd crammed into the little village hall. The uniform gave her an unaccustomed air of austerity, yet it's very severity actually enhanced her pale, ethereal beauty and slim figure. Those watching her were struck by this new gravitas.

'Ladies and Gentlemen, we are gathered this evening for a noble purpose.' Her tone was strong and determined. 'That purpose is to show the young men of Henham and Wangford that their strengths and skills as fighting men are urgently needed to defend our country against a most brutal, cowardly enemy. I urge *every* man here tonight, between the ages of 19 and 30, to come forward and volunteer if they've not already done so. We need each one to play his part in defending England's honour.

'This will not be an easy war to win. We're already seeing the price some of our fighting men are prepared to pay. Some have been wounded in battle, others taken prisoner. Those who've given their lives have made the ultimate sacrifice. Do not let that deter you. Your King and your country need you and will be forever grateful.'

Helena looked down at her clasped hands, gathering her thoughts. Then she raised her head and smiled at those about her. 'As you know, his Lordship and I have converted Henham Hall into a Red Cross hospital. We have there a fine band of doctors and nurses who're treating sick and wounded soldiers and sailors. A large number of patients are there already and many more will come as the battle intensifies.

'We need everyone to do everything they possibly can to help the hospital by donating money or small luxuries for the invalids; items such as soap or cigarettes, books or nightshirts. I shall be making a wider appeal through the columns of the local newspapers because this is most necessary work and we urgently require additional funds. I'm sure I can rely on the people of Wangford and Henham to be generous.'

Her brief appeal over the Countess stepped lightly from the platform to take a seat in the front row, a flutter of applause following her.

Now it was time. The moment he'd been dreading. William rose slowly to his feet and called for volunteers to come forward. There was a moment's silence; an agonising lull. Would anyone respond?

Then one by one the young men, sprinkled throughout the audience, rose from their seats. They edged their way along the rows, bumping past neighbours' knees as they did so. William watched each one keenly from his lofty vantage point on the platform. Some provoked a smile, others a stab of intense pain. He tried hard not to reveal his emotions as the familiar faces passed before him.

The men formed up in lines at the foot of the platform, shuffling their feet to ensure the ranks were straight. Thirty-five of his boys prepared to fight.

William fought back tears as, with backs straight and heads erect, the recruits sang the National Anthem with vigorous pride.

Next day seven motor cars left Wangford for Ipswich carrying the volunteers to the recruiting station. Only one man was rejected.

East Anglian Daily Times

Monday September 7 1914

Letters to the Editor
The war and our villages.

In our country districts the families of the labourers are likely to experience hard times during the coming winter. Together with the extra harvest money there has also come the increased cost of provisions, etc, the result of which may be the money which will have been put by for the rent, winter coal and clothing will be, to a great extent, of necessity already spent by the time that winter is upon us. Besides this, the earnings of the unmarried sons which might have been depended upon for those requirements, will be in many cases no longer available, the young men having joined the forces.

Under these circumstances it would be of real assistance to many families in our villages if the present school attendance by-laws, which now compel practically all children to attend school until they reach the age of 14 years, could be for the time relaxed and that during the continuance of the war children over 12, who could obtain employment, should not be required to attend school. Many people would willingly find them light employment in house or garden and though the amount of their earnings might not be very great, yet it would go some way to procuring for them what at that age they need quite as much as education – sufficient food and warm clothing.

Signed 'a village inhabitant'.

Chapter Thirteen

Tuesday September 22 1914

'Do you think we'll ever have a child?' Ernest lay naked and sweating on the small iron-framed bed where he'd been making love to Lizzie, his elbow crooked against the thin mattress, head resting on a clenched fist. He murmured his question close to her ear, almost as an afterthought.

He gazed down at her, trying to imagine what this pale, boyishly thin body would look like with a new life expanding inside it. A bulging abdomen, breasts laden with milk for a baby. He, patting the bulge proudly, feeling its limbs flexing and kicking. But it was hard. The picture in his mind was incomplete. The image didn't sit comfortably with the Lizzie he knew.

Here she was, lying relaxed beneath his scrutiny after giving herself unconditionally and uncontrollably to him. Nightdress rolled up over her small breasts to expose the slimness of her waist and belly. Her long blonde hair lying in a riotous tangle across the white pillow. Not five minutes earlier he'd wound his fingers amongst those tresses as the two of them had writhed and groaned in mutual pleasure. Now, with his free hand he gently stroked the firm flesh and delicate mound of hair.

Lizzie stared back at him, resenting his gentle blue eyes basking in her, devouring her. All passion spent she modestly tugged at her nightgown to cover herself. It was not merely the chill of a September dawn cooling her heated flesh that made her shiver. He tried again. 'Would you like that? A baby? Do you think it'll happen one day?'

She turned her head away. It wasn't a discussion she wanted right now. Or at any time. She felt annoyed he'd raised the subject after they'd coupled with such abandon. She shrugged her shoulders carelessly. 'I don't know. Perhaps we're doing something wrong. Perhaps God doesn't intend us to have children. Not just yet, anyway.'

Of course she'd thought about it. Often. Wondered what it would feel like, the actual, terror-filled moment of giving birth; the pain, the pushing, the blood and anguished cries. But there were gentler images, too; suckling the baby, cradling it in her arms and cooing it to sleep. Everyone she knew had children. Sometimes she envied those loving mothers who wheeled their infants out in prams in the park and proudly watched them toddling and tumbling on the grass. But mostly she dreaded the experience. Felt only pity for working class parents who struggled to feed a constant stream of new mouths.

Her older sister, Hilda, had born six, one of whom had died in early infancy, and now at the age of thirty she was old and tired and without hope. Each new pregnancy brought only dismay and recriminations between husband and wife. Its confirmation greeted with tears and heads held in hands as they sat in faded hand-me-down armchairs on either side of the kitchen range where the whole family gathered for warmth.

Then there were the wearisome nine months, cycling round all too frequently, when Lizzie watched as Hilda, struggling with sickness and a body close to collapse, slaved over the washing, the cooking and the constant cleaning. And always, always the nagging hunger of a mother who deprived herself so that her babies had sufficient to eat.

There was never enough food in Hilda's house. Her husband, Edward, worked at the nearby Ransome Sims and Jeffries engineering factory, making agricultural and horticultural machinery; ploughs, thrashing sets and tractors, but earned a pittance. Certainly never enough to keep them all. And now, with the outbreak of war, orders had been cancelled both at home and abroad. As a result the thousands of men who worked there were employed only from day to day. The family which had always lived from hand to mouth now faced the prospect of real starvation unless the company won coveted war contracts.

Hilda had loved Eddie. Once, in the past. She'd confided in Lizzie that in recent months she and her husband had resorted to sleeping with a bolster down the middle of the bed. A physical wall on which was invisibly written 'Enough is enough.' If that was how having children corrupted a loving relationship she was secretly glad she was childless.

Barren. Frigid. Those were the disparaging words people used for married women like her. Her mother pitied her, others pointed a chastising finger. 'What, no babbies along yet?' As though she was keeping her legs closed to her husband. If only they knew! She could afford to hold her head high. Her back was broad.

Lizzie swung her legs over the side of the bed and reached into a chest of drawers. She took out a scrap of newspaper, torn raggedly around the edges. She held it up in one hand, waving it with calculated casualness, knowing it would intrigue him.

'I thought I might take a job. Helping with the war effort. Work in an office, a factory, something like that. Here, look. It's in your own paper.' She leant against the side of the bedstead, looming over her husband, holding her slim body erect and cocking her head sideways. She'd have looked coquettish were it not for the defiant glint in her eyes, daring him to refuse her. 'What do you think?'

She handed him the cutting, angling it under the pale light seeping through the small window so he might see to read. She'd countered his question with one of her own. One where she was confident she'd be the victor.

Ernest sat up abruptly, gathering the counterpane about him in some confusion. The time for nakedness had disappeared as rapidly as the early morning mist. He took the paper quickly, giving it a cursory glance. He could barely make out the words without his spectacles.

'Well. My goodness!' He tried to gather his thoughts as quickly as he'd covered his bare buttocks. 'It's not something I'd thought of. You working. Doesn't seem right, somehow. And a factory, well… that doesn't sound like suitable work for women. It's a man's job. It'd tire you terribly, you ask Eddie. And what about looking after the house? And the cooking? How'd you cope with all that and a job, too?'

The question hung between them, unanswered. She didn't have an answer. Yet there was something alluring about a job. A frisson of independence quivered in her mind, just contemplating it. Working with other women, producing something of value. Helping the war effort. 'I'd cope. I'm sure I would. Other women do, so why not me? Do you know that women are being asked to take men's job as tram conductors, too? Perhaps I should do that instead. Work on the trams in Ipswich. Might be interesting. More interesting than staying at home cooking, anyhow.'

Ernest always struggled hard to deal with Lizzie when she adopted this mantle of petulance. He sighed and shook his head. Lying flat on his back he stared at the ceiling, studying the filigree fan created by delicate shards of sunlight filtering through the holes in the worn blind. In the obdurate silence that occupied the space between them he sensed only warfare.

He pursed his lips and was about to say 'We'll talk about this later' when there was an outburst at the front door.

Knuckles clenched in a frenzy, someone was hammering fit to break through the solid panelling guarding the Victorian terraced house from intruders. There were high-pitched cries from below of 'Ernie, Ernie! Wake up. Wake up!'

'Who on earth can that be?' He sat up, startled by the commotion.

'How do I know? You'd better go down. I'm not dressed.' Lizzie slumped back onto the bed, shrugging her shoulders petulantly.

'Neither am I, damn it.' Ernest grabbed his nightshirt and with arms waving over his head as he struggled into it, he hobbled to the window overlooking the street. Flinging up the bottom sash, he leaned out, the tails of the shirt barely covering his pale buttocks. 'Who's there? Who is it?'

'Ernie! You're late. You're late for work! It's gone half past seven. It's me, Johnny. The Chief's sent me round to get you. You must come quickly. Something's happened.'

'What? What on earth's going on?'

'There's been a terrible disaster. You must come. The Chief wants you. Now!' And with that John turned hurriedly away and ran through the winding back streets that led him to the newspaper office.

Ernest turned from the window, his slight form blocking the daylight, creating a dark shadow. 'God Almighty, what can have happened? I can't believe I'm late for work. The Chief will be furious. The clock must have stopped.'

John's shrieking voice with it's overtones of panic sent him rummaging quickly in the wardrobe and chest of drawers for clean clothes. He chose a white shirt and dark suit. Somehow he thought they'd be appropriate. 'We'll talk about this idea of yours later. This evening, over supper.'

Lizzie sat up in bed, clutching her knees to her chin, watching his every move. 'If it's anything like last time you won't be back for supper. I'll be lucky to see you a-fore midnight.'

'Maybe.' He bent his head to lace the sturdy black boots that served him through winter and summer alike. The muscles around the smashed bone in his leg pained him as he arched his back low and he bit his lower lip to stifle an involuntary yelp. He didn't want Lizzie to hear his suffering. 'Must go. No time for breakfast.' He touched his lips to her cheek and was gone.

The Chief was unusually subdued, his ebullience and forthrightness blanketed beneath a foreboding which communicated itself the instant Ernest reached the top of the stairs at the end of the corridor leading to the editor's office. He sat hunched over a slip of copy paper. His shoulders, uncharacteristically slouched, had collapsed inwards onto the gaudy flowered waistcoat stretched across his belly.

The old man's stick, normally displayed intimidatingly in the manner of a schoolmaster's cane on top of the desk, was propped in a corner by the hatstand instead. It spoke volumes. On this occasion it was not required. There was no need for him to use it to lambast the battered, green leathered desk in order to emphasis this story's importance.

'A message came for you.' The editor sniffed his disapproval. 'Before you deigned to turn up at the office – late. Alfred took the call. A Lieutenant Briggs, I think he said. Know him?' He barely glanced up as Ernest, leaning lopsidedly on his cane, stood before him.

'Yes Chief. I met him about a month ago. While I was covering the disaster which befell the *Amphion*. I asked the Lieutenant to let me know if anything happened concerning the fleet in Harwich.'

'Well, he's kept his word. Alfred took a note over the telephone. Better read it.' He thrust the piece of paper across the ink-stained leather to his War Correspondent.

Ernest skimmed the uneven type produced by Alf's old Imperial, serious eyes moving rapidly from line to line. Then he read it twice more. Slowly, squinting through his spectacles. Hardly able to believe its content, muttering the words into the subdued stillness.

'Three British cruisers torpedoed and sunk by German submarines in North Sea off Hook of Holland early this morning. *HMS Aboukir, HMS Hogue* and *HMS Cressy*. All ships belonged to the third fleet. Large number of casualties. Possibly being brought to Harwich.'

He looked up and grabbed his glasses from the bridge of his nose. 'Dear God. *Three* ships. *Three* of our ships. How could such a thing happen?'

Sir Frederick Wilson raised bloodshot eyes heavenwards, his side whiskers sweeping dolefully back and forth as he shook his head. 'Who knows? That's for you to find out. Take the car down to Shotley Barracks. Bound to be people down there who'll know what's going on.'

'Yes Chief.' Ernest carefully folded the message and slipped it into the pocket of his jacket. 'Perhaps I should take John with me? It's most likely the Harwich fleet'll be called on to search for survivors, in which case they'll bring them back into port. With two of us there we won't miss anything.'

Sir Frederick nodded in acquiescence. 'As long as Alfred can spare him from other duties, I agree.' Then, as an afterthought, he added, 'This war's not going at all well for us, yer know Hart. Most folks are saying it'll be over by Christmas, but I'm not convinced. I fear the losses we've sustained at sea and on the battlefields in France could prolong the fight far into next year. It'll mean you serving as War Correspondent for quite a while yet. Are you up to it, d'yer think?' He glanced down at Ernest's black walking cane.

Ernest was nonplussed by both the assumption and the question. 'Yes Chief. Of course. But there's a great deal to do. So many things going on throughout the county every day. If the situation deteriorates I would appreciate an assistant. John perhaps?'

The corners of the old editor's mouth twitched and he held Ernest's gaze hard. 'He's a promising young man. We'll see about that.' With that he flapped the back of his hand towards the doorway in a gesture of dismissal.

It was with a sense of *déjà vu* that Ernest found himself once again standing on the gravelled pathway overlooking the River Stour at Shotley. Below was the narrow jetty where six weeks previously he'd watched steam pinnaces and Red Cross boats scurrying to and fro, ferrying the badly burnt and maimed sailors ashore to the barracks hospital. He stared at the calm waters sparkling in the sunlight. The grey hulks of warships anchored along the deep channel of the river and out into the bay mirrored back their doubles in the glassy surface.

A perfect Indian summer day, he thought. *Who could imagine there's been a disaster out at sea on such a day as this?*

Dejectedly he eased the throbbing pain in his leg by leaning heavily on his cane and plunged one hand into his trouser pocket. The bent penny he'd picked up weeks previously scraped the tips of his fingers. He ran them absently across its roughened surface, like Aladdin rubbing a magic lamp. Only instead of conjuring up a genii there appeared the nightmarish vision of the blood-soaked body of the sailor being born uphill on a stretcher, with the sound track of a barely-audible clink as the penny fell to the ground. It was a constant prick to his conscience. The true owner of this coin must surely be dead, yet he, its usurper, was very much alive.

But this wasn't the same as the sixth of August. Then the sight of casualties and German prisoners being ferried ashore had shocked and surprised him. Not because he was faint-hearted in the face of such bloodiness, but because it had opened his eyes to a morality that was totally unexpected and alien. The brutal, dishonourable and impersonal way the Germans had used mines to deliver death and destruction to so many innocent men. The arrogant, self-satisfied smirk of the blond Teutonic prisoner as he cast his eyes over the crowd of English onlookers.

The enemy. He'd seen his face for himself and it had made his heart tremble.

In the intervening six weeks he'd become attune to it. Become inured to the shocking sight of torn flesh, the smell of blood and the high-pitched screams of men in pain. He'd quickly adopted the reporters' hard protective carapace. Yet beneath it, barely concealed, his disquiet and anger boiled like lava at the earth's core.

This time was different, too, for he had John at his side. Ernest quietly acknowledged that his reasons for insisting the young reporter accompany him weren't entirely based on news priorities. Reading newspaper headlines baldly proclaiming thousands dead on a French battlefield meant nothing in terms of flesh and blood. He wanted John to be as shocked as he had been. Shocked out of the notion that war was glorious and honourable; that it was an adventure he couldn't afford to miss.

He wanted him to see the casualties of war. Witness the horror of it all. The waste of young men's lives. He wanted John to see the individual tortured faces and mutilated bodies lying in the barracks hospital not a dozen miles from his own comfortable home in Ipswich. Wanted to force him to realise what kind of hellish future these men would face. Young men with old men's bodies that would mock and torment them for the rest of their lives.

'What are you expecting to happen, Ernie?' John lolled languidly at Ernest's side, tall and angular, hands resting arrogantly on his hips, defying the senior man to reveal his inside knowledge like a conjurer producing rabbits from a hat.

'If we've lost three of our cruisers off the Hook of Holland then doubtless we'll see many of the dead and injured brought ashore here at Shotley Barracks and to the hospital that's been set up in the Railway Hotel in Harwich.' Ernest pointed across the broad expanse of river to the grimy building on the opposite quayside. 'You must prepare yourself for some grim sights, Johnny.'

John gazed down at his polished boots scuffling in the dust. He'd never seen a dead body before and was in some trepidation at the prospect. What if the very sight of a corpse should make him faint? He looked up and saw Ernest's blue eyes smiling at him.

'I'll not let you down, Ernie. I'll be a good assistant, you mark my words.'

'I've never doubted that and neither has the Chief. You're a promising reporter and this could be your chance to witness at first hand a disaster of epic proportions. Or at least obtain verbatim eye-witness accounts of the disaster, which are what the Chief will want for tomorrow's edition. You've remembered your notebook and a goodly supply of pencils, I hope?'

In reply John tapped the breast pocket of his brown jacket. 'Hang on a moment.' He grabbed Ernest by the arm. 'Something's happening. Look!' He pointed towards the river.

A dozen or more warship propellers had swung into motion and were churning the glassy surface into a foam while seamen were running about the decks, casting off the lines and hawsers which held the ships fast to buoys in the river's deep channel. Within a short space of time every ship in the harbour was steaming out to sea at top speed.

'I've not seen so many leave quite so rapidly before.' Ernest tapped his pencil on a front tooth after writing feverishly in his notebook for several minutes. 'Must have received a wireless message. Most definitely something more than ordinary patrol duty.'

For hours the harbour was denuded of warships, the last lapping of an ebbing neap tide the only movement.

It was seven o'clock in the evening before the ships returned, appearing out of the evening haze as a snaking grey line along the horizon as they made their way down the Shipway Channel. As each warship rounded Languard Point cheers went up from the waiting crowds on the river banks. It was only as each drew slowly into the River Stour that Ernest noticed some were flying flags at half mast.

The crowds watched in horrified thrall as small boats flocked to the great grey hulks. Men were lowered on make-shift stretchers, others climbed down, unaided, on rope ladders. Eighty of the survivors landed at Harwich's Parkston

Quay and were transferred to the *Woolwich*, the depot ship for submarines. Then *HMS Lowestoft* took up her moorings abreast of the pier on the Shotley side of the river. Once again the little Red Cross boat glided to and fro between warship and the pier, ferrying wounded seamen ashore.

It was a well-ordered routine. Those who could walk staggered up the narrow pathway between the crowds of onlookers. The more severely wounded were gently lifted onto stretchers and carried the short distance to the hospital in Shotley Barracks.

Ernest glanced quickly at the young reporter at his side. The colour had drained from his cheeks and he was clutching one hand to his forehead.

'All right, old chap?' Ernest tapped his shoulder in a comforting gesture.

John nodded quickly. 'Perfectly. Just a bit fatigued, that's all. Standing in the sun all day, yer know. Not used to it.'

'Of course. Tell you what. We'll find the ferryman and get him to row us across to Harwich. See what's going on there. Come with me, the water will cool you off.'

They found the old ferryman sitting in his rowing boat beside the jetty, waiting for customers. He recognised Ernest. 'Back again, then? Whenever there's something bad going on I sees yer down here. Turnin' up like a bad penny.'

Ernest grinned half-heartedly and enquired if the military hadn't changed its mind about allowing the motor ferry to run.

'Whatcher think?' the boatman snarled. 'Wouldn't be havin' to row you across in ones and twos if they had, would I?'

There was no arguing with him so Ernest and John fell silent while the ferryman pulled heftily and painfully on the oars, groaning and wheezing at each stroke. When they reached the Harwich pier Ernest asked the time of the last crossing.

'Looks like I'll have customers all night at this rate,' he answered, taking the few pence Ernest profered for the fare.

Crowds of people had gathered on Harwich pier and quayside and there were loud protests when Ernest and John elbowed their way through to the front. 'We're from the Daily Times,' John said loudly and importantly as he pushed and shoved, but he was to be disappointed if he thought his exalted status would part the ways automatically.

Shortly after eight o'clock that evening the first batch of survivors came ashore. Onlookers scuffled to make a parting for them to pass through, those at the back of the crowd who had been standing on wooden fish boxes toppling in the crush.

The survivors brought ashore at Harwich seemed to be all officers. They appeared in odd garments, some wearing large wraps, others a piece of sacking around their loins. For the most part they were bare-footed. Fresh batches arrived at ten or twenty minute intervals and as each batch came ashore a loud cheer went up from the spectators. The men walked smartly through the two lines of onlookers, who were kept back by a strong guard, to the hospital set up in the Great Eastern Hotel.

Ernest noted that many were wearing llama jackets with a hood attached. He nudged John's elbow. 'See those jackets? That's what the men wear when they're engaged in night watches during cold and wintry weather.'

John nodded. 'How many men do'yer reckon have come ashore so far?'

'I've counted thirty so far,' replied Ernest, consulting his notebook. 'But I'm sure there'll be hundreds more by the time this operation's over.'

'I think they must've all been recovered from the water,' said John. 'They're all wet through.'

At nine o'clock the hospital boat ceased running and Ernest assumed that all the wounded had been safely landed. The crowds, though, were not satisfied and if anything increased rather than diminished in the hope of seeing further survivors. Their patience was rewarded when at half-past nine the last batch was brough ashore. Loud and prolonged cheering could be heard from the sailors on board the *Dido*, the depot ship.

'Wonder what that's all about?' John said.

Ernest shrugged. 'We might discover that later. Keep your eyes and ears open. It might mean a counter success – perhaps one of our ships has knocked out a German sub. Who knows? Come on, let's see if we can get into the hospital. Talk to the officers if we can.'

They abandoned their prime position on the quayside and headed across the street.

Every ward, every corridor and even the entrance lobby of the Great Eastern Hotel was crowded with the injured. The neat rows of empty, white-sheeted beds he'd seen previously were now occupied with dischevelled officers; their make-shift wraps falling in drenched folds from their shoulders. Some were lying immobile on their beds with obvious injuries waiting to be tended by rustling Red Cross nurses moving efficiently from patient to patient. Others sat head in hands, bemused and dazed, the damage they'd suffered far less obvious.

'You take that corridor,' Ernest pointed John to the ward that had once been his favourite dining room, 'and I'll take this. We'll meet back here in the lobby in an hour. You know what's needed. Talk to as many of the chaps as you can. Be patient, listen well and make a verbatim note of what they have to say.' John nodded and Ernest watched him go.

'Ah, Mr Hart.' Ernest turned to see who was hailing him from among the maelstrom of bodies. It was Lieutenant Briggs. 'I thought I might find you here.'

The young officer narrowed his eyes knowingly. Ernest was grateful Briggs had taken the trouble to make that telephone call. At their first meeting he'd thought the officer foppish and insensitive, but now he found himself grudgingly warming to him.

'Thanks for letting us know what was happening,' Ernest said, shaking Brigg's hand.

'Not at all, not at all. This is a dreadful, dreadful disaster. It should never have happened. I fear that when we've heard what the survivors have to say we'll find there were errors in the execution of this mission which played right into the hands of our enemy.'

'Errors, you say? What exactly could've gone wrong?'

By way of answer Briggs turned to the lobby window and gazed out across the River Stour to where the destroyers had returned to their moorings. He swung round to face Ernest. 'Well, I don't think it's any secret that these were old ships, built at the turn of the century - antiquated by today's standard. Certainly ancient by comparison to the destroyers out here,' he waved his hand at the grey hulks swaying on their buoys.

'Despite all their armaments, their heavy guns and torpedoes, they're very vulnerable to attack. That's why they always go out on patrol with a destroyer escort. But this time, unfortunately, the destroyers weren't there. They'd been confined to port because of stormy weather and so the cruisers'd gone out alone. Perhaps they didn't anticipate a submarine attack because of the high seas,' Briggs explained, knowing he was dealing with a layman.

'First the enemy got our ships with mines, now torpedoes. And by all accounts the casualties they've inflicted this time are out of all proportion. It's just terrible, terrible,' Briggs hung his head and his shoulders slumped miserably.

'I see,' Ernest was writing furiously in his notebook. 'These vessels must have had some purpose in sailing, or the Admiralty would surely have kept them in port?'

'Yes, of course.' He hesitated and lowered his voice. 'What I'm about to tell you is only surmise, only hearsay. It's only what I've heard from some of the men we're treating in Shotley Barracks. You may wish to verify it for yourself.'

Ernest waited, giving Briggs space to collect his thoughts.

'You have to understand that all ships operate under strict rules. These patrols were supposed to maintain a speed of 12 or 13 knots and zigzag to avoid becoming targets, but this order was widely ignored by old cruisers like these which weren't able to maintain that speed. Now I don't know whether this happened, but......' Briggs raised his eyebrows and shrugged nonchalantly.

Realising Lieutenant Briggs may have been talking out of turn in hinting that the command of the cruiser squadron was not all it should have been, Ernest acquiesced. 'I'll be extremely delicate in my questioning. Thank you.'

An embarrassed silence fell. Both filled the space by absorbing themselves in the frenetic activity in the lobby behind them as more casualties were moved into the wards, or mattresses laid out to fill every available space for new occupants.

'I realise it's very early to gain any idea of how many lives have been lost, or how many have survived, but......' Ernest held the young officer's gaze, leaving the question hanging in the air.

Briggs recovered his composure, seeming glad of the opportunity to impart purely factual information rather than dwell on the disaster and rumour about its cause. He pulled a hand-written list from his uniform trouser pocket.

'The nearest estimate of the losses from the three cruisers that one is able to form at present is,' he paused and bit his lower lip as though afraid to utter the terrible news, 'that one thousand four hundred are missing and between seven and eight hundred are accounted for.' He looked down at the list and read haltingly, 'Of these, three hundred have been brought into Harwich. Fifty of those are currently quartered on *HMS Dido*, between sixty and seventy have been taken to Parkston Quay and given accommodation on *HMS Woolwich*.

'There are about thirty officers at this hospital while another one hundred and twenty are being treated for their wounds at Shotley Barracks.' Briggs sighed deeply. 'That's all I can tell you at the moment. I've heard a number of chaps may have been picked up by Lowestoft trawlers and a couple of Dutch steamers have taken men to Holland.'

Each figure was carefully noted. Ernest checked his pocket watch. 'I'd best be getting around the wards. I'll not get in the way, I promise you.'

Briggs trusted the journalist to keep his word. Knew his confidence wouldn't be betrayed. 'Fine. I'm required back at the barracks, there's work to be done with the men taken there. I must leave you to find your own way around. Perhaps we'll meet again?'

'Of course. And thank you again. You've been most helpful. I realise these are trying times...' his serious eyes peered at Briggs over the rims of his spectacles yet he tried to smile encouragingly, feeling the young officer's anxiety. 'This war....' he faltered. 'It's taken a terrible toll of our ships. Where do you think it'll end?'

Briggs bit his lip again and grimaced an answer. As he wheeled away on well-polished boots and straightened his back, Ernest might otherwise have mistaken it for a gesture of arrogance or indifference had he not seen the strained lines on the aristocratic face. He watched him leave the hospital and head down to the quayside to hail the ferryman for a return trip to Shotley.

The first ward off the narrow, gloomy corridor was in a state of milling chaos. Men still soaked, hair and clothes straggling and sodden, lay waiting for their wounds to be bandaged. A few were being shuttled off to the operating theatre, but the remainder had a tormented wait. Doctors and nurses were too few to tend any except the most critically injured.

Exploding shrapnel and flying shards of metal had pierced and gouged their patients' faces, ripped gaping holes which the men's shipmates had desperately plugged with torn shirts, arms wrenched from uniform jackets – anything to hand. Yet there were few sounds to betray the pain and fear which hung about the ward. An occasional dull, breathless groan, a cry through clenched teeth, for the rest only a cool and tacit acceptance that this was the ironic hand war had dealt them.

It's a miracle any of them managed to swim or stay alive in the water with such terrible wounds, Ernest thought.

A knot of four or five men was sitting on a couple of the beds at the end of the ward, talking and smoking amongst themselves. He sidled up to them and nonchalantly put his hand on the shivering shoulder of a llama-jacketed officer. The man glanced up, expecting an orderly bearing hot drinks or food. None of them had eaten for many hours. His face fell with disappointment when he saw the slender figure leaning on a black walking cane, untidy blond hair dishevelled after his river crossing. Certainly not a young man with the bearing of an officer.

Ernest introduced himself. Several voices piped up with a cheerful 'Sit down. Come and join us. What do you want to know?'

'I've heard three cruisers were sunk by submarine torpedoes in the North Sea off Holland and that there've been a large number of casualties, but I know no more of this accident.'

'Accident you call it?' A lieutenant from *Aboukir*, huddled in a grey blanket, his thin, drawn face accentuating reddened eyes, leapt in immediately. 'It were no accident, I tell yer. It should never've happened. We should never have put to sea without the destroyers. The whole thing was a monumental blunder and our superiors know it. Other chaps in the service call us the 'Live Bait Squadron' and so we've proved. Hardly surprising the Hun found us an easy target.'

Another, sensing his bitterness, chimed in. 'I'm a Royal Naval Reserve Lieutenant with *Hogue*.' He held out a bloodied, bandaged hand to Ernest in greeting. 'It's hard to piece together exactly what happened, but I recall it was *Aboukir* that was struck first. On the port side. She quickly developed a twenty degree list and it was clear she was a lost cause and would soon turn turtle and sink. Only one of her boats survived, so her crew had to jump into the sea. It was a terrible sight.

'We all thought she'd hit a mine. So did her Captain, John Drummond, who signalled to both *Hogue* and *Cressy* to come closer close and help as we were only a few hundred yards behind her. We stopped and hoisted out our launch and lifeboats and sent them off. But as *Aboukir* rolled over and sank a submarine fired two torpedoes at *us*, hitting us amidships and flooding our engine room.' He choked back the tears as he recalled his own ship's demise.

An older officer, his dark moustache flecked with grey, touched him lightly on the arm. 'Let me tell him, old chap.' He smiled at Ernest and seemed to have accepted his ordeal with remarkable cheerfulness. ' Our Captain, Captain Wilmot Nicholson, ordered the men to grab what they could – hammocks, wood, furniture – that kind of thing – take off their clothes and get into the boats on the booms. As the ship heeled over the men in the port battery jumped overboard. Some, who feared they'd be pulled under as she lurched to starboard, clung on to whatever they could on the decks, but huge waves washed them away.'

'And what of *Cressy*? Was she able to get rescue boats to the men in the water?' Ernest asked.

'Huh!' A tall, willowy man leaning against the end of the iron-framed bed laughed, but there was no mirth in it. 'We sent all our boats from *Cressy* to pick up *Aboukir's* men. As they were returning to us *Hogue* was struck and it was then that I saw a periscope on our port bow about three hundred yards off. Well, we immediately put engines on full speed ahead to try to run the sub down. Our gunner was convinced he'd hit first the periscope and then the conning tower and that the sub had sunk. But I was standing alongside him and I'm sure the shell only struck floating timber.

'Five minutes later I saw another periscope on our starboard quarter. Then a torpedo struck us, but we remained steady. A second missed, but a quarter of an hour after the first they sent down a third. That's what finished us. It hit us in the boiler room. *Cressy* heeled rapidly and turned keel up. Thankfully we'd thrown all the mess tables and stools overboard and all the timber that was lying on deck, so the men had something to cling onto in the water. Many of them floated like that for hours before being rescued by cutters, steam pinnaces and trawlers. The Harwich light cruisers and destroyers arrived some time later and helped pick up survivors, too.'

Ernest wrote rapidly. 'Any idea how many submarines attacked you?'

A short, skinny young man sporting a borrowed jacket that swamped his narrow frame, said 'We guessed there were four or five, but it could have been one whose luck was in. A lone wolf picking us off, one by one. For sport.'

'And were you all rescued from the sea?'

'Most of us, yes,' said the senior man. 'I was lucky. Five men were clinging to the piece of floating wreckage I was hanging onto. One of them was the surgeon from *Cressy*, Dr Gerald Knowles Martin. He encouraged us to rub one anothers' legs alternately with our feet to keep the blood circulating and avoid losing warmth. God knows how we managed to hang on for so long. The waves were ten feet high.'

'After the *Cressy* was struck the second time, I heard our Captain, Capt'n Johnson, shout 'Every man for himself!' said the tall, willowy man. 'God. That was the most frightening thing I've ever heard anyone say in my entire life. I was washed off the deck by a big wave. Down and down I went, deep under the water. I'm not a strong swimmer and I thought I'd drowned. That I'd never come up again. But something within me propelled me upwards. The will to survive, I suppose. As soon as I got to the surface I took a deep breath and struck out to avoid being drawn under by the suction. The last I saw of the *Cressy* she was keel up with perhaps fifty men clinging to her. Some supported themselves on hammocks, but after a time the hammocks became waterlogged and dragged them down. That was it,' he said philosophically.

'The last I saw of our Captain, Captain Johnson, he was in the water trying to swim away from the *Cressy* as she sank,' said another. 'Even then he was thinking of others, like he always did. I heard him instructing the men around him to keep their mouths closed and breathe through their noses. I fear many of them couldn't swim.'

'After Capt'n Johnson gave the order "Every man for himself!" the sea was alive with men, struggling and grasping onto whatever they could to support themselves,' said the willowy man, now leaning against the ledge of the long window at the end of the ward, feverishly puffing on a pipe. 'To make matters worse the Germans kept firing at us. It was a sight I'll never forget.'

A well-built man, an engineer, wandered up to join the group. He was anxious to tell Ernest of his experiences, his close brush with death. 'I spent three hours, three whole hours, floating on a piece of wreckage with another man after *Hogue* went down,' he said. 'We were quickly swept far away from the steam pinnaces and rescue boats and were beginning to give up hope when we spotted the sails of a couple of Lowestoft trawlers in the distance. I was all for letting go a'the plank and swimming for it, but my friend stopped me. He said I'd be a bloody fool if I did. The sail was at least five miles away. Luckily though, the trawler *Coriander* saw us and picked us up. We were almost dead with exhaustion, I can tell you.' He shuddered at the recollection.

'She rescued other chaps, too. The master, Captain Phillips, and his crew picked up one hundred and fifty officers and men altogether. The surgeon you mentioned, they found him and pulled him aboard after he'd spent more than two hours in the water.

'We were sailing back towards Lowestoft along a'the other trawler, the *JCC*, when *HMS Lowestoft* came alongside. She send a launch to take us off the fishing boats. That's how we ended up back here in Harwich,' he explained.

'And what of the doctor? The surgeon, you met on board? Was he injured too?' asked Ernest.

'No, I don't think so,' he answered. 'Otherwise he'd be here in this hospital with us, and I've not seen him. He's most likely helping the doctors tend the men taken to the hospital in Shotley Barracks – that's the sort of chap he is. He wouldn't sit back and do nothing when there's so much going on.'

The lieutenant in the llama jacket, who was from *Aboukir*, looked at the others thoughtfully. 'And what became of all the young midshipmen? I've not seen none in here so far. I fear we may have lost a few. After we were struck I saw Midshipman Wykeham-Musgrave – one of the cadets, he's only about fifteen - swimming towards *Hogue* for all he was worth. I could see he was a strong swimmer. I was relieved to see him pulled on board. But what happened to him when *Hogue* sank? Poor lad. Like the rest of us, I suppose. Swept back into the water he'd thought he'd escaped from.'

'Well, I think young Wykeham-Musgrave was one of the lucky ones,' chimed the engineer from *Hogue*. 'He was among the *Aboukir* chaps who we took aboard. When we were struck, too, he jumped from the deck, like I did, and swam for it. I saw his head bobbing up a couple of times as he struck out for the *Cressy.*'

'Yes, that's right, he did make it and he's here in this hospital,' said the tall, elegant officer. 'One of the Red Cross nurses I was chatting to told me. He's in the top-floor ward, along with some other cadets. She was pretty shocked to find such young boys among the casualties, I can tell you.

'He told her it had been a thrilling experience and that being shipwrecked three times in one morning must be something of a naval record! It seems he was joking about it, so he must be feeling pretty chipper. I gather that when *Cressy* was hit he got clear and after swimming about for a long time found a plank to hang onto with one of *Hogue's* Midshipmen. The Dutch trawler, *Titan*, picked the two lads up several hours later, along with about 300 other survivors. That's how they all came to be here in Harwich. They transferred from the fishing boat to a destroyer which brought them in.'

Ernest was shocked. 'How many of these little boys were on your ships?'

'A fair number,' answered the llama-jacketed lieutenant. 'They were mobilized from Dartmouth. I, for one, don't think they should be afloat during engagements with the enemy. This isn't Nelson's war, yer know. This is the twentieth century. In my opinion they should be training ashore so that when the war's over we have a ready supply of young officers who can take up the duties which others, through death or injury, have relinquished.'

'But it's tradition. It's the Navy's custom to have budding young officers on board ship in wartime,' objected the senior officer. 'There must be at least a thousand midshipmen and cadets in His Majesty's ships – all prepared to lay down their lives for King and country. Like the rest of us.'

Ernest sat with his mouth open in amazement, about to ask further questions, but the conversation was interrupted by the welcome sight of an orderly ladling soup from a tureen into enamel bowls. The group drifted away one by one, glad of the diversion.

Ernest slipped his notebook into his jacket pocket and reached under one of the beds for his cane. As he limped awkwardly between the rows of beds he nodded a thanks to each man he'd spoken to. He'd found their calmness, their philosophical acceptance of what the enemy had meted out to them, before they'd even had the chance to fire a single shot in this war, astonishing.

As he went to open the door to the ward a nearby voice called him. He stopped and looked round. The man was obviously a senior ranking officer. His presence, like his tone of voice, was commanding.

'The Germans got the better of us for once. But just you wait. Our turn will come before long.' He sounded positive, almost cheerful. Ernest moved closer. The officer grinned widely at him. 'I hope I can get a ship tomorrow. I just want to get my own back with them,' and with that he gave Ernest an airy wave of a left arm encased in bandages.

Ernest pushed open the double doors at the entrance to the Great Eastern Hotel and paused on the topmost stone step. He was grateful for the brief moment of solitude to gather his thoughts, with this view across the river, while he waited for John.

As he did so a short, sturdy man in a motley assortment of clothes, including a ship's cap that wasn't his own, but had been given to him by one of the *HMS Ganges* lads, caught him up.

'Off now?' the seaman asked, as he stopped to light a cigarette.

'Yes. How about you?' Ernest replied. He saw the young man was carrying a small bundle under his arm.

'Going for the four o'clock train, home for a spot of leave. Back to Chatham, to wait until they find me another ship.'

Standing face to face in the autumn sunshine Ernest was horrified at the extent of the sailor's injuries. His entire face was covered in a bloodied cross-stitching of cuts. From his forehead, eyebrows and eyelids down his nose and cheeks to his chin there was barely an eighth of an inch of pink flesh left unblemished by the exploding torrent of metal, glass and wood.

Ernest smiled sympathetically. 'Been in a bit of a fight I see.'

The seaman put a hand up to his mutilated cheek. 'A fight yer call it? No, it wasn't no fight. They caught us completely by surprise. No, no,' he shook his head. 'That's not what I call a decent, honourable fight. Not like in Nelson's day when ships did battle fair and square. No, no. The enemy simply picked us off one by one, just as he felt like it. Almost contemptuous of us, he was. Taking potshots at ducks on a fairground stall couldn't have been any easier.'

Ernest murmured something inconsequential and surreptitiously took out his notebook and pencil.

'We'd been parading from a certain spot to another place, going to and fro for days and turning almost at the same place and about the same time. They'd doubtless been watching us. They knew when to make the attack. This was the first time our destroyers hadn't been with us. If they'd been with us this job wouldn't have happened. We'd have had the chance to fight back. As it was.......' he petered out, his emotions wrapping around the words he struggled to retrieve from his traumatised mind.

'We thought the *Aboukir* was mined and hurried to their assistance and got a broadside for our trouble. When the *Aboukir* and the *Hogue* had gone down the sea appeared full of men, floating in the water and everywhere was strewn with wreckage. A submarine came right up amongst them. The *Cressy* opened fire and I'm sure she sank one, if not two, before she herself caught one amidships and she, too, was put below. There certainly was no fight in it.'

There was no cheerful acceptance in this officer, only bitterness. Bitterness at the loss of so many men, so many close comrades. Bitterness at the loss of his ship and that it hadn't been in a fair fight.

John joined them and they walked together in silence to the station, where crowds of onlookers were waiting to cheer the survivors onto the special train awaiting them.

Ernest wondered if the seaman had yet chanced to see his face in a mirror. He imagined his shock when he caught a first glimpse of himself in a shop window or reflected back as he gazed from the train window out across the yellow, harvested fields.

And what of the reaction of his wife and children, if he were fortunate enough to have them? Ernest thought. His wife would touch the deeply-pitted gouges in his face with the tenderness of a loving woman, gently patting her precious cold cream into each raw wound to speed the healing process.

But his children would be repulsed by the stranger at the door, hiding behind their mother's skirts as they faced the demon they'd so often conjured up in their worst nightmares.

East Anglian Daily Times

Thursday September 24 1914

Packed like sardines. Lowestoft trawler saves 350 men.

Considerable excitement was evinced in Lowestoft yesterday when the trawler *JCC* was towed into the harbour with 34 rescued men from the naval disaster, including two officers. The men were received on board *HMS Spanker* and later the skipper, George Jacob, told his story of the disaster.

'We were,' he said, 'fishing 65 miles south-east of Lowestoft and about seven o'clock on Tuesday morning saw three cruisers sink. We were quite close and saw the first ship go down in about six minutes. The second remained afloat about two minutes and the third did not see more than two or three minutes. We cut our trawl and went to try to save life. We could see many chaps in the water and picked up about 350 altogether. Some we took from the water and others reached us in boats.

'Our vessel was soon as full of men as she could be. We were packed on deck like sardines in a tin and those we could not take on board we towed astern in boats and launches. There was a call for volunteers to go in a launch to pick up other men from the water and my third hand, W. Chapman, went with two naval men. We had no more tidings of them.

'About an hour and a half later we saw two trading steamers and after we had gone ten miles towards Lowestoft we saw *HMS Lowestoft* and about six destroyers with her. We loaded a launch with 150 men to put aboard her, but the *Lowestoft* told us he had sighted a submarine and would scout about for a time. After about ten minutes she found it was safe to take the men aboard and we sent nearly all the men to her and some to the torpedo boats. When about five miles from Lowestoft we sighted the patrol boat *Spider* and as there was no wind she towed us to Lowestoft.'

Chapter Fourteen

Friday September 25 1914

'What's *that?*'

John was turfing pencils, notebook and cigarette packet from the pockets of the brown jacket he'd hung on the coatstand. He threw each item carelessly onto the nearest desk as he burrowed into the depths, seeking a box of matches. As he did so a small, white feather hung momentarily in the air behind him before floating to the floor. There it settled, curled amidst discarded newspapers and pencil shavings.

'What's what, Alf?' John turned, clutching the matches, and glanced absently at the chief reporter.

'That.' Alf pointed to the floor. 'It fell out of your pocket.'

John looked in the direction Alf was pointing. His face immediately coloured with embarrassment. 'I..I..I'm sure I don't know.'

'Oh, I think you do,' Alf chided knowingly.

Stan, sitting nearest the door, shuffled his chair forward and bent to pick it up. 'Well, well! What have we here, then? Could it possibly be a white feather?' He held it close to his freckled nose in an exaggerated way, as though intent on examining it more closely. 'Well, my goodness me! So it is. A white feather, eh? Huh!' he sneered. 'Given to you by a young lady, if I'm not mistaken.'

'Er... well... yes.' John wasn't sure whether he should admit to ownership of the feather or not.

'So, *you* got one too, did yer?' With that George, who'd whipped round in his chair as soon as he heard the words "white feather", tugged open his desk drawer and pulled out a larger white feather. His appeared to be a tail feather whereas John's had the downy appearance of one plucked from a bird's breast.

'I got given *this* one yesterday,' There was bitterness in his voice. 'From a young lady a-standing outside a'the station. She sidles up to me, all flirty-like and I thought she were a-goin' ter get fresh with me. "Ho, ho! Me luck's changed!" I thought.

'Then she says, "Why's a fine, athletic young man like you not in khaki yet?" and thrust this in me 'and. It left me a bit speechless, like. So I just shrugs me shoulders and walks away. Huh! Well. She didn't like that. Not one bit. She starts a-yelling and a-shouting after me. "Yer should be in Kitchener's New Army!" said she. "You a coward or a cripple?" said she. Everyone getting off the train heard her, she were makin' such a fuss and a toodoo. What must they a-thought o'me?'

Hearing he wasn't alone, John looked relieved. 'Yes, it were a pretty young lady gave it t 'me, too. This morning. I was just getting off the tram and she came up to me. Nicely spoken lady, too. Educated-like. A girl like that, I was a bit surprised. Approaching men she don't know. What would her ma say?'

'It's the war, stupid,' Alf huffed. 'The White Feather Brigade. It's idiotic young women giving out white feathers to young men who haven't joined the army. It's a new thing they've come up with to try and shame chaps into joining up. They're all over the country, not just here.'

George clenched his thin lips so they disappeared beneath his moustache. 'I tell yer, it's not right. I'm no coward, but she made me feel dreadful. Ashamed. I tell yer, I was bloody upset by it.'

'There's no need. Don't be bullied into doing something you don't feel is right.' Ernest's quiet tones came from the doorway where he stood leaning on his stick. They turned to look at him and in their upturned faces he saw the pained expressions of men treading a wary path through a wholly new and unexpected minefield.

'A chap must do what he feels best able to do. Three have already gone from this office, so wouldn't you think that'ud be enough? And God knows what earthly use those three'll be. None of them has ever held a gun before let alone been trained to use one. Perhaps we should all remember the saying 'the pen is mightier than the sword' and see that by reporting the war as faithfully and accurately as we can, we're helping the war effort just as much as any fighting man.'

'Well said, Ernie.' A rush of relief spread around Alf's rosy cheeks. The others nodded.

John twitched a thumb in the direction of the editor's office and in awed tones said, 'Have you been.....down there....with 'im?'

'Yeeesss,' Ernest drew the word out to an exaggerated length and with it a sigh of intense exasperation. 'I'm afraid so. The Chief's just taken a call from Captain Mayne. He wants to see me. At the police station. Now.' There was a weariness in his voice that betrayed his misgivings at a confrontation that was none of his choosing.

'What's all that about?' Alf enquired, wondered if Ernest wasn't in some sort of trouble.

'I'm not sure, but according to the Chief, Captain Mayne's in a terrible temper. The worst he's ever heard. His language was *most* intemperate. Ranting and raging about the piece in this morning's paper about the German submarines and the three ships sunk in the North Sea. What he thinks *I* can do about it, heaven only knows.'

'Oh dear.' Alf grinned as encouragingly as he could. 'Glad it's you got to go and not me, Ernie.'

The roar of the Chief's voice echoing down the corridor, the sharp tap-tapping of his stick on the bare wooden boards like the Crocodile's warning, sent chairs scraping back to desks so that when he arrived at the door he found his reporters with heads bowed over notebooks and newspapers or fingers flying vigorously over the keys.

'Right Hart! Best get off to see the Chief Constable now. Mustn't keep *him* waiting, even though you deem it acceptable to be late for me!' There was a note of sarcasm in his voice and he laughed, but without humour.

'Yes Chief,' Ernest murmured, hastily stuffing a notebook and pencils into his pockets then grabbing his black cane.

'Here. Take the last couple of day's papers with you. You may need to refer to them,' Sir Frederick took them from under his arm and handed them to his chief reporter.

'Thank you, I suspect I might.'

Ernest was ushered into the Chief Constable's large office on the first floor of County Hall to find Jasper Mayne and his deputy, Superintendent George Staunton, standing deep in conversation as they peered from a long sash window into the cobbled courtyard beneath. On one side of the quadrangle was the police station, at right angles to it the county jail and the two adjoining sides were devoted to offices of the county council.

Ernest had come across Superintendent Staunton several times before in his reporting career, usually while covering criminal investigations or court proceedings. He'd always got on well with the senior officer, who was amiable and quietly-spoken, although Ernest suspected that beneath the unassuming exterior beat an ambitious heart.

He and Ernest were about the same age. Ernest reckoned Staunton to be about 28 and having already made it to superintendent he was almost certain of advancement up the constabulary heirarchy. An advancement which would take him ultimately to the top job. Mayne's job. Yet he didn't present as formidable or as charismatic a figure as Mayne. Short and slight, his dark hair close-cropped and with a fine dark moustache that accentuated deep-set eyes, he had the long, narrow, elegant face and smooth complexion of a romantic.

As Ernest was shown into the dark pannelled room, lined with shelves of files and legal manuals, it was Staunton who turned and stretched out his hand.

'Mr Hart, come in, come in. Glad you could get here so promptly.' He waved him to a hard wooden seat in front of the Chief Constable's desk and sauntered round to take a chair on the opposite side.

Mayne, meanwhile settled into a leather armchair beside the window, having barely nodded a welcome to the reporter. Hart wondered who would conduct this interview and who would be the driving force behind it.

'Now then, now then,' Staunton was thinking aloud as he shuffled papers, searching for a place to begin. He looked up and smiled at Ernest, pulling from the bottom of the pile that morning's copy of the East Anglian Daily Times. 'Ah, here it is. Yes. Now, this report of the sinking of the *HMS Aboukir*, *Hogue* and *Cressy*.'

'Yes?'

'Well, I'm sorry to say there are several points in your eye-witness report with which we'd take issue. Perhaps you'd like me to explain what they are and why we think they're most unhelpful to the Suffolk Constabulary at this present time of national emergency?'

'Yes, by all means.' Ernest wondered what Staunton was driving at. He quickly flipped the paper open at his report from Harwich, which included interviews with several of the injured sailors.

'From what you've written here,' Staunton jabbed his finger at the centre pages, 'you seem to be implying that the loss of these three ships was due to grievous errors by our own Royal Navy. That it was the fault of Navy commanders that the destroyers, which normally protect these ships, stayed in port while the cruisers, notwithstanding the gales, had been ordered to sea.'

'Yes.'

'And do you think that's wise?'

'Wise?' Ernest considered Staunton's use of the word. He peeled off his spectacles and chewed the end of a wire arm for a moment. '*Wise*? Well, if you mean is it *true,* then yes, I think it was. Why?'

Staunton pursed his lips, hollowing his cheeks so that the fine cheekbones became even more pronounced. 'When I say *wise* what I mean is, was it *sensible* for you to write something that would, inevitably, lower the morale of those who read it, the populace here in Suffolk? Put them in fear of the enemy at their door and instill in them a lack of confidence in our Navy and its leaders, not to mention our own fighting men?'

Ernest heard the leather armchair behind him squeak as Jasper Mayne shifted impatiently. Turning his head slightly he saw the Chief Constable's mouth twist in an involuntary gesture of agreement with what his Superintendent was saying. His ice-grey eyes narrowed and as they did so the corners wrinkled into dark crevices, giving him a predatory appearance.

Ernest realised that the ill feeling pervading the room, which had been generated by the newspaper report, was now directed personally against him, as its author.

'That's not what I intended.' He swivelled his gaze back to Staunton.

'But it could be construed as such.'

'I only reported what I'd been told by the men themselves. Particularly the officers who'd been rescued and who were being treated for their injuries in hospital at Harwich.'

'Soooo,' the policeman hesitated. 'Why did you emphasis *blame* for this incident, rather than dwell on the bravery of the men who found themselves in this dreadful predicament?' Staunton's face was now devoid of any amiableness and the menace in his voice was all the more effective for it being delivered with quiet evenness.

'I beg to disagree,' Ernest replied. 'If you read Thursday's report, here.' He stopped and for what seemed an agonising age rustled the pages of the paper back and forth, folding and re-folding until he came to his account.

'You'll find that I say something along the lines that the men had born the situation with wonderful coolness and were exceptionally cheery in the circumstances. I also wrote, just as I'd been told, that the officers stood at their posts and gave commands as though on some grand manoevres and the men cheerfully obeyed. And here I say,' Ernest cleared his throat self-consciously before he quoted verbatim, '"The captain of one of the ill-fated ships remained at his post until the decks were awash. He went down with the ship, but being a powerful swimmer he was able to keep afloat, though he was rescued almost exhausted". These are indeed reports of exceptional bravery and high morale in the most trying circumstances.'

'But see here,' George Staunton picked up his copy of that morning's paper and held it in front of Ernest, tapping several times at the page. 'Today's paper. Under the headline "Survivors leave Harwich. More thrilling rescue stories". You say that if the destroyers had been with the convoy, as normal, these ships would never have fallen prey to German submarines. You're implying that the fourteen hundred men who died would still be alive, and three of our ships wouldn't now be at the bottom of the ocean, if the Admirals and Commanders who make these decisions hadn't made such an elementary blunder.'

'That's what I was told. It's not something I invented, I can assure you.'

'I'm not implying you made it up, but this is a heinous slander on the British Navy and its commanders!' George Staunton banged his forehead with the heel of his hand in exasperation. He was beginning to dislike Hart's dogged calmness. He bent his elegantly-uniformed chest across the desk and held Ernest's gaze in unblinking interrogation.

'Who do you think you are? You, a mere newspaper reporter. What can *you* possibly know of naval strategy?'

In reply Ernest took his notebook from his jacket pocket. 'I admit to knowing nothing of military matters, but I always take a verbatim note of everything people tell me,' he said, flicking back several pages. 'It's what Sir Frederick demands of all his staff. He believes it's the only way to write accurate and interesting reports. I can point you, if you wish, to the exact phrases used by the seamen I spoke to.

'In fact I was told a great deal more about the way these cruisers were operating off the coast of Holland. About how they failed to adhere to orders to keep the ships to a speed of thirteen knots and proceed in a zigzag pattern so the enemy couldn't get a fix on them. Neither did I use the opinion of one of the *Cressy's* officers that had *Cressy* and *Hogue* adhered to *military* considerations rather than humanitarian ones, they'd have quickly turned tail when *Aboukir* sank, consigning the *Aboukir's* men to a certain watery grave, in order to save their own vessels and skins. But since this information was given to me in the greatest confidence I didn't make a note of it and so didn't use it in my article.' He looked up from his notes, peering over his wire spectacles at the handsome face opposite.

'Huh.' Staunton shifted his eyes momentarily to the Chief Constable sitting with tense erectness in the leather armchair. 'I've no doubt that an Admiralty court of enquiry will investigate this entire incident in due course and reach its own conclusions. Nevertheless, we – Captain Mayne and I – consider it irresponsible to print anything that might undermine public confidence in those who're executing this war.'

Ernest thought this was an end to the grilling and rose from his seat to leave, but Staunton was merely changing tack.

'Now then. There's another matter on which we feel you've been somewhat negligent and which now demands to be rectified and immediately impressed upon the general public.'

With this he nodded at Jasper Mayne, cueing him to intervene in the conversation. Ernest turned to face the Chief Constable, wondering how much more criticism he could bear without buckling into total subservience.

'Mr Hart, I've read these articles most carefully.' Jasper Mayne leaned forward in the armchair until his knees were almost touching Ernest's shins. On his lap he had open a leather-bound police notebook which he now refered to. 'And there's a significant comment from one of the officers you interviewed which points, absolutely conclusively, to the work of spies in this sorry incident. You write that this chap tells you the Germans had "doubtless been watching us. They knew when to make the attack".' Mayne's finger traced along the handwritten note he'd made. 'Now does that not reveal conclusively that the enemy had prior knowledge of when this convoy of ships was leaving port and whence it was sailing?'

The reporter hesitated. 'I think, sir, the officer meant that because the ships had stuck to a regular course day after day, turning at the same hour, they'd made their presence known to the enemy.'

'Absolute balderdash!' Mayne leapt from his chair and paced the room. 'I've never heard anything so preposterous. It's as plain as the nose on your face. This had to be the work of *spies*. Or possibly one single spy, working alone. How else would German submarines have known where our ships were heading for? Don't you realise, man, there are enemies not only within our gates, but frequenting areas where they're forbidden, such as the naval bases in Shotley and Harwich? There should have been a clean sweep of alien enemies from within this coastal area weeks ago, but it appears they're still with us.'

'If that's the case, how do you propose identifying these people?' Ernest shot a glance between Mayne, who was standing full-square with hands on hips, blocking the light from the window, and Staunton, who'd momentarily slumped back in his chair.

Staunton was first to answer. 'It's certainly a problem and I doubt the ordinary police officer would know how to deal with it. The alien spy, almost by virtue of his occupation, is usually a very insidious creature. Often those who may be the least suspected by their immediate circle of acquaintances turn out to be the most dangerous. I believe the suggestion made in the House of Lords the other day by Lord Leith of Fife, that more vigorous steps should be taken for rounding up alien enemies, particularly applies to our own part of the East coast.

'There shouldn't be a native of the countries we're at war with permitted to be at large in the prohibited area, even if they've been naturalised. These men might well have retained associations with their former compatriots. They may have strong family ties with near and dear relations fighting for the Kaiser and Fatherland. I think that makes them dangerous and they should be suspect.'

'That's possibly a logical conclusion to draw,' Ernest said mildly, rubbing the lenses of his glasses against his shirt-front.

'Oh, they're very clever, these spies,' Captain Mayne moved closer to him. 'The better educated they are the more dangerous they're likely to be. It needs a clever man to make a good spy. We've had hundreds of them living amongst us for years in places like Harwich, Felixstowe, Ipswich, Yarmouth and Lowestoft. In fact all along the East Anglian seaboard. Some of them are long since naturalised and have become well-known and well-regarded members of this community.'

The Chief Constable's tone grew more menacing. Ernest refused to look at him, concentrating instead on the notes he was making.

'Sometimes they teach our youth at public schools. They've joined our clubs and public bodies. They've even become Territorials and have free access to all the sources of information open to loyal Britons. Many have become, in manner and appearance, if not more British than true Britons. At any rate, superficially unrecognisable from the genuine article.' Mayne paused for breath, his face reddened and contorted with anger. He tweaked the ends of his neat grey moustache nervously between forefingers and thumbs as he fought to regain control.

Ernest felt this tirade was meant not so much as a personal rebuke but as a primer for action. 'So, what are you expecting of me? I assume that's why you've asked me to come and see you? To write something concerning alien enemies for the Daily Times?'

Staunton nodded. 'Yes, Mr Hart. We'd appreciate it if you could draw the attention of your readers to the possibility there may be a spy in their community. It is, after all, the bounden duty of every individual who suspects another of being in association with the enemy to communicate the fact to the authorities. I appreciate that there's a natural feeling of repugnance under ordinary circumstances and conditions to acting on suspicion and vague rumour to the extent of informing the police. But these aren't times for ordinary scruples.'

Ernest scribbled rapidly in his own idiosyncratic mix of shorthand and abbreviated words as Staunton spoke. A verbatim note was essential, he'd decided. It would be his only protection against the ire of the Chief Constable. For now he'd set aside his own scepticism about the existence of spies, his belief that spy-mania was being generated by hysteria and ignorance. This was far too important an issue on which he, alone, should make a decision. He'd write his report as accurately and faithfully as possible and leave it to Sir Frederick to decide what to publish.

He looked up to see the Chief Constable looming over him, both heavy knuckles curled against the edge of the desk as he stood inches from his shoulder.

'Now, Mr Hart,' Mayne's lowered voice was ominous. 'We come to an even baser kind of man against whom we have little protection. I refer to traitors who call themselves Englishmen and are so by birth, but who've entered into a Judas-like compact to betray their country. Men who've cultivated business relations with our enemy, who've lived in their countries for a long time and who've entertained their people. These men are sometimes dragged into a devilish conspiracy, through greed of gold.

'For these spies no punishment could be too severe. But they're the hardest of all to find, not merely because of their numerical insignificance, but also because so few of us would suspect their intentions.'

Staunton sat back, nodding agreement.

Ernest wondered if he were hearing aright. *True born Englishmen, spying for Germany? Are these policemen mad?* He'd noted every word, yet found it beyond belief.

Mayne dragged him back from his misgivings. 'I repeat: all the precautions which can be taken should be taken. Among these are the clearing out from the prohibited area of all natives of the enemies' countries, whether naturalised or not. Have you *got* that, Mr Hart?' He banged a fist on the desk in emphasis.

Ernest flinched visibly. 'Yes sir. But if the Daily Times publishes such a report what effect d'you think it'll have? How can people possibly know who may be a spy and who may not?'

'I would hope that the populace of every town, village and hamlet in Suffolk will examine carefully every single member of their community, English born or not. Cast back in their minds who might have been to Germany, who might have German friends, who may have a German relative, even by marriage. Then we must rely on their consciences to dictate that as true and loyal Englishmen they will report those aliens and traitors to us,' he replied. He raised an eyebrow at Staunton, seeking acquiescence.

Staunton moved his head slightly as though to signal the lowering of a curtain on the performance.

'You're asking people to spy on each other? To report to the police a friend or colleague or neighbour who they suspect might have Germanic connections, however tenuous?' Ernest tried to suppress the outrage in his voice.

'Exactly,' the superintendent replied without hesitation.

'And if these people should *mistakenly* accuse someone? If the police or military take action against a so-called spy in error? What recourse does that person have?'

Mayne puffed his chest out and flexed his powerful shoulders. 'We're at war, Mr Hart. The Defence of the Realm Act makes it very clear that any action we may take will be for the greater good. This is a national emergency in which the nation's security is paramount. Individual freedoms and rights are subservient. They count for - *nothing.*' He flicked his fingers in arrogant dismissal.

Ernest slid his notebook into his pocket. 'I see.' He peered over the spectacles which had slipped down his nose. It was a glare of calculated insolence.

'I think that will be all, Mr Hart. At least for the time being.' Interview over, Superintendent Staunton abruptly extended a well-manicured hand in farewell.

Ernest gathered up his newspapers, notebook and the cane he'd propped against the Chief Constable's desk and bade both men a subdued 'Good morning.'

East Anglian Daily Times

Wednesday October 7 1914

Howitzer Brigade. Men are still wanted.

From an announcement it appears men are still wanted for the 3rd East Anglian Howitzer Brigade RFA, of which the Earl of Stradbroke is the Colonel. For this branch of soldiering men accustomed to or fond of horses are specially needed. They must be men of good intelligence. If they cannot ride when they join they are taught and they will find field gunnery is quite interesting work. For the position of driver the men need not be more than 5 foot 4 inches and a good man would not be rejected if he were even a little below that height. If a man attains 5 foot 6 inches he may aspire to the position of gunner.

We are glad to learn that a very good class of man is coming forward and the reserve battery is gradually filling up, but the reminder that more are wanted will probably bring them along a little faster. Capt Norman Everett, who is in charge at the RFA barracks in Ipswich will be glad to have his numbers complete. Recruits are also being received at Lowestoft where Lieut H A Adnams of Southwold is in charge. The men at the barracks in Ipswich are going on with their training as far as possible and as the clothing and equipment comes along for them they join the brigade camp at Bury St Edmunds.

In reply to the congratulations from the Brigade forwarded by telegram to Field Marshal Earl Roberts on his 82nd birthday, the Commander, Earl Stradbroke, has received the following: "Please accept yourself and express to all ranks of the 3rd EA Howitzer Brigade my best thanks for your and their kind congratulations on my birthday".

Chapter Fifteen

Thursday October 15 1914

Helena paused in the doorway to the ballroom at the start of her morning rounds, scanning the tidy rows of iron-framed beds. In each one lay a wounded soldier or sailor. It was the same in the drawing room and the music room, her husband's snug and the dining room. Sixty beds filled the ground floor reception rooms of Henham Hall and now 55 of them were occupied.

There was no mistaking her for the dozen or so other nurses, swishing ghost-like from patient to patient. She wore the red canton cotton dress which marked her rank of Honorary Commandant, a regulation long white, linen apron and unstarched white cambric cap, pinned in a fantail at the back of her neck.

As she moved from one bedside to the next, men who had been casualties of the French and Belgian battlefields or the mine-strewn North Sea, acknowledged her presence with a 'your ladyship' or 'ma'am'. They automatically raised a hand to touch their forehead or lift an imagined cap. With each she took time to enquire about their progress and the doctor's prognosis. She asked each one about when their wives and mothers might be able to travel to see them and whether they needed money to help pay their relatives' rail fares.

The men were from every part of Britain, having fought with Scottish regiments as well as English. There were even two Frenchmen; a sergeant with the 2nd Chasseurs à Pieds, who'd had a French bullet removed, and a private with the same regiment.

She alone ran the military hospital. Without her husband at her side she bore a terrible responsibility. As Colonel of the 3rd East Anglian Howitzer Brigade, the Earl had volunteered his men for foreign service and was now awaiting the call to France at the brigade's quarters in Middlesex. She was dreading the day when he'd telephone to bid her and the children farewell. But for the moment she put that thought out of her head. She had more than enough to occupy her.

When she'd persuaded George to turn Henham Hall into a hospital, she'd little guessed what a monumental, all-consuming endeavour it would prove. There had been scant funds to meet either its running costs or the wages of the doctors and nurses. As a voluntary Red Cross hospital it received no assistance whatever from the Red Cross so Helena spent much of her time begging gifts from wealthy friends and writing letters to newspapers soliciting donations of all kinds to help her patients.

She especially needed medical aids: dressings, lint, cotton wool, gangey and gauze, invalid chairs, baths, air cushions and ambulances. She cajoled at public meetings for food, groceries and health supplements such as malt extract, cod liver oil and port wine. She appealed for night-shirts and clothing to be sent to the hospital. She begged for 300 pairs of socks. Everything, she said, was welcomed, but especially money. She promised that anything sent to her that wasn't required for immediate use at Henham would be forwarded at once to the English Hospital in France.

Helena even made an appeal in the press on behalf of her husband's men, stationed in Barnes, with no club or entertainment nearby. 'Gramaphones and games, etc, are badly needed. Also blankets and shirts,' she wrote.

She was surprised at how easily she'd overcome her scruples about writing begging letters. Acquaintances, especially those in high places, found her letters amusing and indulged her. The general public, reading her torrent of letters to the newspapers, thought it endearing and succumbed with an outpouring of generosity. She herself had, after all, been quick to respond generously to charitable appeals. When it had been revealed the previous Christmas that the cat-loving Countess has subscribed five shillings to the Ipswich Cats Shelter they'd warmed to her, feeling she was one of them rather than a remote member of the aristocracy.

Sister Methold was coming to an end of her rounds with Dr Mullock when she found Helena seated on the edge of one of the beds in the small ward, which had been created in George's study for the most critically injured. It was occupied by an infantryman from the 2nd Argyll and Southern Highlanders, severely wounded in the chest and spine during the battle of Le Cateau. He lay motionless as she held his large, red hand softly in hers.

'We'll get you home to Scotland soon, very soon,' she said, but there was no answer.

Sister Methold looked pityingly at the Countess and shook her head slowly. Her message was clear; the Scot would be with them for a long time yet. She doubted if he'd ever move his limbs again.

'We're expecting more casualties over the next few days,' Helena said, leaving the soldier to his half-conscious nightmares and joining the two medics standing at the foot of his bed.

'Heaven knows where we're going to put them. We've only five empty beds left and unless we can discharge some of the less seriously injured then we won't be able to admit them,' said Sister Methold sternly.

'I know, I know. But we can't refuse, can we? We'll simply have to find extra beds and nurses if that's the case. The London hospital is already full and so is the Ipswich and East Suffolk. If it weren't for Red Cross hospitals like ours and Lady Byng's I simply dread to think what would become of these men.'

Sister Methold shot a grim look at Dr Mullock. 'We'll see. Perhaps Dr Mullock and I could re-examine each man's record to see if we can't send some of them elsewhere.' With that the two of them left the small ward, its half-dozen patients in turn groaning and shifting their limbs painfully beneath the cool white sheets.

How familiar this room is, thought Helena, *yet how unfamiliar.* The shabby sun-bleached velvet curtains hanging beside the French windows overlooking the terrace, the Earl's favourite armchair now pushed into a corner. Although the dog's favourite rug had been rolled up and stored in the attic with the rest of the furniture, George's books still lined the walls. She fingered the rows of volumes, undecided on which to lift from its dusty resting place.

Which one was George's favourite? It would be nothing too erudite or taxing. 'This one,' she murmured to herself and lifted out a plain bound book from the shelf full of farming manuals. '"The breeding of Suffolk Punches". That's it.' She turned the pages with their grubby, well-thumbed corners, pages of drawings and diagrams and advice on how to breed horses with larger hooves more suitable for working the Suffolk soil.

At heart her husband wasn't a soldier but a farmer. He would, she felt quite sure, cheerfully abandon the aristocratic trappings, the position at court, the honour of being ADC to the King and instead absorb himself in his hobbies; breeding horses, cattle and sheep. Perhaps, she smiled, she should include breeding children in those passions, too. This was how she loved to think of George; slouched in his mother's old armchair absorbed in a dusty farming manual.

She replaced the book where she'd found it. Then quietly, so as not to wake the sleeping forms, pushed open the French windows and stepped onto the terrace.

From here she had a wide view of the lawns and the expanse of parkland beyond. She could hear the methodical 'clack, clack' of shears as a couple of gardeners trimmed hedges and neatened borders in readiness for the autumn. Soon the trees in the park would turn amber and gold and the air would be full of the smell of bonfires. How the children loved those days, kicking through drifts of leaves on expeditions into the woods. With George leading the search for fungi, they'd compete loudly for the honour of discovering the first hedgehog or dormouse hibernating among the hollowed roots of one of the old trees.

A game of cricket was in progress on the lawn nearest the terrace. The patients had conjured up a bat and ball. A set of stumps had been driven into the manicured grass. Assembled from a kitbag or two, she guessed.

More than a dozen soldiers and sailors in various states of injury and incapacity, were intent on the game. She watched in amusement as the bowler hobbled gamely to the crease, letting fly at the batsman at the end closest to her. The batsman, leaning heavily on a wooden crutch jammed under his left armpit, was forced to wield the bat one-handed in an ungainly attempt to score runs. He'd recruited a more agile team-mate, swathed in head bandages, as his runner.

There were among this motley crew, she noted, no cricketing whites. The traditional garb of flapping flannels and crisp linen jackets, which had graced the Hall's lawns in past summers, had been replaced by the more sombre, dark-stained whites of bandages and plaster casts.

The batsman fetched the ball a hefty blow with his free hand, twisting his wrist painfully as he did so. 'Oh, well played Bertie!' The cry went up from a group lolling on the bottom step of the terrace below her. There was a dribble of applause from those on both sides who were able to put their hands together. Bertie's runner leapt forward and crossed paths with the batsman who'd been waiting at the opposite crease. 'Four! It's a four!' yelled one of the bystanders. 'No, a six!' cried another. 'Yer can stop running!'

But Bertie's triumph was short-lived. His ball skied towards the makeshift boundary of jackets and boots where a young sailor, one arm bunched into a sling, was waiting. He tottered backwards until his body was poised, every sinew stretching upwards beneath the falling ball. Then with a shriek of triumph he scooped it one-handed from the air. 'Out! Out!' he yelled to no-one in particular.

The effort proved too much. He overbalanced, tumbling backwards head over heels, his injured arm cradled into his chest for protection.

Helena watched intently. The joy and exuberance of these men, who'd only recently seen such suffering, astounded her.

'Well held, Charlie!' 'Oh splendid catch!' The shouts were accompanied by more enthusiastic applause.

Charlie struggled to his feet, wincing and clutching not only the ball, but his arm. He held his prize aloft in triumph and his grimace turned to a broad smile.

At that moment a figure in brown overalls erupted from the rose garden and charged across the expanse of greensward towards the knot of players waiting to greet the next batsman. 'Get off my lawn! You're not allowed to play there! Get them stumps out! Go on, clear off!' The head gardener's face was purple with rage. 'How dare you! What would Her Ladyship say if she could see you!' He shook his fist close to the bowler's face.

The young men looked at him with a mixture of surprise and amusement. Some shrugged their shoulders while others, yanking at the stumps, reluctantly made to leave the pitch.

'What is it, Simpson? Is there a problem?' The clear, authoritative tones of the Countess rang out from her vantage point on the top step of the terrace.

Tommy Simpson's head whipped round in surprise. 'Oh, me lady, you're there. I didn't see you, beggin' yer pardon. But these fellows are ruining your lawn with their stumps. Made great holes in it. I'm sorry your ladyship, I'll make sure they're repaired right away.'

Quickly Helena strode across the grass. She raised her hand to halt the patients disconsolately dragging their pained bodies from the makeshift pitch. 'No, no, please don't leave. Do carry on with your game.' She smiled gently. 'I was so enjoying watching you. I haven't seen a good game of cricket at Henham since last summer.'

She turned to Tommy Simpson with a gleam in her eye. 'Simpson, don't you think a few small holes in our lawn are a small price to pay for the pleasure a game of cricket is giving these chaps? After all, they've been fighting a war. They've been wounded. Come, come now. Let them be.'

'But me lady......' His face crumpled into a protest, knowing how particular the Countess was of her gardens.

'No 'buts', Simpson. My wish is that they carry on playing and enjoying their game. Is that understood?'

'Yes, me lady. So longs as you don't mind 'em out here, oi'll leave 'em be. Thank you, yer ladyship.' He touched the peak of his cap at her and without another word headed quickly back to the rose garden.

'Yes, yes, do carry on,' she nodded to the players as they tentatively replaced the stumps.

'Thank you, ma'am,' Charlie had relinquished his position in the outer field to see what all the fuss was about and was standing at Helena's side. He casually threw the ball back to the bowler. 'Play on, Chalky!' he called to him.

'That was a splendid catch you made.' Helena smiled into Charlie's wide, freckled countryman's face. Then nodding slightly towards the sling supporting his arm 'You've been with us a while, haven't you, Able Seaman.....?' She paused, expecting him to supply his name.

'Able Seaman Charles Wesley Potter, ma'am, serving on His Majesty's ship *Woolwich*. Been here these past six weeks, since the action in Heligoland Bight. Gave the Hun a proper trouncing, we did. Sank three of his ships, with no losses of our own. And apart from a handful, there weren't many casualties among our men, either. I were one of 'em a'course. If I says so meself, m'am, it were a fine victory.' He clutched at his left arm, still aching in its sling.

'So how did you receive your injury, Able Seaman?'

'I were one of the after gun crews and was at me station at the time we were in action. I caught a German Maxim bullet in me forearm, see?' He raised his bandaged arm and waved it nonchalantly at her. 'Even know which ship fired the damn thing. It were the German Destroyer V-187.'

'And were you badly hurt?' Her green eyes stared at him attentively from beneath the severe Red Cross cap.

'No, no, ma'am. Just a flesh wound. It's none too serious. They brought me ashore at Shotley and operated on me in the barracks hospital. Then I was transferred up here. To your hospital, ma'am. I've been told by Sister Methold I'm to be allowed home later this week. Just for a few days, before I rejoins me ship.'

'I'm glad to hear it, Mr Potter. You were indeed one of the fortunate ones. Some of these other chaps weren't so lucky, as I'm sure you're aware.'

'Oh yes ma'am, I know. I've seen 'em. And heard 'em. Chaps dyin' right there in their beds beside me.' He paused to watch the game resume. A new bowler had taken the ball, another batsman was at the crease.

'I knows it sounds funny to say this, but this war's a bit like a game o' cricket, don't yer think?' He held her gaze with his hazel eyes. She wondered what he was going to say next. 'One day we bowl the Hun a Yorker and kick up 'is stumps, the next he sends our batsmen packing with some fine catching. 'One day we're on the winning side, the next day *he* is. 'Cept.....' he paused, gathering his thoughts together. 'It's not a game at all. No-one shakes yer hand as yer walks off the pitch at the end of the day and says 'well played', do they? Not like the cricket matches in our village, anyhows. And some chaps don't live to play in the next match.'

Helena couldn't fault the seaman's logic nor find any argument with the simple analogy he'd applied to the complexities of this war. Any war.

She thought back to the numerous conflicts her father, grandfather and uncles had fought in. War had perhaps been simpler then, in Wellington's day, but never, ever a game of cricket. Never had war been governed by such gentlemanly rules. War was a paradox. It brought out the best in men, such as the brave actions of her uncle Charles Crauford Fraser, who'd put his own life in danger to rescue comrades under enemy fire during the Indian Mutiny. But it also brought out the worst, the cruellest of natures. She thought particularly of the mines laid by the enemy in the sea around the Suffolk coast. They had already snatched the lives of several innocent trawlermen.

She was nodding her dark curls in wry agreement, but Charlie failed to notice.

Pulling himself up to his full five foot five inches of Suffolk country labouring stock, he let out a hearty laugh. 'We'll beat 'em in the end, don't yer worry ma'am. That's if me and me brothers have anything to do with it,' his freckled cheeks glowed with confidence. 'Me father's sent *six* of us to fight for King and country. Not to mention the three score or more of other lads from our village who've joined the colours.'

Six sons. Helena wondered how she'd have reacted if any of her four sons had been of an age to accept a commission in the army or join the navy as a midshipman. *What would I do if I had to say goodbye to all four of my boys?*

She stared at her shoes, unable to look him in the face. Charlie Potter's father may have waved them off proudly with the rest of the lads from their remote village on the Suffolk coast, but what of their mother? Having born six sons, how would she face losing them?

She was saved from further discomfiture by Sister Methold hurrying across the lawn in her direction.

'Your ladyship, your ladyship!' the matron called breathlessly. 'There's been an emergency. You must come at once! I've just taken a call from the schoolmistress at Southwold. She says boatloads of refugees from Belgium have just arrived in the harbour. They're in a terrible state. Hungry and wet through. She asked if we had any food and clothing to spare and if we could bring it down immediately. What do you think, your ladyship? I said we'd do what we could.' Sister Methold's composure had deserted her and her usually pale complexion was flushed.

'Of course, of course, Sister Methold. We must go immediately.' She turned briskly to dismiss Charlie. 'Excuse me, Able Seaman, but I must leave you to your game.'

'Yes your ladyship. And thank you.' He touched his forehead and made his way back across the lawn where his comrades greeted him with quizzical glances. *What could he have had to discuss with the Countess?* they wondered.

Helena was immediately decisive. 'Ask cook to set aside some of the supper she's preparing and get one of the nurses to sort out spare clothing,' she said, turning her attention to Sister Methold. 'I'll get the car sent round at once.' She hurried up the steps of the terrace and into her husband's study, matron behind her. 'Oh, and I think we should ask some of the other ladies of the village for their help, too. Get one of your staff to telephone Lady Eden and also Mrs Smith at the school. I'm sure she'll have children's clothing and some good wholesome food that can be spared from the school kitchen.'

By late afternoon, when Alma arrived at Southwold harbour in the pony trap laden with tureens of hot food and a linen basket full of hand-me-downs and blankets, Helena was already on the quayside, surrounded by a clamour of children and mothers begging for food, bowls and spoons outstretched.

Alma had commandeered the remaining cans the milkman had on board his cart when he'd called at the school door and she had added their contents to the pea soup and curry that she and Ida had been preparing. Fortunately, too, they still had in the house a large bundle of clothes she and William had collected from among the villagers to send to Belgian refugees in London and which was awaiting the carrier to take them to the station. Now there was a greater need for them right here on their own doorstep.

She was greeted by a pitiful sight. All afternoon a small fleet of Ostend trawlers bearing a desperate human cargo had been navigating its passage through unfamiliar tides and shoals around the harbour entrance and was now moored along the quayside.

The refugees' arrival had quickly become a local spectacle. As each boat tied up and disgorged its passengers the bedraggled newcomers were loudly cheered. They'd returned the compliment with a feeble wave, overwhelmed by this unexpected display of emotion by their English hosts.

It was a scene of utter chaos. Of desperation and misery. The grief of the fugitives, driven across the inhospitable North Sea by the exigencies of war, was pitiable in the extreme. Alma had never expected to witness anything so hellish.

Belgian families and their possessions had been tipped out across the rough planking of the quayside like so much sea-born detritus. It was hard to tell, in some cases, which were human bodies and which were bundles of bedding, clothing and items of furniture.

Women and children predominated and after spending two days and an entire night at sea on the open decks of fishing boats they were in a terrible state. Women fainting and ill, young girls weeping and shivering, elderly matrons tired and hungry, babies screaming, children sobbing, others just staring. All with wet clothes clinging to their trembling flesh.

Some of their menfolk carried bundles of family belongings, tied up in sheets or blankets and slung back and front of them. Small family heirlooms, so precious they'd been grabbed in preference to more practical necessities as the refugees fled their homes in Antwerp. There were canaries and parrots squawking in cages, fancy china, bundles of books and other treasured articles.

The stench defied description. Alma clutched a handkerchief to her face in an attempt to filter the smell through faint lavender. The pungent odour of fish engrained in the trawlers' decks had become entwined with that of unwashed bodies and soiled clothes. Clothes stained with urine and faeces, for being packed like sardines there had been no privacy, no allowances made for female sensitivities or the frailties of old age. Soiled with vomit as the nightmare of seasickness had overtaken them after being tossed for thirty six hours on the North Sea.

People, people, people. Not one smiled as she passed. Alma wondered at what inhumanities had been inflicted by the invading enemy that these people had willingly subjected themselves to such humiliations.

Alma pulled the pony to a halt beside a group of fishermen's stone huts and stood on tiptoe in the trap. There, at the farthest end of the harbour, she glimpsed Lady Stradbroke with the Mayor and Mayoress and a group of other distinguished townspeople, standing shoulder to shoulder behind a long tressle table. Before them were set rows of metal pots beside which stood a toppling mountain of bowls. Alma clicked her tongue at the pony to walk on and drew up beside them.

'Oh Mrs Smith, thank goodness you've arrived!' Helena exclaimed, an unexpected agitation in her voice. 'We're *so* in need of whatever sustenance you're able to provide.'

Bent over a hot tureen, she was oblivious to her appearance. Unruly curls strayed from the back of her Red Cross cap and her cheeks burned with a flush that was not simply the result of her exertions. Alma detected desperation, even panic in the Countess. A fear she might be in danger of being overwhelmed by desperate, outstretched hands. She was ladling hot soup into bowls, which were being grabbed as soon as it was served. Others along the line were pouring milk for crying children. There were hordes of them, many without parents. Orphans of a war that was still only two months old.

A couple of local fishermen had been detailed to help unload the arriving wagons, carts and carriages with their bounty and they set to, clambering up the step of the little trap to carry away Alma's pots of soup and curry.

'While we're distributing meals to these poor people, would you like to help with the clothing?' Helena suggested. She pointed to the crowd behind the fishermen's huts. 'You'll find Agnes round there.'

The fishermen lifted the bundles of clothing from the trap and followed her to the clothing distribution area. 'This is a rum owd do, miss, in't it?' said one as they struggled through the press of bodies.

The refugees seemed to be of the fishing and poorer class, though there were a few more respectably-dressed artisans and wealthy people among them. Most of the fugitives were scantily dressed, but fortunately the weather wasn't cold and those who really needed garments badly – and she could see there were certainly very few who did not – had surged towards the piles lying in disorganized mounds on the ground.

Chaos was about to break out.

'Form a line!' Alma shouted, dropping her bundle to the ground. It was an involuntary cry. The command of a schoolmistress accustomed to orderliness. She expected children to wait in line and these fugitives were no different. She shouted again above the cries of foreign voices, 'Get into a queue!' And then, when there was no response but a confused shrugging of shoulders, she yelled in French, 'En file indienne!' She waved her arms at them to indicate what she wanted. A straight line. No pushing, no shoving. They understood and shuffled into a reluctant and patient queue.

She watched their longing eyes as they awaited their turn and then the obvious intense delight when they received a little warm covering to replace their wringing wet garments.

Coats, dresses, shirts and trousers, even hats and shoes had been donated by well-meaning local people. All were distributed freely and with the minimum of fuss. Someone had even thought to bring small toys for the children.

The women were more anxious about their offspring than about themselves, ignoring the piles of adult clothing and instead pulling woollen jerseys and jackets over the shoulders of smaller infants while urging older children to find something to keep the chill sea breeze from their bones.

Alma watched as some of the men substituted canvas shoes for their traditional wooden ones. They strutted about like dandies for a time while their wives showed off their new acquisitions. It could, she thought, have been a fashionable parade had it not been for the dire circumstances in which these people had arrived on English soil.

Fed and clothed there was now a desperate need for warmth and shelter. With great alacrity the Mayor, Charles Fowler, commanded that anyone in the town with a motorcar should drive to the quayside and help convey them into town. Some were taken to The Swan Hotel, others to the Constitutional Club and a few found comfort around cottage fires in the narrow terraces of the town.

Later a special motorbus arrived to convey all the refugees to Lowestoft. As they were driven away crowds gathered to see them off, waving and cheering until the bus disappeared from view.

The kind-hearted folk of Southwold were unaware, as they cheerfully distributed aid to the Belgians who'd fled Antwerp, that the same scenes of destitution and misery were being played out further up the coast. Hundreds more refugees aboard two dozen fishing smacks had arrived in Lowestoft harbour on the same tide. Others had made their way to Folkestone on cross-Channel ferries.

As the sun sank behind the distant spire of Walberswick church, the exhausted army of volunteers packed away their tables, tureens and what little remained of the clothing.

Gathered outside the Old Ship, the Mayor made a short, impromptu speech, thanking them for their kindness. He bent a deft bow in the direction of the Countess. The front of her uniform was streaked with green and brown soup stains, her sleeves were soaked and rolled up over her elbows. Her dark hair tumbled in dishevelled ringlets and her cap sat awry. Her delicate features looked gaunt and tired. Never had he seen her looking less aristocratic, but never more breathtakingly beautiful and vulnerable than she did at this moment.

With his eyes fixed on her, he cleared his throat and spoke quietly. 'I'm most grateful for the spontaneous generosity of so many of you, and most especially honoured that the Countess Stradbroke has seen fit to add her own efforts to this worthy cause. I'm sure our friends from across the North Sea will not forget the kindness of Suffolk folk.' There was a short ripple of applause, then the group quickly broke up as they bade each other a weary farewell.

Alma returned home with a heavy heart. Only weeks before she'd sat with William in the pony trap in this same square, witnessing young men marching off to join the colours. Young men, not long out of the schoolroom, full of bright hope and camaraderie. It was a spectacle she'd found both puzzling and shocking. Shocking for its youthful innocence, its lack of animosity or militancy. Bravado they had a-plenty, yes. Bravado in their bold promises to send the Hun packing from 'Gallant Little Belgium'.

This spectacle, though, had shaken her belief in humanity, in the essential goodness of man to man. It had been one of incomparable pathos. These innocent foreigners had become flotsam, tossed up on the Suffolk shore as an unexpected consequence of the war; women and children, the frail and elderly, and men with despair etched on their faces at the sight of their families' hard-earned security reduced to tatters and borrowed shoes. And all for a war that was none of their creation.

'Get them out!' Jasper Mayne thumped his clenched fist hard on the desk. 'I don't want them here!' His fist hit the desk again. Superintendent George Staunton wasn't going to argue. It was never a good idea to argue with the boss when he was in this kind of mood.

'These.......refugees. Belgian, you say?' Mayne sneered. 'How do you know that? How do you know there aren't spies amongst them? Taking advantage of the situation – and the good nature of the people who're offering them shelter and succour?'

Staunton pursed his lips, searching for a diplomatic reply. 'I don't, sir. You're quite correct. They may not *all* be what they seem.....' His voice petered out, lacking further inspiration.

'I have a meeting of the Executive Committee of the East Suffolk War Relief Fund in fifteen minutes. Make sure I have all the latest intelligence concerning what's been going on in Lowestoft and Southwold this afternoon.'

It was late evening when the committee met. Without the Earl of Stradbroke in the chair to act as a moderating influence, Mayne tended to get his own way. And on the issue of foreign aliens he was determined his will would prevail.

Ernest Hart was slumped in his usual seat to one side of the council chamber when vice-chairman, Charles Lomax, slid into the chairman's ornate, high-backed chair. He watched with only passing interest as the Chief Constable stomped heavily to take the adjacent seat. Two dozen or so committee members sat facing them around the circular chamber.

Ernest was beginning to weary of some of the tasks which, because of his new role as War Correspondent, now came his way. The practical coverage of events day to day; the skirmishes at sea and the subsequent casualties, the reports of spies, his frequent visits to the numerous hospitals that had sprung up to treat the war wounded, he enjoyed, even found satisfying despite the long days they entailed.

But endless committee meetings to discuss the local war effort also went with the territory and these left him bored and impatient. Lizzie always knew when he'd been covering such a meeting. He was the most disagreeable character on God's earth. At least, that's what she told him, and he wasn't in a position to argue with Lizzie. Now she was working in an office at Ransomes' factory, doing her bit for the war effort, she'd become even more scathing of the soft and worthless job that took him to the Daily Times each morning. That, again, was her opinion.

Ernest gave an involuntary shrug as he thought of the arguments that they batted back and forth on the topic as an almost daily routine. Each time Lizzie set upon him with her sharp tongue he felt his leg twitch with pain. It had become an automatic, involuntary reaction, reminding him of his own physical shortcomings. Now, as he sat waiting for the meeting to begin, his fingers felt along the indentation of the scar beneath his trousers and he rubbed it gently, soothing the constant ache.

He was lost in a reverie of Lizzie; a fantasy of tenderness and passion, when he glanced up and found himself the object of Capt Mayne's ice-grey gaze. It made him uncomfortable. Something in the steeliness of those eyes galvanized him. An intensity of white heat, a rage desperate for release.

Ernest sat up and collected his thoughts. *Something's amiss. What can it be? Is it something I've done? Or written?*

Lomax dealt with the customary formalities in a perfunctory way. He was content that the stage belonged to Jasper Mayne this evening.

'I have an important announcement to make to the Committee,' the Chief Constable began, leaning forward to ensure he was in the full view of all the members, sitting in raked tiers around the room. He waited for the murmur of conversation to subside.

'This important announcement concerns the question of refugees in the prohibited area of the county. When the alien restriction order first came into force the prohibited area in Suffolk might roughly be described as the section of a circle with Harwich at its centre, passing through Brantham, Ipswich,

Woodbridge and Aldeburgh – the area surrounding the fort of Harwich.' He paused to ensure he had their entire attention. Only Ernest sat with head bent, writing quickly as he took notes.

'Since then, however, it's been extended until it now embraces the whole of East Suffolk.' There were nods of acquiescence around the chamber as that point was understood.

'Lately, I have learned, Belgian refugees have been coming into the county. Now.' He paused and glanced at the notes Superintendent Staunton had prepared for him. 'I have no power to deal with them except as alien friends. My duty is merely to register them. But I'm sure you will agree, *that* is not sufficient.' The Chief Constable was pleased to see heads nodding more vigorously from all sides of the room.

His tone hardened. 'I believe there are grave objections to their being in the prohibited area. Many of these refugees speak only Flemish. This language is *so* closely allied to *German,*' he leaned heavily on the word, 'that it's extremely difficult for the police to carry out their duties. How, you may ask, is the average constable to be expected to differentiate between Flemish and German? *And,*' he paused for effect again, 'if he's unable to do so, how can he possibly determine whether there are *spies* lurking among these alien friends?

'Why, only a day or two ago I was notified of the fact that *thirty* – yes, thirty – German spies had been discovered amongst the aliens landing at Folkestone, having arrived there aboard the cross-Channel ferries.' There were gasps and exchanged glances of amazement among the councillors.

Capt Mayne's spine straightened. The lines etching his face darkened. 'I don't want these people here. I don't want them staying in Suffolk. All the refugees who've landed – and I'm aware that nine hundred have arrived in Lowestoft and a number in Southwold – but *all* of them, every single one of them, *must leave the county.*' He pounded his fist on the desk to accentuate each word. '*Immediately.* I want them sent to other places, outside the area.'

He would brook no disagreement. There was silence. Some, who had helped deliver food and clothing to the refugees earlier in the day, shuffled uncomfortably in their seats, glancing furtively at others for a sign of opposition. There was none.

Finally the vice-chairman spoke. Lomax was an elderly solicitor and a liberal at heart. His tone was conciliatory and subdued. 'I'm sure we're grateful to the Chief Constable for this information,' he said. 'I imagine there's no-one who isn't aware that this is a prohibited area and everyone, in the interests of the county, is bound to see every possible safeguard is carried out.

'However, we should extend a welcome to any refugee who lands here, on our shores. It is our humanitarian duty, and instinct, to do so. But perhaps in view of what the Chief Constable has told us, we should now be more wary. I would suggest that information about these refugees should at once be sent to the Chief Constable so that arrangements can be made for their transportation to non-prohibited areas.

'Meanwhile, We have not only to consider the danger of spies,' he peered pointedly over his wire spectacles at Capt. Mayne. 'But we also must consider the fact that on the East Coast we are in a very exposed position, and this is a matter of great importance for the well-being of the children.'

'Here, here' muttered voices from the tiers of maroon plush seats, relieved that Lomax had poured a little balm on Mayne's intemperate demands.

But Mayne's uncompromising stance on the Belgians only reinforced Ernest's conviction that the man was obsessed with spies. *He cares nothing for the plight of these poor people*, he thought. *Spies, spies, spies. That's all I've heard him talk about in recent weeks.*

The meeting broke up quickly and Ernest slid from his insignificant station at the edge of the chamber. He felt used. Humiliated in his impotence to fight Mayne's absurd and hysterical notions.

If, as his editor demanded, he were to accurately reflect the truth of the meeting, he would have no option but to report Mayne's fantastical obsession in full. Verbatim. Anger welled up inside him. As he limped back through the rain-splattered darkness to the office to type up his story he asked himself whether it was right and just that the newspaper should be the constabulary's mouthpiece.

East Anglian Daily Times

Wednesday October 21 1914

Dispatch from Paris. War of Invisible Millions. Miles of Trenches and Barbed Wire a Vivid Picture.

This war might well be called the war of the invisible millions. Apart from occasional bayonet charges and cavalry actions there is little about it that is spectacular and as the interminable battles in the four countries progress, it is the shells and bullets from guns and rifles that cannot be seen that are spreading death and wounds among the soldiers of the warring nations.

Miles upon miles of trenches, miles upon miles of barbed wire, thousands of invisible infantrymen and the never-ending roar and rattle of invisible cannon and machine-guns. That is the battle field of today.

The movements of troops are carried out under cover of night and broadly are regulated thus: three days in the first line of trenches, three days in the second line and three days rest. No words pass as reliefs are made. In a deathly silence one company crawls in whilst another crawls out. Here and there, possibly, a few handshakes. The sentries are silently posted as the new defenders resume an interrupted sleep until the dawn.

But the gunnery never sleep. And over the trenches, from sunrise to sunrise, shells scream their active defiances from one line to another. As dawn breaks a lowly spoken, almost whispered word of command, brings to their knees the figures hitherto recumbent on a straw-strewn, spade-turned earth. And while company officers are making a search of the enemy's position for any sign of life, which would enable them to get a range, the men make briefly, efficient examination of their arms.

Then they wait. The officers continue to sweep with their glasses the open fields and apparently peaceful woods, seemingly destitute of other than vegetable life. Presently the keen eye detects a movement in the area which is known to include the enemy's trenches. With quick judgement the officer gives his men the range and an order to fire by company swiftly follows. Quickly the men rise above their trenches, rattle a volley at the enemy and disappear even more quickly to await further commands. Meanwhile officers are observing the effects of that volley.

So it goes on all day. Volley after volley, range after range. Now and then a shell bursts among the riflemen and some fall back to their rest which ever shall be unbroken. The bodies lie untouched till night for their places are filled by men from the second line who often have to kneel upon the bodies of their fallen comrades. Each movement from the second line to the first is balanced by a corresponding movement from the resting line to the second. Thus the fighting, the killing, the wounding, the filling-up of gaps continue until night's fall brings a few brief hours of maybe troubled rest.

Above: William and Alma Smith with pupils at Henham and Wangford School.
(courtesy Douglas Howeld)

Below Left: The Countess of Stradbroke. Artist: J.J. Shannon. (courtesy Frances Boscawen)

Below Right: The 3rd Earl of Stradbroke, in the uniform of Colonel of the 3rd East Anglian
Howitzer Brigade, Royal Artillery. (courtesy Robert Rous)

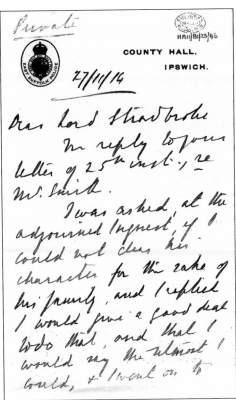

Opposite, Top Left: The Earl and Countess of Stradbroke with their four sons at Henham Hall. John, Viscount Dunwich, left

Opposite, Left: The bathing pool at Henham School. Benny Crowe, fourth left, marked with a X. (courtesy Douglas Howeld)

Top Left: Captain Jasper Mayne, Chief Constable of East Suffolk Constabulary (courtesy Suffolk Police Museum)

Top Right: First page of a letter from Capt. Jasper Mayne to the Earl of Stradbroke

Below: *HMS Amphion*, sinking after striking a German mine, the first British naval casualty

BEWARE OF SPIES.

DON'T TALK. THE ENEMY HAS EARS EVERYWHERE.

DON'T imagine that everyone who SPEAKS ENGLISH is to be trusted, and that every UNIFORM covers a FRIEND.

DON'T exchange confidences with CASUAL COMPANIONS or when travelling at home or abroad.

DON'T trust STRANGERS who write to you, who offer gifts or hospitality, or who tell you their secrets.

DON'T carry about with you or show MAPS, PLANS, ORDERS, or any naval or military document.

DON'T hesitate to PREVENT and to REPORT at once any leakage of information or any suspicious action.

DON'T mention naval or military matters in your LETTERS. They have a habit of getting into print to the advantage of the enemy.

DON'T imagine that private DIARIES or NOTE BOOKS will keep secrets. They sometimes get lost or stolen.

DON'T leave written SCRAPS OF PAPER about. BURN them. They might tell tales.

DON'T forget that a CHANCE WORD or a SCRAP OF PAPER may help your enemy and SLAY YOUR FRIEND.

W.16061—6748 100,000 3/16 H W V (P 1514) P. 16/901

Left: Handbills warning of spies and saboteurs were issued at the outbreak of war

Below: The most famous recruitment poster of the war. Alfred Leete's 1914 image of Lord Kitchener

"YOUR COUNTRY NEEDS YOU"

Part 3

The First Casualty

Chapter Sixteen

Wednesday October 28 1914

Somewhere, like a fresh spring bubbling from the ground that metamorphoses first into a trickling stream and then into a full-flooding river, the rumour started.

Why and how it started was a mystery. Who started it was equally mysterious. For without a shadow of a doubt, someone did. A word. Just one word. That was all that was needed in such febrile times. Egged on by incessant newspaper reports about spies, and admonitions that preyed on everyone's sense of patriotism that they should report likely suspects to the police.

One misplaced word.

Without that person's first word dropped, however casually, into a conversation, there would have been no rumour. Without that first malicious, insinuating thought being implanted into another's fertile mind the rumour might have died. It would have been an end to it. And without the tongues and minds of a second, third and fourth, multiplying hourly and daily, there would have been no well-spring of gossip and tittle-tattle and innuendo to churn the rumour into a torrent of lies.

A torrent that became, by the end of October, an unstoppable flood that would sweep even the strongest swimmer over the shoals and out of his depth. So it was in Wangford and Henham during the autumn of 1914.

The word was 'German'.

'He's not from around here. He's a stranger, he talks different. He's not a Suffolker.'

'He looks different - not like the rest of us. He's got the dark hair and complexion of a foreigner. He acts different, too.'

'He's had German students to stay with him.'

'He was sent a postcard from Germany only this summer. My girl told me when she came home from school. Saw it with her very own eyes. Foreign writing on it, too.'

'His son studied in Germany. Never returned home. As far as anyone knows he could still be there.'

'He went to Germany hisself, d'yer remember? To fetch his son home when he was took sick?'

'I've heard his son's serving as a Lieutenant in the German army. Joined the Hun. Killing our men.'

'His daughter's married to a German.'

'He's friendly with a German sea captain.'

'I actually saw him sending signals to German submarines with a lantern from Southwold clifftop, not too long ago.'

'I'm not surprised, in that case, that people are saying he's a German spy.'

'Wouldn't be surprised, meself, if he turned out to be a German all along.'

'I always wondered why he came here in the first place. He says he's a Devon man. Well, now we know better.'

'Newspapers all say we should tell the police if we think anyone's acting suspicious-like.'

And so they did.

He was William Smith.

East Anglian Daily Times

Wednesday October 28 1914

A moving dispatch from Northern France on the British advance from Ypres. Night attack in glare of blazing bushes. German charge broken.

In my dispatch of yesterday I was able to state that the British force at Ypres, after a glorious stand for five days against overwhelming odds, drove back the enemy for fifteen miles. News which reaches me today fully bears out the accuracy of my information.

The German forces were, I'm told, under the command of the Bavarian Crown Prince. It is even reported he has been wounded. After repulsing German attacks on the line of the Ypres Canal on Friday morning and inflicting enormous losses on the enemy, the force advanced north and east across open fields, driving the enemy before them. Before nightfall they had captured Langemarck and established entrenched positions beyond the village.

It was here that the enemy was routed and repulsed with great loss. As darkness fell upon the village the roar of cannon ceased and a peaceful night followed a desperate and exhausting day.

Suddenly there was a shrill whistle. Bushes soaked with petroleum burst into flames showing a glare over the scene.

Masses of men sprang up from the beet crops within a few hundred yards of our trenches. With bugle sound and yell and song they came dashing forward, headlong to our position. Though taken by surprise our brave men were not unprepared. They took their places in the trenches and held them, pouring a terrific fire into the advancing host, volley after volley, fifteen rounds to the minute by one fellow alone and deadly work, also, by machine gun fire.

Answering with the rifle and machine gun the enemy advanced still with bugle and shouts of 'hoek, hoek'. They were in dense masses, they fell in hundreds. They got within thirty yards of the trenches then they recoiled. Three blasts of the whistle. The retreat had been sounded.

Our men sprang out of the trenches and were in amongst them with the bayonet. The slaughter was terrific. There were hand to hand encounters in the dim flare of the burning bushes. Many of the enemy threw down their arms, pleading for mercy. No quarter was given on either side. The work was too desperate for that. The bayonet and the bullet did the work.

The enemy was driven back on Roulers. A battery and several machine guns were captured. Thousands of prisoners were taken, including a General and several other officers.

Chapter Seventeen

Monday November 2 1914

A wet Monday morning. Slanting sheets of rain lashed horizontally, driven by a cruel north-easterly straight off the sea. William and Alma grimaced resignedly at each other across the breakfast table as the rain rattled against the windowpane. Neither spoke. Rain. Always a bad start to the school week.

The children would soon be arriving, cold and soaked after a long walk or cycle ride across fields or down rutted cart tracks. Sodden coats, jackets, caps and leaking boots would be discarded in the little cloakroom and the classrooms would be permeated throughout the day with the dank, animal smell of drying woollen socks and children's hair.

Some would have been up since early morning, feeding chickens and collecting eggs or harrying the cows in for milking. They'd be bedraggled, muddy and exhausted, full of bad humour. The fumes from the coke stove that Ida Spencer prodded into life would induce a heady drowsiness and there would be little hope of dragging their minds back to their studies.

Alma sighed and rose from the table. An early start was called for. She left the pile of official letters addressed to William on the hall table, beside a large jug of golden chrysanthemums picked from the garden. No time for Will to open them now. They could wait until evening. Even then, he was so pre-occupied with organising a concert to raise money for the Countess's hospital, that she doubted the fat manilla envelopes from County Hall would see the sharp end of his paper knife until the following day. His mind was in a whirr of string quartets and operatic arias, music hall turns and the fact that the Countess herself would be performing one of her favourite songs from operetta; 'The Wine Song' out of 'The Laughing Husband', a song which showed off her fine mezzo-soprano voice.

By the time they'd locked the schoolroom doors in the darkness of late afternoon and skirted the puddles in the windswept yard, the chrysanthemums they'd picked on a glowing Sunday morning had shed their curling petals and sprinkled the topmost letter with a dusting of pollen.

It wasn't until after supper that William reluctantly swept up the mail and threw himself into an armchair by the fireside, dumping the letters in his lap with exaggerated sighs and grunts of exasperation. Dick having taken up his favourite position, stretched full-length along the rug to bask in the warmth of the glowing logs, merely twitched an ear, acknowledging his master's presence.

Alma studiously ignored the fuss he was making. Perched on the chaise longue beneath the window, she concentrated on the piles of exercise books stacked on either side of her, steel pen tapping methodically as she dipped it into the red ink-well she'd placed on a side table.

'You know my dear,' William said, half hoping she'd lay down her pen, 'I do believe next week's concert will be one of our most successful. Everyone's so eager to take part, it's terribly gratifying. Her Ladyship will be delighted when she sees how many tickets have already been sold. Well over two hundred. Would you believe that?'

'Mmm. That's excellent,' Alma's head remained resolutely bend over her pupil's books. Her pen continued to scroll neat comments in red on the bottom of compositions. *Excellent work, Daisy. Do not allow the tails of your letters to grow too long, Victoria. Untidy writing. See me,* on Harry's. She had no wish to prolong the marking session with interruptions.

'Ah well,' he sighed and reached up to the mantlepiece for his paper knife. He resigned himself to an hour or two's wading through tedious reports and committee minutes. 'I'll take Dick for a walk after I've dealt with the post. What a pile again! I sometimes wish our education officers would just let us get on with the job of teaching and not bother us with yet more Inspectors. I expect that's what half of these are about.' He laughed, but with little humour, as he slashed with melodramatic gusto at the first of the manilla envelopes. Particles of pollen fell and dusted his cuffs a light gold.

There was silence as he read. Alma sensed it was not a contented silence. For several minutes she couldn't even hear him breathing. She peered surreptitiously over the rims of her spectacles, suspecting he might have dozed asleep before the glowing fire, just as the dog had.

But instead she could see that his close-cropped dark head was shaking and he was running his fingers through his hair. Puzzled or exasperated, it was a typical reaction to the tedious nonsense the bureaucrats in County Hall pestered him with. She smiled to herself. Will was generally an amiable man, but after a wet Monday in the classroom it took very little to irritate him.

'What the....what the devil?' He paused, then with a further vigorous shake of the head, repeated, 'What the devil is *this* all about?'

Still she refused to be drawn into conversation. Her marking had to be completed before bedtime.

'This can't be meant for me. There must be some mistake.'

Resignedly she glanced up, laying the steel pen carefully in its holder. The depth of William's frown surprised her. His face had turned ashen. 'What is it? What on earth's the matter, my dear?'

'This letter. It must be meant for someone else....It's from....from.... the Chief Constable.' Scattering the rest of the letters across the dog's flanks he rose slowly and crossed to her. He laid a single sheet of typewritten paper over the exercise book in her lap. 'Read it.'

She picked it up and held it close to her face, the slanting light of the gas lamp illuminating each word.

'Read it aloud, Alma. Read it. It's very strange....I don't know what to make of it.'

She read in her teacher's matter-of-fact tone, though as she reached the final paragraph she faltered and her voice shook. Shook with puzzlement and uncertainty.

'"Whereas by the Defence of the Realm Act, 1914, His Majesty has power during the continuance of the present war to issue regulations for securing the public safety and the Defence of the Realm, subject to and in accordance with that Act, and whereas by the Defence of the Realm Regulations, 1914, it is ordered by Regulation 24a as follows:

Whereby the behaviour of any person is such as to give reasonable grounds for suspecting that he has acted or is acting or is about to act in a manner prejudicial to the public safety or the safety of the realm, the competent naval or military authority may by order direct him to cease to reside in any area (specified in the order) within or in the neighbourhood of a defended harbour or area, and any person to whom an order relates shall within such time specified in the order leave the area specified in the order, having first reported his proposed residence to the competent naval or military authority, and shall not again reside in that area without a permit for the purpose from that authority:

And whereas an order dated 30 October 1914 has been made by the competent authority under the within regulations, you, your wife, and family (if any) are hereby required to cease to reside in the county of Suffolk, or in any proclaimed or prohibited area, and to report your departure to the police before you leave and your arrival to the police at the place to which you go.

Dated the 31ˢᵗ day of October 1914

J.G. Mayne, Capt.

Chief Constable of East Suffolk."'

She laid the notice down on the exercise book she was marking. 'How odd. How very odd.' Their eyes met in mutual bewilderment. 'It can't be meant for us, certainly. That's obvious. But nowhere does it give the name of the intended recipient. So who *is* it meant for?'

'That's what I don't understand. Could it, perhaps, be someone else in this village and the postman has delivered it to us in error? Whoever it is, it's a shocking letter to have to receive.'

'Well, there's one way to find out, my dear. Retrieve the envelope and check whose name is on it.' She picked up the exercise book and pen once more.

William rummaged through the letters scattered across the worn hearthrug and the dog's prostrate back. Only one had been opened. Fortunately he hadn't thrown the discarded envelope on the fire, as was his normal habit.

He held it with both hands. It was addressed to him. He heard his own name like a faint echo deep from within his soul, issuing from his throat. '"W. Smith, esq. Headteacher, Henham and Wangford Schools, Yarmouth Road, Henham."' He stared at it, unable to believe the neatly typed words before him. This ominous notice *had* been sent to him. He and Alma were its intended recipients. His mind was in turmoil. The implications of this single sheet of white paper, with its County Hall address, were too terrible to contemplate.

'Alma, it's addressed to me. To me. Can you believe that?'

Alma sighed and laid her work down for a second time. 'It's absurd. It's obviously a mistake,' she said dismissively. 'Yes, it's totally absurd. A very poor joke on someone's part, I'd say.' She tapped the pen nib adroitly against the side of the inkwell and began leafing through another blot-stained exercise book.

William's hand stopped her, clutching at hers with an unexpected ferocity. His voice shook slightly. 'No, dearest, I fear not. It's clear that I'm the person it's intended for. Look, look....' he held the envelope out to her. 'Look at the envelope. See for yourself. It's addressed to me. There's no doubt about it. "W Smith esq." Not only that, the writer has addressed me as "Headteacher, Henham and Wangford Schools." There's no ambiguity in it.'

'But Will......I don't understand....'

'Neither do I. I see no rhyme or reason to it. If this notice is genuinely intended for me then I need to get to the bottom of it. I suspect there's malice here. Someone making mischief. I wouldn't be surprised. I'm sure that there's the odd person, even in this village, who would wish us ill. Someone who's envious of our position, our happiness together, our success in the school. Wouldn't you say?'

'Let me read it again. More carefully. I need to take in exactly what it says,' Alma picked up the notice from amongst the exercise books. She read silently for a moment or two, then pointing at the beginning of the second paragraph looked up and said, 'What behaviour? What behaviour do they suspect of you that could possibly be prejudicial to the public safety or the safety of the realm?'

'I don't know Alma. I honestly don't know. Look, if I did I'd tell you. But I... we...neither of us have done anything wrong. We've not been involved in this war in any way, so I'm as in the dark as you are. I'm totally mystified.' He was holding her hand tighter than ever.

'But do you realise what it means? Look! Look!' she stabbed her finger at the third paragraph. She read the passage again. '"....You, your wife and family are hereby required to cease to reside in the county of Suffolk". Will! Don't you realise? It's telling us to get out of Suffolk! Leave our home, the school, the children. Our entire livelihood would be taken away from us if this were a true document. It can't be true. It can't possibly be right that the Chief Constable thinks we're a threat to the safety of our country. I've never heard anything more ludicrous or monstrous. So why's he saying it? Why? Why?' Her cheerful dismissiveness had given way to agitation. Tears welled brightly in her eyes.

'Dearest, if I had any inkling I'd tell you. We have no secrets you and I. You know that. You do believe that, don't you?' Will pleaded.

'There must be something......something that's triggered this notice.' Alma shifted the books from her lap and stood to face him. 'Perhaps.....perhaps it's something you've said? Something inflammatory or out of turn? Something that might have impuned the skills of our fighting men in the face of an overwhelmingly better force? I recall you being very outspoken when this country declared war on Germany. People in the village, with sons or husbands called to the colours, may have been resentful of your opinion. People who may have suspected that your outspokenness betokened disloyalty to your country.'

Will was shocked. He looked into the questioning grey eyes gazing up at him. 'What? What are you suggesting, Alma? That I've said something treasonable? That I've been disloyal to my country? Or perhaps you think, because we have German friends, that I've aided the enemy, or inadvertently passed secret information to the Germans? Is that what you're accusing me of? Of being a spy? A traitor?' His voice rose angrily and he took both her shoulders in his strong hands so she was forced to face his anger. 'Go on! Tell me, tell me! Tell me that you, of all people, think I'm a traitor!' His hands clutched her so fiercely she flinched.

Never, in the whole of their married life, could she recall him speaking harshly to her. His expansive, sunny nature left no room for such malevolence. This sudden explosion of rage, this doubting of her love and understanding of him, frightened her.

She took a deep breath to steady herself. 'Will, how can you say that? Of me? Your wife? Of course I don't think you're a traitor. I know you'd never betray your country. But you can be very .... what shall I say? ....intemperate in what you say. I know you believe you're speaking only the truth, but others may find it hard to take. You've never made any secret of your contempt for the government and its lack of preparedness in taking the nation into this terrible war.'

'I haven't said anything that you can't read in the daily newspapers,' he retorted. 'There are eminent politicians and scholars expressing exactly my views on this war. If this letter,' he banged it violently on the side table sweeping the red inkwell off with a clatter onto the carpet, 'this damned letter is really meant for me, then why doesn't it spell out what crimes I'm supposed to have committed? Why? There's not so much as a hint as to whether someone's taken exception to something I've said. If that *is* the case, how can someone be branded as acting in a manner prejudicial to the safety of the realm simply because they speak the truth.? Yes, the truth, Alma!'

'Perhaps....perhaps it's not what you've said. Perhaps it's what you've done. What *we've* done,' she said slowly as a grim idea formed in her mind. 'Supposing the *police* have heard we have German friends? Our little frauleins, who came to stay here four years ago? Or maybe someone's told them that Alex studied in Germany all those years ago? Maybe, maybe.....Is that the sort of thing the police can hold against you? That these tenuous connections to Germany could be construed as grounds for treachery?'

William released his hold on her, his shoulders slumped. 'Oh my God, I can't believe it. If having friends in Germany constitutes a good reason to banish us from our home, our school, our livelihood, then the world has gone utterly mad. It's complete lunacy. I can't conceive of a government which would condone such treatment for something so insignificant. Can you?' His voice dropped to a hoarse whisper. 'Is that what this is all about? Our German friends? Alex being cared for by the Reimann's when he was sick? Is this now the sacrifice we have to make for knowing those people?'

Alma sank to the chaise longue and clasped her head in her hands. 'Surely not. Besides, why should the Chief Constable be interested in who *we* know? We're just ordinary school teachers. Nothing special.'

William suddenly grabbing her hand and dragged her to her feet again. 'The postcard. What did you do with the postcard?' he blurted out.

'What postcard?'

'The postcard from Germany. From the little frauleins. From Marianne and Eva. You remember, the one they sent earlier this summer. What did you do with it?'

'Well.......I pinned it to the wall of my classroom the day it arrived. And.... and...'

'Yes?' he demanded.

'I asked the children in Upper Standards to write a composition describing it. The mountains, the green meadows, the pretty flowers. It looked so different from our own landscape, I thought they'd find it interesting.......' Her voice petered out. An unpalatable truth was dawning on her. 'Do you think.....do you think someone has told the police about our postcard? And anyway, it was totally harmless, totally innocuous. The sort of thing friends send to each other all the time. No, no. I don't think the postcard has anything to do with it. I'm quite sure it hasn't.' Yet she didn't sound at all sure.

'No, no. I mean, what have you done with it *now*? Now the war has started? Is it still there?'

'I don't think so. I vaguely remember taking it down not long afterwards.'

Will was becoming increasingly impatient. 'Yes, Alma, but *then* what did you do with it?'

'Well......I suppose I must have put it in my desk drawer for safe keeping.'

'Right.' He pulled her towards the sitting room door. 'We'll find it. See if what it says could be construed as treachery, or "prejudicial to the public safety" as the Chief Constable so charmingly puts it. Though I very much doubt a holiday postcard is evidence of treachery, I wouldn't put anything past that man. He has spies on the brain, if the newspaper reports are anything to go by. He sees spies everywhere.'

On their way out into the darkness, Will grabbed the lantern from the hook by the scullery door. Then leaning against the driving rain they hurried across the schoolyard. In his haste he fumbled the key in the lock of the schoolhouse door. By the dim light of the lantern Alma could see his hands were trembling. She laid her hand reassuringly on his arm, but he never looked up.

They almost ran down the short corridor to the Higher Standards classroom, where eerily empty rows of desks and backless forms gazed up at them as they stepped onto the small platform which raised the teacher's desk and high chair. While Will held the lantern over the open desk lid Alma rummaged through its contents. Each item was taken out and placed on the platform; register, board cleaner, chalk, red pens and pencils, spelling book, a book of tables, a book of arithmetical problems, her favourite book of poems, and the bible, prayer book and hymn books she used each day.

But of the postcard there was no sign.

'Where is it? Where is it?' Will demanded. But he realised it was a fruitless search.

'It's not here. It's definitely not here. I know I put it away in my desk. I'm absolutely sure.' Alma's eyes were full of tears as she glanced up into the light of the lantern. 'I'm sorry Will. I'm so sorry......'

'So.' He pursed his lips and sighed. 'If it's not here, you must have left it somewhere else. Or lost it. Or......or......someone, some child, no doubt, must have taken it. Perhaps they liked it so much they took it from your desk and put it in their pocket to take home to show their parents. That's not beyond the bounds of belief, you know,' he tried to sound comforting and reassuring.

'But if that were the case.....then the very fact a child has had the temerity to steal something from their teacher's desk is a very serious matter. They must be punished, and quite severely.'

'But Will, if a child has taken it home to show their parents, perhaps the parents felt it was un-patriotic. Though I still don't see how it could precipitate such a notice as the one sent by the Chief Constable.' Alma felt defeated and exhausted. There seemed no explanation for the extraordinary notice with its cataclysmic consequences – exile from Suffolk, from their life, from all the people they knew and loved.

'Let's go home. I need to think about this.' Will stepped down from the platform and leaned his buttocks against the front row of desks. He watched Alma replace the contents of her desk then lower the lid with a gentle thud. For what seemed an eternity she remained immobile, her hands gripping the edges of the desk, white knuckled, head bowed in utter perplexity and misery.

Will noticed the light of the lantern glinting against the slender gold band of her wedding ring. Never in their married life had they encountered such turmoil, such a potential threat to their happiness. Not even when Gladys died. They had wept, both of them, over their daughter's passing, of course, because her sunny disposition had lightened all their lives. Yet death had blessedly released her from a painful body and for that they'd given thanks to the Lord.

But this notice, this letter. This banishment from Suffolk for an unfathomable crime against the nation. It meant an unknown destination, an uncertain future, but even more crucially it impuned his patriotism, his loyalty as a true and honourable Englishman. It meant his total humiliation, a stripping away of his respectability. His reputation would be in shreds.

Both deep in thought, they were oblivious to the downpour that drenched them as they crossed the schoolyard back to the house. Everything was as they had left it. The fire still burned brightly in the grate in the cosy sitting room, Dick sleeping before it, the scattering of unopened envelopes between his paws. The inkwell had rolled across the floor, spreading the red ink stain in an irrevocable, immovable stain, but Alma was so immersed in a torment of doubt she never noticed the ruined carpet.

'What shall we do, Will? What shall we do now?' she said, as she sank into one of the fireside chairs.

'I've been thinking about that as we came back,' he said, stroking her hair reassuringly as he perched on the arm of her chair. 'I must inform the Earl, because as chairman of our school managers he needs to know what's happening. After all, if we're to be banished from the county then someone else will have to be appointed to take over the school, and His Lordship will have to ensure that happens promptly. Though he may have difficulties finding suitably qualified candidates as so many young men are leaving the profession to join reservist regiments.'

'How can you talk to the Earl? He's away, serving with his regiment. It's impossible,' Alma said dismally. 'And anyway, how can you talk so reasonably about someone taking over the school at such a time? When our whole livelihood is at stake? We need to fight this order. We need to find a way of getting it rescinded. A way of persuading the Chief Constable that it's all a dreadful mistake, that you've done nothing wrong, nothing that could possibly pose a threat to our country.'

Will gazed into the embers, seeking inspiration. 'But who, apart from you, knows me for what I am? What I truly am? Who knows me best? As a public-spirited person whose only desire is to serve his community and his country?' he mused.

'Perhaps you should ask the Countess for help. She knows you better than most,' Alma raised her eyebrows questioningly. 'And she has influence. Undoubtedly, she's a woman of great influence and forcefulness. Why not go up to the Hall and see her?'

'What, this very evening?'

'Of course. There's no time to lose. Besides, she's a wise person and I'm sure she wouldn't mind an unannounced call, given the gravity of the situation. She's likely to be in touch with the Earl, too, as I know the Hall has a telephone.'

Will patted her lightly on the shoulder. 'Alma, bless you my dear, you always have the best ideas. I'll go at once. I'll take the trap. It won't take long.' He kissed the top of her head before springing energetically to his feet. 'I'm sure the Countess will help sort out this terrible mess. Exert her considerable influence with the Chief Constable. Yes, yes, it's a very good idea,' he said, though his confident tone was pure bravado.

William's thoughts were in turmoil as he drove the pony at a fast trot up the long drive through the Hall's parkland. It was an utterly wild night and he was alone. The driving rain beat against his face, drenching the overcoat he'd thrown on as he'd rushed to the stable to harness Polly to the trap. Now he was overwhelmed by a sense of helplessness, boiling over into a confused hysteria which constricted his throat, strangling him with a tightening knot of impending disaster.

With one hand clutching Polly's reins he wrenched at his coat collar with the other, throwing his chest open to the downpour in a physical reaction to his mental torment. Through the billowing silver sheets of rain and the rivulets trickling from his eyelids he could just make out the majestic ancient trees bending with eerie sighs to the storm's lash.

Rounding a bend in the road he was confronted with a sight he'd never witnessed in all his years visiting the Hall. The fine Italianate Georgian mansion was lit up like a Christmas tree, twinkling a myriad reflections in the dark pools along the rutted drive. Every window on every floor glowed with light, accentuating the imposing solidity of the building.

William was astonished. The brightness, the grandeur of such an illumination quite took his breath away. Yet the vision of beauty, he realised, was a direct result of the war, just as was his own predicament. Each lit window represented an occupied bed in a hospital ward. Each ward would be a scene of suffering and compassion. Now he, too, was journeying to the Hall to seek compassion and succour for his wounds. He drove the pony harder, her hooves splashing through the puddles, fracturing the lighted vision into a million flying droplets.

William knew his visit at such a late hour and in such appalling weather would be unexpected. Ringing the bell which would jangle in the butler's pantry, he stood in dread that it would be ignored. After some minutes he heard the light tread of the butler, James Hill, on the stone floor. Then the door opened a discreet distance, barely allowing James to peer out into the darkness.

'Is that you, Mr Smith?' A familiar brow creased as he attempted recognition.

'Yes James, it is. May I come in?'

The butler pulled the heavy door towards him and ushered William into the bright hallway. Before he could ask what business brought William so unexpectedly to the Hall, Will had shaken off his drenched overcoat and hat and handed them to him. 'Is her Ladyship at home? I need to see her on a matter of grave urgency concerning the school.'

'Why yes, Mr Smith,' said the man who'd been one of William's most diligent pupils when he'd first arrived as Henham's schoolmaster. James's lean, all-knowing face refrained from questioning or curiosity. He accepted that for his old master to arrive in such a state of wildness with his hair and clothes unkempt and disarrayed and his boots muddied, a disaster must surely have occurred.

'Her Ladyship has, as you're probably aware, turned the entire ground floor over to the Red Cross Hospital and is now living in rather cramped conditions on the first floor. I'm sure you'll understand......'

'Of course, of course,' William answered hastily, following James up the wide staircase to the upper floor.

Outside the Countess's sitting room door James motioned him to wait. William watched his retreating back as he knocked, and on a command to 'Enter!' slipped in. The young man, he thought, became the formal black uniform with great aplomb. He'd turned out to be a credit to his widowed mother.

William was momentarily lost in thoughts of a fair-haired boy with a warm smile, always with his hand in the air to give a correct answer. A model pupil.

'Her Ladyship says she will see you now.' The sudden reappearance of the butler startled him.

'Thank you James.'

Helena was still in her Red Cross uniform and was seated at a small desk piled with papers. The room was cosily furnished with odd armchairs and a sofa, unlike the grand drawing room downstairs, which now housed a dozen or more patients. A fire burned in the grate and although Helena was alone, William sensed an easy contentment about the room, an intimacy that was never present in the more intimidating setting of the formal room.

'Mr Smith! Come in, come in.' Helena chirped cheerfully, but as she rose from her chair her elbow dislodged a pile of letters and sent them floating across the dark red carpet. 'Oh dear!' She bent to retrieve them and smiled up at him as she grovelled on her knees. 'All these letters to respond to. They're from patients who've left our hospital and who've written to let me know how they're getting on. Isn't that wonderful? Such lovely men.'

William immediately crouched next to her to help shuffle up the letters. Some were scrawled in pencil on lined paper, others on thick blue notepaper. Those in his hands had come from addresses at other hospitals, far away.

'You know, I quite miss them when they've gone, but it's nice to know they still think of us here. Such lovely appreciative letters, too....' She dumped the jumble of letters back on the desk and belatedly shook hands with William.

'Now then. What brings you out on such a dreadful night? You must have got drenched to the skin. Come and sit by the fire.'

'It's very good of your Ladyship to see me without prior notice,' William began. Then remembering that formalities were called for in the Countess's presence he enquired after her health and that of her husband and children.

The Earl, she told him, was busy training new recruits in the Howitzer Brigade and was hoping the numbers would reach a full complement soon so that they could entrain for France. He was well and glad to be doing his bit for the war. Then her bright green eyes clouded. 'But I miss him dreadfully. And the children too.'

'Why, ma'am, where are the children?'

'I decided it was best I should send them away. A military hospital is no fit place for children, especially the girls. They are very sensitive to suffering and I did not want them upset. They've gone to stay with their cousins at Dennington Hall, with their governess and maids. I see them as often as I'm able, but the work at the hospital keeps me very busy. We seem to get more and more casualties sent to us by the week. I really don't know how we're going to cope......' She sighed and smiled wanly.

'I'm sure it's for the best, your Ladyship.' He nodded encouragement.

'Now then. I'm sure you didn't come here in this awful weather to discuss the health of my family,' she fixed him with a sharp gaze. 'James intimated there might be a problem at the school?'

'Yes, your Ladyship. What I've come to discuss with you, well.....I think it could certainly pose a problem for the school. I'm afraid something rather ....rather....well, I don't really know how to express it. Something rather extraordinary, rather disconcerting has happened.' William reached into the pocket of his jacket and took out the Chief Constable's letter, carefully folded in its brown manilla envelope.

'I've had a letter from the Chief Constable, Captain Mayne, your Ladyship. I only opened it about an hour ago, hence my arriving at such a late hour. You will see, if you would be so kind as to read it for yourself, that it makes the most extraordinary accusations regarding my patriotism and loyalty to King and country. As a result of these mistaken accusations he's demanding that my wife and I leave Suffolk immediately.'

'Leave Suffolk?' Helena's back straightened in surprise. 'Leave Suffolk? I've never heard anything so absurd! Why on earth should Captain Mayne ask *you* to do that?'

William took the notice from its envelope. Helena, ever astute, held out a slender hand encouraging him to share his burden with her, to trust her. But it occurred to him in that moment that the Countess might think ill of him. That she might even start to doubt his integrity as a result of the Chief Constable's banishing order.

No smoke without fire, he thought. *That's what she'll think. That's what they'll all say when we're gone.*

'So, what have we here?' She held the notice in both hands and read in silence. William's eyes never left her face. He wanted to catch every nuance of her reaction to what was written there. The little nods she gave as she read the preamble of the first paragraph, the puzzled frown over the second and the raised eyebrows of astonishment as she took in the full implications of the third.

'I simply don't understand why this has been sent to you, Mr Smith. There must be a mistake,' she said briskly, dismissing the letter as an aberration.

'I don't understand it either, your Ladyship. But there's no mistake as to its intended recipient. I wish there were. You see,' he held the envelope out to her, 'my name is on the envelope. It was addressed to me. It arrived this morning, with the rest of the post, but unfortunately time forbad me from opening it then. Had I known what was awaiting me I would have dealt with it sooner. I'd have made a proper appointment to come and see you earlier in the day so that I didn't cause you this inconvenience and disruption.'

'Nonsense, my dear Mr Smith! I'm extremely relieved you did come to see me. I would have been most annoyed had you not. This is a completely monstrous letter and it must be rebutted. No question about it.'

'Yes, your Ladyship. But what do you suggest is the best way of going about it? You know Captain Mayne, I'm sure. How may I best convince him that I'm a totally loyal Englishman who would do nothing to prejudice public safety or the safety of the realm, as he's accusing me of doing?' He slumped in the battered leather armchair in front of the fire and clasped his hands to his face.

Helena was perplexed. *If only George were here, he'd knock this stupid notice on the head immediately,* she thought. But George wasn't there. He was holed up in a training camp somewhere in Middlesex with his men, kicking his heels as he awaited orders to embark for France. How she missed him. Missed his wide embrace, his generous smile and his calm common sense.

'I would suggest....' she paused, searching for a logical solution. 'I would suggest you pay a visit to Captain Mayne himself and demand an explanation for this notice. Go to Ipswich, to County Hall on the first train tomorrow morning. I'm sure that's what his Lordship would suggest. Impress upon him that you are a natural born Englishman who has never given cause for doubt about his patriotism and loyalty. I'm sure that'll do the trick.'

'Do you think he'll agree to see me? After sending a notice like that? He may feel that's an end to the matter and he's washed his hands of it. For all I know I may not be the only one. There may be other people who've been similarly devastated by such a banishment.'

'I would hope he would be able to offer you a suitable explanation. Dear Mr Smith, don't despair,' she pleaded, gazing at his forlorn expression.

'I can see only the worst of outcomes, I'm afraid. That Alma and I will have to leave Henham for somewhere....who knows where?....and leave behind our school, the children.......' His voice tailed off to a whisper as he fought back the tears.

Ah, yes......the school.' The long-term ramifications of this notice jolted her. She had a responsibility to the school, in her husband's absence. Who would run the school if Mr Smith and his wife were not there? 'Yes, yes, the school. I will talk to his Lordship on the telephone tomorrow morning about what is to happen to the school *if*....and I say *if,* rather than *when,* you are forced to leave. But the whole thing is preposterous, absolutely preposterous!' Her dark curls shook with anger and disbelief.

'I will do as you suggest. I'll pay Captain Mayne a visit tomorrow. He may be inclined to relent if he sees how sincere I am in my love of this country and my desire to do nothing but good in this community.'

'Absolutely! I couldn't agree more.' Helena smiled encouragingly and rising from her chair took his hand affectionately. 'I will speak to his Lordship first thing. He may be able to intercede on your behalf, too. Dear friend, don't despair, please don't despair. Never give up hope, however bad things are looking. It's our family's motto, you know – *je vive en espoir.*'

William nodded, holding her hand for a moment in his strong fingers. 'You're most kind, ma'am. I admit, this notice has had the most frightfully depressing effect on both myself and my wife. I will take heart from your support, though, and tomorrow will make the journey to County Hall.'

'And you must, most definitely, let me know, straight away, what the outcome is. Good luck and God bless you, Mr Smith. Henham and Wangford can ill afford for you to move elsewhere.'

William accepted her good wishes as a sign of dismissal, bowed slightly and closed the door behind him with a quiet finality.

As he drove the pony trap away from the Hall, down the long rutted drive, he was unaware that Helena was watching him go, standing half-hidden behind the long velvet curtains at the bay window. She shivered slightly in her thin uniform as the wind rattled the ill-fitting sashes, though she was oblivious to the small puddle forming on the carpet at her feet where the rain had seeped in. She watched until he disappeared into the wild night, head hunched low into his shoulders as he battled against the elements.

Poor man. Poor, poor man, she thought. *He must fight this, he must.*

Never give up hope. Fight to the last breath in your body. That was the guiding principle by which generations of her family had lived by. Helena was a Fraser, born with rods of iron through her soul and spine, inherited from battles past. Battles fought by her Scottish ancestors against the English. It was a Fraser, after all, who had married the great King Robert the Bruce's sister, Mary.

As a child Helena had begged to be told, over and over again, the story of Mary's mother, Marjorie, Countess of Carrick.

A determined woman, of Scots Gaelic descent, Marjorie was a formidable operator. The story went that she'd been so determined to have the elder Robert Bruce - Robert and Mary's father - for her husband, that she'd held him captive after he'd returned from a crusade. She'd refused to release him until he agreed to marry her. 'What spirit, what grit,' her father always said when the story ended. Then added, teasingly, 'You have Marjorie's spirit, you must live up to her.'

'Yes Papa,' she'd invariably answered, though from her mother Amelia she'd inherited her fun-loving high spirits and the gentle, compassionate nature that had made her a surprisingly good nurse.

With her two older brothers, Sandy and Hugh, egging her on she'd quickly learned to fight her corner, become her own kind of formidable operator. Although Sandy and Hugh still called her Baby, though she was now in her forties, she knew she could beat them in a fair fight any day. As a child she'd been as brave and fearless as they, could walk as far as them across the moors, ride faster and jump higher than they could. She'd even shot big game on a gruelling four-month expedition through Africa, two years previously.

Ah, Africa. The recollection brought back memories of a more desperate, close-run fight. The fight to keep dear George alive through his grievous illness. He'd been taken ill with malaria and typhoid fever and when they returned home from their African journey his condition had worsened. She'd feared he would die. Now he was facing another fight, this time against the formidable guns of the enemy on European soil.

'Oh George, what would you do now?' she muttered to herself. 'what would you do to help our poor friends? This war, this infamous war isn't like any other battle we've faced.'

𝕰𝖆𝖘𝖙 𝕬𝖓𝖌𝖑𝖎𝖆𝖓 𝕯𝖆𝖎𝖑𝖞 𝕿𝖎𝖒𝖊𝖘
Monday November 2 1914

Fierce battle.

Fighting on a violent scale has followed the resumption of the German offensive in Western Flanders and Northern France. Although the battle line is swaying this way and that the enemy has made no progress in his attempt to force the road to Calais and, in the region of Ypres, the allies steady advance continues.

Progress is also being made along the coast and there are unconfirmed reports that the allies, still effectively supported from the sea, have occupied Mariakerke, two miles southwest of Ostend. All the Belgian coastline from Knocke down to Ostend is now occupied by the Germans, who notwithstanding their frightful losses in the past three weeks, are still reported in enormous strength. Entrenchments have been thrown up and preparations made for the conflict near at hand with the advancing allies.

Chapter Eighteen

Tuesday November 3 1914

There was no sleep for William and Alma that night. Throughout the long hours of darkness and far into the cold, opaque dawn, they talked. Endlessly revisiting past remarks and actions that might have been misunderstood. Remarks and actions that had unsuspectingly plunged them deep into this abyss. Tortured hours, spent wondering how their peaceful lives could have been shattered so completely by such an absurd accusation. Casting about for reasons as to why everything that had appeared good and noble for so long had been sullied, their honour impuned and their reputation stamped into the dust.

As they tussled and dissected their predicament the answer always ended in the same phrase: its because of the war. The war, the war.

William paced the floor, clutching the left side of his temples as anxiety wormed its way into every nerve and sinew, causing a blinding migraine, while Alma ministered aspirin and endless cups of tea. They sat gazing into the stubborn embers of the fire, William dispiritedly stirring them into life with his foot.

They walked together, hand in hand, with Dick bounding ahead, to the brink of the bathing pool where the first scudding clouds of the morning met the moonlight in black water. There they stood and wondered if they had seen their last swimmers, their last glorious summer, redolent with the joyous shrieks of children. Was this to be an end to it all?

'What of the children? What will they say? What will they think of us? I must clear my name, I must. Otherwise, how could I ever return and hold my head high among them again?' Will picked a stone from the bank and threw it, hard, into the middle of the pond. The moonlit shadows juddered and skittered away, circling the intrusion.

Alma squeezed his hands between her slender fingers. 'After thirty years at this school you must surely realise that all the children, not only this generation of children, but their parents before them, have all come to love and respect you. I'm sure once you prove this is a dreadful mistake the whole incident will blow over.

'You said yourself, Captain Mayne has shown, by his public pronouncements to the newspapers, that he's obsessed with spies. We must explain to the children, if we're forced to leave, that we're innocent of such gross charges.' There was desperation in the pale face, drawn into anxious furrows.

'There are so many practical considerations, too,' Will responded, hardly hearing what she'd said, giddy with a rising panic. 'Where will we go? To my brother's in Drewsteignton? Or to your family in Bream? We're like a ship in mid-ocean, caught in a storm without a compass. We don't know which way to turn. And what of the animals? Polly and Dick? Who will care for them? We can't take them with us. And what will we do for income? This order robs us of our living. How shall we live?' William's head was bursting with the pain of such incomprehensible choices. He felt like a condemned man, awaiting the hangman for a murder he hadn't committed. Above all he constantly turned every cell of his heart and brain inside out over the question; how would he be able to clear his name?

They sank into bed at dawn, exhausted, but though they lay there with eyes closed neither slept. William had decided he needed evidence of his family's innocence of any charge of disloyalty, any hint that they may be harbouring German sympathies, let alone actively aiding the enemy. He spent hours searching through drawers in cupboards and trunks in the loft for correspondence that would repulse his accusers. He found the most recent letters from Alex in Guatemala; old letters from Alex when he was studying in Aachen; a couple of formal missives in stilted English from the Reimanns, one discussing plans to send their daughters to study English at Henham, the other informing him of Alex's illness; Christmas cards from members of both the Smith and Morse families in Devon and Gloucestershire. Innocent letters between relatives and friends.

Hardly the stuff of spy hysteria, he thought, as he carefully tied them into a bundle with string.

Later that morning Alma drove him to Blythburgh station in the trap. They exchanged a gentle, forlorn kiss goodbye and she watched him board the train and take a seat by the window. His eyes followed hers as the train slowly pulled from the platform. Neither waved. Their arms were as heavy as their hearts.

By the time Blythburgh had disappeared Will was lost in his own obsessions. *What if? What if? What if I can't convince the Chief Constable the charges are a lie?* The bleak November fields, being ploughed into shallow brown furrows by teams of Suffolk Punches, the hedgerows frost-bitten and devoid of colour, the muddy farmyards and toiling labourers, he was blind to them all as he was carried on his way to Ipswich.

From Ipswich station to the crenulated magnificence of County Hall was a brisk quarter-hour walk through the town's main streets. William was glad of the normality offered by the anonimity of a large town. The chance to mingle with shoppers and stall-holders, dodging trams and horse-drawn vehicles of all descriptions. The noise and the bustle jolted him from his isolation. He was glad to be an insignificant face in a crowd.

Yet since he'd last been in Ipswich the atmosphere had changed markedly. Many of the young men, he noticed, were in khaki and those with a girl on their arm strutted like peacocks while their female companions held their heads high. 'My man's in uniform, quite a prize,' their poise announced to the world at large.

This war, this war, he thought, *how it makes fools of us all.*

Still unsure as to whether the Chief Constable would be available, or would receive him even if he were, William summoned his composure then pushed open the heavy doors at County Hall's entrance and headed down the wide corridor that led to the Police Station.

The Chief Constable was in his office, he was told by a seargent at the front desk. In a meeting. If he cared to wait until the meeting ended he might be seen. And so it was, as the County Hall clock chimed eleven, he found himself ushered into the Chief Constable's office on the first floor.

'A Mr William Smith to see you, sir.' the young sargeant announced to a handsome, uniformed man sitting behind a large oak desk. Will hung back, some paces behind him.

'Thank you sargeant, that will be all.' A discreet instruction to close the door firmly behind him as he left. It came from Captain Mayne, seated in the leather armchair by the long sash window.

William turned to face him, but all he could make out was a bulky silhouette against the light. A silhouette of a tall, imposing figure in inky-blue uniform, with crisp grey hair and equally crisply-cut moustache, sitting straight-backed with a familiar arrogance. The steely eyes may have been shielded by shadows, the telling downturned corners of the hard mouth merely an indecipherable blur, but Will knew they were there. He remembered their last, wordless encounter and was filled with trepidation.

He, by contrast, was under perfect scrutiny. Brief shafts of watery sunlight percolating through the window illuminated his face, accentuating the deep furrows of anxiety around his mouth, forcing him to blink and screw up his eyes. He felt at a distinct disadvantage, sensing the interview would prove more of an interrogation than the reasoned conversation he'd hoped would demonstrate his innocence of any charge of prejudicial behavour.

The uniformed man behind the desk spoke first, the voice formal and without a hint of welcome. 'Good morning Mr Smith. I'm Superintendent Staunton and I shall be assisting Captain Mayne with his investigations.' George Staunton scrutinised William coolly. He didn't invite him to sit down.

No chair had been left in front of the desk, deliberately. He was being forced to stand throughout.

William stiffened his athletic figure and stood erect, dignified.

'You have, I believe, come in response to the notice sent to you yesterday under Regulation 24a of the Defence of the Realm Regulations of 1914?'

'I have. Yes, indeed I have. I am most perturbed by it. Most perturbed. As soon as I received it I straightway determined to enquire the meaning of it. I am most anxious to know why it was sent to me. I believe it to be a mistake. Totally unjustified.'

William launched in hard, foregoing the niceties of preliminaries. Nothing mattered to him except clearing his name, seeing the order cancelled. Had he been a more reckless man he would have taken the notice and torn it into tiny shreds before the eyes of these policemen there and then to demonstrate his distain and disgust, but he wasn't. His pride forbad such an action. He had a reputation as one of the county's most respected headmasters to maintain.

'Very well,' Captain Mayne leaned forward and stared hard at him. He'd seen this man before, but where? He struggled to place the face. Where *had* he seen this face? The sallow, bronzed skin, the sleek, unnaturally glossy black hair and moustache, the proud bearing of this well-honed body ? This face had already once provoked his suspicions, he recalled. This face had leapt out at him in a crowd somewhere. He'd suspected then this man was a foreigner in their midst. An alien. So unlike the sons of Suffolk with their long, languid forms and pale brown hair. He couldn't for a moment place him. But to find him standing in front of him at last. Ah, that gave him great satisfaction.

If William was discomfited by the Chief Constable's unwavering stare he refused to show it. 'It's a matter of great importance that I find out *why* that notice was sent to me,' he insisted.

Mayne flipped open the dark brown leather-covered notebook on his knee. William noticed the words 'East Suffolk Police' and Mayne's number tooled in gold on the front, just like any other policeman's. 'We need to ask you a few questions first. Get a few things straight before we can discuss the reason behind the notice. Superintendent?' He nodded to Staunton.

As William turned away from the light to face Staunton, Mayne remembered. *Yes, that's it. The public meeting in County Hall to set up a local Defence Committee. This man, Smith, was sitting in the front row, observing everything but saying nothing. So was he recruited to the Committee? This man, who was now under suspicion of spying for the enemy? How very dangerous. How fortunate we've caught him in time.*

'Yes, Mr Smith. Perhaps we can start with you telling us a little about your history, how long you've been resident in Suffolk, where you've come from, that sort of thing,' Staunton threw the suggestions out casually. 'First of all, we'd like to know, are you an Englishman?'

'Yes of course I'm an Englishman,' William said testily. 'Of course I am, surely that's obvious? I'm a Devonshire man. I was born in Devon, in the village of Drewsteignton on Dartmoor, the son of the village blacksmith. I lived for twenty-two years in Devonshire. All my family are there, still.'

'You don't have the brogue of a Devonshire man,' Staunton said brusquely.

'No, well, that's simply because I've been living in Suffolk for so long. I've been schoolmaster at Henham and Wangford school for these past thirty years.'

'You don't speak like a Suffolk man, either.' Staunton sneered. 'And you don't *look* like an Englishman. Where are you *really* from?'

'I told you, I'm an Englishman. I'm from Devonshire.' He was becoming irritated.

'Very well.' The deeper, more resonant voice was that of the silhouette by the window. William turned towards it and as the light caught the flicker of white pages being turned over in the leather-bound notebook, something dropped out. A small card. It rested on the gleaming parquet floor until Mayne slowly bent down to pick it up. He glanced for a few moments at the brief lines of handwriting on it then handed it to William.

'Have you ever seen this before?'

Will gasped. It was the postcard from Germany. From the little frauleins. The postcard he and Alma had so frenetically sought the night before. 'Yes, of course. It was sent to my wife and I earlier this summer. Where did you get it? How did you come by it?' He couldn't hide the tremour of panic in his voice.

Mayne ignored the questions. 'It's from Germany, is that correct?'

'Yes. Yes it is. It's from the two young girls, students, who lodged at the schoolhouse while they were learning English. That was many years ago, of course,' he added hastily.

'How many years?'

'Er....er....' he closed his eyes and gazed up at the ornate chandelier hanging above his head. 'I believe it was in 1910.'

'You say this arrived earlier this summer? Can you tell us when?'

'No, I'm afraid I can't. I think it was well before the outbreak of war. Yes, definitely before the war,' he answered firmly.

'And do you recall what was written on this postcard - from *Germany*?' The suspicion was unmistakable.

'No, not precisely. I know the frauleins very kindly invited my wife and I to stay with them at their home in Aachen, but of course the war has made that impossible.'

'Read it.' Mayne leant forward and thrust it at him.

The dark pannelled room was unlit, forcing William to hold the postcard at a slant towards the light so he could decipher the words.

After a brief moment Captain Mayne prodded him. 'It says, does it not, that the writer's father had recently gained command of a submarine?'

'Yes, yes it does.'

'An enemy submarine, presumably. A *German* submarine?'

William looked down at the card. There was no answer.

'You know this man? This young girl's – Marianne I think it was – father? You know him?'

'Yes, I do.'

'How *well* do you know him? Perhaps you could give us some details as to where you met him and under what circumstances?'

Where to begin? William cast back over the years. Alex's sojourn at the Reimann's house while studying German in Aachen, his illness, the kindness of Herr and Frau Reimann and their two daughters, Marianne and Eva, and both their sons in nursing him; his own journey to Aachen and brief meeting with the family before bringing Alex home to recover his health. All this he described briefly and unemotionally. It was a matter of personal history; neither good nor bad, neither marking him out as a patriot nor a German sympathiser.

'Would you say, as a result of your residing with this German family in Aachen that you got to know them *well?*' Mayne said finally.

'Well enough. They were very kind to my son. I was extremely grateful to them.'

'So. You've been to Germany yourself, met Germans while you were there, eh?' chimed in Supt. Staunton.

'Yes, but that was long before the war,' William protested. 'I saw no patriotic reason why I should not have gone. Besides, my son was only seventeen at the time and he was very ill. He could not have travelled home without my assistance.'

'Your son. Where is he now? Still in Germany?' Staunton's words were hard and staccato, like rifle fire.

'No, no. He left there some years ago. He's in Guatemala in Central America. Teaching modern languages in a college there.'

'Guatemala?' Staunton turned to Mayne with raised eyebrows. 'Sounds a highly unlikely place for an Englishman to be. I believe that particular area of America is popular among Germans as a place to colonise and work, is it not?

'I wouldn't know,' Will answered shortly.

'I don't think you're telling us the truth, Mr Smith. We've been informed that the reason your son is absent from this country is that he's fighting with the German army. That he's actually a Lieutenant in the German army. Is that not so?'

William was taken aback. 'Good heavens! What a suggestion. It's absolutely untrue. Who on earth would say a thing like that? He's a teacher, an ordinary teacher. Like me.'

'I see. And I believe you have a daughter?'

This change of tack threw him. 'Yes, yes, my elder daughter, Evelyn Edith. She's married and living in Maidenhead in Berkshire and is expecting a child, her first. My other daughter, Gladys Valetta died some years ago when she was only 18. She was blind and paralysed from birth,' he added, although he thought the information superfluous. *Why should they want to know about my children?* He was mystified.

'And this daughter, Evelyn Edith. What is her married name?' Staunton pried.

'Why? Why do you ask me these questions?' He was beginning to feel rattled.

'Just answer Supt. Staunton's question, if you please,' Mayne interrupted. William glanced towards the figure in the window and saw he was making notes in the leather-bound book.

'Green. Her married name is Green.'

'We have reason to believe that is not the case. That in fact your daughter is married to a German.'

William shook his head in exasperation. 'That's nonsense, total nonsense. Where did you get such an idea? She's married to an Englishman, John Frank Green.'

'And what of your own nationality, Mr Smith? Can you *prove* you're an Englishman? Or are you a foreigner? A German, in fact?' Staunton leaned forward across the desk and peered unblinking into his face.

Incensed at this final onslaught, William's temper broke. He shouted, 'Of course I'm not German! That's a wicked, heinous lie! A slur on my reputation and my patriotism! I told you, I'm English. I was born in Devonshire. Who has been saying such a thing? If you think I'm a German, prove it!' His face flushed with anger and his chest heaved uncontrollably. *What in God's name were they trying to prove?*

'That's not for us to prove,' Staunton replied. 'It's for you to prove to us that you're English. *You* must prove you are who you say you are.'

The airlessness of the room stifled him, he wanted to wrench open the stiff white collar beneath the well-pressed black suit. Instead he thrust his chin into the air. *I won't be beaten. I must fight this.*

The leather armchair beside the window creaked as Jasper Mayne rose to his feet. The inquisitor stepped very deliberately towards his victim. Pulled up to his full six foot two inches, he towered over William. A face the consistency of steel. A final *coup de grace.*

'Now then, Mr Smith,' Mayne said quietly, rubbing at one end of his moustache with his fingers, as though deep in thought. 'We have it, on good authority, on unimpeachable authority, that you've been seen acting suspiciously in a sensitive military area, namely the harbour and clifftop at Southwold. We very strongly suspect you've been contacting your friend, the German submarine commander, Herr Reimann, or perhaps other enemy shipping in the vicinity of the Suffolk shore. Sending signals with a light. Signalling information concerning the movement of British warships in and out of Harwich. Admit it, Smith, you've been acting as a spy for the enemy. Admit it, why don't you?'

William stared at the down-turned mouth, now so close to his that he recoiled from the ill-smelling breath emitted with those incredible words. He was speechless. *What were they saying? Had he misheard? A German? A spy? Alex fighting for the German army? His daughter married to a German? What unbelievable questions!*

'These are preposterous suggestions. I'm not a German, and neither I nor any of my family are spies. I can prove it.' He pulled the bundle of letters bound up with string from his pocket and thumped it onto the desk. 'If you care to read these you will see I'm telling the truth. I don't know where these rumours about me have come from, but all I do know is that they're malicious and completely untrue. Idle village gossip, I suspect. I have good and honourable friends who will vouch for me. The Countess of Stradbroke, for one. Why don't you ask *her* if I'm a German? She will no doubt tell you what an outlandish suggestion that is.'

William's dark eyes blazed as his gaze travelled from one policeman to the other.

'Besides, if you truly believe I've committed a treasonable act, why not charge me? Put me on trial? Put me on trial as a traitor! At least then I could plead my innocence – and prove it – before a judge and jury in a court of law instead of being found guilty of some trumped-up charge which has been brought about because of malicious gossip. A charge and a verdict to which I'm allowed no defence!'

'Mr Smith, pray control yourself. You're not being charged with anything,' soothed George Staunton.

'Then why did you send me this notice?' Will took the folded sheet of white paper from his pocket and waved it wildly in their faces. 'It arrived completely out of the blue, without any warning or previous discussion. No-one from the constabulary came to see me to ask whether these accusations were true. Quite preremptorily you demand that I and my wife move from the county, from our work and our home. Is that fair? Is that justice? Is that what this country's become now there's a war on? A nation in which the police and the military can ride roughshod over an individual's liberty and good reputation?

'And how many more of these notices have been sent out? I suspect I'm not alone in being the unsuspecting victim of your ....your....your *mania* for rooting out aliens.' His chest heaved violently as though he was about to explode.

'All right, all right Mr Smith. I think we've heard enough, although in order to satisfy ourselves that you are who you claim to be I'd like to see your birth certificate,' Staunton said, taking the bundle of letters and pushing them without a glance into a drawer.

It was a straw, the slenderest of straws. 'My birth certificate? Of course, of course. I'll post it as soon as I return home.'

'We will also require a day or two to go through these letters and papers,' Mayne added. 'I will therefore defer your removal from the county for two days. That will be until the *sixth* of November, instead of the fourth. Do you understand? The order is deferred.'

'Yes. Yes I do.' Calmer, he stared down at his well polished best boots, aligned neatly side by side.

'There's nothing further to say, Mr Smith. We have more enquiries to make. I'll bid you good-day,' Mayne concluded, Staunton nodding assent. No handshakes were extended and as he went to put his hand on the doorknob the Superintendent called quietly after him, 'Oh, Mr Smith, I think you've forgotten something, haven't you?' He paused. 'The postcard. The postcard from Germany. I think *we'd* better keep that.'

William had slipped it into his pocket without thinking.

'You haven't yet told me how you came by it,' Will said, reluctantly producing it.

'No, I haven't.' Staunton was abrupt. There had been too many questions and too few answers from this schoolmaster. The interview had produced nothing by way of tangible evidence. 'And it's not something I'm prepared to reveal, either.'

The walk back across the expanse of gleaming floor was agonising. William placed the postcard, with its tantalising view of the Bavarian Alps, on the desk and left without another word.

Outside the claustrophic emotions of the pannelled room William found the corridors of County Hall calm and subdued. He was in a daze, in need of tranquillity and fresh air where he could breath more easily and recover his composure. He stepped through a doorway and found himself in the cobbled central courtyard. He felt dizzy, his head hurt and he wished he could sit down for a moment. There was a stone bench in the centre and he sank gratefully onto it. Momentarily he glanced up at the long sash window of the Chief Constable's office on the first floor. *Is someone watching me?* he wondered. The dust obliterated any sight of a face that might be lurking there.

Above it were the Tudor-style battlements that made this grey brick Victorian building look like an ancient castle. He'd discovered it to be an impenetrable fortress, harbouring a world of secrets, of scheming and of malicious accusations. He had no right to be here.

'I say, old chap. What are *you* doing here?' He felt a friendly squeeze of his shoulder and looked round.

'Oh George, it's good to see you.' It was his old friend and colleague George William Busby from Yoxford School. 'It's hard to explain. Do you have a moment?'

'Yes, a couple of minutes.' Busby sat next to him on the bench. 'I'm on my way to an Education Committee meeting, but it can wait. You look most dreadfully upset, old chap. What's going on?'

William related as succinctly as he could the entire story of the past two days. The arrival of the notice demanding his removal from Suffolk, his conversation with Lady Stradbroke and the interview he'd just left with the Chief Constable and his Superintendent.

'They accused me of being a German, George. A *German*. Can you believe that? Me, of all people!' He laughed, but Busby detected near hysteria in it.

'My dear Will. What an absurdity. Whatever next. I don't know......it's this crazy war. It's affecting people's minds, people's judgements. I don't think the Chief Constable is any exception. Everyone's become paranoid about spies.' Busby said in a kindly way, trying to reassure his friend.

'I know. But I'm neither a German nor a spy and a traitor. You know that as well as anybody does. I just hope I've been able to convince the Chief Constable. How could anyone say such awful things when I've spent my life teaching children to be loyal to their country?"

'Don't worry, old chap. If this stupid business goes any further I'll get the National Union of Teachers onto it. Our legal chappies will make representations on your behalf, take up your case. It's what the Union is good at, sorting out its members' problems. Anyway, once you've sent the police your birth certificate this whole stupid business will blow over, mark my words. Seriously. Don't take it too much to heart. Now, I must dash or I'll be late. I'm sure you're going to be head of Henham and Wangford School for a good few years yet. *Nil desperandum* old chap!' and with an airy wave of his hand the portly figure of George Busby disappeared through a door in the opposite side of the courtyard.

Busby's amiable good sense cheered him. He arrived home from the station in the station waggon to find Alma waiting for him at the gate. As he leapt down from his seat she grabbed at his arm.

'Well? Well? How did it go? What did he say? Can we stay?'

He smiled and put his arms around her. The waggoner was oblivious to the significance of the scene as he turned the horses around and headed back to Blythburgh.

'Yes, my dear, it went well. Captain Mayne said we might stay longer. I'm very hopeful I've been able to clear my name, especially now I've been able to produce letters proving Alex is living in Guatemala and not Germany. Would you believe it? They actually suggested Alex was fighting for the enemy; as a Lieutenant in the German army?' He forced a laugh so that she might see how much more relaxed he felt about the matter. 'Anyway, whatever happens I've been assured that the NUT will take up my case. I met old Busby down at County Hall, which was a bit of luck, and he told me he'd get the union onto it. Good news, eh?'

'Come. You must tell me all about it over supper,' she urged, tugging at his arm.

'First, my love, I must harness Polly and drive over to the Hall. I promised I'd let Lady Stradbroke know the outcome of my interview. I won't be long, I promise. But don't wait on supper for me. I don't feel hungry.'

Lady Stradbroke, he was told, was busy on her rounds. He found her in the ward that had once been her husband's snuggery. Hesitating to push open the door for fear of intruding, he asked a passing nurse to inform the Countess of his arrival.

Helena immediately rushed out, rubbing her hands down her apron. 'Good afternoon Mr Smith. You must excuse me, I was in the midst of helping to feed patients. It's good of you to come so soon. Tell me, how did you get on with our friend the Chief Constable?' Her attempt at making light of the affair wasn't lost on him.

'I hope.... in fact I think, your Ladyship, that I may have convinced him of my innocence,' William said earnestly. ' I think I impressed on him the fact that someone was spreading malicious rumours with the intention of harming my wife and myself. Although, I have to admit, what hurt me most of all, in fact shocked me beyond belief, was that his Superintendent, a man named Staunton, actually accused me to my face of being a *German*!'

'A German? You? Oh my dear Mr Smith, how ludicrous! I've never heard anything like it in my life. Wait till his Lordship hears this. I fear he'll be more than a little angry that the police have set their dogs on you on the back of such idiotic village gossip.' Then Helena chuckled. 'Though on second thoughts he'd probably laugh aloud at the stupidity of our police force.'

'I took several letters and papers to show them which I felt would bolster my case. I've left them at the police station as they wish to study them thoroughly. They also want me to send my birth certificate to prove I'm an Englishman and that I was born in Devonshire, exactly as I told them.'

'But have they *exonerated* you, Mr Smith?' Helena pursed her lips anxiously. 'Have they withdrawn the notice to move from Suffolk so that you can remain here?'

'No, your Ladyship, they haven't.'

Helena's eyes opened wide with exasperation. 'What? That's disgraceful, absolutely disgraceful! I'm absolutely stupefied...I simply don't know what this country's coming to. Not exonerated you? Not cleared your name of these stupid charges? It's outlandish!' She stamped her foot and thrust both hands deep into her apron pockets, staring hard at William, hoping for a more acceptable answer, but none was forthcoming.

'The only thing Captain Mayne would say is that the order has been deferred and we can stay in this area until Friday the sixth of November.'

'But that's only three days, Mr Smith! Three days. Oh, I simply don't believe it. George will *have* to be told.' In utter exasperation she turned on her heel and disappeared back into the ward without a word of farewell.

William arrived back at the schoolhouse just after four o'clock to find Pc Charles Revell, the village constable, standing in the doorway, deep in discussion with Alma. As he unlatched the garden gate Alma turned to him and with relief in her voice said, 'Thank goodness, here's my husband. You can tell him for yourself what you've just told me.'

'Good afternoon, constable. What is it you have to tell me?'

'Yes, good evening, sir.' In his mid-thirties Pc Revell was tall, almost six foot, and skinny with a sallow complexion, dull brown hair and eyes that made him look sullen.

'Tell Mr Smith about the telegram, please constable,' Alma urged. 'Tell him what you've just told me.'

Charles Revell cleared his throat nervously and took the telegram from his pocket for a second time. 'I've had a wire from the Chief and in it he's asked me to tell you that yer time is deferred.'

'All right, thank you, constable. I know that already,' said William testily. 'The Chief Constable told me himself when I was at Ipswich police station this morning. Was there anything else?'

'The Chief just says to inform you that action is deferred.'

'Very well. It's as I thought. Captain Mayne's not withdrawn the notice.

He's not withdrawn any of the charges. Nothing. The position hasn't changed at all.' With that William turned his back on them both and stormed the length of the gloomy hallway.

Alma ushered the constable quickly out into the porch. 'Thank you constable. Good afternoon to you.' The heavy door clattered to a close behind him.

East Anglian Daily Times
Thursday November 5 1914

Six lives lost. Another Lowestoft drifter mined.

Information reached Lowestoft yesterday that another Lowestoft steam drifter, the *Will and Maggie,* had been sunk by a mine during Tuesday night. Four of her crew were brought into Lowestoft by the *Quistite,* but six are missing, including George Gower, skipper, and son.

The skipper of the rescuing boat, who was not many fathoms away, says the explosion was a terrific one and that the unfortunate men must have been blown to pieces. He cut his nets to go to the *Will and Maggie* and found he had mines in his own. Two of the rescued men were somewhat injured. One had a cut at the back of his head and the mate several teeth knocked out and jaw hurt.

The smack *Unity* brought in a mine which she had picked up. The fishing fleet, generally, report mines were exploding spontaneously in the North Sea from 6 pm Tuesday until 3 am yesterday. But none but the *Will and Maggie* appears to have been injured.

The drifter *Effort* reported having seen considerable wreckage floating, which corresponded with the parts of a Dutch fishing vessel. The skipper, George Durrant, fears she may have been the victim of a mine. Although not yet officially ordered to do so, the herring fishing fleet are, after Tuesday's incidents, remaining in port on their own initiative and as a measure of prudence.

Chapter Nineteen

Wednesday November 4 1914

'It's hopeless. Utterly, utterly hopeless!' William yelled down the corridor, slamming the sitting room door on the constable's taciturn confirmation that there would be no reprieve, merely a deferment of their exile.

He threw himself into his favourite armchair by the fireside, repeating the phrase obsessively, over and over again. Angrily at first, then declining into a muttered, *soto voce*, 'Its hopeless.' With each utterance he pounded his forehead with the heel of his hand as he desperately sought another answer, a more positive one, to his nightmare.

Within the space of twenty-four hours his life of unexceptional tranquillity and contentment had been thrown into a pit of misery and confusion. The decline had been rapid and absolute. He was a beaten man.

The mental torture now manifested itself physically, eating into every bone, muscle and sinew of his body. He was wracked by an all-consuming pain. Incapable of movement, he made no effort to raise his head as Alma closed the door softly and came to stand beside him. It was as though the morning's interview, and the effort of having to stand erect under the gaze of his interrogators throughout, had taken its toll, robbing his spine of its vigour.

'The postcard,' he mumbled. 'The postcard from the little frauleins.'

'What about it? Have you found it?' Perched on the arm of his chair, Alma was suddenly hopeful.

William shook his head slowly. 'The police have it. Captain Mayne showed it to me.'

'How on earth....how on *earth* did it end up in his hands? What did he say? Did you explain? Did you explain to him who the little frauleins were?'

There was no answer. William reluctantly raised his head, but it was with great effort. The face he turned on Alma was ashen and hollow, that of an elderly man for whom life no longer held enchantment or meaning. His natural buoyancy and good humour swept away in a whirlpool of depression.

'How can I face such ignominy? Such humiliation? I feel like a common criminal,' he muttered into knitted fingers as Alma laid a comforting hand on his shoulder.

'I shall never be able to hold my head up again in society. I shall be an outcast, a leper in my own village. I failed, Alma, I failed. I failed to get the order rescinded, failed to clear my name. More than anything when I stood before those two policemen, those.....inquisitors.....I wanted to hear Capt Mayne say "We're mistaken. We made a mistake. These acccusations are merely the product of rumour and malicious gossip and we withdraw them totally. You may stay where you are".

'But he didn't. I failed. All I heard were the words "action is deferred". Deferred. What good is that? It's deferred only until the sixth! Then the whole world will know, Alma. When we've left this house and this village, everyone will be told it's because the police think I'm a danger to my own country. That I can't be trusted to live here on the East Coast.

'When we're gone *everyone* will think I'm a traitor. Can you believe that? I'm mortified that people will think I'm capable of such treachery, that I'm not a true patriot. Oh Alma, I couldn't bear that. I couldn't bear to go on living, knowing that's what people think of me. My reputation will be stained forever. And what makes it worse is that I've brought disgrace on you, too. I've failed *you*, Alma.'

Alma knelt down beside him and gently tugged his hands from his face. The glow of the fire illuminated them both and for a moment they could have been mistaken for a couple enjoying the contentments of marriage; the warmth and tenderness, the overflowing of loving hearts. But the wide-eyed pain in both their faces would have immediately dispelled such an image.

'Will, don't talk this way. Please, please, don't say such things. It's not true, you haven't failed. We must go on fighting this order. You say George Busby has promised that the union will fight your case. Well, that's a cause for hope, isn't it? It's a start. Give them time to organise something. We'll go away somewhere, anywhere. I don't mind. It'll give us time and space away from Suffolk to think things through. It won't be for long. The union will get the order rescinded, I'm sure. They'll convince the police that dissent isn't disloyalty. Besides, this war will end soon. Everyone says it'll be over by Christmas. Then all this stupid hysteria about spies will be forgotten and we can come home.'

'I fear that's not the case, my love. This war won't be ended at Christmastime, nor even in the spring. It might not even be over by *next* Christmas. The situation is hopeless, I tell you, hopeless.'

'Will, my darling, you're so distressed at the moment, you can't see a way out of this nightmare. But in time you will. We both will,' she pleaded.

He shook his head mournfully. 'No, no Alma. You don't understand. How could you? You're a woman. But to every decent Englishman honour and reputation mean everything. Without his reputation an Englishman is nothing. And these.... these qualities....they mean everything to *me*. I've worked hard to live my whole life in an honourable way, with a true spirit of self-sacrifice, so that I might promote the well-being of those around me. The fact that anyone here, in this village, should now regard me as a traitor to my country is more than I can bear.'

He fell silent and stared with unseeing eyes into the fire. Alma knelt before him, her head resting on his knees, lost in her own thoughts of a future neither of them relished.

Half an hour passed before William sighed deeply and said, 'We must pack. I'll go and get the trunk and bags from the attic. We'll start tomorrow so we're ready to leave on Friday. I'll wire my brother John to see if he can take us at Forge Cottage. If not, I'm sure George would have room at Chagford.' He pushed his aching body from the chair with a great effort of will. 'But first I need to put the school's affairs in order, make sure the records are all up to date. I'll be in my office if you need me.'

He walked with heavy steps past the little stone hay barn, through the gateway that separated the house from the school then across the yard. All around its perimeter were drifts of fallen leaves waiting to be swept up and burnt in a blaze of autumn colour and light. The year was coming to its end.

He unlocked the front door. The building was still warm from the coke stove in Lower Standards classroom and there hung about it the remains of the pungent odour of a hundred and fifty children's bodies.

Silence. Every room was silent. The children had all gone home, so had his assistant Hilda Barber and the pupil teacher, Florrie Howeld. Ida Spencer would arrive in an hour or two to clean. It gave him time to linger in each room, observing and remembering. There was nothing he loved more than his school. There was nowhere else he'd rather be. He'd poured his entire being, his intelligence and love, into this place. This building, these children.

Two generations of families, parents and children, had passed through these doors. When he'd first arrived at Henham, in 1884, the children had been sullen and unruly, unwillingly dragged to the classroom from their labours. Now they were neat in appearance, well-behaved, steady and busy in their work and equally hearty in their play. He'd introduced a revolutionary modern curriculum so the children were well-versed not only in arithmetic, reading, writing and Bible studies, but enjoyed practical training in gardening and poultry-rearing.

He could hear the children now. The diligent scratching of slate pencils on slates in the infant classroom, the squeak of pens on paper in the Lower and Higher Standards, the chatter and laughter of a class howing in the vegetable garden or feeding the hens. But most of all he heard the squeals of delight of swimmers plunging into the pool he'd created at the bend of the river and the shouts and clatter of cyclists as they careered furiously along the village lanes in training for championships.

'Where did I go wrong?' William mused, gazing from the window of the Higher Standards classroom out across the darkened garden and down to the bathing pool. 'What did I do to turn these people against me?' He shook his head. There were no answers to be found in these silent rooms with their empty desks. No child answered him back.

Each classroom etched on his memory, he turned to his small office at the front of the building. A neat pile of registers lay on his desk, along with his own record books and the punishment book. He reached into one of the drawers where he'd carefully filed away copies of inspectors' reports. He lifted one out.

Ah, Mr Grindrod.' His eyes skimmed the one-page report. '*If you could see me now. Would you write now that it's a pleasure and a stimulus to visit this school? Would you write those words if you were here with me at this moment?* He shoved the file back in the drawer. The registers were perused, the record book signed and the punishment book brought up to date. He sat there until every last piece of paperwork was completed.

'It's done,' he told himself. He locked the door behind him and went back into the house.

Alma looked up from her book. She was finding it difficult to concentrate. From overhead she could hear movement in the attic, a shuffling of footsteps then a thunderous crash as boxes toppled over. The cavernous space echoed and magnified the sounds so that she cringed, imagining the house had been hit by a storm. She rushed to the bottom of the stairs.

'Will? Are you alright up there?'

A muffled voice replied in the affirmative. William appeared, dragging a large leather trunk after him. 'This will have to do. We don't have time to pack much,' he said shortly.

'I'll start first thing in the morning. Before school,' she replied.

'Tomorrow we must also find new homes for the animals. Perhaps Charles Acton will take Polly and the trap. Do you think one of the Boggis boys would look after Dick and the poultry?'

Alma nodded. 'I'll ask. I'm sure they will.'

'I'm going out.' He took his overcoat from the stand in the hallway. 'I'll take Dick for his walk.' The Labrador was lying in his basket in the scullery and leapt up when he caught sight of his master. 'Come on, old chap.' Will unhooked the lantern from the nail just inside the door, set it on the draining board and touched a light to it. The wick burned brightly for a second before he twitched it down to a mere glimmer. Just enough to light their way.

They headed down to the bathing pool, skirting its edges where there was nothing to be seen of the summer's lilies except a green luminosity in the water.

While Dick rushed on, Will paused on the bank. Hundreds of children's faces smiled up at him out of the water. Happy faces, full of promise. All except one. Benny Crowe's. He always saw little Benny Crowe, with his cheeky smile and upturned pug nose, poised somewhere on the edge, taking the plunge, never to surface again. That day had been the worst of his life, until today.

He wandered along the river bank, following the dog's instincts. The bronze-bellied Suffolks in the field on the opposite bank raised their heads in curiosity. One whinnied a welcome. *Perhaps it's a call of farewell*, he thought. *Animals have such finely tuned instincts.*

Onwards they walked, through meadows and woodland, across the turnpike and up through the Henham estate and across ploughed fields. He lost track of time, pushing a relentless pace, despite the pain in his limbs and the throbbing of his temples. The horror of shame, the dread of living with disgrace and vilification driving him onwards.

'I can't go on,' he murmured to the dog padding loyally beside him. 'I simply can't go on.' He retraced his footsteps, returning to the pool. He felt an urge to throw himself into it, but couldn't. He couldn't bear to sully its waters with another death. Couldn't imagine lying face downwards in the decaying remains of the lilies where he'd found the child.

He sat, knees hunched beneath his chin, on the top step of one of the bathing huts where the children changed for swimming. Bent almost double, his chest tightened. Choked by the miasma of deceit and lies which clouded his oxygen, he held his breath, willing it to be his last.

But it'd be a crime and a sin. A sin against God. I'd be consigning myself to the everlasting fires of Hell. My body left to rot in unhallowed ground. That was what his church had taught him.

Yet at this moment, staring into the dark water of his pool, he feared neither God's punishment nor the Devil's torments. He had no faith. There was no God. Not the God of kindliness he'd taught children to worship in school and Sunday School, nor an all-seeing God the Father, who peered into the inner workings of the soul. His life had been his own. So, too, would be his death. He couldn't pinpoint the moment when faith had abandoned him. Perhaps it was when Benny died in this same water.

It was so late when he arrived home that Alma had retired for the night. His footsteps on the stairs roused her and she sat up as he entered the bedroom. 'I'm not asleep, Will. Are you alright?'

He sat on the edge of the bed, head in hands. 'My head aches terribly. I can't seem to shake it off. I walked miles with Dick, but it didn't help.'

Alma padded across the darkened room in her nightdress to the dressing table and lit a candle. Its glow reflected a golden haze in the small mirror behind it, casting deep shadows around her. She pulled a bottle of tablets from the drawer. 'Here, take some aspirin. They might help. You should try to sleep now, William. You had no sleep last night and today has been a terrible strain on you. Come to bed, Will.'

William caught his reflection in the mirror. He barely recognised himself. *If this is what I've become then it's better I end it all.*

Without a word he wrenched off the boots he'd polished for his interview at Ipswich police station then slowly undressed. His best black suit was put back on a hanger in the cupboard. He blew out the candle and with it the disturbing reflection. Still in his underwear he slipped into bed beside his wife.

'Good night, Will. We'll get through this dreadful business and everything will be all right again, you'll see. Don't despair.'

He kissed her face then touched his lips to her hair. 'Good night, dear. Goodnight. God bless you.'

He listened to her breathing as she drifted into sleep, felt her shifting restlessly at his side as the nightmare of what was happening to them impinged on her subconscious. He lay there, eyes open, hour after hour into the dawn, unable or unwilling to fall asleep.

At seven o'clock he crept from the bed. Closing the bedroom door behind him he stepped lightly with bare feet down the creaking staircase and into the scullery where he'd left his serge overcoat.

Dick struggled to his feet, leaving the warmth of his basket.

'Not this morning, old chap,' said Will, stroking the dog's head for the last time. The dog, sensing his master's misery, slumped his chin warily on front paws.

William plucked the lantern from its hook as he had done the evening before, and lit it. Holding it high he scanned the scullery, swinging it slightly to left and right. There, on the end of the draining board was what he was searching for.

The razor he shaved with each day. He picked it up and held it in his right hand, as though about to shave, examining the sharp, shiny blade. He ran a finger along its edge. *It's sharp enough,* he decided.

He blew out the lamp.

Wrapping the overcoat tightly around him he strode barefoot across the yard to the hay barn that divided the house from the school. It was dark and cold inside, but it didn't matter. He stepped inside and drew a deep breath.

'Forgive me, my love.' He flung wide his overcoat and holding the razor open, drew the blade fiercely across his throat. A single movement, a single moment of unutterable violence and desperation.

Chapter Twenty

Alma had seen dead bodies before, but never one where life had been extinguished with such ferocity.

She'd stood vigil with William by Gladys Valetta's bedside until their child breathed her last, faint breath, then closed her blind eyes. She'd covered the defiant, upturned nose of Benny Crowe with one of her best linen sheets as he lay on the schoolroom floor.

But this was different. This was murder, no matter whose hand had drawn the blade.

She'd searched the house for him. Called his name. Then called again across the yard. No answer. In the silence thrown back by the frosty air a terrible misgiving clutched at her throat, strangling her. Hardly able to breathe she pushed open the door to the hay barn. The last place she imagined he'd be.

Surely he wouldn't? He couldn't?

A body. Just as she'd feared. There it was, a body so bloodied and mutilated she barely recognised it as that of her husband.

Alma leant to support herself against the doorframe. Clutching her shawl around her shoulders with one hand to ward off the early morning chill, she raised the lantern higher with the other. As she swayed uncertainly, so did the lantern, unleashing shadows across the rough-hewn walls.

The hem of her woollen dress rustled against the straw as she reluctantly stepped inside. Her movement sent a rat scuttling from a dark recess to make its escape through the open doorway.

William was lying face downwards, the straw surrounding him stained dark red. As Alma swung the lantern above her head the light glinted on his glossy black hair, matted with still warm, viscous blood. It played along the length of his out-flung arms until, at his fingertips, it caught the sharp reflection of a razor, half-buried in the hay. His own razor, its bone handle worn yellow with years of constant handling.

She stood the lantern on a hay bale and sank to her knees. Her hand wavered over the well-worn overcoat. Gently she touched the sturdy shoulder beneath, pushing his body so that it rolled over, slowly and without energy, slumping onto its back.

A jagged gash across his throat had cut the windpipe, almost severing head from shoulders. From it still poured a lurid red stream of flesh and fluid.

The unseeing brown eyes stared back at her out of a face the colour of autumn mist.

'No, no, no! Oh God, it can't be.

Such despair. Such hopelessness.

She knelt, cradling his body in her lap until the crimson flow turn the colour of decaying leaves. One last time she kissed the full mouth, feeling the familiar stroke of his moustache against her cheeks. Ran her fingers through the dark hair. Softly closed his eyelids.

She extinguished the lantern and sat gazing at the end of life.

The finality of it all overwhelmed her.

Even the shouts and racing feet of children arriving in the schoolyard next door failed to move her. She heard anxious calls at the schoolhouse door, but ignored them. Nobody came searching for them in the hay barn. When the voices died away she swayed to her feet and, holding tightly to the doorframe, took a deep breath. Lifting her head high she screamed into the dull air, 'Murderers! Murderers! The lot of you! You've killed him!'

But the unforgiving mist threw back her words. The classroom windows and doors were deaf, shut tight against the cold.

Chapter Twenty One

Hours later she stumbled into school. William's blood had dried into her blouse and skirt and stained them dark red. Her face was pale and puffy from weeping and her hands bore the stains of his violent end. Pieces of straw were caught in the woollen shawl around her shoulders. Hilda Barber, teaching in the infants' classroom, was shocked by her appearance.

'What's happened to you? What's the matter?' She rushed to Alma's side and sat her gently in the teacher's chair. The small children stopped scratching pencils on slates and looked up. They sensed something was wrong.

Alma barely gasped, ' He's dead. They've killed him.'

'Who? Who's dead?' She need not have asked. Alma's face was eloquent enough. For one moment Hilda thought she'd mis-heard and that Alma had said "I've killed him". It was impossible. Surely she couldn't have murdered her husband?

'Get Doctor Acton.' Alma whispered. She swayed back and forth in the chair, on the point of falling into a faint.

'I'll send a child.' Hilda's plump figure scuttled rapidly from the room to seek out an older pupil from Higher Standards. She soon returned carrying a glass of water. 'Here, drink this. I've sent Charlie Boggis for the doctor. He won't be long.' She wound a comforting, motherly arm around Alma's shoulders.

Dr Charles Acton arrived, thinking one of the children had been taken ill.

All Alma could do was shake her head and lead him to the stone hay barn. She pointed inside. Dr Acton gasped. He'd not expected to see his friend there. He knelt down in the hay to examine William's body. Then, when he was satisfied there was no hope, slowly got to his feet.

He led Alma into the house and into the small sitting room where he made her comfortable on the chaise longue by the window. Her shawl was trailing from one shoulder and he tucked it around her. 'Lie here, Alma my dear. I fear you're in a state of shock.' He went to his black bag. 'Take this. It's a mild sedative.'

He sat in silence by her side, watching her face intently. After a while he said calmly, 'I'll get the police. They need to be informed. I'll be back later to see how you are.'

Pc Charles Revell arrive unnoticed at the barn. He made a cursory inspection of the body and its wound and retrieved the weapon from the hay. Revell had no doubt as to the cause of death. It wasn't murder. It was suicide.

An hour or so later the undertaker's apprentice arrived with a coffin on the back of a hand-cart. Victor Howeld was only sixteen and had been one of Alma's ablest pupils. She was shocked that such a delicate task should have been assigned to one so young and impressionable.

'He's in there, Victor,' she pointed as they stood together at the door to the barn.

The boy's hands shook as he held a lantern in front of his face to get a closer look. He could see his old headmaster lying in the blood-soaked hay and was fearful of going in. The thought of touching the familiar body under such circumstances made his stomach heave. He was afraid he'd vomit at the sight of so much blood. He gulped and breathed deeply.

'I'll manage. Thank you, Mrs Smith,' he turned to her, hoping she'd leave him to deal with the corpse in his own way. Alma drifted away, numbed.

Victor lifted the body clumsily onto the cart and covered it with a cloth. He wheeled it down the brick pathway and out onto the turnpike which led up to Wangford village.

'Sad ole do, Vic,' George Mallett, the wheelwright and undertaker, said, when he returned with the body.

'Yes, guv. Very sad. 'E was a decent teacher, 'e was. Taught me a lot.'

'Wonder why he done such a thing? Oi s'pose its suicide and not murder?'

Victor hadn't considered there would be any doubt.

'Don't know, guv. Who would want to murder Mr Smith?'

'Ah. I've heard rumours about him. Not very pleasant rumours, either. There's some in this village who don't think he's been a-sayin' or a-doin' the right thing in this war. I don't agrees with 'em. I thinks it's stupid gossip, but I do know there's some as wished him ill. Well, he's gone now, more's the pity.'

'Oh?' Victor stared at him with enquiring eyes, but his employer only answered with a meaningful shake of his head.

'Will there be an inquest before the burial?' the apprentice asked.

'Yes. Most likely at the school. His own school. It's a real tragedy, it is. A tragedy for all them kids there, and for the church. We'll put Mr Smith's body in the chapel of rest until the funeral. Will you see to it, Vic?'

Victor blew his nose on the filthy rag hanging from the snake belt around his leather apron and hastily wiped away the tears gathering in his eyes. It would be a great honour, he decided, to prepare his old headmaster's body for burial.

East Anglian Daily Times

Wednesday November 4 1914

Germans flooded out. Precipitate retreat from the Yser. Guns and wounded abandoned. Vigorous offensive by the allies.

In one quarter of the battle field in Flanders, at any rate, the Germans are in retreat, abandoning guns and both dead and wounded. They have evacuated the inundated valley of the Yser and are retiring to the east. The Belgian army, which has so gallantly contested the enemy's advance in this region, reports that everywhere they have found indications of a precipitate retreat. A vigorous offensive is being assumed by the allies, whose advance is particularly marked in the neighbourhood of Ypres, whose capture, it will be recalled, the enemy regarded as of first importance.

Chapter Twenty Two

Friday November 6 1914

The Lower Standards classroom was crowded long before the coroner opened William Smith's inquest late on Friday afternoon. Pressing into the familiar high-ceilinged gloom, villagers and former pupils jostled for places on the wooden benches alongside teachers and estate workers.

Journalists from not only the county's newspapers, but also London papers, converged on Henham School scenting a story seething with controversy and highly-charged drama. Clutching notebooks they crammed the front seats, anxious to catch every nuance of the tragic tale as it unfolded.

A tale of how a good and honourable man, having lived a life of self-sacrifice, had been unjustly hounded to his death, wrongly accused of being a traitor to his country.

Although he was one of them, Ernest tried to distance himself from his metropolitan counterparts, deliberately positioning himself at the farthest end of the row. Their rough manners and vulgarity appalled him. Yet he too, was part of this frenzy of public curiosity, part of this voyeuristic press, intent on mopping up the titillating sewage of a scandal.

Deep within his soul Ernest felt a burden of responsibility for the dead man. He couldn't rid himself of the guilty feeling that he, personally, was in some way to blame. That this event, which had spawned such a public furore, was his fault. Since the outbreak of war he'd written stories concerning German spies after being tipped off by reliable informants. No matter that the accusations turned out to be false; the stories had generated frenzied excitement among readers.

Whatever his own misgivings he'd given full rein to Captain Mayne's obsession with spies. His warnings of the enemy concealed within; the Englishmen prepared to betray their country for a handful of silver. Then there were his diatribes against the Belgian refugees, his insinuations that spies had secreted themselves across the North Sea under cover of their distress.

Ernest broke into a sweat, his face flushing red with shame, at the recollection of what he'd written. Highly coloured, inflammatory prose. How many more poor innocents had been wrongly accused because of what he'd written? He dared not wonder too deeply.

There had been an argument about who was to cover the inquest in the reporters' room on Wednesday afternoon. It had only been resolved when the editor himself intervened. Ernest had won, but it was a sombre victory.

'You'd better take a look at this,' John had said, waving a sheaf of copy paper slips under his nose. 'Good story. Got it from the coroner's office when I made my calls this afternoon. What do you think, eh?'

Ernest read quickly. "We regret to learn that Mr William Smith, for many years headmaster of the Henham and Wangford schools, was found lifeless on Wednesday morning in a shed at the rear of his residence, his throat being cut. The circumstances surrounding the tragedy will in due course be investigated by the County Coroner, who was promptly informed of the occurrence".

John had gone on to describe the prominent position Mr Smith had held in the locality. "The range of his interests was considerable and his tragic end will evoke sincere sympathy for those he has left behind".

'Hmmm. Well, it looks like an ordinary suicide to me,' shrugged Ernest, handing John his copy.

'There's more to it, Ernie. I've heard, off the record, that this Smith fellow had been accused of spying for the Germans and had been told to get out of Suffolk. That turned his head and he cut his throat. Suicide.'

'You can't say that until there's been an inquest. It'll undoubtedly all come out then,' Ernest said with disinterest and turned back to his typewriter.

Stan's unruly ginger head erupted from under the desk where he'd been searching for a lost folio. 'What's this? An inquest coming up? I always do inquests. Sounds like a good 'un. Let me have a look.' He grabbed the pieces of paper from John's hands.

'Hey, hang on a minute!' John protested. 'This is a war story. Spies and Germans, it's about the war. I think Ernie should go.'

'Inquests are my responsibility. I'm covering it and that's flat.' Stan's freckled face had grown red with annoyance.

The sudden row re-ignited Ernest's interest. He looked up from pounding the keys. 'Hey, John's right, Stan. If it concerns the war I suppose I should rightly go.'

John wrested his story back, seeing he'd started a row that was going nowhere. 'Let the Chief decide. But I'll lay a wager he'll say Ernie should cover it.' He passed the bundle of papers back to Ernest, who made for the corridor, quickly followed by Stanley.

They found Sir Frederick leaning over the iron railings around the balcony overlooking the stone, watching the comps. He'd heard the row down the corridor and had been about to intervene when they approached him.

'Come into my office you two. What's all this racket about?' He flopped into the battered chair behind his desk and undid the tight buttons of his waistcoat, exposing a rotund belly bursting the buttons of a tea-stained shirt.

It was left to Ernest to explain, handing John's copy over to him to read.

'Doesn't mean a lot to me,' Sir Frederick grunted. 'Who's this chap Smith? Anyone we know?'

'No Chief,' said Ernest. 'Never heard of him before.' He outlined briefly what John had found out.

'Spying for the enemy, eh? Now I wonder who could have accused a seemingly innocent man of that?' He raised an eyebrow significantly in Ernest's direction. Stan was mystified by the gesture.

'Mmm. My guess would be.....well.....maybe the Chief Constable himself?' Ernest replied, questioning his own answer.

'Exactly. Bullseye, young Hart. Captain Mayne again. The man with spy mania on the brain. You know all about that, don't you Hart?'

'Indeed I do, Chief. Indeed I do,' Ernest sighed and smiled towards Stan. 'So you see, Stan, this is undoubtedly one for me.'

The Chief rubbed at his whiskers impatiently. 'Hold on, Hart, hold on.' He pointed his stick at Stanley. 'You. Head up to Wangford tomorrow and poke about a bit before the inquest on Friday. Understand? See what yer can find out about this Smith fella. Local connections, what people think of him, that sort of thing. So you'll both be covering the story. Satisfied?'

'Of course, Chief. Thank you.' Stan shot Ernest a sly grin. They were quits.

'Now clear off, the both of you. And I don't want to hear arguments in my reporters' room again, d'yer hear?'

They chorused 'Yes, Chief' and left.

Ernest had arrived early at Henham School to ensure a front row seat and while he waited for the inquest to begin he poured over Stan's summary of the information villagers had given him the day before.

He's certainly done his research thoroughly, Ernest admitted. He'd discovered William Smith had been closely connected with the religious, social, educational and public life of the district for thirty years. A Sunday School superintendent, he'd scarcely ever missing being present in church. He'd also sung in the Church Choir, been a Parish Councillor and a hard worker for the Unionist Party.

Stan had heard that Smith, with the help of his wife, had organised many highly successful children's events and other popular entertainments. Ernest was surprised to read that at the time of his death he'd had been busy arranging a concert for the wounded in Henham Hall Hospital.

'There was nothing he wasn't ready to turn his attention to,' one informant had told Stan. 'In this connection it's impossible to forget his wonderful success as a swimming instructor.' As the originator of school gardens in Suffolk he'd succeeded in demonstrating they were of inestimable value. 'It must have been a particular satisfaction when he found his idea was generally adopted,' Stan had written.

Ernest quickly skimmed the sheaf of thin folios. He was struck by the liveliness of the man, his unusual approach to education, his enthusiasm for sports and outdoor activities. There was a colourful account of how Smith had constructed a bathing place for his pupils. Originally there'd been no more than a ditch at the back of the school to work on, but by his own labours, and with the assistance of his schoolboys and their parents, it had come to fruition. He'd taught hundreds of children to swim and achieved a high measure of success in swimming competitions.

He'd been chairman of Wangford Bowling Club and associated with Halesworth Football Club. The athletic and cycling sports meeting which he promoted each year at Henham Park was one of the best in the Eastern Counties and attended by the country's leading athletes and racing cyclists.

Stan had ended his copy with the words 'Mr Smith will indeed be greatly missed in the district where he had worked so loyally and was so highly esteemed.'

No-one had so much as hinted to Stan that he was unpatriotic or disloyal in any way. Or that anyone had disliked him or held a grudge. Everyone who the reporter had spoken to had willingly conceded that Smith's life was nobly spent in the service of others. *So why did he die like this?* Ernest tapped his pencil against his front tooth and frowned.

He was musing over the paper slips when a plump man collapsed, puffing and panting, into the seat next to him.

'Is this seat reserved for newspaper journalists, or might I sit here?' he asked Ernest breathlessly. He'd been hurrying, anxious not to arrive late.

Ernest peered up at him through his steel-rimmed spectacles with a glimmer of half-recognition.

'Yes, yes, of course.' He smiled at the red-faced man in the well-filled tweed suit. 'I believe we've met before, but I'm afraid I can't quite recall where,' he said apologetically, folding Stan's copy in half and stuffing it into his jacket pocket. He would certainly use it in his inquest report.

'Ah ha! Then I have the better of you,' the man laughed. 'We've sat together, you and I, once before. At the meeting in County Hall when Lord Stradbroke set up the East Suffolk Defence Committee. Now do you remember? I'm George Busby, headmaster of Yoxford School and you, if memory serves correctly, are the war correspondent for the Daily Times?'

'Yes, yes indeed. That's right. What an excellent memory you have! Now, of course, I do recall it. You were with a friend, another headmaster. Dark-haired chap, smartly-dressed. I remember he was extremely worried about the effect the war would have on his children's education and the well-being of poorer families. I made a note of what he'd said at the time. I fear that his concerns have been born out. But your friend's not with you today, I see.'

248

Busby's joviality evaporated. 'My dear chap, It's very good of you to remember him, and remember him for his kindly, thoughtful qualities, too. I'm afraid that this inquest today is into that very same friend's tragic death. The man you met was indeed William Smith. He was a dear friend and a remarkable teacher. One of the best and noblest of men. His passing is a terrible, terrible loss.' Busby's voice broke and he reached into his breast pocket for a handkerchief and blew his nose loudly.

Shocked by the revelation that he'd actually met the man whose death he secretly felt he'd caused, Ernest clutched his hand to his forehead and closed his eyes. He'd sat next to the dead man not a couple of months previously. A man he'd noted for his ferocious opinions, his dark flashing eyes, his very different bearing and appearance. A foreigner, he'd suspected, but of course had never given voice to his suspicions. Suspicions tragically shared by the Chief Constable from his lofty position on the platform.

'Well, well. I am terribly sorry...terribly.....shocked,' he stuttered.

Busby patted the younger man's arm. ' I quite understand. Well, we must do our best for him. Do the best we can to clear his name. We're here to see justice is done. I'm sure you'll make that very clear in your report. I expect the coroner will call me to give evidence on behalf of the County Association of Teachers. The members are dreadfully concerned that if this can happen to a fine headmaster like William then who else might be accused unjustly, perhaps for trying to explain the reason for this war to his pupils?'

They were interrupted by the entrance of the coroner with his jury and the main witnesses. The crowd crammed together on the narrow benches hushed to a mere whisper and then to complete silence as the witnesses took their places in two row of chairs, placed on either side of a long oak table at the front of the classroom.

One row had been set aside for Alma, Dr Charles Acton and the Countess of Stradbroke. They were joined by the barrister Henry Lynn and also Edward Ruckes from NUT headquarters in London. Opposite them sat members of the jury with the Earl's estate manager, William Mitchell, acting as foreman. A single seat had been placed at the end of the table for the coroner, Arthur Vulliamy.

Supt John Page and Supt Herbert Clarke, shifting uncomfortably in their seats, were the sole representatives of East Suffolk Constabulary.

The Countess of Stradbroke, dressed in sombre Red Cross outdoor uniform, was the last to enter. She, of all the witnesses, would command the greatest respect. She sat erect, a determined set to her mouth, ignoring the whispering that greeted her arrival.

Supt Page spoke first. He rose to his feet, conscious of his dignity and position in the neighbourhood, cleared his throat nervously and stammered, 'I'd like to express my own, and the police force's, deepest sympathy for the widow and family at this very sad occurrence.' Captain Mayne, he added, was unable to be present because he'd been called to an important meeting in Ipswich.

There were mutters of 'disgrace' and ' shame.' A lone voice made clear his disgust with a loud 'he should be here.' Heads nodded in agreement. Supt Page sat down quickly, feeling the hostility at his back.

Arthur Vulliamy turned to Alma sitting beside him. He touched her arm gently. 'Now you, my dear. I would like you to give your account of what happened.'

A sigh, barely audible, like the north-east wind swishing through reeds along the banks of the River Wang, floated from the spectators. Here was the grieving widow, the bowed and broken spirit still numbed by finding her husband's bloodied corpse.

Alma pushed back her chair and stood reluctantly. Her eyes, shrouded by a fine black veil, were cast down at the table where every day she and William had eaten lunch with the children. How could she describe the moment she'd found Will? How could she put into words her horror? How to express her despair and hatred for the gossips who had driven him to such a terrible death?

'Perhaps you could start by telling us your late husband's age?' Vulliamy prompted.

'My husband was 52 years of age.'

'And what happened on the morning of Wednesday the fourth of November?' he enquired.

'William got up about seven o'clock, leaving me in bed. I went downstairs and commenced packing. But when my husband didn't reappear I went to search for him.' Alma faltered. The crowd in the schoolroom held its breath. All knew what she was about to say.

'I went out to the hay shed of the stables and found him lying in the hay. Face downwards and with a razor by his side.' She bit her lip hard as the tears welled in her pale grey eyes.

'Had anything recently happened that would disturb his mind?'

'Yes. He suffered the greatest of distress and anguish through receiving a notice.'

'Do we have a copy of that notice?' asked the coroner, addressing the police witnesses.

'Yes, sir.' The coroner waited while Supt. Page searched among his papers for a copy of the Chief Constable's order and passed it across the table.

As Arthur Vulliamy read the notice aloud it seemed that all the power of the state to overwhelm and dominate the individual was contained in that single piece of paper. Its only excuse was the Defence of the Realms Act, 1914.

For the listeners in William Smith's schoolroom this was the first they'd heard of such an authority.

The Coroner's tone was measured and deliberate. But as he reached the final paragraph it was tinged with incredulity.

'"You, your wife and family are hereby required to cease to reside in the county of Suffolk or in any proclaimed or prohibited area and to report your departure to the police before you leave and your arrival to the police at the place to which you go".'

When he finished there were more mutterings of 'shame' and 'disgraceful.'

The Coroner looked up from the notice and directing his remarks to the jury told them, 'An addition has been written on the notice. It reads: "Will leave prohibited area of Suffolk on Friday sixth November 1914 and it's signed J.G. Mayne, CC (Captain), East Suffolk". He has dated it the third of November 1914.'

A tall, elegantly-dressed man now rose to his feet. His appearance was greeted with an appreciative murmur, as though an invisible hand had raised a scarlet curtain and this actor had stepped into the spotlight, centre stage. An actor whose reputation had gone before him.

Henry Lynn, they anticipated, would not belabour the constabulary witnesses with one of their own wooden truncheons. No. Rather he would dissect them, tear away at the flesh of their argument, with the subtle delicacy of a scalpel-wielding surgeon.

Several dozen pairs of eyes fixed on the long face with its finely sculpted cheekbones and neat moustache. Watched the theatrical toss of the head as he flicked away stray curls of dark hair from his forehead.

Henry Lynn began on a quiet, explanatory note. 'The notice was sent to Mr Smith in its first form on Monday the second,' he told the Coroner. 'He was then interviewed by Capt Mayne at Ipswich on Tuesday the third. Capt Mayne put the addition on the notice, which extended the time of leaving by a couple of days.'

He then turned to Alma. 'Mrs Smith, where was your husband born?'

'In Devonshire', Alma replied.

'How long has his family lived there?'

'I believe the brother of my husband has five or six generations who have lived in that house and carried on that business.'

'Do you know when your husband left Devonshire?'

'He went to Culham College between 1882 and 1883,' she said.

'From the time he went to Culham has he always lived in England?' asked the barrister, anxious to establish William's roots as a true-blooded Englishman.

Alma's voice became hard-edged and defiant. 'He never left England but once. That was when he went to Aachen to bring home our son, Alex, who was ill.'

'Your son had been staying there to learn the German language and you had taken Germans in exchange?'

Alma said that was so.

'Mr Lynn,' the Coroner interrupted. 'I suggest you confine yourself to the question the Jury has to decide.'

'Sir, I believe my questions are germane to this inquiry,' Henry Lynn's mellifluous voice rang with authority. 'I want to show whether or not there's any justification for the notice sent by East Suffolk police and which upset this man to such an extent that he went mad. My object in asking the question is to show what the dead man's life had been and what kind of a man he'd been. That there was no reason for this notice as he was a loyal Englishman all his life.'

'I don't think that will affect the question,' said Arthur Vulliamy.

Henry Lynn disagreed. 'It will affect the Jury as to whether the deceased was upset by the notice, which caused his temporary insanity. They are entitled to know what the effect of the receipt of such a notice on this man was without any previous inquiry or explanation.'

But the Coroner persisted. 'I think the fact of the notice is sufficient without going any further,' he told Lynn.

Again the barrister shook his head adamantly. 'The Jury ought to see whether the notice was justifiable. And I also want to clear his memory. If not justifiable, the more reason for that notice being the cause of his insanity.'

There was a sudden whispering and rustling in the room. The Countess of Stradbroke had risen to her feet. She made it very clear she wished to speak. Henry Lynn gave way gracefully.

'*I* saw Mr Smith after he got the notice. I can bear out what counsel, Mr Lynn, has said. I don't think a matter of this sort should be hushed up. What broke dear Mr Smith's heart was the fact he was accused of being *German*!' Her anger rang to the vaulted roof. There was a stunned silence.

Vulliamy relented. Clearing his throat as though about to apologise, he turned to Alma. 'Was there anything in his life that would be sufficient for his having to leave the district?'

'He was loyal to the country,' said Alma passionately, 'I will stake my honour. There was nothing in his conduct or life that made it dangerous for him to remain at Henham.'

Henry Lynn glanced at the notes in front of him. He looked straight into Alma's strained eyes. 'It has been said your daughter married a German,' he said.

'That's absolutely untrue!' cried Alma. She pointed to a young man sitting in the crowd with her daughter Evelyn Edith. 'There's my daughter and her husband.'

'He doesn't look like a German,' Lynn said wryly, casting his eyes over John Frank Green, who had come dressed in his best tweed suit. He did, indeed, look the picture of an English country gentleman. He smiled sypathetically at the pregnant young woman in mourning black.

Vulliamy interrupted, 'Did the receipt of the notice affect your husband's mind?'

'The charge killed him. He has been killed through that.'

'Did he seem worried by this notice?'

'Yes, he was anxious to show that the charge was a lie.'

Determined to find out what had happened after William returned from his interview with the Chief Constable, Henry Lynn coaxed gently, 'What did he say the night before he died?'

'When he returned home I met him at the gate. He told me that Capt Mayne said we might stay longer. He was very cheerful then because he had hopes of clearing himself. He seemed brighter. I think what made him brighter was that he knew the NUT was going to take up his case. Although I must say that he'd been in terrible distress since Monday, when the notice was served on him.'

Once again Helena interjected. 'Capt. Mayne told *me* there was nothing in it except village gossip,' she said crisply. 'What distressed Mr Smith most terribly was that one of the officials named Staunton at the police station accused him – to his face – that he was a German. To his very face!'

Alma nodded. 'He saw Staunton and in an interview with him he was asked: "Are you an Englishman?" My husband replied "I have lived 22 years in Devonshire and 30 years in Suffolk". But Staunton told him: "You have not the brogue of a Devonshire or Suffolk man".'

She was sure that Capt Mayne had never sent her husband a message saying it was merely village gossip. 'My husband even left the correspondence we'd had with our German friends for Capt Mayne to read,' she added.

Henry Lynn took a piece of paper from his bundle. 'Capt Mayne telegraphed on Tuesday the third to the police at Wangford after his interview with your husband. This telegram said "Inform him that action is deferred and that he need not move for the present." Did you know that?'

'They didn't tell him that,' said Alma. 'They didn't tell me that, either. That would have saved his life.'

'Didn't Mr Smith see the constable, and didn't the latter say the period was extended?'

Alma agreed. 'Yes, the constable said it was deferred.'

Once more the indignant Countess was on her feet. 'Why wasn't that telegram *given* to Mr Smith or Mrs Smith to read for themselves, may I ask?' Turning to Alma she said softly, 'Was that telegram *ever* handed to your husband?'

'Not that I know of,' said Alma.

'I simply can't understand it,' declared Helena. ' Capt Mayne said he'd sent a telegram that Mr Smith had been reinstated, or words to that effect. There was some muddle the night before Mr Smith's death. When he came to visit me, to tell me about his interview at Ipswich Police Station, Mr Smith was under the impression that he was going on the sixth.'

At this, Arthur Vulliamy turned to the Jury. 'Would you like Capt Mayne to attend this inquest? It would seem he has various points to answer.' William Mitchell, the foreman, quickly agreed and the Coroner said he would adjourn the inquest for the Chief Constable's attendance.

As she continued her evidence Alma told the inquiry her husband hadn't slept a wink on the Tuesday night, nor the night before. 'He told me he'd got such a bad head that in the middle of the night I got up and gave him some aspirin.'

One of the jurors wanted to know exactly what the policeman had said to her husband when he called at the schoolhouse.

'The policeman came into the passage. I didn't ask him to sit down because I was told he'd laid false information against my husband,' she explained. 'He said something to this effect; "Mrs Smith, I have had a wire from the Chief and he says that the time is deferred". The policeman said he'd come to deliver the message personally and I told him my husband wasn't at home. My husband then came in and the policeman said something to the effect: "Your time is deferred",' Alma recalled, wracking her dulled memory for the exact words.

Helena was on her feet again. 'Mr Smith didn't take the telegram to mean that it entirely *exonerated* him?' she persisted. She was warming to her role as advocate for the dead man.

'My husband thought that Capt Mayne had sent a message confirming what he had told him..... as to the two days' extension. He didn't understand that the time was further deferred. If he had he ....he....he,' she faltered, 'he would have lived.'

A murmur of sympathy arose from the room.

Henry Lynn wanted to question the local constable for himself so Pc Charles Revell was called.

'On the afternoon of the third, about four o'clock, I received the following wire from Capt Mayne; "Re Smith, Henham. Inform him that action is deferred and he need not move for the present. Acknowledge receipt". Pc Revell read from his leather-bound notebook.

'Did you show that to Mr Smith?' demanded Lynn.

'No, I read the contents to him,' said Pc Revell.

'Did he say anything about it?'

'He said "All right, thank you".'

'Did you read the telegram to *Mrs* Smith?'

The policeman could see where Lynn's questioning was leading. He replied reluctantly: 'I told her the contents of it.'

Lynn locked Pc Revell's gaze. '*Why* did you not read it to her?' His tone could have carved ice.

'I told her I'd received a telegram from the Chief Constable and I read those words in it.'

'Tell me the words you said,' insisted Lynn, banging the table with a fist.

'I....I.... told her I'd received a telegram from the Chief that the action against her husband had been deferred and that he need not move at the present.'

Again Lynn insisted. 'Mrs Smith said nothing in her evidence about you saying: "He need not move at present". Did you read the telegram to *Mr* Smith?'

'No, I said the same as I said to Mrs Smith.'

'And yet you said that you *read* it ....*read* it....to Mr Smith.'

'I *told* him everything that was in the telegram,' said Pc Revell, growing flustered.

'Why did you not *read* it?' Henry Lynn's fury was evident to everyone there. His tone carried a loud and clear message. *This constable is culpable.*

'My instructions were to inform him of the *contents* of my telegram.'

The room was silent. The barrister bowed his head as though collecting his thoughts for a renewed barrage. His audience waited. Lynn decided to change tack, his tone quieter, more menacing.

'Have you ever known anything about Mr Smith to make you suspicious?'

'No, sir.'

'How long have you been in the village?'

'Three years.'

'You know Mr Smith pretty well?' Henry Lynn said casually.

'Very well indeed,' said Pc Revell warmly.

'Have you ever known anything of the slightest disloyalty on his part?'

'No, sir.'

'Have you any idea of anything being said about him of his being disloyal?'

Pc Revell paused and shook his head. 'Only....only... well....only rumours.'

'What rumours have you heard?'

'Nothing but rumours, which I reported to my superior officer.'

'Aha!' exclaimed Lynn, banging his file on the table. 'We are *coming* to it now. You reported *rumours* to your superior officer. Will you repeat them here?'

'I...I... cannot repeat rumours,' stammered Pc Revell lamely.

'I want the report to your Chief Constable.'

'It belongs to my superior officer,' the constable replied obstinately.

Lynn glanced around the room. All eyes were on him as he dug deeper into the mire of the gossip and rumour that had cost William Smith his life.

'When did you stop his Lordship,' Lynn began deliberately, 'and tell him there had been two spies in your district?'

Pc Revell was aware that Lord Stradbroke's wife was listening closely. 'His Lordship asked me whether there had been spies in the district. I said the only German I knew in the district had stopped at Mr Smith's.'

'When did these people live at Mr Smith's?'

'Over three years ago, before I came into the district,' replied Pc Revell.

Anxious to protect the young constable from further interrogation, Supt Page leapt to his feet and insisted, 'The contents of the telegram *were* explained to Mr Smith.'

Lady Stradbroke had heard enough. She left her seat and walked across the room to where Ernest Hart and the other newspaper reporters sat in a huddle over their notebooks. 'I hope it is clear to the Press that Mr Smith was an Englishman and his daughter was married to an Englishman.'

The reporters, overwhelmed at being addressed directly by the Countess, nodded vigorously. Ernest bit his lip and kept his eyes on his notebook. Was this remark directed at him, personally, for what he'd written? The insinuating stories about spies, the blandishments to report neighbours, however flimsy the evidence against them?

He felt vulnerable and dared not meet those glowing green eyes for fear of betraying his guilt. His leg went into a spasm of sharp pain and he pressed his lips even tighter together for fear he might cry out or groan.

Helena returned to her seat, disgust and anger evident for all to see.

Henry Lynn waited until she had sat down and the muttering in the crowd subsided. He then produced, with a dramatic flourish of his elegant hand, a copy of William Smith's birth certificate from his bundle. 'A copy of Mr Smith's birth certificate was forwarded to Capt Mayne,' he said. 'It shows, quite clearly and without any shadow of a doubt, that the deceased was born on the twenty-third of July 1852 at Okehampton.' The *coup de grace*. He felt he had made a cast-iron case for William Smith to be exonerated.

But determined to have the final word, the Countess once more leapt to her feet. She held in one gloved hand two small sheets of flimsy, lined paper covered in neatly pencilled handwriting. 'I'd like permission to read this letter which I've just received from my husband, who's serving with the colours,' she said, addressing the entire room in a voice that rang clear and cold with rage.

No-one spoke.

'This is what he says: "I have just heard with the utmost horror about poor Mr Smith. It is too dreadful to think that his death should have been caused by those who had occasion to be very grateful to him. Certainly he was a long way the best man in the village, and the influence for good exercised by him and Mrs Smith will be a great loss to the church, as he's been indefatigable in taking the Sunday School. In fact I don't think he can be replaced as an influence for the spiritual and general welfare of the village".'

Lady Stradbroke paused for her husband's words to sink in. She turned the page and continued to read. ' "I often said of Wangford that great harm was always being done by tittle tattle. I never thought such a tragedy would be enacted as now has taken place. These males and females (one cannot use the words men and women), who have maligned Smith and set about tales concerning him, must know in their own hearts that they are, in reality, just as much his *murderers* as if they had drawn the knife across his throat with their own cowardly fingers".'

There was a gasp from the entire room. The Earl of Stradbroke had accused the villagers of being 'murderers'. His own people.

Helena looked up. She wanted the harshness of her husband's verdict to sink in. After a long pause she read on. ' "In these sad times, when all our best and bravest are sacrificing their lives for their country, it is awful to think that the mean and petty creatures of the earth have the power to hound, by false pretences, to their doom those whom they wish to spite. No doubt you will feel as I do, as you realise what help Smith was in keeping things straight and, of course after the inquest has satisfactorily cleared the case, you will be glad to help show the great respect all the best people in the village feel".'

She quietly lowered the pages of her husband's letter to her side and put a hand to her mouth to hide the tears that were gathering. She had done what she could to clear William Smith's name.

A shocked silence greeted Lord Stradbroke's letter. The Coroner was the first to break it. He cleared his throat and said gently to the crowd, 'I have had cases in the past where tittle tattle has done great mischief. In one case it killed a woman.'

Henry Lynn wondered if perhaps this was the Coroner's way of exonerating the actions of the police. He said tartly, 'But tittle tattle ought not to cause a notice like that.'

With that stinging rebuke the Coroner said he would adjourn the inquest for a week so that he could hear evidence from the Chief Constable. He rose from the head of the table and the crowd parted to let him leave.

As the reporters scurried away together in a pack, anxiously comparing notes, Ernest remained, stunned, in his seat until the room had almost emptied.

He watched as Lady Stradbroke moved to sit close to Alma. He caught her whisper 'Alma, my dear, you must rest now. This has been a terrible ordeal for you. And tomorrow you have William's funeral to bear. I will do what I can to help you, rest assured.' With that she stretched out her gloved hand and clutched Alma's firmly in hers.

Ernest retrieved his stick from beneath the hard wooden bench and limped from the schoolroom. When he reached the door he looked back over his shoulder. The two women, heads bent, still had their hands clasped together in shared grief.

On impulse he turned across the yard towards the small stone barn between the school and schoolhouse. He wanted to see for himself where this man had ended his life. He rationalised that it would add colour and verisimilitude to his report, but in reality it was a desire to experience more closely the horror of the event that drew him there.

As he pushed open the gate in the wall he saw that George Busby had followed the same urging. He was leaning against the rough wooden doorframe, smoking a pipe. Wreaths of sweet-smelling tobacco drifted towards him, mingled on frosty air.

'I wish he hadn't done it.' Busby's eyes were filled with tears. 'Such a huge waste of a man. A man who gave and had so so much more to give to his family, his friends and his work.'

It could be William Smith's epitaph, thought Ernest.

'There was no need for it,' Busby said, wiping his eyes and recovering his composure. 'No need for him to kill himself. I'd have fought for him. So would the union. We'd have cleared his name eventually, he knew that. But that wasn't good enough for him. He felt his honour had been impuned, damaged irreparably.'

'So why do you think he did it?' Ernest peered up at him over the wire rims of his glasses.

'He was a ....what shall I say?....a *complicated* man.' Busby thought for a moment. 'A very complex character. Wonderful company, of course. One minute full of energy and enthusiasm, dashing around hither and thither, laughing and joking, always at the centre of things. But then at other times he'd be overcome with depression and despair.'

'Even so, why? When his life seemed so perfect?'

'He never came to terms with the conditions some of his pupils lived and worked in. He used to say it was such an unnecessary waste of life. I remember when one of his best cyclists, Francis Martin, was crushed to death in Wangford Mill, he was inconsolable. The poor boy had only just started work and was inexperienced in the workings of the mill. He found himself drawn into the cog wheels by his clothing and that was an end to him. William railed against the unfeeling attitude of the foreman, but nothing changed.

'And then there was the tragic death of Ben Crowe. William always blamed himself for his death, but of course there was nothing he could have done to prevent it.' He stared absently into the dark recess of the barn, imagining William's corpse lying there.

Ernest studied the friendly, open face, one corner of the mouth chewing on the stem of his pipe. A spark of burning tobacco fell from the bowl onto the hay beneath their feet. Ernest quickly ground it with his boot.

They lolled against the inside wall, both musing their own thoughts for some time, Busby puffing noisily on his pipe while Ernest stirred the hay absent-mindedly with his stick. For an instant he thought he caught a glimpse of blood-stained stalks, but it was too dark to be certain.

Blood on the straw.

Of course. That's it. Ernest froze, his stick poised in mid-air, pointing into the darkness. *That's it. Blood on the straw.* The sudden realisation that he'd found a solution to his own agonising accident after so many years left him stunned, immobile.

There was a commotion outside the butcher's shop in Carr Street, next to the newspaper office. Someone was peering into the adjacent stable where the butcher kept his horse and cart. Someone else shouting over and over again, "He's cut his throat! He's cut his throat!" That's when I stepped into the road to take a look. Then the black horses were upon me. That's it! That's what I couldn't remember. The butcher cutting his throat. Blood on the straw.

After several minutes emersed in his own recollections Ernest said, 'Can I ask you something?'

Busby turned to him. 'Of course.'

'It's difficult to put into words and I haven't mentioned it to anyone before, but......' he faltered.

'Yes?'

'I've been writing a lot about spies and spymania recently. Reporting the arrests of people suspected of being enemy aliens, that sort of thing. I've covered meetings, when people like the Chief Constable have held forth on the subject of spies in our midst. And the paper's published them all quite prominently, of course. Do you think......erm....do you think?...' again he hesitated.

Busby looked sympathetically at the young man. 'Do I think you've aggravated the situation with your sensational stories of spies?'

'Yes, I suppose that's what I'm trying to say.'

Busby drew on his pipe and puffed a sweet-smelling white cloud into the barn.

'It's difficult to know. Which comes first? The very sensible warnings to be on the look out for people behaving suspiciously and your reporting of them, or the hysterical reaction of the public? Because it seems to me that this pseudo-patriotic hysteria about spies is what caused the malicious gossip about William, and caused it to spread in this village. Gossip and tittle tattle which ultimately harried him into the grave. But what you're asking is; should you blame *yourself* for this happening?'

Ernest nodded, but no words could come.

Busby paused as he tapped his pipe out on the wall. 'Ah well now, that's a very deep question indeed. I really don't know what to say on that. If anyone's to blame it is the press as a whole and their seeking after sensational news to titillate their readers. No one individual journalist should be made to bear such a responsibility. No, no indeed,' he concluded.

'I wish I could believe you're right, but I feel most dreadfully that I helped precipitate this poor man's death.' The words rushed out.

Busby laid a hand gently on Ernest's narrow shoulder. 'My dear young man, I applaud your candidness with me. You must take heart from this honesty. You have it in your capacity as a journalist to right wrongs, to repair situations and I'm sure that's what you'll strive to do.' He tapped his pipe finally on the edge of the door frame to knock out the last dregs of spent tobacco. 'Have you mentioned your misgivings to your editor?' he asked.

'No. I don't think I could. He's a good editor, but…'

'But?'

'But I doubt whether he'd understand. If I told him how I felt he'd most likely say I was going soft in the head. He'd think I wasn't coping and give my job to someone else. Alf Gilbert, perhaps. I couldn't bear that. It would be humiliating.'

'Ah, the old demon pride raising its ugly head again,' Busby chided. 'I suspect your fear of humiliation and disgrace is akin to that felt by poor dear William. Our reputations make martyrs of us all, don't you think?'

Ernest shrugged. 'Maybe so.'

'Come,' the headmaster said at last, stuffing the pipe into his breast pocket. 'We'll find the station wagonner and get him to take us back to the station. We can talk more about this on the train.'

East Anglian Daily Times

Friday November 6 1914

Fight for Ypres. Most desperate battle of the war. Battle still in progress. British outnumbered by four to one. Times Telegram from PA Northern France, Thursday Nov 5. Eye witness dispatch.

The battle of Ypres is still in progress. It has now become a battle of artillery. The infantry have, for the present, at all events done their work. The British infantry have done it well. They have repulsed the enemy in spite of their overwhelming numbers. The German army has been driven back eastward, back into their own trenches. Here for the present they are safe under cover of their big guns.

The battle of Yser, thanks largely to the waste of waters stretching between the opposing armies, is practically over. The Germans are credibly supposed to have realised the futility of trying to break through and to be meditating a retreat to the north. Further south the enemy has made his supreme effort between Ypres and Lille.

Here, as I indicated yesterday, a great and sudden blow was struck and it was the British army that received it. Some of the heaviest fighting during this war ensued, but the Germans, speaking in a general sense, were repulsed with appalling slaughter. Fighting is still furiously in progress, but having failed in the first place the enemy, it may be assumed, in the light of past experience would do no better in later attempts.

The German losses, I am credibly informed, have amounted during this great attack on the British lines to well over 50,000. The fury of the German attack has undoubtedly spent itself although I think it is rather early yet to emphasise suggestions of German demoralisation. The enemy has a way of recovering himself after the severest defeats and even after a course of starvation rations, which must be recognised. Even if he is an unscrupulous foe he is dogged and brave and docile to command.

Chapter Twenty Three

Saturday November 7 1914

'Earth to earth, ashes to ashes, dust to dust,' Alma murmured as she dressed in unfamiliar black widow's weeds. These were the words the Reverend Trevor Edwards would utter as William's body was consigned to the newly dug grave beside the vestry door. She dreaded hearing them. They were so final.

'How's it come to this?' She addressed her reflection in the mirror on the wash-stand as she fiddled with the positioning of the hat and veil on her peppered curls. Satisfied, she stabbed it through with a long hatpin. She couldn't get the phrase out of her head.

Dust to dust. This can't be happening to me. Surely this can't be happening? Will, tell me it's all a bad dream. A nightmare. Why, only last Saturday we were helping the children dig over the soil in the school vegetable garden, ready for spring planting.

Her dressing was complete. She gazed at herself in the small mirror and for the first time in her life loathed what she saw. The soft greens and greys or delicate floral prints she usually wore had been replaced with the harshness of sombre mourning. It did not suit her. It enveloped her, body and soul, crushing her into a subserviance of sadness. She fingered the stiff fabric of the new dress.

'This isn't me at all,' she muttered, shaking her head in disbelief. Transfixed by the image, she sat motionless, unable to move or think rationally.

Behind her, in the mirror's middle distance, her eyes re-focused on the most painful reminder of her loss. The large iron-framed feather bed she and Will had shared for thirty years and where she'd given birth to their three children. Over the years she'd failed to notice how the patchwork quilt she'd stitched so diligently as a newly-wed had faded and frayed. Now she noticed and it hurt.

So many years. God was good to us. Life was good. Why did it all have to end like this? Why did you leave me? Why did you have to do it? I just don't understand. She clasped her hands to her face and sunk her head in silent prayer. *Dear God, help me to forgive them. It's very hard.*

A quiet knock at the door broke into her thoughts.

'Mother, are you ready? Everyone's assembled in the school, waiting for you.' Evelyn spoke softly as she opened the door.

Alma nodded and turned from her mirror. Evelyn was beautiful in a pale, translucent way. The young woman in her late twenties was heavily pregnant and the strain of carrying her baby, maybe even twins her doctor had warned, was etched in the blue shadows around her eyes. Evelyn had so longed to produce a grandchild for her beloved father and that longing was about to be fulfilled. She'd dreamt of the day she would place the baby in his arms for the first time. Imagined his coos of delight as he danced the child around the schoolroom. But now the child would never gaze up into its grandfather's smiling brown eyes and her father would never feel the tiny hands gripping his fingers.

Evelyn's misery was magnified by her anxiety for her mother. She could see Alma's grasp on sanity teetering on the brink of total collapse. And she had another, unspoken fear. That Johnnie, having joined the Territorials, would soon be sent to France with his regiment.

Evelyn took Alma's arm and led her downstairs.

'If only Alex could have been here, too,' Alma said wistfully, thinking of the son she'd not seen since boyhood, as they made their way across the yard to greet the mourners.

Evelyn agreed. It was years since she'd seen her brother. Always working in some far-flung, desolate corner of the world. 'Johnnie sent a telegraph to the college where he works in Guatemala, just as soon as we heard about poor father,' she said. 'But who knows how long it'll take to reach him? It could be weeks before he gets it. Don't fret mother, I'm sure he'll be back.'

A large crowd of mourners had gathered in the schoolroom waiting to take up their positions in the funeral procession. William's two brothers, John and George, had brought their families from Devon. Alma's sister, Minnie Valletta, and her husband Charles were there from Bream in Gloucestershire.

Alma was overwhelmed to see the large number of schoolteachers who had come to pay their tributes. They'd come from across the county, representing teaching unions and associations. They had taken the news of William's death particularly hard. So many knew him as an inspiring teacher. If such a terrible tragedy could befall him, who might be next to suffer such injustice? She was comforted to see Hilda Barber and Florrie Howeld, their assistant and pupil teacher, standing nervously together in a corner of the room.

Local people, who were anxious to show they had given the vicious rumours no credence, smiled sypathetically at Alma as she moved about the room. Members of the clergy, the postmaster, members of the Parish Council of which William had been a member and the bowling club where he'd been chairman.

The largest contingent of mourners, though, had walked in procession from Henham Hall estate, led by William Mitchell. Standing in respectful silence were the Earl's butler and steward, his head gardener and head carpenter.

The head gamekeeper had gathered around him at least two dozen estate workers. *So many of our children. If only Will had known what people here really thought of him, he'd be alive now,* she thought.

The press of bodies threatened to overwhelm her. Close by she noticed the inky blue uniform of policemen. Two of them, at her husband's funeral. *How dare they! How dare they come here. Today of all days.*

Superintendent Herbert Clarke and Inspector Walter Ruffles averted their gaze as she passed without a word. *Why are they here?* she thought. *That terrible letter from Captain Mayne which drove William mad. Drove him to this insane act. They're the guilty ones.* She wanted to round on them and point her finger and scream, 'Murderers! You're to blame for William's death!' But the words wouldn't come. Sadness quelled her anger, and besides she could feel Evelyn's comforting hand at her elbow.

Outside the yard echoed not to the joyful shouts of running children, but with boots stamping in the frostbitten dust to pacify chilled bones and the subdued muttering of yet more mourners.

Beyond them, out on the winding turnpike which would lead the funeral cortege to the church, the Countess sat waiting in her carriage. She was alone and composed; icy-faced and impassive. Waiting to show that she, Lady Stradbroke, believed William Smith had been a loyal Englishman and a true friend. She confidently expected her very presence in the procession to proclaim his innocence to the world. Proclaim her distain for the vile-tongued village gossips who had destroyed him.

In front of her carriage the hearse bearing William's coffin presented a sombre sight, its four black horses draped and standing patiently. She watched as their breath formed writhing spirals into the frosty air while the undertaker and his assistant held their heads steady.

Earlier that morning Helena had ordered that some of the estate workers take precious winter bedding straw from the barns to scatter on the cobbles of the main street. 'As a mark of respect to Mr Smith,' she had told William Mitchell.

The funeral cortege moved off. A slow, painful procession of black, winding its way up the narrow street from the school through the village. At its head the hearse, followed by the pony and trap bearing Alma with Evelyn and Johnnie. The Countess's carriage took its place behind the family and following her, in slow-trodden formation, a sea of black sadness.

The tolling of a single church bell and the muffled, deadened drumming of horses hooves and wooden wheels on straw-littered cobbles the only sounds to break the clear air.

As the procession passed across the border from one parish to another, more than a hundred children from the school, each carrying a bunch of white chrysanthemums, signifying truth and honesty, were there to meet it. With them stood more representatives of the different organisations and societies with which William had been connected and almost the entire staff of Henham Hall; housemaids and grooms, footmen with ploughmen.

Alma gazed down from her seat in the trap. So many people lining the street. So great an outpouring of grief and affection. *Why didn't they take to the street and proclaim the rumours false last week? Last month, even?* She was not to be comforted by their sympathies. *Now he's dead and nothing can bring him back.* She pressed a handkerchief to her eyes to stem the tears.

The horses were pulled to a halt at the church gate. The polished oak coffin was carefully lifted from the open hearse then slowly born aloft into the church on the shoulders of pallbearers from the Henham Estate. Behind them followed the officiating clergy and the choir.

Children of all ages lined up on either side of the pathway in final salute to their headmaster. Many were in tears, whether they were old enough to understand the full impact of his death or not. Walking behind her husband's coffin, Alma searched their faces as she passed. There was genuine grief in these innocent eyes. They had loved him as she had. They shared her tears just as William had shared his life with them.

Those waiting patiently outside heard the service from within the church. Heard the full-throated singing, the heart-felt responses to the prayers for forgiveness and redemption.

Stanley and John had been given the task of covering the funeral for the Daily Times. They moved quietly among the villagers, pencils and notebooks in hand, questioning. 'What kind of man was Mr Smith?' they asked. 'Why do you think so many people have come to show their sorrow and grief at his suicide?' 'How could anyone say he was a spy?'

The villagers were eager to provide honest answers that would satisfy them. 'Mr Smith has always been a great patriot who strove to leave the world better than he found it,' answered one.

'No one but a patriot would have interested himself to the extent Mr Smith did in his fellow men. The large numbers you see today are here because they want to testify to this,' said another.

'How can they say he was a traitor to his country?' demanded one woman. 'Why, he was in the midst of organising a concert to raise funds for the wounded soldiers at Henham Hall just before he died. How can people have said such dreadful things about him? All he cared about was teaching children.'

The journalists faithfully recorded their comments. The obituary they would write would underline the shameful nature of this man's death. This was undoubtedly a big story. A *cause célèbre* that would sell newspapers.

The last 'Amen' echoed from within the cavernous flint church. The church door was flung open and the coffin carried out. As it arrived at the graveside by the vestry door the children crowded round, scattering their posies of white chrysanthemums over the polished lid. It bore the simple inscription: "William Smith, died November 4th 1914, aged 52".

These simple flowers were all that was buried with him, except for the small bunch of golden chrysanthemums Alma had picked from the school garden before sunrise. She gently tossed the tiny posy onto the coffin. She heard the earth tumbling onto the lid. 'Earth to earth, ashes to ashes, dust to dust,' the clergyman intoned distantly. It was too much. She sank to her knees at the graveside, sobbing uncontrollably.

The journalists watched and noted everything. This was a drama that had everything; the wrongful accusation of a wholly innocent man, spy mania, police bungling, the war, a gruesome death, the love of a bereaved widow and the unwavering support of the dead man's aristocratic benefactor.

They diligently noted the messages on the wreaths placed on the grave after the mourners had moved away. These would be avidly consumed by their newspaper's readers, they agreed.

They noted that the Countess of Stradbroke expressed her regard with the words 'A loyal Englishman and true friend.' Her husband's fine wreath bore the words 'Col. The Earl of Stradbroke, CVO, CB, ADC, to his friend Mr William Smith, in grateful recollection for all the good work he did for the people and children of Wangford and Henham parishes during the thirty years he resided amongst them'. The Earl's son, Viscount Dunwich, wrote 'To Mr Smith, who taught me to swim'. The Earl and Countess's other children also sent a floral tribute.

There were countless others; from the scholars, teachers and former pupils, from fellow-workers in the Sunday School, from employees on the Henham Estate and from many old friends.

Evelyn and her husband gently led Alma away. Away down the long pathway through the graveyard and into the main street. The pony walked quietly, its hooves and the wooden wheels of the trap swishing through the straw. It bore the three of them on the lonely journey home.

There seemed no relief from the nightmare in the days that followed the funeral. Alma was in shock. She spent hours in her room, either gazing out of the window at the harsh, monochrome landscape with its ploughed fields and frost-tinged hedges, or at a small photograph of William by her bedside. She ate little and hardly slept. Visitors who came to offer their condolences were politely turned away by Ida Spencer, the housekeeper. 'Mrs Smith isn't well enough to receive visitors,' she would explain, closing the door of the schoolhouse quietly in their wake.

Ida was worried about her mistress's sanity. At night she'd hear Alma roaming the rooms and corridors, calling her husband's name. Sometimes the scullery door would bang to a close. Peering from her top floor window Ida often spied Alma in her nightclothes, weaving demented patterns back and forth across the darkened schoolyard.

Ida now took over the complete running of the house. She ensured the fires and lamps were lit and the shopping and cooking done. She tried to tempt Alma to eat nourishing broths and puddings, but her mistress refused, pushing the food away. Ida also reluctantly assumed dog-walking duties, taking Dick on his customary morning and evening forays into his favourite hunting territory along the river bank.

It was here, one morning, that she was approached by Charlie Boggis, one of the older pupils. Charlie and his brother Clement had spent some years boarding with Will and Alma when they were younger. Their parents had considered the three-mile walk from their home in Southwold too far for such small children. He'd become part of the Smith family, just as Ida had done over the twelve years she'd spent in service with them.

'Miss Ida,' Charlie panted as he ran up to her. 'Is that ole Dick?'

'Yes, Charlie. Now master's gone there's no-one to take him out. More's the pity. He's a dog that needs a lot of walking. Long walks and rabbiting, not just leaping into the pool to rescue the likes of *you* when yer can't swim.'

'That wus when I wus a little'un. I'm in the life saving team now, Miss Ida,' Charlie retorted proudly. 'And I bet I could rescue *you* if yer fell in.' He pointed to the bathing pool, its murky depths now covered in a thin layer of ice.

Ida huffed and shook her head. 'Well I can't dilly dally chatting to you. I've got lunch to prepare for Mrs Smith.' She gathered her shawl tightly around her shoulders and turned to head back to the schoolhouse. 'Besides, there's snow on the way I shouldn't wonder.'

Charlie looked thoughtful. 'Miss Ida, if you're too busy I could walk Dick for you. I could take him out before school and then again before I cycle home.'

Ida smiled. Dog walking wasn't her favourite chore. 'If yer like. Dick knows you and would come back when you called. Come round tomorrow morning, at eight. Call at the scullery door, mind, so you don't disturb Mrs Smith.'

To prove he could be masterful with the wayward black Labrador, Charlie let out a piercing whistle and yelled, 'Dick! Dick! Come here, Dick!' To his astonishment the dog bounded back immediately and sat panting between them.

'There, Ida. I can do it,' he said proudly, patted the dog's head, murmuring all the while, 'Good ole Dick, good ole Dick.'

They walked together to the schoolhouse and when they reached the gate Charlie glanced up at the bedroom windows. Alma was watching them, a dark, shadowy figure, half hidden by the heavy drapes.

'Is that Mrs Smith?' He sounded curious. 'It don't look like her.'

'Yes, Charlie, but she's not feeling herself at the moment.'

'She looks so sad. It was terrible about Mr Smith killing himself like that. And her finding him dead in the little ole hay shed with his throat cut and blood everywhere.' He stopped and looked at Ida, immediately wishing he hadn't said it.

'What'll she do now?' he said, rapidly changing tack. 'Do you think she'll still be our teacher? We miss her, so. And Mr Smith, of course. They've sent us a new headmaster this week to take his place, but it's not the same.' Charlie rattled on, but Ida had lost interest.

'I'll see you tomorrow at eight to collect Dick,' she said abruptly and with that she and the dog disappeared through the scullery door.

While the gossip among children at the school was about their new headmaster, everyone else in Henham and Wangford could talk of nothing but William's death. They were still in shock at the way he'd died. While some claimed he'd been murdered, others argued that rumours he'd been a spy had driven him to take his own life. 'Fancy the police banishing Mr Smith from the county!' Some weren't convinced of his innocence, though. 'No smoke without fire,' they'd parrot, and recall the German frauleins who had stayed in the schoolhouse and Alex's prolonged absence abroad.

Nobody was prepared to broach the subject of who was to blame. The fact Lord and Lady Stradbroke had made it clear they had no doubts left them feeling uneasy.

'It'll be up to the jury at the inquest to decide,' Tom Baxter, the postmaster, said sensibly whenever one of his customers broached the subject. 'But everyone in Wangford and Henham must bear some of the blame. We all heard the rumours. Why, practically everyone who came into this shop used to whisper about hearing there were spies in the neighbourhood. And even if you and I didn't indulge in the tittle tattle ourselves, we didn't exactly rush to Mr Smith's defence, did we? Who among us actually stood up and said, publicly, "What nonsense! William Smith is no more a German spy than I am"!'

His customers would shuffle their feet uncomfortably.

'None of us,' they'd admit ruefully. 'And you're right. We should have. He was a good man. The best in the village. That's what Lady Stradbroke said at the inquest last Friday.'

'Wait until the resumed inquest hears what the Chief Constable has to say. He must have heard something pretty shocking to have sent that letter,' was Mr Baxter's final word on the matter.

East Anglian Daily Times

Monday November 9 1914

Editorial

When Parliament meets on Wednesday one of its most important duties will be to consider and revise the operations of the Press Bureau. The nation, at enormous cost and suffering, is making a gigantic war, but it is not allowed to know what is really going on.

Patriotism is a flame which burns brightly by stories of heroism and tales of daring, but no such inspirations ever come through the agency of the Press Bureau. The news it permits to filter through is of the scantiest kind, and if it were not for the more communicative French Bureau we should know little or nothing of our soldiers at the Front.

The effect on recruiting is very prejudicial, for English enthusiasm is stirred best by knowledge. A glorious defeat moves us almost as much as a victory and there was no time when recruits came more freely and gallantly to the standard than after the retreat from Mons.

We sympathise with the position of the gentlemen who form the Press Bureau. Their duties are probably as distasteful to them as was the work of the gentlemen who formed the Star Chamber in the days of Charles. Bodies placed in posts of dictatorial authority invariably go too far. The Press Bureau has been hurriedly placed in the position of determining what the British nation shall know and what it shall not, and in the endeavour to serve its masters has gone much further than the masters desired.

The military authorities were naturally anxious to prevent news 'of use to the enemy' from getting through, but this does not imply the suppression of all intelligence.

A week ago there was a naval engagement off Yarmouth, the news of which the Press Bureau took pains to suppress. Is it because the British public is regarded as incapable of sustaining news of disaster or mishap? What possible gain could it be to the enemy to be told of the engagement long after the German ships had sent their news home by wireless?

When the British had an opportune and gallant encounter with the Germans between Harwich and Antwerp, sinking four of the enemy's destroyers, publication of the news was also objected to by the Press Bureau. Both victory and disappointment came under the same regulation ban.

King George has spoken well, our politicians and orators have stopped their differences and uttered inspiring words to the British people, but no help comes from the war side – only silence and long lists of wounded.

Is this the way to promote recruiting, to keep up the levies constantly required at the front to meet the strain of the German millions? Would it not be better to take the nation into trust and confidence?

We submit that the Press Bureau is a feeble and unsatisfactory instrument in regard to the dissemination of news, that if continued, its operation should include the provision of quick and adequate intelligence instead of suppression or excision, and that the British public should have all news promptly - good as well as bad - care being taken that we profit and that the enemy profits nothing.

Englishmen do not care to hide their heads in the sand. Public interest in the war is at its highest pitch and our leaders must not despise national enthusiasm.

Chapter Twenty Four

Friday November 13 1914

Even Alma, in her numbed state, was curious to hear what Captain Jasper Mayne had to say. He was her husband's accuser, his interrogator and tormentor. She wanted to hear his voice. The voice that had caused William such pain. Hear him speak the same words he'd thrown in William's face. His accusations, his taunts. Hear him justify the letter that signed Will's death warrant. She would listen to that voice and search his eyes for the betraying signs of guilt. Or perhaps he felt no guilt for what he had done.

For the rest of the villagers, the appearance of someone as illustrious as the county's Chief Constable in their midst caused huge excitement. It burnished the gruesome death of their headmaster with an added frisson of speculation.

Ernest Hart and half a dozen other reporters from London newspapers were among the large crowds which had gathered well before the resumed inquest began that afternoon. Once again they commandeered the seats at the front of the classroom, anxious to catch every word.

Outside, the schoolyard buzzed with excited chatter as the crowd grew ever larger. The more agile amongst the onlookers leapt onto the wall to ensure a prime position. Hundreds of people had come from across the county to see Captain Mayne arrive to give evidence. At last the truth would be heard.

Jasper Mayne presented an awesome figure. Straight-backed and impassive, he arrived seated in the back of the local superintendant's horse and trap having being collected from Blythburgh Station. As immaculate as ever, his left breast was conspicuously adorned with military campaign ribbons and medals which glinted in the autumn sunshine. As he stepped down from the trap he halted momentarily, taken aback by the size of the gathering craning to catch a glimpse of him. Then he strode through the open school door, head aloft, deliberately avoiding their gaze.

The Coroner, Arthur Vulliamy, with the jury at his side, was already seated at the head of the long oak table awaiting his entrance. He offered Captain Mayne one of four seats reserved for police witnesses. At Mayne's right hand, looking ill at ease, Superintendent George Staunton, shifting in his seat. At his left Superintendent Herbert Clarke, who was based at Halesworth, nervously folding and re-folding his arms while PC Charles Revell's staring eyes revealed his terror at further cross-examination.

Inspector Walter Ruffles, Revell's superior from Southwold, a fair complexioned, robust middle-aged man, sat fingering his police notebook, absently turning the pages back and forth.

Once again the man who would pick away at the fabrication they'd woven, sat at the opposite end of the table. Tall and composed, his unruly hair falling across his eyes, Henry Lynn KC, prepared to confront the Chief Constable.

This time Alma would be spared the agony of giving evidence and was thankful to be seated with her daughter and son-in-law in the front row. She could hardly bear to look when the Chief Constable swept past her, his polished boots brushing against the hem of her black mourning skirt as he did so. With a great effort of will she forced her gaze upwards to take in the impassive face, the cold grey eyes and the meticulously-manicured moustache.

This is the man who killed my husband. I must see him for myself.

The Coroner opened proceedings by reminding the gathering that it was Captain Mayne who had signed the order issued by the military authorities calling on William Smith to leave Suffolk under the Defence of the Realm Act.

Henry Lynn was first to address the jury. He stood and waited for the whispering to cease before starting. When he did so his voice was resolute, tinged with suppressed anger. 'We're here today to hear exactly *why* East Suffolk police thought William Smith was either a German or a German spy,' he said. 'On what did they base this suspicion? What was the reason for issuing the notice banning him from Suffolk?'

He turned with a dramatic flourish of his arms towards the jury. It was their pronouncement at the end of this inquest that everyone was waiting for and he wanted to make an indelible impression with his opening remarks.

The first witness, Superintendent George Staunton, was called. Yes, he told Henry Lynn, he knew Mr Smith. He'd seen him just once, at the police station in Ipswich.

'He came to ask you, didn't he, why the notice was issued?' asked Lynn.

'He came to see the Chief Constable', Staunton replied.

'But he saw *you*,' persisted Lynn.

'I was present, yes,' Staunton agreed.

'What conversation took place between you and Mr Smith?'

'He was telling the Chief Constable his history, and said he'd been thirty years here,' replied Supt Staunton, holding his small leather police notebook open at the page where he had made notes of the meeting. 'I said, "Where were you born"? He said, "I was born in Devonshire". I said, "You don't speak like a Devonshire man."

'"No," he said. "I've been thirty years in Suffolk". I said, "You don't speak like a Suffolk man, either". That was all I said.'

'Didn't you say, "You look like a German?' accused Lynn.

'No,' Staunton said, then quickly added, 'nor even thought of it.'

'Had you any reason from the conversation you heard to suspect that he'd ever been a spy?'

'Never.' Staunton denied he'd played any part in the investigation into Mr Smith's case. 'The Chief Constable would deal with that,' he said warily.

'So far as you know, no investigation was made of any kind whatever?' said Lynn.

'So far as I know *every* investigation was made. I know nothing one way or the other.' Staunton was cagey.

Police Constable Revell, who'd given evidence at the previous week's hearing, was again called. He had told the jury that he'd told Mr Smith there was no need for him to leave the district 'for the present'.

Henry Lynn suspected someone was lying and he was about to find out who.

'According to you, constable, Mrs Smith's evidence was untrue?' said Lynn.

'It wasn't untrue,' admitted the constable.

'Mrs Smith said you mentioned *nothing* at all about *not* having to remove for the present, but that action was *merely deferred*.' Lynn exaggerated the final phrase, allowing it to linger heavily in the air. The banning order, he hoped to imply, had been left hanging over William Smith's head like an executioner's guillotine, only pausing momentarily before dropping to do its deadly work.

Revell thought for a moment and replied sullenly, 'She must have misunderstood me. I told her plainly in the house and I told Mr Smith on the road.'

'When you saw him, did he say, "I know"?'

Revell said he had.

'With regard to these rumours you spoke about, did you ever make inquiries as to whether they were *true*?' Lynn prodded further, anxious to reveal and ridicule the bungling ineptitude of the local constabulary.

'I did as far as I could,' Revell stammered.

Lynn was insistent. 'What did you do?'

'I inquired of people who came to see me.'

'What did you find out?'

Revell shook his head, refusing to be drawn. How could he admit that all he'd heard were malicious rumours and mere tittle tattle? 'I cannot go into that. I reported to the Chief Constable.'

Lynn leaned a little closer to his witness. 'What did you report?'

'I cannot go into that,' the young constable repeated.

Arthur Vulliamy interrupted. 'Did you find anything to lead you to believe he was a spy?'

Revell admitted he hadn't.

Rumours, rumours. Henry Lynn wondered if anyone had ever asked William Smith directly to his face, about the rumours that were circulating about him. 'Did you ever speak to Smith about these rumours?' he asked the policeman.

'I spoke to him, but not about the rumours.'

Extraordinary, thought Lynn. *A man is banished from the home he's lived in for thirty years and no-one tells him why.*

One of the jurors wanted to probe further. He asked, 'Of whom did you make inquiries in regard to Smith?'

Revell stood his ground. 'I can't answer that.'

Inspector Walter Ruffles, Revell's superior, was the next to be cross-examined by Henry Lynn. The KC was warming to his task, knowing that the prevarication and fudging would reach its zenith when Mayne himself took the stand.

'Had you heard the rumours about Mr Smith, too?' Lynn asked him.

Ruffles said he had. Pc Revell had mentioned them to him, but he refused to disclose the nature of the rumours.

By now Lynn was becoming riled. So much dissembling. So much secrecy, especially among the police hierarchy. He sensed the large audience watching in the schoolroom shared his unease.

'I'm sorry, but I must ask you. Is it the practice in Suffolk to make inquiries when anything of this kind is reported to you, and when all you've heard is rumours?'

'We make careful inquiries as a rule,' said Inspector Ruffles.

'Were they made in this case?'

'No.'

'Do you know of anybody who made them?'

Ruffles shook his head, negatively.

Now a fourth police officer took the stand. Supt Herbert Clarke was clear that William Smith had been made aware of a telegram sent to Pc Revell by the Chief Constable, saying the removal notice, which had been served on him, was now deferred. 'The telegram was telling him that he need not go away from the village at present,' explained Supt Clarke. 'I saw him as he was returning home in the station waggon after his interview at Ipswich Police Station. Mr Smith appeared to be very pleased. He leant from his seat and called out to me, saying, "Isn't it a good job I carried those papers up with me to see the Chief Constable? It will show that my boy is living in America and not in Germany".'

Clarke said he'd understood that Mr Smith hadn't got to go away.

Lynn persisted. 'Did you understand that the charge against him was *removed*?'

'I gathered it would be removed.'

'That the whole thing was cleared?'

'That was my opinion.'

Henry Lynn was even more mystified. No one had yet spelt out what the specific charge against William Smith had been. This high ranking police officer was saying it would be removed and the matter cleared up. Why had no-one told Smith, though?

'As Superintendent of the neighbourhood, you knew Mr Smith?'

'I have known him for thirty years.'

'You found, as a rule, he had been a perfectly good citizen?' Lynn realised this was a leading question. The Coroner fixed him with a stare and Lynn thought he was about to object to his line of questioning. But Clarke's answer surprised him.

'I think he was a very... er...what shall I say?... very *excitable* man.' Supt Clarke hesitated, searching for a word to describe the headteacher.

'Has anything, anything at all, in his life during the last thirty years, given you an idea that he was disloyal?' pressed Lynn.

Clarke knew he was on flimsy ground. 'From what I've heard I think he had been very indiscreet with his tongue and actions during this present crisis.'

Lynn snapped. 'Give me an example?'

'From what I've heard'..... But he wasn't allowed to go any further.

Lynn banged the table hard with his fist. 'From what you've *heard*! Rumours again! Was it ever your duty to inquire as to whether there was any *truth* in these rumours?'

'Everything was forwarded to the Chief Constable and he would make inquiry. You couldn't go about the village making inquiries,' explained Clarke lamely.

'What was *your* opinion of Mr Smith's character?' said the barrister, his voice tinged with irony.

'I believe he was a loyal subject of his country, but very excitable, which would lead him away at times.'

Lynn glared at the witness. 'I know a lot of loyal subjects who are very excitable, but does that lead you to think they are anything in the nature of *spies*?'

Clarke admitted, 'I don't think he was.' He sat down, looking defeated and perplexed.

'Call the next witness, the Chief Constable of East Suffolk, Captain Jasper Mayne.' At the Coroner's summons a rustle of whispers passed through the crowd.

The Chief Constable stood, as though to attention, pushing back his chair noisily. His eyes met Henry Lynn's, his unwavering gaze confronting the dandified scorn of the counsel's. Both realised this was to be a crucial confrontation.

'Capt Mayne, I believe you wish to make a statement to this inquest,' Arthur Vulliamy inquired.

Jasper Mayne held a typewritten sheet in one hand. He twisted the end of his moustache with the forefinger and thumb of the other. Playing for time, steadying his nerve.

He began by expressing his sympathy for Alma Smith and the bereaved relatives. It was terse and official.

'I thought it best,' Mayne said, turning from the Coroner to the audience ranged along the benches, 'to read a written and considered statement in view of the various and inaccurate statements made at the last hearing, and the misconceptions which doubtless sprung from them,' he explained. He looked down at his paper.

'I cannot, in any circumstances, in my position as Chief Constable, and as an officer of the Crown, reply to any question framed or put with the object of eliciting information as to the nature or substance of confidential or privileged documents. Nor can I answer questions as to the grounds for the order served on the late Mr Smith by the police to leave, temporarily, that proclaimed area under the Defence of the Realm Act.'

Jasper Mayne relished the look of amazement in Henry Lynn's eyes. He'd succeeded in slamming the door on further embarrassing questions.

He went on: 'Information with regard to such matters isn't relevant to the present inquiry which, I gather, is to determine the cause of Mr Smith's death and the state of his mind at the time.

'The war has called for the passing of legislation of an unprecedented nature,' he declared. 'Among public officials who have to carry that legislation into effect I venture to suggest no one holds a more responsible and anxious position than the Chief Constable of one of those Eastern Counties on the coastal frontier. The one dominant and governing factor I have to bear steadily in mind is the safety of this country,' he added, puffing out his chest with self-satisfied importance.

Mayne was anxious to move on to refute several of the damaging accusations made against the police at the previous Friday's hearing. He held up a handful of newspapers. Ernest Hart and the other journalists in the room shuffled in their seats and exchanged rapid glances. Was the Chief Constable about to rip into their reporting of the opening of the inquest? They waited expectantly as Mayne flicked through the pages of one of them.

He held a copy of the Daily Times aloft. Ernest closed his eyes, praying the Chief Constable wouldn't mention him by name, singling him out for public scorn. Then Mayne opened the paper wide and peered at the centre pages.

'According to these newspaper reports a member of the public stated that "What broke the deceased's heart was that he was accused of being a German",' Mayne read in a voice well-used to commanding attention. 'That accusation was never made by the police. Nor has it been alleged by the police, as has been suggested, that Mr Smith's daughter married a German. A member of the public said that I told her there was nothing in it except village gossip. I never said anything of the kind.'

Mayne's disparaging reference to the Countess of Stradbroke as 'a member of the public' wasn't lost on the Chief Constable's audience, nor on Henry Lynn. *Is he being deliberately demeaning to the Countess?* wondered Lynn. If so, he'd expose Mayne for the arrogant fool he was.

Mayne went on. 'The member of the public in question called me up on the telephone at Ipswich.'

Henry Lynn leapt up. 'Her name is Lady Stradbroke. You needn't describe her as a member of the public.'

'She *is* a member of the public,' retorted Mayne distainfully.

He's digging himself even deeper into the consciousness of the jury as a bumptious idiot, thought Lynn, glancing over to the twelve men sitting quietly to one side of the Coroner. *Perhaps he doesn't realise that the jury foreman is the Earl's estate manager.*

Lynn shrugged his shoulders with considered carelessness. 'I suppose so, and so are you.'

'She called me up with reference to this order served on Mr. Smith. The next I heard was – the telephone was rather indistinct – "All slander and village gossip". I'm not giving the exact words, but the sense of it. I didn't quite grasp the import of the remark. I said, "In all districts there's village gossip and slander". The conversation continued but there was nothing more on that particular point. Lady Stradbroke also said, "What distressed Mr Smith most terribly was that one of my officers, Staunton, accused him to his face that he was a German". I have heard Supt Staunton's evidence that this isn't true,' added Mayne.

The Chief Constable then switched to Alma's evidence. He told the jury that Mrs Smith had said her husband had been interviewed at Ipswich police station by Supt Staunton. 'But *I* conducted the interview *myself,*' he said. Staunton had sat in on the interview.

Yet again he attacked the Countess. His simmering resentment of the way she had criticised police handling of the Smiths was obvious. Mayne recalled: 'Lady Stradbroke said, "Why wasn't that telegram given to Mr Smith or Mrs Smith"? Well, it wasn't the constable's duty to hand a telegram from his superior officer to a member of the public.'

The Chief Constable's explanation sounded lame, Lynn judged, and he felt sure the jury would think so, too.

Mayne went on, 'I'd also like to repudiate the statement by Lady Stradbroke that I sent a telegram 'reinstating' Smith – or words to that effect. And I deny, absolutely, that there had been a muddle of any kind where the telegram was concerned.'

Anxious to protect the reputation of his officers he added, 'I also think the statement made by Mrs Smith that a certain policeman laid a false accusation against her husband is a cruel reflection on that officer. Mr Lynn here,' he waved his arm across the table at the barrister, 'has made the most determined effort to fix Mr Smith's death on the police and in particular on that subordinate police officer.'

'I said it, and I meant it,' retorted Henry Lynn.

'That charge, I venture to think, is made without an atom of evidence and without any ground whatever. It's quite uncalled for and a monstrous charge to make.' Mayne was shouting now, leaning across the oak table so that his reddened face was only inches from Lynn's.

Lynn backed away. 'I want to get the evidence - if you can give it to me.'

Mayne sneered. 'I know you do.'

'*Will* you give me the evidence on which you based this charge?' The barrister dropped his voice. It sounded threatening.

'I have explained. I cannot.' Mayne stood, glaring his defiance, arms crossed over his tightly-buttoned uniform.

'I know you can't. Have you got any evidence to justify the charge?'

'The answer is obvious. Yes. It wasn't a charge, anyway.'

'Isn't it *worse* than a charge to discharge a man from his professional life – at once?'

'You know he got an order to leave a proclaimed area,' answered Mayne, refusing to admit he'd pressed any charge on the headmaster.

But Henry Lynn wasn't satisfied. 'What investigation, if any, took place in this case?' he asked.

'A full investigation - by me,' was the Chief Constable's answer. He turned to the jury. There was a certainty in his demeanour which was designed to convince those listening, but instead sowed only resentment in their minds.

'I want to know - *what* investigation?'

'I cannot tell you.'

'Why not?'

'Because it's privileged. I want this to be perfectly clear. You're not a court of inquisition on *me!*'

The audience gasped. This inquest was turning into a battle of wills between the barrister and the Chief Constable. The elegant, urbane young lawyer had the portly, pompous policeman on the defensive. In this extraordinary make-shift court room it was the Chief Constable who appeared to be on trial, his very reputation at stake.

Mayne's intransigence infuriated Lynn. He was deliberately evading questions that were at the heart of the case.

'I ask you to answer any question unless the Coroner says it's wrong. You aren't the person to decide. I want to ask you; what investigation was ever made about this man?'

'I cannot tell you.'

'Was he ever spoken to about the matter?'

'Probably not. As far as I know, not.'

'Then he wasn't spoken to?

Mayne sneered in reply, 'You all understand that under these unprecedented circumstances, in any case of this kind, you can't hold an inquiry.'

'I know that, but you say that you made investigation. So, only when an investigation proves to be right, you take action?' Henry Lynn tried to sound reasonable.

'In cases of espionage?'

'Yes,' said Lynn.

'That has nothing to do with this,' said Mayne. 'We never accused Mr Smith of being a spy .... or of being a German.'

'Then what *did* you accuse him of?' pressed Lynn, feeling that at last he might get to the truth.

But Mayne shook his head. 'I'm not going to tell you. It's not relevant. This is one of the reasons that led to the Order.'

'I want to know what led to the Order. That's what I'm trying to get at.'

'You can't get it. It's not in my power to give you a confidential Order.'

They had reached an impasse. Neither was giving ground. The coroner eyed the two adversaries and decided to intervene.

'The Order was given by the Home Office?' Arthur Vulliamy asked.

'No,' said the Chief Constable, 'by the competent military authority.'

'On what information did they act?' he said patiently.

Mayne wouldn't be drawn. 'Partly on my own and partly on the Chief Officer of Police. It's perfectly clear that the Chief Officer of Police could make a report and the competent military authority, presumably – I can't speak for him – would form his own conclusion and issue the Order.'

'Are you saying you're not going to tell the jury anything at all about the information given by you to the competent military authority?'

'No.'

The Coroner rubbed his hand across his ridged forehead in bewilderment. 'You gave certain information to him?'

'Yes.'

'And the competent military authority then ordered that Mr Smith should leave this district?'

'He then issued an order,' said Mayne, 'which I have got.'

'And consequently *you* sent the notice?'

'Yes.'

Henry Lynn sighed. Mayne was proving the toughest nut to crack in his legal career. But crack this arrogant Chief Constable he would. And anyway, it made a change from defending petty criminals.

'You,' he stabbed his finger across the table at Mayne, '*You* signed the Order.'

'Does the military authority, to whom you report, make their *own* inquiries?' Vulliamy asked.

'Not necessarily,' said Mayne warily.

'That seems to be the difficulty in this case. They don't make inquiries,' he sniffed in disgust. Members of the jury glanced at each other. The Coroner's remarks were significant, pointing them towards their final verdict. 'If they had made inquiries, what would they have found out?' he added, peering long and hard at Mayne over his wire-rimmed spectacles.

'I don't know. I couldn't say. But he wasn't accused of being a German or of being a German spy.' Mayne was determined to press home the innocence of his police officers in this untidy mess.

Vulliamy continued. 'Was it considered bad for him to continue to live here?'

'Yes, and that it was undesirable for him to live in a proclaimed area, having regard to all the circumstances.'

Henry Lynn jumped to his feet. 'As far as you know, did you ever know anything at all except these silly rumours against Mr Smith?'

'Yes.'

'What?'

'I can't tell you.'

'You say deliberately that you know something against Mr Smith and that you won't tell the jury?' Lynn sounded incredulous.

'I am not called upon to reveal anything connected with the reasons which led to the issuing of the Order,' insisted Mayne.

'I don't ask you anything about the reasons that led to the issuing of the order. I ask you: "Do you know anything personally against Mr Smith's character?'

'His character as a loyal Englishman?' Mayne queried. Lynn nodded. 'Certainly I think he was a loyal Englishman. Supt Staunton has already told you that.'

Lynn couldn't believe what he was hearing. Mayne was changing his answers every few minutes. 'Did you ever know anything before or after his death against his character as a good, straight-forward, loyal Englishman?'

'I think he said injudicious things and behaved injudiciously.'

'What did he say injudiciously?'

Mayne pursed his lips. 'I can't go further than that.'

'I ask you again,' Henry Lynn pressed hard, 'what inquiry you made and what the result was?'

But Mayne was obdurate. 'That I can't tell you. I am perfectly able to tell you, but it's not in my power to do so.' It was a strange answer.

Henry Lynn then turned to the note the Chief Constable had added to the margin of the Order, giving the Smiths a brief respite until Friday November 6th before they were forced to leave Suffolk. Why, he asked, had he done this?

'Mr Smith brought me correspondence, which he wanted me to read. He also said he'd produce his birth certificate,' explained Capt. Mayne.

Another inconsistency, thought Lynn. Calmly he leaned towards the Chief Constable. 'Why did you want his birth certificate if he wasn't accused of being a German?'

A murmur of assent buzzed round the room. People in the audience nodded their heads in agreement. It was a fair point.

Mayne wasn't to be fazed. 'I venture to say that most people, seeing Mr Smith for the first time, would have some doubt as to what he was. And certainly having regard to his manner of talking and intonation, and so forth, that doubt did cross my mind. Staunton also asked him a certain question.'

What on earth is he implying? wondered Lynn. William Smith, with his stocky, athletic build and shiny, jet-black hair, was typical of those with Celtic ancestry living in the West Country or in Ireland.

'Was there a doubt as to whether he was a German or not?' he asked.

'I shouldn't like to commit myself to that,' replied Mayne.

'But you had a doubt?'

'Not as to German nationality.'

'Are you quite sure that doubt wasn't expressed?' pressed Lynn.

'Certainly,' Mayne snapped.

'Why did you want his birth certificate?'

Mayne was undeterred. 'It struck me that his nationality was other than English.' Yet still he refused to say what nationality he suspected.

Lynn turned to the bundle of letters William had taken with him to his meeting with the Chief Constable in an attempt to clear his name. Among them was the postcard from the two German students. 'You read his letters and found nothing wrong with them?'

Mayne shuffled his feet uncomfortably and broke his gaze with Lynn. 'I haven't read them yet.'

'Then why on earth did they make you change your mind?'

'One minute,' Mayne faltered. 'You're making an allegation which isn't correct. I've told you. He handed me the letters and said he'd get his birth certificate. I said the delay was only to allow him to remain here until I'd read the letters and he'd got his birth certificate.'

Lynn insisted: 'That telegram didn't mean the thing was *withdrawn?*'

'No. Deferred.'

'Then this man was still under the stigma of this charge?

'I don't like the word "charge". He wasn't charged with anything,' Mayne started to explain, but the legal niceties of what constituted a charge were lost on Lynn.

'Inferentially he was charged with a good deal,' the barrister retorted. 'He was still to remain under the stigma of this order.'

'He was confused. But there was no doubt Revell stated the substance of the telegram to him.'

'That telegram was in no way a *withdrawal* of the notice?'

'Not an *absolute* withdrawal, no' said Mayne.

Lynn tugged at the lapels of his black gown with both hands. He presented a challenging figure in that tiny court room.

'Are you *now* prepared to withdraw the notice?' He was offering Mayne an olive branch, a way of placating the jury and a hostile audience.

'You are asking me to clear his character?'

'The object is that I want to keep Mr Smith's memory sweet,' Lynn said reasonably.

But Mayne wasn't about to apologise or clear William's name, even after death. He turned to face the members of the jury, striving to inject a note of sincerity into his voice. 'I will ask the jury to believe that I would give a good deal to do what you ask. I can't say more than that he was guilty only of injudicious behaviour and utterance, but that would not justify necessarily the withdrawal of the order, having regard to the special times in which we live.'

One of the jury interjected. 'Were there any other reports, other than Pc Revell's? Or was it *all* just gossip?'

Mayne replied directly to the jury. 'No Chief Constable would act alone on the report of a constable. He would take every means in his power to get to the bottom by personal inquiries and consultation with others.'

Lynn interrupted with biting sarcasm, 'Without consulting the man himself?'

'Under these circumstances, certainly.'

'The man was condemned, untried. We know that.' The injustice of such a verdict threatened to overwhelm him.

Another juror wanted to question Mayne further. 'There was no other report, other than Revell's, which he said was founded on gossip only?'

'I don't know that he said that. The position of a rural constable in making a report is that he's bound to report everything necessary. It was a well-balanced and perfectly unbiased report which merely stated certain things. It became the duty of his superior officer to carry the matter further and to form his own conclusions.'

The juror persisted. 'Have you had any *other* report?'

'No other written report,' he admitted finally.

The Coroner indicated to Capt. Mayne that his cross-examination was over. The Chief Constable eased himself back into his seat, aware of twelve pairs of eyes boring into him from the jury side of the table.

Vulliamy then called the local doctor, Charles Acton, to give medical evidence. He said he had been called after Alma had discovered her husband's body in the stone barn. Without emotion he gave the details. The deceased, he said, had cut his throat but died from asphyxia arising from a cut windpipe, not from loss of blood.

'What sort of a man was Mr Smith?' asked Arthur Vulliamy.

'I found the deceased a very excitable man. He was temperate – he didn't drink alcohol - and was exceedingly sensitive to anything said against his honour,' said Dr Acton. 'But in the two or three years I've known him I have to say that once or twice I've seen him on the border line between sanity and insanity. The very tragic drowning of a little scholar while swimming preyed on the deceased's mind for a long, long time.'

'From that you would conclude that this other thing preyed on his mind?'

'Certainly I should,' said Dr Acton.

Henry Lynn took on the questioning. 'What else do you know about him?'

'I have always known him as a most loyal Englishman.'

'Have you heard any rumours?'

Charles Acton shook his head vigorously. 'None at all. I have never been asked, and as a school manager I think I might have been consulted. I thought the police might possibly have come to me for some idea of his character.'

'Have you heard of any inquiry being made by the police?

'No, I have not. It came as a shock to me. Although several things have upset Mr Smith in the past, I don't think his mind has been unhinged during the last few years, no,' Dr Acton replied thoughtfully.

The final witness to give evidence to the inquest was one of the last people to see William before he died. His old friend George Busby. Busby described for the jury, as briefly as he could, the conversation he'd had with William the afternoon before he died. 'Mr Smith told me that they – the police – had accused him at Ipswich of being a German,' he said. 'That got on his mind, I'm sure.'

As he walked back to his seat the audience buzzed with excitement. This dramatic court-room tussle was drawing to its finale. How would it end? What would the jury make of it all? Everyone had an opinion and whispered it loudly to their neighbour.

The elderly Coroner took off his spectacles, polished them on a white handkerchief and placed them carefully back on his nose. It was time to sum up. Briefly, succinctly, but with the full force of his long experience. It was undoubtedly the most controversial inquest he had ever officiated at.

Henry Lynn fixed him with an unerring stare. So much was riding on this case. A man's reputation. The chance to right a wrong, make amends for an injustice.

'The whole point in this case,' began Arthur Vulliamy, 'is whether the deceased, William Smith, was of sound or unsound mind at the time of his death. If he was of unsound mind, what caused it to be so? Was it the notice ordering him to leave Suffolk? And before making such an order did the police make a thorough, exhaustive inquiry?'

There wasn't a sound in the room as everyone strained to hear his quiet reasoning.

'I personally, don't think the police thoroughly investigated this case because they didn't even ask the man involved whether there was any truth in the rumours,' he said, his gaze tracking deliberately around the room. 'They seemed to have taken the rumours direct to the Chief Constable, who acted on them. The Chief Constable didn't order an inquiry before he reported to the military authorities. The military authorities immediately took action. They ordered Mr Smith to leave the place where he had been living for 30 years, where he was respected and highly thought of.

'I can quite understand,' he added, 'that that would be enough to upset the man's mind, particularly if he was sensitive and excitable. But I have found nothing whatever against this man's character.'

His summing up completed, Vulliamy once more removed his spectacles and laid them on the pile of papers before him. 'I think this is a most lamentable case and I'd like to express my personal sympathy with Mrs Smith for the terrible affliction she's gone through. It was *most* uncalled for.'

He nodded at Henry Lynn. This was his moment.

Lynn briefly clasped his forehead as he rapidly gathered the threads of the case together. For the dead William and his widow Alma, for the many worried and indignant teachers in the teaching union which had hired him, he had to make an unassailable case. His statement would have to withstand the onslaught of the police and the military. He wanted once and for all to put paid to the hysterical spy-mania now gripping the British public.

'I don't think there's a single person in this room, not even excepting Captain Mayne, who will leave and say that he believed there was the slightest slur of any kind on the character of Mr Smith,' declared Lynn, his voice ringing out across the schoolroom.

'It's unfortunate, to say the least, that that notice was served. I'm surprised beyond imagining that the police haven't had the honesty and the candour to come here today and say: "We have made a mistake and are sorry for it".

'There's not the slightest doubt in the world that the effect of the notice, which was absurd and unfounded, on the mind of an excitable, though loyal, Englishman was to turn his brain, and result in this terrible trouble.' Henry Lynn paused. The eyes of every juror were unwaveringly on him.

His voice rose to a crescendo. 'The police by their action in a spy panic have *killed this man*. I'm not saying it was intentional. I'd be the last man to say that. But the effect of that notice was to cause the man's death as irrevocably as though his sentence had been pronounced by a Judge!'

He turned for the last time to the jury. 'It's for you, the jury, to say whether you believe the action of the police was justified or not. If this case had been properly investigated they would have found there was no reason at all for issuing this order and the order might have been countermanded.'

The jury filed out and into the smaller infants classroom next door. It was the signal for everyone in the room to exchange opinions. The conversations grew louder. Those waiting outside for the verdict could hear the excitement mounting, knew something was about to happen.

The jury were out for an interminable time. It made Henry Lynn anxious. Why such a delay? Surely it was an open and shut case? After what seemed hours the jury returned and a hush descended on the room.

The Coroner asked the foreman, what verdict they had returned.

William Mitchell replied: 'We are quite agreed that the deceased committed suicide whilst of unsound mind, caused by false reports against his patriotism. The jury are also of the opinion that the police are very much to blame in not obtaining local information before acting on reported rumours.'

After expressing the jury's sympathy with the widow and relatives the foreman sat down.

Their criticism of East Suffolk police was exactly what Henry Lynn had wanted to hear. He turned to the NUT committee members sitting behind him and smiled. He hoped the verdict would, in some way, assuage their anger. Nothing, he knew, would heal the pain suffered by Alma Smith.

The Chief Constable rose abruptly and without a word marched quickly from the schoolroom. He pushed his way through the crowd in the playground to the waiting trap at the gate.

Jasper Mayne knew his reputation had been severely wounded by this incident, but his pride remained intact. He had not admitted to any mistakes, nor had he so much as hinted that William Smith was innocent of guilt.

This is wartime, he reasoned, *and the greater good is paramount. Individual liberty means little under such circumstances.*

East Anglian Daily Times
Saturday November 14 1914

Avalanche of Iron and Fire. Terrific artillery duel at Ypres. PA War special. Paris, Friday.

The Journal's correspondent at Furnes, about midway between Dunkirk and Ostend, telegraphs to his paper as follows:

Despite the violence of the bombardment, despite the terrible avalanche of iron and fire which has rained upon Ypres and its surroundings, the Germans still make no progress in that direction. While they have brought up still more formidable artillery, that with which the Allies are opposing them is even more formidable. Our shells are inflicting veritable carnage in the enemy's ranks. They have raked them in their trenches and thanks to the dexterity of our gunners rarely miss their mark.

All the prisoners brought into our lines were still under the influence of the terror with which our projectiles had filled them. These, they say, not only swept the whole trenches, but where they fell above the subterranean galleries caused earth slides which buried those within them and who had thus prepared their own tombs.

In the neighbourhood of Ypres the infantry has for the moment been put in the background. It is practically solely a terrific artillery duel which is going on. The infantry remains in the trenches and can only approach the enemy by digging galleries and then opening them.

Everywhere the vigour of our troops and those of our Allies are doing marvels. The Germans can continue bombarding the ancient capital of Western Flanders, they can reduce its artistic treasures to powder, but it is not at Ypres that they will find an opening by which they can gain the road to St Omer and Calais.

Chapter Twenty Five

Monday November 16 1914

Helena's days were filled with nursing duties while evenings were fully occupied writing letters to former patients and their families. She was most particular that each patient, after leaving Henham Hall Hospital, should receive a personal letter in her own hand, enquiring after their progress. Often, if their wounds were serious, they would be undergoing further treatment at a hospital closer to home. No-one was missed. When they replied she wrote to them again.

There were also daily admissions records to be kept. She entered every patient's name in a small register, along with the date he was admitted, his age and regiment. Then she'd make a note of the injuries and the battlefield on which they had been sustained; Aisne, Lille, Le Bassée. 'Shrapnel shoulder and back,' 'leg amputated,' 'bullet in left arm,' ' bullet wound left hip, shrapnel through sciatic nerve,' 'bullet wound in back.' She'd become accustomed to seeing the most terrible injuries, summarising them in a curt phrase.

While she performed menial tasks that did not require a trained nurse, such as changing dressings, feeding men unable to feed themselves, or holding a drinking cup to their mouths so they might sip water or milky tea, Helena grew to know her patients well. Their cheerfulness in the face of excruciating pain stirred in her an admiration and deep affection. By each man's name she'd write a short comment. 'A good-natured, cheerful boy,' 'a particularly nice man,' 'a particularly nice, sharp boy. Very helpful and nice to the Belgian soldiers,' 'a tall, dark, silent Scotch boy,' and of one; 'I think a little off his head.'

She recorded her developing experiences in running the hospital. 'My first operation. A nice little man in the dining room. The bit of shrapnel has been taken out of his foot.' There were amusing incidents, too. 'Had a moustache which he cut the ends off to please me. Had some interesting stories.' Finally she would enter their date of discharge. Or passing.

The register was an unscholarly work; ink blots and crossings out, hastily scribbled notes in unrestrained, looping scrawl, in pen or pencil, whatever came to hand. It revealed the increasing pressure and exhaustion she was suffering. New casualties were being admitted almost daily, brought from Ipswich by ambulance after arriving by special train from Southampton. Every bed was occupied.

There was little time for anything else in her life. The children had been sent with their governesses and nurses to stay with cousins at Dennington Hall.

Her visits to see them were becoming less frequent. She desperately missed both them and George. More than anything she longed for his telephone calls, longed to hear his cheery voice bellowing 'Nellie! Is that you? How the devil are you?' down the crackly line.

Helena turned to the last letter in the tray on her desk. It was almost midnight and her eyes hurt.

'One last letter, then I really must go to bed,' she murmured. She sliced open the blue envelope with her silver paperknife and quickly read the preamble. Someone craving her pardon for their temerity in writing directly to her, but hoping she might help.

She was on the verge of dismissing it as a mere begging letter when the name 'Mr Smith' sprang off the page. Flipping it over she glanced at the signature at the bottom of the second sheet. *Jean Ludwig. An unusual name. Sounds German. Could it possibly be?*

Quickly she scanned the neat handwriting. What Jean Ludwig had to say intrigued her.

"I have just been reading the report of the inquest on poor Mr Smith, whose death is the horrible result of a horrible slander, for I notice it mentions that Germans had been living in the locality.

As my boy, who unfortunately bears a German name, Fritz, has been living in Southwold since April, it has caused the keenest sorrow to think he may be one of the innocent ones drawn into this awful fiasco. He had a notice served on him on Monday, too, worded in much the same way, if not quite (but I was too upset to read it thoroughly) requesting him to leave the county in three days.

May I state the facts of the case? Mr Ludwig senior was brought over from Germany when a little boy and had never set foot in the country since, nor had he any German friends. He married an English woman. His son – my husband – was born in Banbury and had never been in Germany in his life.

My boy was also born in Banbury, in 1893, and also has never been in Germany. My husband died in 1895. After losing both his parents I wished to be independent and took the post of schoolmistress in Halesworth Boys School in 1899 and have held that post ever since. My boy was educated at Beccles College, passed the exam for Lloyds Bank, was failed by the doctor and so took up motor engineering. But he left Messrs Botwood's of Ipswich last February, his health completely broken down.

In April he was offered the post of Insurance Agent at Southwold. Being an open air life I urged him to accept it. No doubt enquiries have been made by the police in their anxiety to capture somebody and they have come to the conclusion it was 'suspicious' that a motor engineer in February should turn up as an Insurance Agent in April. So easy is it to weave a web of suspicion around a person who is handicapped by his name.

He left here for my brother's inland home in Worcestershire on Wednesday morning. The latter has taken the matter up keenly and says he will have the whole thing threshed out, even if it has to be laid before the Home Office.

His solicitor has gone into the matter and says it is the most absurd thing in the world. He is *not* an alien, both his father and he being British born and the Superintendant to whom he had to report himself at Bromsgrove said that as things were he couldn't ask him to sign the papers he was supposed to sign.

My boy was beside himself with indignation when the notice was served on him and when he reached home sobbed with the shame of it. He is the only member of the family burdened with a German Christian name and that simply out of compliment to the family surname. In the meantime he has lost his post and my home is left desolate.

We have come to the conclusion, your Ladyship, that suspicion has been woven around his every movement by an over-zealous police. Such as waiting about on the front in preference to the street for a lady friend.

I don't think my boy had ever spoken to poor Mr Smith in his life and although I knew him by sight I did not know him personally. How I regret my boy's correspondence was not opened. He has no German friends to correspond with.

I've taken the liberty of enclosing a photo of my boy. Is it the face of a plotter or traitor, your Ladyship? Will you pardon this endeavour to vindicate poor Mr Smith and my dear son and only remember a mother's love will dare anything?

I am your Ladyship's obedient servant,

Jean Ludwig".

'Well! How extraordinary. How very extraordinary,' Helena murmured. She put the letter down on the pile in front of her and stared at it for a long time. It's contents mesmerised her. *So it's not just poor William Smith. There are others. Other innocents. Other people whose lives are being ruined by this hysteria about spies. But what on earth can I do about it? And all because the poor boy has a German name. Why, even the Royal Family has a German name, Saxe-Coburg-Gotha. And nobody considers them a risk to the nation.*

Wracked with frustration and fatigue she cupped her chin in her hands and gazed out of the window into the black night. Gradually her head drifted downwards until her arm slid across the desk, her pale cheek resting on it. Within minutes she had fallen into a deep sleep.

She didn't hear the door opening quietly, nor the boots tiptoeing towards her. She barely registered that a hand was lightly touching first her shoulder then her hair.

'Nellie, Nellie. Wake up. It's me.' George whispered into her tumbling, dischevelled hair. He bent over her, a shadowy figure in khaki uniform.

Helena was dreaming. Dreaming she was with George and the children, playing hide-and-seek in the woods. He'd found her hiding and was ruffling her hair.

'George, George,' she said sleepily. 'Is that you?'

'Yes, my darling. Sorry to wake you, I know it's late.' He squatted beside her chair and put an arm around her waist.

'What are you doing here?' She squinted through bleary eyes, half imagining, half believing.

'Got a couple of days leave, old thing. Sorry I'm so late. Had to get a cab all the way from Ipswich.' He circled her with his strong arms and lifted her from the chair and into his embrace.

'Oh George!' She put her head on his shoulder and wound her arms sleepily around him. 'You don't know how I've longed to see you. I''ve needed you here so much. It's been awful, absolutely awful these past few days. We're all in a state of shock. You can't imagine, George, what a dreadful effect the death of poor William has had on us all. And poor Alma, she's completely beside herself with grief. We've had the funeral and the inquest and still the police won't admit they're wrong. I just don't know what to do for the best. It's dreadful.' Her words rushed as a torrent, tumbling incoherently.

'My poor Nellie,' he soothed. 'I wish I could have been here. Especially for William's funeral. But it hasn't been possible to get away. I promise I'll go and see Alma tomorrow. See what I can do to help.'

He kissed Helena tenderly. 'You look so terribly tired, Nellie. You're working too hard. Burning the midnight oil again, I see. What's all this, then?' He waved a hand at the untidy piles of papers scattered across the intricately inlaid desk.

'Patients. I have to write to all my patients,' she said. 'They're like members of one large family. An awful lot's happened since you went away.' She picked up the letter on top of the pile. Jean Ludwig's plea for help. 'And this. You wouldn't believe what's happening to our people, George. Terrible things. It's not just poor William being accused of being a German. There are others, too. What's going on? What's this war doing to people? It was never like this before the war started.'

She handed him the letter to read.

He reached into his uniform pocket for spectacles and peered at the precisely formed, feminine handwriting. As he read he huffed in disbelief, occasionally muttering 'Dear me, dear me' to himself. When he put the letter down he peered over his glasses at Helena.

'This takes the royal biscuit, it really does. It's almost as bad as accusing William Smith of being a German, although in this young man's case I can see why the police should be suspicious. His name must have caused them some apprehension. Even so, there were obviously no checks made before someone dashed off a copy of the Defence of the Realm order to remove him from Southwold.'

'The order sent to William and Alma was even worse,' Helena said indignantly. 'It accused William of acting in a manner prejudicial to public safety or the safety of the realm. William, of all people! I just can't believe it's possible. An order like that, based purely on village gossip and innuendo. It's obvious that no-one in the police asked any questions or made any enquiries about the veracity of those rumours, either.

'And then for William to take his own life because of the shame of it. Well, it's unforgiveable. Unforgiveable. I can't tell you how angry I am about it. I can't stop thinking about it. For something like that to happen in Henham, well.....' Helena shrugged her shoulders in despair, lost for words.

'I think a strongly worded letter to the Chief Constable's in order,' George said, pacing the small sitting room. 'Don't you? Coming from me, in my capacity as Chairman of the County Council as well as a Territorial Colonel and an Earl of the realm. That surely must elicit a reasonable apology from Captain Mayne, don't yer think?'

'If anything helps change that man's mind then we must do it.'

'Right, m'lady,' he said with renewed vigour. 'I'll dictate and you take a note.'

Helena turned up a fresh sheet of notepaper and a pencil. Far into the night the two of them tussled with the form of words they should use to persuade Mayne to admit his error. Begging him to redress his mistake, to admit he had acted too hastily and without scrupulous checks into both the rumours and William Smith's background.

What, George wanted to know, were the "injudicious behaviour and utterances" that had condemned this poor man to exile and propelled him to a horrible death? Had he, in fact, been guilty of espionage?

When they were both happy with the wording Helena slipped the scrawled notes into the top drawer of her desk. She would get it typed neatly later.

George stretched out his strong hands and, clasping her slender white fingers tightly between them, led her into the adjoining bedroom.

Several days later, after George had returned to his regiment in Middlesex, a letter addressed to him arrived from County Hall. Among the pile left on Helena's desk was Captain Mayne's reply.

"Dear Lord Stradbroke,

In reply to your letter re Mr Smith I was asked at the adjourned inquest if I could not clear his character for the sake of his family and I replied I would give a good deal to do that, and that I would say the utmost I could, and I went on to make it quite clear that there was no suggestion made that Mr Smith was a spy or had been guilty of espionage, but that the grounds for the Order were his utterances and general behaviour.

The conclusion arrived at being that in the interests both of himself and the country, he was not a person whom it would be wise to have in this Proclaimed Area. No suggestion was ever made by the police that he was a German. (I heard that for the first time at the Inquest.) Persons suspected of espionage are handed over to the military authorities to stand their trial by Court Martial.

I took no steps to "redress a mistake" as you rather suggest in your letter. The instructions I sent the day before Smith's death (which were communicated to him) saying that his removal was deferred, were (as I said at the Inquest) sent because, at my interview with him on the previous Tuesday, he gave me a large bundle of letters to read and also promised to obtain a copy of his birth certificate, and pending my reading the one and receiving the other, I felt that he should have a remand.

You now ask me to say that I believe I made a mistake. That I cannot do. If I had thought so I would have said so, at once.

I am ready to state all the circumstances before the proper authority, if desired, but I certainly was not prepared to do so on the demand of the Counsel employed by the NUT at the Coroner's Inquest.

Obviously such a demand was *ultra vires* and had no bearing on the specific matters the jury had to determine.

Yours very truly,

J.G. Mayne".

Helena flung the letter across the room in disgust. It was as unemotional and inflexible as the man. Mayne was flatly denying that the police had raised doubts concerning William's nationality, or that they had suggested he might be German, even though Helena clearly recalled William recounting such a conversation when he returned from his interview with the police.

It contained no revelations of the true reasons why he'd suspected William of treachery. There was no hint of a posthumous reprieve. Not the slightest movement to restore his reputation. Mayne's official stamp of condemnation would remain intact.

It was the final verdict on William's honour and it was a damning one.

East Anglian Daily Times

Monday November 16 1914

British Officer's Iron Cross. Wounded German rescued under fire. Paris, Saturday.

One of the noblest and at the same time, most dramatic stories of battlefield heroism that the war is likely to produce reached Paris today. It is as follows:

During a recent combat German troops attacked the British trenches, but were repulsed. They retired to their own trenches, taking with them their wounded, but one of the latter was overlooked and left behind. A comrade, observing him, left the German trenches to effect a rescue, but was almost immediately killed by the British fire, a score of bullets piercing him.

A British officer, however, realised the situation and, having given the order "cease fire" himself went out into the open to pick up the wounded German. He was struck by several bullets and badly wounded, but the Germans, as soon as they saw what his object was, also ordered the "cease fire". Thereupon the British officer staggered to the fallen man and carried him to the German lines.

A German officer received him with a salute and, calling for cheers, pinned upon the breast of the British hero an Iron Cross. Then the Britisher returned to his own trenches.

He was recommended for the Victoria Cross for this notable example of chivalry, but succumbed to his wounds.

Signed Alfred J Rorke, Central News.

Chapter Twenty Six

Christmas 1914

Only one person alighted from the mid-afternoon train when it arrived at Blythburgh Station from Ipswich. The ticket collector assumed the young man who stepped hesitantly onto the platform was a foreigner, visiting for the Christmas holidays.

Tall and lean, his face was deeply burnished by the sun. An unusual, broad-brimmed, black fedora pulled low over his eyes revealed extravagant black curls tipping over his collar. A woven Mayan shawl, an intoxication of reds, yellows and purples, hung casually around his shoulders.

The young man carried a small trunk in one hand and a bulging Gladstone bag in the other. They contained the full extent of his worldly possessions. He stood and watched the train pull away into the early dusk in the direction of Southwold with a look of amusement as though it were a novelty. He was about to turn for the exit when a sudden gust whipped the shawl from one shoulder. Dumping the bags on the edge of the flatform, he grasped the shawl and wrapped it tightly around his neck then buttoned the flimsy black jacket.

Ted Alexander Montague Smith had come home ill-prepared for such weather and in that brief, shivering moment, marooned on Blythburgh Station platform, he questioned for the first time whether his patriotic intention to join Kitchener's New Army hadn't been a mistake. How would he acclimatize to such weather? Hunched into his inadequate jacket, the collar turned up and the scarf sheathing his ears, he picked up his bags and after handing over his ticket, quickly strode from the station to hail the station waggon.

'Henham, please. Henham School,' he called to the waggoner who was sitting on a bench smoking a pipe, awaiting customers.

'Yessir, certainly sir. Henham School yer say?' The waggon creaked and groaned as he lowered his cumbersome form into the driving seat and unhitched the reins. He looked suspiciously at the foreign gentleman with his gaudy scarf and dark complexion and thought it best not to indulge in conversation. You couldn't be too careful with foreigners. They weren't to be trusted.

Alex Smith heaved his bags into the waggon. *Home. This grey, frost-bitten landscape is my home,* he thought. *The land of my birth. I've come all this way, travelling half-way around the world, to fight for this. To fight for King and Country. My country.* 'Mmm,' he sighed a sigh deep with reservations.

After two years he'd grown acclimatised to the heat and dust of Guatemala, with its brilliantly coloured vegetation and exotically dressed, dusky-skinned women. One woman in particular. It was this unassuming, khaki-coloured landscape, with its undemonstrative and unassuming people, which felt like a foreign land.

As the dusk faded into darkness, the sight of twinkling candles on Christmas trees in the drawing rooms of large houses along his route home reminded him it was almost Christmas Day. He expected this Christmas to be a subdued affair, now England was at war with Germany. So different from the ornate celebrations that would mark the event in Guatemala City.

A number of Germans worked for German-owned coffee holdings in Guatemala, and when Alex had read newspaper accounts of how many of them were leaving to fight for their Fatherland, he resolved to do likewise. He'd thrown up his job teaching English, French and German to Guatemalan students, and undertaken the long and expensive journey home.

He'd travelled cross-country along cart roads and rivers to the Caribbean coast, by tramp steamers hopping from port to port up the eastern seaboard as far as New York, then he'd bought a six-day passage by Transatlantic steam ship to Liverpool. Several train journeys later he'd reached this remote rural outpost.

Home at last. Soon he would be re-united with his parents. He sensed there would be something of the Prodigal Son about his return. Deeds done or deeds neglected would be forgiven.

Blue with cold, Alex allowed himself a faint grin as he glimpsed the school through naked trees as they rounded a bend in the turnpike. He'd already resolved on a practical joke to fool his parents. Before ringing the door bell he'd pull the hat further over his eyes to obscure his face. The rainbow-coloured scarf would have to be concealed in his pocket. Too much of a giveaway, he'd guessed. Then, when his mother opened the door – he knew it was usually she who answered to callers - she'd think it was a perfect stranger. She'd politely enquire who he was and why he was there. Then he'd throw off his hat and announce, 'It's me! Alex! Happy Christmas!' Her face, her look of dumbfounded amazement, would be priceless.

The waggoner helped him down with his bags at the school house and bade him 'Merry Christmas.' Alex returned the greeting and pushed open the gate. Stopping for a moment he took in the familiar surroundings. The solid brick and flint house, the school next door, the playing field and the dark soil of a newly-dug school garden. The last light of dusk glinting on a sliver of grey water caught his eye. He realised that not yards away was the bathing pool where his father had taught him to swim. He wondered if Suffolk Punches still cantered through the meadow beyond the willows and rushes.

So familiar, yet something about it seemed unfamiliar. It had changed. What was it about re-visiting a loved place many years on? Alex couldn't put his finger on it and shrugged.

Just as he'd schemed during tedious hours of travelling, he unwound his scarf and stuffed it into his jacket, pulled the wide brim jauntily over one eye and pulled the bell. He heard it jangling in the hallway. It echoed emptily back to him. He listened intently at the door. No busy feet came tapping on the stone floor to answer his summons. He rang again. Still no answer. Not even a bark from Dick to let the visitor know the premises were guarded. Nothing. *How disappointing*, he thought. *Just when I'd hoped to surprise them. They love my tricks, always did. So did poor little Gladys. She used to laugh louder than anyone.*

Alex stepped back from the porch, but a quick glance at the windows confirmed there were no lights on at the front of the house. He wandered round to the kitchen and scullery at the rear. None showed there either. The school next door was also in darkness, but he'd expected that, being so close to Christmas.

'Mmm. They're out. I wonder where? Perhaps there's a service in church, seeing as it's Christmas week. Expect that's where I'll find them,' he muttered, slightly puzzled. Surely Dick would have launched himself at the scullery door with a loud 'Woof' after hearing a strange footfall on the gravel? And then, horrified, he clamped his hand to his mouth. *Supposing old Dick's dead?* He'd expected the dog to be there. He'd always been there for him as a child, a constant playmate.

Good, faithful old Dick. But four years had passed since he'd left home to study in Europe and then teach in Central America. He shouldn't expect to find everything as he'd left it.

He pushed the hat back from his eyes, wrapped the scarf back around his neck and studied his bags for a moment. He could leave them safely on the doorstep, he felt sure. It would make the long walk from school to church less tedious if his hands were free of their burden.

The turnpike was enveloped in darkness when he set out. The nearest houses in Wangford's main street were some way off. He could see their lights as dim pinpricks on a black velvet tapestry. When he reached them his spirits rose. *Not too much further to the church.* He leant on the iron gate and it squeaked open. The church looked promising. Every window blazed with light and the sonorous notes of the organ drifted from them.

Alex unlatched the heavy oak door a crack. Enough to peep inside. The church was empty. Emboldened, he opened it wider. It swung to a close behind him with an echoing thud. The organ voluntary stopped abruptly. 'You're too early young man. Carol Service is tomorrow evening. Six o'clock,' a disembodied voice thundered down from the organ loft.

'Thank you,' he called back. 'Sorry I disturbed you.'

Outside in the darkness once more he considered where to go next. His mother and father must be with friends, enjoying supper, he imagined. The thought made him hungry. He hadn't eaten for hours. Not since he'd purchased an unappetising pie from a stall while waiting on Liverpool Street station for his connection to Ipswich. He closed his eyes and recalled a past Christmas when, as children, they'd played party games after supper at the doctor's house. *Charles Acton's place*, he thought, *that's where they'll be.*

Jessamine Cottage was just around the corner, in Church Lane. He knocked and waited. No tricks this time. He was no longer in the mood. The doctor himself opened the door.

'Yes?' he enquired. 'Can I help you?' He showed no sign of recognition.

Alex removed his hat, but not with the dramatic flourish he'd planned for his parents. 'Doctor Acton, it's me. Alex. I've just arrived home and found no-one was there. I wondered if my parents were here? With you?'

'Alex? Is it really you?' Charles Acton flung the door wide. 'Oh my dear boy, come in, come in. At last! At last! So you received Evelyn's telegram, then? Thank goodness!' He grabbed the young man by the elbow and pulled him inside.

'Telegram? What telegram? I haven't received any telegram. Why should Evie send me a telegram?' Alex frowned. Then his face relaxed. Perhaps she and her husband had at last produced an offspring.

The welcoming smile instantly disappeared from the doctor's face. 'Oh my dear chap, come and sit down. Sit by the fire. I expect you could do with a drink. What'll you have? Whisky? And something to eat, too, of course. You must be starving after your long journey.'

Alex admitted he was and after Charles had persuaded his housekeeper to quickly rustle up a late supper, the two men settled into armchairs on either side of a cheerful fire.

'Doctor Acton, I've not corresponded with my family for.....oh, goodness me....a very long time. Longer than I care to remember. Probably well over a year. I'm afraid I'm a terrible letter-writer. Mother writes to me quite regularly, but I rarely reply. Very remiss of me. I have to say the Guatemalan mail system is somewhat erratic, so perhaps Evie's telegram is still on its way.'

The doctor nodded and was about to interrupt and explain about the telegram when Alex rattled on enthusiastically.

'You're most likely wondering why I'm here? Well, I've thrown up my teaching job and I'm going to join Kitchener's Army! What d'yer make of that, eh? I heard about the war only a few weeks ago and resolved, like thousands of other chaps, to join the colours. So, here I am! Prepared to serve King and Country, as they say.' He finished with a triumphant flourish of his hand.

How like his father he is. The dramatic gestures. The spontaneity of his actions. 'Yes, yes indeed. Most creditable. Most....' Charles Acton faltered and looked balefully at the young man. His thoughts churned madly. *He doesn't know about William. How am I going to tell him? It's fallen to me to break the news. Oh God, give me strength to say the right thing!*

Charles's voice was soft and soothing. He leant closer to Alex, his hands clasped across his knees. 'Alex, my dear chap. I'm afraid this Christmas will be very, very different. Not at all how we would normally celebrate it. And I say that, not simply because of this dreadful war, although I must say it's causing us all incalculable grief. No, it's something else. Something more....how shall I put it?...more at the very *heart* of this particular village....and more particularly at the heart of your family and mine.

'We're all under a terrible cloud. A cloud of despair and mourning, Alex. That is how you find us on the eve of Christmas, I'm afraid. All of us. But most particularly,' Charles looked down at his hands. The knuckles gripping his knees were white. 'Most particularly of all.... your dear mother. She has had to bear the worst loss of all. You see, Alex......,' he swallowed, holding back his own emotion at the loss of his dearest friend. 'Your father is no longer with us.'

'No longer.....with us?' Alex's spine stiffened. He distrusted what he was hearing. 'You mean....he can't be?...he's...he's....dead?'

'Yes, I'm afraid he is. I'm desperately sorry that this shocking news should have to come from me, rather than your own family, but your mother has gone away. To your uncle John's home in Devon. She needed to get away from the village for a while. To recover. To mourn your father. To come to terms with what's happened.'

'It's not possible! I can hardly believe it. He was always such a fit man, so sporting and active. I wish I'd known earlier,' Alex chided himself, 'I'd have come home much sooner to be at his bedside. What did he die of? Did he suffer for long?'

'No, no Alex, it wasn't like that.' Acton paused and gazed into the firelight. The realisation now dawned that it was not only the fact of William's death that had to be broken. It was the savage way in which he'd taken his own life and the cause of it that had to be revealed, too.

Slowly and patiently Acton described how his mother had called for him after she'd found William with his throat cut in the barn. The public outcry when it was discovered what had driven him to such an act; the verdict of the inquest jury; the questioning of the Chief Constable; the outpouring of public grief at his father's funeral; the departure of his mother for her brother-in-law's home on Dartmoor, where she hoped to find solace and peace.

Alex listened to all this with gathering disbelief. He sank his head into his hands, but there were no tears. Such wild, dramatic stories befell other families, not his own. He felt empty and remote. Numbed beyond weeping.

'I must go to my mother,' he said. 'She needs me. There's nothing to keep me here, now. I'll wire her that I'm coming. I'll catch the train back to London tomorrow and then take another to Devon. I can be there in two days, I expect.'

Acton stood up and put a hand on Alex's shoulder. 'You must stay here tonight, Alex. The school house has been locked up since she left. Besides, you wouldn't want to be there on your own. Not now.'

'Thank you. I should like that.' He remembered he'd left his bags on the schoolhouse doorstep. 'I must fetch my bags. I left them in the porch at home.'

'Now don't you worry about little things like that. I'll get cook's boy to run down for them.'

Acton left to make the arrangements and returned bearing a tray with supper. 'Eat this, it's one of cook's specialities,' he said, topping up Alex's whisky. 'And over supper you can tell me about what you've been doing in Central America and your life there. So very different from here, I've no doubt.'

A wan apology of a smile played for an instant around Alex's mouth, but his deep eyes were filled with uncertainty.

East Anglian Daily Times

Wednesday January 6 1915

Christmas truce in the trenches. Exchange of pleasantries with the enemy. Burying the fallen.

The Press Association has received the following letter from a subaltern at the front: December 31 1914.

Christmas has come and gone – certainly the most extraordinary celebration of it any of us will ever experience. We were due back in the trenches on Christmas Eve and the battalion's official Christmas Day was consequently held on Wednesday the 23rd. For the time being all ranks put aside the grim recollection of the events of the past week and gave themselves up to keeping the day as pleasantly as possible. There were stacks of presents for officers and men and no lack of comfortable hampers full of good things.

In the yard of the farmhouse where my company was billeted there is a huge cauldron. In this no less than 125 pounds of pudding in tins were boiled at a time. We turned out to see them dished out. It was a Gargantuan spectacle. The next day we returned to the trenches groaning under loads of comestibles and condiments destined to alleviate our lot on the morrow. That night it froze hard and Christmas Day dawned on an appropriately sparkling landscape.

A truce had been arranged for the few hours of daylight for the burial of the dead on both sides, who had been lying out in the open since the fierce night fighting of a week earlier. When I got out I found a large crowd of officers and men, English and German, grouped around the bodies, which had already been gathered together and laid out in rows. I went along those dreadful ranks and scanned the faces, fearing at every step to recognise one I knew. It was a ghastly sight. They lay stiffly in contorted attitudes, dirty with frozen mud and powdered with rime.

The digging parties were already busy on the two big, common graves, but the ground was hard and the work slow and laborious. In the intervals of superintending it we chatted with the Germans, most of whom were quite affable, if one could not exactly call them friendly, which indeed was neither to be expected nor desired. We exchanged confidences about the weather and the diametrically opposite news from East Prussia. The way they maintained the truth of their marvellous victories because they were official (with bated breath) was positively pathetic. They had no doubt of the issue in the East, and professed to regard the position in the West as a definite stalemate.

A tiny, spruce little Lieutenant, spoken of, to his manifest chagrin, as "Der Kleine" by his comrades, attached himself to me, and sent his Bursche back for a bottle of cognac, and we solomnly drank "Gesundbeiten". He was an amiable little soul really, with the typical Prussian officer snap in his speech. Every few words were punctuated with "nich?"

Meanwhile time drew on and it was obvious that the burying would not be half finished with the expiration of the armistice agreed upon, so we decided to renew it the following morning. At the set hour everyone returned to the trenches and when the last man was in, my little Lieutenant and I solemnly shook hands, saluted and marched back ourselves.

They left us alone that night to enjoy a peaceful Christmas. I forgot to say that the previous night – Christmas Eve – their trenches were a blaze of Christmas trees and our sentries were regaled for hours with the traditional Christmas songs of the Fatherland. Their officers even expressed annoyance the next day that some of these trees had been fired on, insisting that they were part almost of a sacred rite.

On Boxing Day, at the agreed hour, on a pre-arranged signal being given, we turned out again. The output of officers of higher rank on their side was more marked and the proceedings were more formal in consequence. But while the gruesome business of burying went forward there was still a certain interchange of pleasantries. They distributed cigars and cigarettes freely among our digging party who were much impressed by the cigars. I hope they were not disillusioned when they came to smoke them. Meanwhile the officers were amusing themselves by taking photographs of mixed groups. The Germans brought us copies to send to the English illustrated papers as they received them regularly.

The digging completed, the shallow graves were filled in and the German officers remained to pay their tribute of respect while our chaplain read a short service.

It was one of the most impressive things I have ever witnessed. Friend and foe stood side by side, bareheaded, watching the tall, grave figure of the padre outlined against the frosty landscape as he blessed the poor, broken bodies at his feet. Then with more formal salutes we turned and made our way back to our respective ruts.

Chapter Twenty Seven

January 1915

Alex arrived in Devon on Christmas Eve. Slumped on a bench on Exeter station platform, watching the last passengers unloading their baggage, he wondered if his uncle had received his telegram. There was no way of knowing. He'd left Suffolk before there had been any possibility of a reply. He would simply have to wait. Wait and hope that John Bragg Smith would come and collect him in his horse and cart.

And if he didn't? Alex shuddered. The station was draughty and an inhospitable place in which to spend Christmas.

He scrunched the shawl more tightly around his throat. As a last resort he could book himself into the Station Hotel, but his meagre savings were disappearing alarmingly fast. He could ill-afford to spend money on hotels now he'd come this far.

The London train which had deposited him on St David's Station disgorged its final dribble of passengers and headed westwards. Porters busied back and forth, earning a few pence for carrying mountains of luggage. The holidays always brought a welcome influx of visitors to the town from Bristol and London.

Alex waited. He maintained a casual air, as though accustomed to lounging around on hard wooden benches for hours on end, but as he watched the minutes ticking past on the station clock his heart beat faster. *They don't know I'm here. I shall be stuck here, in Exeter, all over Christmas.*

An hour passed and with it the crowds. He was alone. His solitariness provoked curious stares from porters and the ticket collector. One asked him if he was being collected. 'Yes, I'm expecting my uncle from Drewsteignton. Any minute now,' he replied abruptly. The porter doubted this was true.

Then, just as he was doubting it himself, he saw a grey-bearded man walking the length of the platform towards him. Alex stood up. Was this his uncle? He had no means of recognising him. They had never met and his father had never possessed photographs of his family.

'Uncle?' Alex asked hopefully.

'Alex m'boy! It *is* you! Well, well! I thought it might be. Yer looks just like yer father did as a young'un.' John Bragg Smith took his hand in his great rough-hewn one and shook it with jovial vigour. 'Well, my loverly, we're glad to be havin' yer here, I can tell yer.'

'Uncle John, it's so good to see you. And so kind of you to......'

'Shush, shush, me boy. I won't hear of it.' John picked up both Alex's bags and nodded in the direction of the ticket collector. 'Got the pony and trap outside. Come on, me boy. If we get a hussle on we'll be home before dark.'

He strode out into the station yard and handed Alex up into the trap, passed up the bags, then settled himself into the driver's seat next to his passenger. He clicked his tongue at the sturdy Dartmoor pony, which took off at a brisk clip.

'We've been looking forward to you comin' to Devon to see yer poor dear ma ever since yer father's funeral,' he said, flicking the reins across the pony's back.

'I realise that now. Oh, I do so wish I'd known earlier,' Alex sighed, ' but I knew nothing of father's passing. Nothing, until I arrived at Henham three days ago. Doctor Acton told me. I've been so worried about Mama ever since I heard. How is she?'

'Not good, me boy. Not good. She never sleeps. I hears 'er moving about her room all hours o'the night. Our doctor's been to her and given her something to help her sleep and that helps for a while. But then she sinks back into her mourning again. It's terrible to see. Terrible. It's like she's in a distant land, far away from us. We're all shocked by Will's passing. O'course we are. It were a dreadful way to go. But yer mother ...well... she sometimes says she can't believe Will's dead. She says she must have imagined it. But of course she didn't.'

'Poor Mama. If only I'd known.....'

'Don't you go a-frettin' yerself, young Alex. I'm sure she'll cheer up when she sees you. She was in a whirl when your telegram arrived. "What, my Alex? Comin' here?" she kept sayin'. "Tomorrow?" "Yes, yes", we'd all say and laugh at her cus she was so disbelieving on it.'

They were soon out of the city and heading along the Okehampton road. As they climbed higher onto Dartmoor a fine grey rain descended to meet them. Cold and clammy, it clung to their clothes. Alex hugged his arms tightly around his body in an attempt to combat the bone-chilling dampness. His uncle, noticing his discomfort, moved closer to give him what little warmth he could.

The track became more rutted and rock-strewn the higher they climbed. Alex began to wonder if there could be any form of civilisation at its end. Suddenly his uncle reined in the pony with a 'Whoooah!'

'Are we there?' Alex was mystified for he could see nothing but high hedges and trees. No sign of a village or even an isolated farmhouse.

'No, Alex. But this is a favouite spot where yer Ma comes to walk. You might find her here,' he waved his hand in the direction of an even narrower track. 'If yer do, we'll take her home. It's a good two-mile walk and in this mist she could well lose her way. She don't know these moors like us.'

'Why should she come here? There's nothing but fields and hedgerows.'

'No? You go take a look beyond that thar hedge. You'll be surprised what's there, I'll be bound,' John chuckled to himself. 'I'll wait here for you. She may already have started for home, in which case we'll meet her on the road, but I'll warrant she's still here.'

Alex dismounted from the trap and made his way uncertainly down the track. He pushed open an iron gate and found himself in a small meadow enclosed by ancient hedges.

The strangest sight greeted him. Three giant, grey granite standing stones stood in a circle, a flat slab balanced across their pinnacles so that it formed a rocky cavern. It was a primitive place, still haunted by its ancient past. He imagined it must once have been an altar. A place where primitive peoples held religious rituals and offered living sacrifices to their gods. Animals, people. He couldn't begin to guess. Or perhaps it was a stone tomb; a grave where the tribe laid its dead.

As he moved closer to the stones he saw a bundle of rags discarded against the farthest stone. A few more steps and he realised with horror that the bundle was human. His mother. She was sitting on the ground beneath the cap stone, her back against the smooth inner face of the rock, head slumped. A dark woollen shawl swathed her entire body. She didn't see or hear Alex's feet swishing through the unmown grass.

His immediate fear was that she, too, was dead. But when he took her hand between his she flinched like a cornered animal.

'Mama, Mama,' he whispered softly. 'Wake up, Mama. It's me. Alex.'

He tilted her head, his hand beneath her chin. Her skin felt cold and damp. He brushed the wet hair away from her cheeks with delicate fingers and watched intently for her to open her eyes.

This wasn't the greeting he'd planned for his parents. The practical joke he'd schemed, where he'd have flung off his hat and yelled gleefully, 'It's me, Alex!' *Oh, if only it had been so*, he thought. *Everything's completely different. This isn't how I imagined my homecoming.*

He put his arm around her shoulders. 'Come, Mama. I've come to take you home.'

Alma half-opened her eyes, but there was no hint of recognition. She drifted back into the cold sleep that had claimed her.

Alex lifted her to her feet and half-carrying, half-dragging her, managed to get her to the end of the track. 'Uncle! Uncle! I've found her! Give me a hand getting her into the trap, will you?'

John Smith leapt down and bodily lifted Alma into the back of the trap. 'Oh my! She's soaked to the skin. We must get her home quickly,' he said, whipping the pony into a fast trot.

'She's going to be alright, isn't she?' Alex clutched his mother even more tightly around the shoulders, trying to warm her frail body. 'She looks so thin and pale. So unlike Mama.' He untied his shawl and wound it round her head.

'Mama, please don't die, Mama,' he murmured.

Then to John Smith he said curiously, 'What's that strange place with the stones? It looks like an ancient altar. Or perhaps a tomb of some sort?'

'Ah, that's Spinsters' Rock. And yer right. It is a tomb. The saying goes, here-abouts, that it was erected one morning before breakfast by three spinsters! I, meself, can't see how three old ladies could ha' lifted them heavy slabs of granite, can you? It's more like it was built by the ancients, the Neolithics, five or six thousand years ago.'

'It's a weird, eerie sort of place, isn't it?' said Alex, wondering why it appealed so much to his mother that she should make a regular pilgrimage there.

'Yer right there, boy. It beats me why yer Ma walks all this way. Maybe it's like a church. She finds comfort there. Maybe because it's stood there for so long. Something enduring. Like her and Will. Never apart. Till now.'

Alex contemplated this theory. Then he said, 'Did father go there when he lived here? As a boy?'

'Oh yes, a'course he did. We all did. We used to make up stories around it. Witches and warlocks, that kind of thing. Ghostly happenings. We'd frighten each other sayin' it were 'aunted. Even so, we'd come down here on our ole' bicycles. What a feeling that was; going downhill with our feet off the pedals. Mind you, it's up and down hill all the way home, too. We had to walk most a'the way. That 's why us young 'uns were always gettin' into trouble with our Ma for being late for supper.' He laughed at the recollection.

Then, after taking a couple of steep gradients, they arrived in the centre of the village. Squat cob cottages and work-shops spilled from the central square into cramped side streets. At the head of the square Alex could see the grey stone tower of Holy Trinity church. Close by was the village pub, the Druid's Arms. The pony had no intention of stopping in the cobbled square, however, but turned, with barely a flick of the reins to his back, down a steep hill.

Half-way down Netherton Hill was the cottage where his grandfather John and grandmother Mariann had raised his father, his uncle John and four other children. They'd lost two of them in infancy, but such was to be expected.

Next to it was the blacksmith's forge where old John had worked, almost to his death at the age of 82. Now the uncle sitting beside him was the village blacksmith. Alex shot a glance at John Bragg Smith's muscular shoulders and the gnarled hands lightly holding the reins. He thought this must have been how his grandfather looked after years of pounding hammer on anvil.

John pulled the pony up outside and the two men lifted Alma out of the trap. John's wife, Elizabeth, was waiting for them at the door. She stood aside to let her husband carry Alma through. He deposited the almost lifeless body in a large armchair by the log fire and stood up, stretching his back.

'Is she alright? Is she breathing?' Elizabeth asked anxiously.

John nodded gravely. 'Jest about. Much longer and I think she'd have died of cold and exposure.'

'I was so worried when she didn't return home. Where did you find her?' Elizabeth demanded.

'Just where I thought. At Spinster's Rock, sheltering from the rain,' her husband replied.

Elizabeth swept him aside and knelt at Alma's feet. She struggled to untie the wet laces of her boots and wrenched them off. 'Alma dear, are you alright? Speak to me. Please, Alma dear,' she begged.

Alma nodded and whispered something inaudible to Elizabeth. Alex was relieved to see her open her eyes and the colour returning to her cheeks.

'We must get you out of those wet clothes. You're drenched to the skin. And look at your boots!' Elizabeth said, holding them aloft with some distain. Dirty boots had no place in her sitting room. Short and plump, with her dark hair drawn into a bun, she was proud of the way she kept herself and her house. Clean white blouse each day, starched and ironed pinafore. She had standards.

'John. Call Winifred and Eva in from the pigs. Tell them their aunt needs their help. And tell them, too, that their cousin's arrived.' Then, when she'd done her duty by Alma, she turned at last to the young man standing shyly in the doorway. 'So you're Alma's boy. Well, well. You looks just like yer father did at your age. Uncanny, the likeness. You have Devonian blood in your veins, no doubts about that.'

Alex smiled. There was no higher compliment than to have Devonian blood. He'd been accepted by his formidable Aunt Elizabeth. Yet hadn't it been just this same blood, this swarthy, dark Celtic complexion and lustrous black hair, that had marked his father out as a foreigner in the eyes of Suffolk villagers? In the eyes of the police?

His thoughts were interrupted by two boisterous teenagers bursting into the room. Black curls flying along with their uncontrollable arms and legs, his cousins Eva and Winifred erupted around him.

'Cousin Alex! Oh, how wonderful! Truly wonderful! Tell us all about Guatemala. Tell us about your journey.' Their demands tumbled over each other as they giggled with coy embarassment at this handsome young man who had mysteriously appeared in their home.

'Girls, girls!' Elizabeth's sharp tones broke across their merriment. 'Attend to your aunt first. Take her wet clothes and hang them in the scullery. Then you, Eva Mary, can find her something warm and dry to wear.'

'Yes, Mama, yes Mama,' their tone was dutiful, but their concern for Alma was genuine enough. They fussed around her, carefully unwinding the long shawl from her shoulders and Alex's gaily-coloured Mayan scarf from her head. Then they extracted her from her overcoat and delicately laid her back in the armchair.

'Poor Aunt Alma,' whispered Winifred to Alex. 'She will be so glad you're here to comfort her. Perhaps she'll be able to enjoy Christmas now you've arrived.'

Alex nodded. He thought twelve-year-old Winifred wise and coquettish beyond her years. She was a beauty who would undoubtedly enslave men's hearts.

Christmas was as jolly an occasion as the Smith's could possibly make it for the grieving widow and her son. The entire family; John and Elizabeth, the two girls and their little brother William, not to mention their older sons, John and George who were of an age with Alex, lavished a natural, unforced affection on them. They may have been strangers to the house, but they were kith and kin and therefore to be cherished. They attended church together as a family; sang carols and songs around the piano while Alma played, and were an attentive audience as with rapt wonder they listened to Alex's tales of life in Guatemala.

Gradually, as the days passed into the New Year, Alma's strength returned. She resumed her walks, this time with her son as constant companion.

He asked her one morning, as they set off in the crisp sunshine, why she'd chosen to travel all the way to her in-laws on Dartmoor rather than stay with her sister Minnie and brother-in-law at their inn in Gloucestershire.

'Minnie and Charles live a very different life to the one I've become accustomed to with your father,' she said simply. 'Can you imagine how difficult it would have been for me at the 'Rising Sun'? Their constant bonhomie and the drunkenness? I'd have found it most distressing. And anyway, I'd have been such a nuisance to them in my sorrow. I wanted solitude, not convivial company. I found it here.' She stopped to lean over a gate to watch a herd of cows being driven back to their pasture after milking. 'I love the wildness of the moors. In a way it reminds me of Henham.'

Yet Alma's unspoken fear was that each step taken across Dartmoor distanced her from Henham. Took her further away from Will. Some days this passing of time and space terrified her. No matter how hard she tried she couldn't claw her way back. William was receding into a different time frame and even when she stretched her arms and hands heavenwards he did not meet her or grab hers to hold. He had slipped from her grasp and been swallowed into the grey air.

He'd become an insubstantial speck, like the buzzards she watched defining malevolent circles higher and higher until they disappeared from view.

On this particular morning she was taking Alex to a high plateau overlooking the Teign gorge, 900 feet below them. She wanted to show him an interesting building that was under construction, which she'd discovered on an earlier expedition. A fine country house, being built in Medieval style, from granite. As they stopped to watch the masons at work at Castle Drogo, lifting the heavy blocks into position with pulleys to form the exterior walls, she said with some awe, 'Imagine building a Medieval castle today, in the twentieth century. Isn't it an extraordinary notion?'

Alex found it amusing that any one, even a self-made millionaire, should want to spend his fortune on such a forbidding-looking home. 'Sir Julius Drewe must be extremely eccentric to want to live in a place like this,' he chuckled.

Day after day they tramped through lush river valleys, waded across trickling steams and clambered rocky crags. At first the conversation was halting. Two strangers converging on the same road. Thrown together by a fate neither had chosen. At first they exchanged superficial niceties; family news, such as the imminent birth of a child to Evelyn and Johnnie, how the coal mines owned by her family in the Forest of Dean were prospering and how her own mother, Theophila's, health was failing.

But Alma revealed nothing of her husband's death and her son did not pry.

Until one day, while they stood together beneath the flat stone of Spinsters' Rock, she faced him and cried out, 'Why, oh *why*, did he have to do it? Why did he have to leave me, Alex? Why did he feel he had to die rather than face his accusers? We could have born the shame together. We could have weathered *anything* together.

'For thirty years I believed he loved me. Loved *me* in the way I loved him. Above everything. Even above you three children, Alex. But now I can't believe he loved me at all. How could he have loved me, if he was prepared to put his honour first? Honour above all things. Even above me. Above our life together. That he could deprive me not only of his life but my own, in such a dreadful way.

'He must have realised, too, that I would be the one to discover his body. That it would be a terrible, terrible sight. A shock I shall never recover from. Do you think such an act represents *love*, Alex?'

Alex was surprised by her outburst. He looked into the familiar grey eyes. They were creased with rage and bitterness. He felt awkward. This was his mother. She was confiding her innermost turmoil to him. How should he answer her?

He bit his lip then said, 'Father *did* love you, Mama. I know that, even though I've not been here these past four years. There's not a shadow of doubt about it.

Everyone could see how much he adored you. But who can tell what passes through another's mind when they're under such a cloud? He must have been more deeply depressed by the rumours than anyone, even you, could imagine.'

She gripped his arm fiercely. 'I'll never forgive him for leaving me like this. *Never.* We were so happy, so content. Life was good. Then without warning it's gone. All gone. It's as though our house has been struck by lightning and is collapsing around me. I'm buried under the rubble and can't escape. I can't breath or think. I hate myself for feeling this way, Alex, but I can't help it. He's left me with nothing.'

'In time you'll see things differently, I'm sure,' he said lamely. 'Perhaps when you return to Henham? Return to the school? And I can't stay here in Drewsteignton indefinitely either, I fear. My money's nearly all gone.'

'Oh my dear, I hadn't realised,' she loosened her grip on his arm. 'How will you get back to Guatemala if you have no money? I'm afraid I have bills to pay and that's one reason I need to get back to Henham very soon. But what about you? How will you be able to resume your teaching post if you don't possess the fare back again?'

Alex cleared his throat. Until now he hadn't dared broach any discussion with her of the true reason for his return to England. His mother's frail tenure on sanity had forced him to bide his time, bite his tongue on several occasions. Now he must tell her the truth.

'Mama, dearest, I feel it's my bounden duty, as a patriotic Englishman, to fight for my King and country. So....I've decided to enlist. When I was in Guatemala I saw newspaper reports of the war and read that Kitchener was calling for a million young men to join up. Well, I'm of the right age, I'm fit and I can handle a gun and ride a horse. I'm sure I could be useful in the artillery or one of the cavalry regiments.

'So my intention, after I've accompanied you safely back to Suffolk, is to find the nearest recruiting office and join the colours. Like so many others have done.'

Alma stood wide-eyed. She clutched her hand to her mouth, horrified. After several moments she said quietly and calmly, 'I urge you to think again. Please, for my sake. Don't enlist. Don't fight. This is an infamous war and I've disapproved of it since the day it began. Your father, too, inveighed against it. I sometimes wonder if that wasn't his downfall. Maybe his forthrightness against the war was misconstrued by some people... ignorant people.... as being disloyal and unpatriotic. But he was only telling the truth.

'What worried him most was the thought that our friends, the Riemanns, would become our enemies because of this stupid war. Think of that, Alex. The people who took you into their home, welcomed you as one of the family.

You want to *kill* those people? Supposing you were to meet on the battlefield, face to face? You and Rudolf and Walter Reimann? They were like brothers to you. Could you take *their* lives?'

Her eyes were wide and beseeching. Begging him to change his mind.

'Well. I'll see. I'll see.' He looked away. She was right. He'd been swept along by a wave of patriotism. German patriotism. The Germans in Guatemala City, hundreds of them, quitting their posts and heading for the Fatherland. Their patriotism had left him under a cloud of guilt that overshadowed his hitherto sunlit life. A guilt that could only be assuaged by donning English khaki.

'Besides,' she paused, hanging her head miserably, 'I couldn't bear to lose you, too. Not after Will. This war has snatched him from us just as completely as if he'd been shot by the enemy. No, you mustn't even consider it. This country doesn't deserve you fighting on its behalf. It doesn't deserve you laying down your life in some muddy field. After all, it was this government's warmongering and stupidity that was responsible for the death of your father. Not to mention the thousands of young men who've perished already on the battlefields of Belgium and France. Many more are being horribly maimed. You have only to see them in the wards at Henham Hospital. Poor, pathetic creatures. Men of your age, crippled for the rest of their lives. If that happened to you....well... well.....' her voice petered out.

'Yes, well, I can understand that. But, please don't make yourself anxious on my behalf, Mama. I'll give the whole matter very careful thought, I promise you.'

She took both his hands in hers and in that moment of calm she was once more the parent, responsible for a wayward, wild child.

'Alex, go back to Guatemala, I implore you. You'd be fulfilling a far more worthy mission in life teaching children than fighting a war. Go back and teach them the languages of Europe. Help to expand their horizons, open their minds to cultures other than their own. If you need money to pay for your fare I have a little money saved from my salary. A hundred pounds or so. You must take it. You will put it to far better use than I.'

He shook his head and pursed his lips. 'Mama, please. Let me think it through in my own good time. But first we should go back to Henham, together. Do you think you're strong enough now? Your future lies back there with the children you love. You know that.'

Alma nodded and sighed. 'Yes. You're right. The Education Committee wrote saying that, if I felt the memories at Henham were too unbearable, they could offer me a post elsewhere. But I refused. Henham is my home. Where I've been happiest. I'll wire Ida so that she may prepare the house for our homecoming. Shall I tell her we'll be back this Friday?'

Alex squeezed her hands. 'Yes, Mama. This Friday will suit very well.'

Chapter Twenty Eight

Saturday January 16 1915

It was dark when Alma and Alex arrived back at the schoolhouse in the waggon from Blythburgh Station. There were lights in the windows and Alma saw them with relief. She hoped Ida was still there and would greet them at the door.

Home. I'm home. She paid the waggoner then turned up the pathway, heart thumping nervously.

'Here we are at last, Mama,' Alex said cheerfully. 'It's wonderful to be back, isn't it?'

'Part of me is glad. But another part of me is dreading it,' she admitted. 'This house is so full of memories.' When they drew level with the small stone barn between house and school she shivered involuntarily. She waved a gloved hand towards it. 'And *that*. That has the worst memories of all. I don't know how I'm going to bear seeing it every day on my way to school.'

Alex took her arm and steered her quickly to the front porch. He rang the bell and heard footsteps running. Ida, still in her cooking apron, flung open the door and exclaimed, 'Oh, Mrs Smith, Mrs Smith! I'm so glad to see you. Come in quickly, come in. It's so cold out there. And Mr Alex, too. Is it really you? Well, well. How you've grown. Quite the young gentleman now, I see.' Ida twittered and fussed like a mother bird, talking to no-one in particular and muttering to herself as she led the way into the sitting room.

'I've lit the fires in all the rooms and removed all the dust covers. And there's a stew cooking on the range. I thought you'd not have eaten much on your journey and would like something hot and filling. With dumplings, Mr Alex. Your favourite.'

'You remembered, Ida. How clever. I always loved your mutton stews,' Alex's eyes twinkled at the woman who had been a constant presence throughout his childhoood.

'We're very tired, Ida,' Alma said quietly. 'We'll retire early, I think. We have no unpacking to do tonight. Our bags had to be left at the station because the waggoner had no room for them. Alex will take the pony and trap and fetch them tomorrow.'

'Very good Mrs Smith. Well, if there's nothing else you need me for, I'll be off. See you in the morning. Good night Mrs Smith. Good night Mr Alex.'

'Thank you Ida.' Alma's smile was weary and as the door closed behind the housekeeper she sighed again. 'Well. What do you think? Does it look the same?'

Alex spun 360 degrees around the little sitting room. 'Pretty much. Yes. Much as I remember it. ' And it was. The fire sparkling in the grate, the clock ticking on the mantlepiece, the same velvet curtains, the battered leather armchairs, Glady's chaise longue still beneath the window. He remembered how she'd lie there every day, listening to the children playing in the yard and the traffic on the turnpike. There was a red ink stain on the carpet which hadn't been there when he left. He thought it unusual. His parents were usually so careful. But he made no comment.

After the supper dishes had been cleared away Alma turned with angular shyness to her son. 'I know this will sound very odd to you. But....would you ...would you come up to the bedroom with me? I'm dreading the prospect of sleeping in that bed tonight. Just to see.....that.....well, there are no ghosts lingering there.'

He nodded. 'Of course. I understand. Do you really want to stay in your old room tonight? Why not sleep in my bed and I'll take your room. It might be easier on your mind. Even if just for tonight, while you accustom yourself to the old place again.'

'No, no. I don't want to be disloyal to Will. I'll sleep in our marriage bed, just as always. I'm determined on that. It's just that.....well...'

'If you need me, Mama, I'll only be next door. You know you can call me if you can't sleep,' he assured her.

When he'd seen his mother safely to her room, Alex sank into one of the leather armchairs before the flickering embers in the grate and smoked a cigarette. Thoughts and emotions were locked in a chaotic battle; should he follow his patriotic intention and join up or should he follow his mother's imploring that he should return to the safety of Guatemala? He sank his head into his hands, yet could find no resolution to this turmoil. Hours later he crept upstairs in his bare feet, afraid he might awaken his mother.

But Alma couldn't sleep. She lay in the familiar bed with the faded quilt pulled up around her face. The smells were as they'd always been. Will's scent still in every fibre of every fabric in the room. His clothes were still in the wardrobe. Even the thick overcoat the undertaker had returned to her when they'd prepared his body for burial. Still with the blood stains around the collar. Although faded to a dull brown, she would always know they were there.

When her restlessness grew too urgent to bear she walked about the room and opened the blinds. A full moon lit every item of furniture as though it were daylight. It lit the face pressed against the glass. An ethereal face.

They were woken on Saturday morning by Ida gently closing the scullery door behind her. After lighting the kitchen range and sitting room fire she took coals up to the bedrooms and re-lit the little fires in the grates.

'I've the school to clean this morning,' she announced as she busied about. 'Being Saturday. And then I'll come back. See what you want by way of orders for the grocer and greengrocer.'

Alma was distracted. 'Yes, yes. Come and see me afterwards.'

At half past nine Alex left to fetch the pony from Charles Acton's field. His mother had reminded him that if he were taking a short cut through the churchyard he should stop and see the fine memorial cross erected to his father by the pupils and parents of the school. Alex was somewhat surprised to find it just outside the vestry door. Somehow he'd imagined it would be tucked away in a discreet corner, or beneath one of the weeping ash trees that overhung the churchyard wall. Suicide was a sin in the eyes of the church, and those who died by their own hand were invariably relegated to a plot beyond the confines of the church. He knelt on the bare earth at its base and offered a wordless prayer.

Polly whinnied with recognition and galloped to greet him when he pushed open the five-bar gate to the doctor's field. Alex laughed aloud at the sight of her; head up, mane flying. He felt a childish joy in the obvious delight of this animal. He led her back along the river bank and harnessed her to the cart which was stored in the cart barn in the bottom field.

They took a leisurely pace along the turnpike towards Blythburgh. From his vantage point in the driving seat he could see over the tops of blackthorn hedges that it was low tide in the Blythe estuary, for the mud glowed dully in the pale January sun.

Drawing close to the lane branching off towards Southwold he spotted a boy throwing sticks into the reeds for a black Labrador to chase. He pulled the pony to a halt and stood up in the trap. 'Is that Charlie Boggis?' he shouted.

The boy stopped and looked around furtively as though he had no business being on the river bank. 'Who wants to know?' he retorted.

'Yes! I recognise you now,' Alex came back cheerfully. 'And whose dog is that? It looks like my old dog, Dick.'

The boy ran up to the hedge, the dog not far behind. 'Who're you? Yer can't be Alex, surely? Alex Smith? Well, my goodness, so tis,' Charlie beamed.

As they drew closer Alex was able to take a closer look at the dog's markings. Suddenly he cried out, 'It *is* Dick! It *is*!' He leapt down from the trap and ran to the hedge, scrambling through the scrubby thorn sticks, heedless of the scratches.

'Dick, Dick! I thought you were dead! Oh thank goodness, you're alive. Dick old boy, old boy, oh Dick.' He flung his arms around the dog's neck and buried his face in the dark fur. 'Oh Dick, thank goodness.....' he repeated.

His eyes filled with tears. Tears of joy, of relief, of pent up melancholy. Tears he could not shed at the death of his father now welled up for the living presence of his dog. He could hardly bear to let him go.

'Di'nt yer know I'd got ole Dick, then? Yer Ma gived him ter me when Mr Smith died. Ida couldn't cope with 'im, what with the walkin' twice a day to keep 'im fit and takin' 'im hunting, rabbiting, that sorta thing, yer know,' the boy explained with a shrug.

'No, no, I didn't. I never thought to ask what'd happened to Dick. It was such a shock to hear of my father's death that it went completely out of my mind.'

Charlie patted the dog proprietorially. 'Well, if yer wants to see 'im while yer back you can, any time. You know the butcher's shop in Southwold, don't you?'

'Yes, I do.' Alex brushed away the tears. 'But I may not be here for long. I've come back from Guatemala to join the army.'

Charlie nodded knowingly. 'Ah. Yes. Two of me brothers have volunteered. Wish I wus old enough to fight, too, but I'm only fourteen. Pr'aps the war will go on another four years and I'll be old enough then.' He sounded hopeful.

'God forbid, Charlie! Four years is an impossibly long time. Don't wish your young life away. You've got Dick to look after, anyway. I can see you're doing a grand job. He looks splendid,' Alex complimented, running his hand over the glossy back. 'Now I must get going. I have to collect my bags from the station.'

He stroked Dick's head wistfully. 'Goodbye Dick old boy. I'll miss you.' He bade farewell to Charlie, pushed his way back through the thorn hedge and leapt with athletic lightness into the trap.

All the way to the station he murmured to himself, 'Dick's alive. Dick's not dead,' chuckling with relief at his mistake.

Alma had made up her mind. She waited until Alex had left for the station, then picked up the jacket and scarf Ida had left on the three-legged stool in the scullery and took them into school. Ida was cleaning the large Lower Standards classroom and it smelt of fresh beeswax and disinfectant. The desks and forms, the floor and the wooden platform had all been thoroughly scrubbed and polished.

Alma breathed in the pungent mix. It was inconceivable she'd never smell it again. She paused in the doorway, watching Ida on her hands and knees, swirling a polishing rag across the floor with muscular movements. Ida looked up and smiled, then went on working. She had two more rooms to do, and the head's study.

'Ida, I've brought your clothing over, in case I'm out when you're finished. I'm going to lock the door.' Alma laid the coat and scarf on the nearest bench.

Ida heaved herself to her feet, arching her back painfully as she did so. 'Thank you, Mrs Smith. I shall be done in an hour, anyway.'

Alma stared hard at her. The young woman, who had been her housekeeper for more than a decade, had helped care for her children and cared as much about the fabric of the school as she and William had its pupils and their education. On impulse she shot out her hand towards Ida. 'I just wanted to say thank you.' She paused awkwardly as Ida took her mistress's hand. 'Thank you for all you've done for my husband and I, and our family.....and of course the school.....these past twelve years. I wanted you to know I've always been grateful, though I may not always have shown it.'

With that she quickly turned and left. Ida stood and listened to the heels of her boots clacking along the wood corridor, puzzled. She shrugged and lowered herself once more onto her knees, working the rags in regular circles across the pitted floor.

One thing more, and then it's done.

Alma knew she would find what she was looking for in a bookcase in Higher Standards. The large leather-bound book she and Will had compiled to teach generations of children about English heroes. Over thirty years they had collected pictures and articles on such famous figures as Wellington and Clive of India, Gordon of Khartoum and Kitchener, explorers like Doctor Livingstone and Captain Cook, doughty women such as Florence Nightingale and Good Queen Bess, and pasted them into the book. She slid it from its place on the shelf, tucked it under her arm and took it home. Other children, not yet born, should have use of it.

She returned home through the scullery door. Methodically, she checked she'd locked it behind her then laid the large iron key on the draining board. From a nail in the scullery she unhooked a long piece of cord that had been used as a leading rein for the pony, and clutching it in one hand, picked up the stool in the other. This she left at the bottom of the stairs.

Purposefully, yet with trembling hands, she climbed the stairs. She leaned over the banister rail and for a few tantalising seconds peered down. *The drop from the top landing to the hallway beneath is far enough.* She looped the cord over the rail and tied a slip knot in one end. She tested it and was satisfied.

She turned for one last glance from the landing window, across the garden to the playing field and beyond to the bathing place. The bloodless light of a January morning glanced off the thin ribbon of the River Wang as it slithered between banks of reed. *How could he bear to leave all this?*

She dragged herself away from the melancholy landscape, back down to the warmth of the sitting room. At her desk she drew a sheet of headed school notepaper from the drawer. Dipping her pen into the black inkwell she dated it, Saturday 16th January 1915, then in her customary, perfectly even handwriting, wrote:

"My Dear Alex,

This book is to be treasured. As you know, your father compiled it because of his admiration for heroic Englishmen. I would like you to take it to Evie and Johnnie before you return to Guatemala so that the twins may see how patriotic their grandfather was and learn from it, just as hundreds of children who have passed through Henham and Wangford School have done.

William and I have had the happiest of lives together. I know he loved me as I did him. No family could have been more fortunate in having such a devoted husband and father. You will understand, I am sure, that I miss most dreadfully. I am nothing without him.

Your father was a loyal Englishman, none more so, yet he died with a stigma hanging over him. His honour and good name were impuned and he could not live with that. I understand that now.

It is the war. Nothing else is to blame for Will ending his life in the way he did. If there had been no war he would be alive still. Alive and enjoying life, as he always did. I'll never forgive this war, nor this government for allowing us to be drawn into it.

The police were only doing what they thought was right, so I forgive them. But as I face my God I find it hard to forgive the gossips in this village who invented the malicious rumours that condemned your father to such a horrible death. They murdered him, even though it was at his own hand. These were people he loved and served with all his heart. God may forgive them.

God forgive me, too, for what I am now about to do. I go to join the husband I love more than life itself.

Your ever-loving mother, Alma."

She blotted the letter then placed it in a white envelope and addressed it to Alex. Letter and book were left together on the desk. *It's done.* She looked at the clock. Half past ten. Alex would be returning soon. There wasn't a moment to lose.

She regretted that it would inevitably be Alex who would discover her body. Alex who would have to cut her down. That her death would be another burden for him to shoulder. But he'd proved himself to be not only strong-willed but self-contained and self-reliant. Remote, even. He would recover.

The three-legged stool from the scullery stood in the hallway, waiting. She climbed carefully onto it and wound the knotted end of the cord around her neck.

Through the glass panel in the back door she could see the yard and the stone barn where William had ended his life. *So close, so close.* Beyond it, the silent schoolyard. In her imagination she heard the joyful shrieks and laughter of children released from their desks for a few precious moments. She missed the sound of children playing. Perhaps if the children had been there she would have paused. Had second thoughts. But this was Saturday and all was quietness.

She murmured the Lords Prayer under her breath. In a firm, resolute voice she added, 'Will forgive me, God forgive me.'

Then she kicked away the stool from beneath her.

Epilogue

Alex stood on the promenade deck of the Cunard liner, watching dockers on the quayside uncoil the last of the heavy docklines. A final act before the ship pulled away to steam slowly from harbour, out into the Irish Sea and then across the Atlantic to New York.

He'd heeded Alma's last wish. He was returning to Guatemala. Back to his job teaching languages. As he turned his face for one last time towards Liverpool docks he knew he was turning his face against his country forever. He had no regrets. He was quite sanguine at the prospect of never seeing England again.

He'd arrived here, in this same city, full of enthusiastic expectation and patriotism. Determined to be a soldier. To fight – and die if necessary – for his King and country. But now? Well, now was different. The intervening month had changed all that.

Changed *him*.

Bitterness gnawed into him and his heart felt as cold as the grey waters rushing beneath him. He scorned the idea of shedding a single tear, let alone spilling a single drop of blood, for England. He'd sacrificed enough already for the nation of his birth and its blinkered bigotry.

He'd cut down Alma's still-warm body. Sat mesmerised through her funeral. Given evidence at her inquest. Disposed of her belongings and administered her will. She'd left him a legacy of £454 12s. 8d. The sum total of his parents' thirty years' hard work and devotion.

He closed his eyes, screwing them tightly shut against the images. He was determined to bear away only pleasant memories.

Dick scampering like a puppy through the marsh grass to greet him. He, leaping from the trap and charging through thornbushes without a thought for the scratches and tears. The smell still in his nostrils of the dog's wet fur mingled with his own salty tears as he buried his face in its neck. The touch on his cheek of silken wisps, as delicate as a baby's. Involuntarily he moved his hand to his face, stroking his skin. Remembering, he sighed and smiled.

And then there were the babies. Evie's twins, Frank and Jane. He'd gone to Maidenhead with the history book, as instructed in his mother's suicide note. Evie had given birth the previous day and he'd been overwhelmed with pride and nervousness when she'd placed her new-borns in his arms. His niece and nephew. His new family.

Alex turned and walked the length of the ship, past the crowds huddled together, lining the rails eager for a last glimpse of home. From the foredeck he could see the white-crested breakers far out in the ocean and the last vestiges of the English coastline outlined in the mist.

In front of him lay the place he'd come to call home. He hoped he could go back and pick up where he'd left off, yet deep within him he resolved to make it the start of an entirely new life. A life he was determined to share with Maria, the love he'd so carelessly left behind.

He'd broken her heart when he'd left her apartment in Guatemala City. The cries of 'No, no, Alex! Don't leave me!' chilled his blood. He winced at the memory. How callous his desire for valour had been.

She'd begged him not to go. 'What if you're killed in battle?' she'd reasoned. 'How would I ever know? Who would tell me?'

Well, now he'd make it up to her. Marry her. Have his own family, just like Evie and Johnnie.

'Mrs Maria Smith,' he rehearsed the words to himself. ' Mrs Maria Smith.' Such an ordinary name for such an exotic flower. He doubted there could ever be another Mrs Smith in the world quite so beautiful, with her flowing black hair, sinewy figure and alluring dark eyes.

'Smith.' He uttered the word again. An ordinary name indeed. He saw before him, in the passing waves, the faces of his parents. William and Alma Smith. Two very ordinary people. They would have agreed with him, said of themselves even, that they were unremarkable people. Just a couple of teachers, living good but ordinary and uneventful lives.

Yet there was nothing ordinary about their deaths. They had become extraordinary people, the manner and cause of their passing a public scandal.

The injustice of their brutal suicides hit him with such sudden force that his heart raced, sending the blood rushing to face. Pain stabbed the indentation of his left temple. He winced again, clutching at it, pushing his fingers into the pain. It was, he realised, the same desperate gesture he'd seen his father make so many times as he struggled with migraine.

'Smith. Yes, I have an ordinary name. But I shall bear it proudly for the rest of my life for my parents' sake,' he said quietly to the silver wake disappearing into perfect lines of perspective.

'There is nothing for me here. My future lies across this water.'

He turned away from the rail, from the distant headland that was the last remnant of English coastline, and made his way purposefully down to his cabin. Now he was content to turn his back on England.

East Anglian Daily Times

Thursday January 21 1915

The Henham Tragedy. Parliamentary Inquiry suggested.

The report which appeared in 'The Times' of an inquest held at Henham in Suffolk disclosed, says the Daily News and Leader, as pitiful a tragedy as any associated with the war. The circumstances are not only pitiful but important for they show what infinite wrong can be done by mischievous rumour and ignorant campaigns against suspects.

The inquest was on the body of a Mrs Smith, the widow of William Smith, schoolmaster of Henham, the principal village on Lord Stradbroke's estate. We quote the report of the case as it appeared in our contemporary.

'Early in November Mr Smith received a notice from the Chief Constable of East Suffolk that under the Defence of the Realm Act he was required to cease living in Suffolk. He had been schoolmaster at Henham for 28 years and the matter so preyed upon his mind that he cut his throat.

At the inquest on his body it came out that a suggestion had been made that his only son, who had studied languages in Germany many years ago, was a Lieutenant in the German army. As a matter of fact, the son had just left Guatemala where he had been teaching languages, and was on his way back to England to enlist. After arriving in England he stayed with his mother in Devonshire and returned with her to Henham.

On Saturday, during her son's absence, Mrs Smith hanged herself from the banister. He made the discovery on his return.'

That is the story. The jury returned a verdict of suicide while of unsound mind. But we look in vain for any comment by them on the shameful causes that drove first the husband and then the wife to take their lives.

Does it really mean that this Suffolk jury had no comment to make, felt that there was nothing in this lamentable story that called for indignant protest? If that is so, we hope that Parliament, when it meets, will be less callous and will demand an Inquiry into the tragedy.

It will want to know on what grounds, other than mere stupid rumour, this couple - who had lived in the village for more than a quarter of a century - were called upon by the Chief Constable to leave their home like criminals?

What evidence did the Chief Constable obtain? What pains did he take to ascertain whether it was true or false? Whatever his steps, we know that the rumour was cruelly, wickedly, false and that as a result of it this unhappy couple have been harried into the grave.

What must be the feelings of the son who, after travelling across the globe to serve his country, finds this desolation of his old home the reward of his devotion?

The story throws light on the crime of those who recklessly invent and spread rumours. It also shows the harm that is done by those newspapers, which for the sake of sensation, fill the minds of the ignorant with idle suspicions of their innocent neighbours.

The case of the Smiths only differs from many that have occurred, in the completeness of its tragic consequences. The double suicide which occurred in Suffolk, says the Daily Graphic, shows the mischief that can be wrought when patriotism is replaced by the mental disease which can best be described as 'pseudo-patriotic hysteria.'

The man who is a true patriot either enlists or quietly busies himself with doing some practical work for his country, or cuts down his personal expenditure so as to be able to help others. Except for enlisting, the true woman patriot does likewise but in addition to patriots of this type, who are happily in the large majority, we have among us a considerable number of hysterical persons who think they can prove their own patriotism by insulting other people.

The suburban young woman, who goes about presenting white feathers to young men not in uniform, represents a typical case of this disease of pseudo-patriotic hysteria. In some cases these silly and usually idle young women have actually presented white feathers to officers home on leave and wearing mufti.

A more serious manifestation of the same disease is the invention of false rumours, such as those that led to the Suffolk tragedy refered to.

In this case a rumour was started that the son of a village schoolmaster was a Lieutenant in the German army. The rumour gained credence and the schoolmaster who had been in the village 28 years was ordered by the Chief Constable to move inland. The disgrace so preyed upon the unfortunate man's mind that he cut his throat. A few week's later his widow hanged herself. In the meantime, their son, who had been teaching in Guatemala, had returned to England to enlist in the British army.

It is hardly necessary to draw the contrast between the true patriotism of this young man, who had crossed half the world to serve his country in the field, and the mean cowardice of the hysterical busy-bodies who had invented lies about him.

Acknowledgements

I am indebted to Terry Hunt, the editor of the East Anglian Daily Times, for permission to quote passages from the relevant EADT editions of 1914 and 1915.

Thanks to Tonie and Valmai Holt for permission to quote from their book 'Battlefields of the First World War - a Traveller's Guide' with regard to the battle at Le Cateau. I am also grateful to author Tim Carew's executors for permission to use details of Le Cateau which he so poignantly described in his book 'The Vanished Army'.

The following people and organisations have helped me write this book. William and Alma Smith's story has been greatly enriched by their particular and specialist knowledge.

Residents of Wangford and Henham: Douglas Howeld, Lady Penelope Gilbey (grand-daughter of the 3rd Earl of Stradbroke) and Marion Tilney (current owner of Henham School and Henham Schoolhouse) for providing information and photographs.

Janet Rigby of Lytham St Annes, for background on Alma Smith's family, the Morses of the Forest of Dean. Frank Green (son of Evelyn Edith Green, née Smith) for information regarding his mother. Paul Greener, village historian of Drewsteignton, Devon, for information regarding William Smith and the Smith family in Drewsteignton.

Robert Rous of Dennington Hall (grandson of 3rd Earl of Stradbroke) and his sister, Frances Boscawen, for historical information regarding the 3rd Earl and Countess and for giving permission to reproduce portraits and photographs of the Earl and Countess.

Suffolk Police Museum for their photograph of Chief Constable Captain Jasper Mayne and details of police equipment and dress of the period. Dr John Bourne, Director of the Centre for First World War Studies at University of Birmingham who supplied details of First World War artillery.

The staff of Suffolk Records Office in Ipswich for their help in my research, particularly in the Stradbroke Archive, which forms part of their collection.

Also Lowestoft Records Office, where the records for Henham and Wangford School are kept, and the Royal Anglian Regimental Museum in Bury St Edmunds.

Lifesavers for information about lifesaving techniques in 1906. The British Red Cross Society for details of the uniform worn by voluntary Red Cross Hospital nurses.

* * * * * *

Bibliography

'The Vanished Army' by Tim Carew, published by William Kimber 1964.

'Battlefields of the First World War - a Traveller's Guide' by Tonie and Valmai Holt, published by Pavilion Books 1995.

'The War at Sea 1914-1918' by Julian Thompson, published by Pan Books in association with The Imperial War Museum 2005.

'History of the First World War' by Liddell Hart, published by Pan Books Ltd 1930.

'Before the Lamps Went Out' by Geoffrey Marcus, published by George Allen & Unwin Ltd 1965.

'The London Magazine' vol. XXII, published by Carmelite House 1909.

'Suffolk Scene' by Julian Tennyson, published by Blackie 1939.

'Suffolk Within Living Memory' compiled by Suffolk Federations of Women's Institutes, published jointly by Countryside Books, SEFWI Ipswich and SWFWI Bury St Edmunds.

* * * * *